I0588298

Spellbound Heart

BOOK THREE IN THE MAIDENS OF FAIRHAVEN TRILOGY

DANA GRICKEN

OLIVERHEBERBOOKS

Cover art by Dar Albert at Wicked Smart Designs

Published by Oliver-Heber Books

0 9 8 7 6 5 4 3 2 1

CHAPTER 1

As a little girl, Iris ran around the back yard of her small home, wearing fake metal armor and carrying a wooden sword. She had begged the fairy godmothers of Fairhaven to make her a real knight, but they all said she was too young. But one day, Iris vowed she would be the brave guard she always dreamed about.

"Take that, evil dragon!" she cried, waving her sword around. "You are no match for Guardswoman Iris Ambrose!"

"Iris, dinner!" her mother called from inside the townhome.

"Okay, Mommy!" Iris set her sword and fake armor on the ground, then entered through the back door. "I'm coming."

Inside the home, Iris's mother had baked a meat pie with magical spices from the garden. It smelled heavenly. As Iris skipped over for a plate, her mother bent down, placing a purple flower in her long, flowing dark hair.

"I found this while gardening at work today," she said. "It's called a Miracle Flower. Apparently, it has healing properties. Mainly for minor wounds. And it looks beautiful on you, don't you think? Look how amazing you are."

Her mother reached for a nearby magical mirror, one that

1

whispered positive words. Iris looked at the flower in the reflection and smiled. It contrasted nicely against her dark skin. "It's really pretty. Thanks, Mommy."

The door opened behind them, then Iris's father walked inside, carrying a briefcase from a day of work as a magical locksmith. He set his briefcase down, then Iris watched as it grew legs like vines and hung itself up on the coat rack. Then the legs removed her father's shoes for him and set them by the door before vanishing.

"I'm home!" her father called. "Mmm, that smells amazing. More food from the garden, my love?"

"You know it." Iris's mother gave her a plate first, then held one out toward her husband while kissing his cheek. "I stole a bite and it's delicious."

"I bet." Her father looked down, patting Iris's head. "Hello, dear. How was your day?"

"I fought a dragon, Daddy. And won!" Iris cried. "I'm going to be a guard one day. I'm going to protect Fairhaven from everything bad!"

Her parents looked on, smiling. Then her mother gestured at the flower in her hair. "And that flower will keep you safe while you're saving the world. How lucky are we have to such a brave daughter, darling?"

"The luckiest," Iris's father replied with a smile.

But now, years later as Guardswoman Iris stared at the magically preserved Miracle Flower in her hand with the sharp edges shaved down, she couldn't help but feel like it had let her down.

Fairhaven was gone.

"So, what do we do?" Gemma asked. Iris had only seen Gemma in passing, walking through the palace to and from the library. "We're the last survivors of Fairhaven. The explosion broke the magical barrier, allowing humanity to see us. We're stranded here. We have nothing—no money, no home. And people hate and fear us for what the senator has done. Where are we going?" Gemma's voice broke and she turned into a human man's arms.

Princess Esme looked to her father, the king, for guidance, but he shook his head. "These patrols were your idea, Esme. If not for you, we'd be dead like the rest of our people. You should be the one to give the next order. Consider it practice for when you take my place." His pale skin and sunken eyes were a testament to the poisoning he'd endured at the hands of traitors.

Princess Esme took a deep breath. "All right. So much has changed—the humans know about us now and our home is gone. We can't magically erase their memories this time, not again. We need a safe place to regroup in the meantime."

Gemma's boyfriend, Ian, raised his hand. "I own a bar not far from here. Horizon Bar. I can close it down for a few days, give you all sleeping bags on the floor. It's not much, but at least you'll have a place to go."

Gemma looked worried. "Ian, are you sure? I know how much your bar means to you—"

"I'm sure. Whatever I can do to help."

"Thank you, that's truly kind. Noah still has his apartment that's open to all of us. In the meantime, I suggest we get some rest." Princess Esme looked down, still heavy with grief. "Today … today was a hard day. The worst Fairhaven has ever seen."

But Fairhaven wasn't there anymore. It never would be again, something that tugged at Iris's heart.

"Noah, Father, Fairy Godmother Odelia," Princess Esme said, "we're all going to Noah's apartment. Gemma and Ian, you can take my soldiers for the night. There aren't many left so it'll be easy to keep them safe. We'll come visit you tomorrow and discuss our next plan of action."

Ian nodded. "Of course. If you'd all like to follow me."

Iris, after turning over the senator's body to police, followed her fellow soldiers out of City Hall. Gemma spoke with some humans on the street, an elderly woman and her grandson, and a woman and her daughter, promising them everything would be okay.

"And I'll explain it all soon, okay?" Gemma told them. "Just bear with me. We need to get these soldiers someplace safe first."

The humans nodded, letting them leave. More unfamiliar humans watched them from a safe distance. The offices at City Hall were still empty, deserted in fear and reeking like magical smoke. Princess Esme went with her father, husband Noah, and fairy godmother, vanishing down the street to Noah's apartment. Iris quickened her pace to keep up with Ian, Gemma, Gemma's father—Mr. Solace, and Gemma's Fairy Godmother Blanche.

"My bar is just down here," Ian said over his shoulder. "Almost there."

They continued walking, counting all the humans out on the street. They murmured and pointed at them in their odd armor as they passed. Once Ian reached his bar, he unlocked the door, gesturing for them all to enter. Ian locked the door behind them, then flicked on the light. It lit up the dark bar and the empty tables. He walked into the backroom, bringing out snacks and some sleeping bags.

"Here. Some snacks in case you're hungry. And I always keep these sleeping bags back there," Ian said, setting them on the floor. "Just in case one of my patrons is too drunk to drive home. Anyway, please, get comfortable. And I'm really sorry about Fairhaven. Losing your home ... that's such a tragedy. I can't think of anything worse."

The soldiers thanked him, grabbing a few peanuts from the bar and sitting on their own sleeping bag. Mr. Solace and Fairy

Godmother Blanche stuck close together. The room turned quiet as Gemma and Ian whispered behind the bar. Iris sat on one of the stools, thinking about the senator's defeat.

She was glad he was dead, but it had cost them everything —their home and way of life. It just wasn't fair.

Footsteps clicked toward Iris, then Gemma cleared her throat. "Um, hi. I don't think we've met before. I've seen you around, but we've never spoken."

Iris turned to her, shaking her hand. "Hello, I've seen you a few times heading in and out of the palace, and I've heard of you. Gemma Solace: the librarian who went to the surface."

Gemma shook her hand, nodding. "That's right. I don't believe I know your name, though."

"Iris. Iris Ambrose. One of the soldiers tasked with keeping Fairhaven safe." Iris paused. "I guess we both know how that turned out."

Gemma frowned. "Yeah. I'm so sorry. I hope you don't blame yourself—"

"Of course, I do," Iris interrupted. "I should've been watching the senator more closely. Maybe then this wouldn't have happened. My parents' deaths ... they're my fault."

Iris swallowed the lump in her throat and blinked away the burning in her eyes that threatened to turn into tears. At least it had been quick. A painless death. By the time anyone down there figured out what was happening, it would've been too late to react. But Iris's heart still ached when she thought of her parents, knowing she'd never see them again.

"First off, I'm sorry for your loss. But you're not responsible. The senator had people on the inside, and he had everyone fooled. He was a charming man, as much as I hate to admit it." Gemma placed a comforting hand on her shoulder. "I don't know how, but we'll get through this. I promise."

Iris faked a smile, though she didn't believe Gemma. She

remained on her stool as Gemma walked behind the bar to chat with Ian again. When the other soldiers laid down to go to sleep —ten of them—along with Gemma's father and fairy godmother, Ian cleared his throat and approached Iris.

"Is the senator's body safe with the police?" he asked. "I mean, do they know the proper protocols to disposing of a Fae's body?"

"I told them to burn the senator. Even though I think he should be blown to smithereens. He's gone for good—no need to worry."

Ian nodded and headed back to the bar. Right now, there was nothing she could do until the morning. So, she picked a sleeping bag at random, lying down and shutting her eyes. The bar filled with the snores of her soldiers around her. She wasn't sure how they could sleep at a time like this, but they had no choice. Gemma and Ian eventually grabbed their own sleeping bags near the bar and stayed close together all night.

When the morning light streaked through the stained-glassed windows, Iris had barely gotten any sleep. Her dark hair —once long and beautiful in her younger days—was up in a tight ponytail. Her eyes had dark circles under them. Her mind was filled with the thoughts of Fairhaven and her people's final moments. She eventually got up, stretching and grunting as the other soldiers did the same.

Gemma and Ian were already awake, sitting at the bar and drinking tea. They held hands and stared up at the television on the wall. Iris walked over, grabbing a stool as the morning news caught her attention.

"... and the city of Toronto is still reeling after learning about a magical kingdom called Fairhaven hidden beneath our storm drains," the reporter said, showing pictures of the desecrated City Hall. "We're currently awaiting word from Prime Minister Lin to see what she decides to do about this revelation ..."

"Who wants to bet the humans already hate us?" Iris asked, glancing around the bar. "I've heard rumors that they're violent."

"The humans may surprise you," Gemma said, glancing at Ian. "Some of them are truly kind. Don't write them off just yet. I know this is a different circumstance, but still. I have faith."

The news reporter went live to a journalist on the street. Iris noticed a group of construction workers trying to repair the storm drains and air out City Hall from all the smoke bombs. The mayor and assistants had returned to work, though they looked nervous and had more guards on duty. A journalist nodded before speaking into her microphone.

"I'm live at City Hall where we've heard rumors of a coup by these magical people," she said, pointing at the building behind her. "They've vanished for now, but the Fairhavener prisoners are in police custody. They think they caught everyone. No word from the prime minister yet, but we're interviewing people on the street in the meantime. Miss, would you care to give your opinion?"

The cameraman panned around, showing a young woman with a squeaky-pitched voice. She grabbed the microphone and looked straight into the camera. "If you ask me, these magical freaks should be jailed. They have too much power."

"Oh my gosh," Gemma said, turning to Ian. "I know that woman. She's the secretary at the news station."

Ian raised an eyebrow. "Really?"

Gemma sighed. "Yeah. I sort of ... used magic to convince her to get me on TV. But it was only to save Barbara's bookstore, I swear!"

Iris didn't know what Gemma was talking about, but it seemed serious. As Ian's eyes widened, the secretary spoke again. "I replayed footage from the news station I work at, you know. And one of those magical weirdos cast a spell on me to get past me and on live television! You should have the footage. The woman who wanted help for some dying bookstore?"

"Interesting," the journalist replied, turning back to the television. "Thank you for your testimony—we'll find that footage and warn people in Toronto that they may be susceptible to mind control. We'd like to urge the public to be cautious. There could be more going on that we don't understand. But that begs the question: how dangerous are these magic people?"

"Too dangerous," the secretary snarled. "And I want them all jailed."

"Back to you," the journalist said before the camera cut to the news station. Iris's people were the number one story across Toronto—and most of the world.

Gemma slid off her barstool, shaking her head. "Oh, this isn't good. I knew I shouldn't have used that potion."

"Hey, it's all right," Ian said, placing a hand on her shoulder. "You tried to do a good thing. You didn't know all this would happen."

"We were told to never use magic on the surface after Fairy Godmother Zamira made it compatible up here," Iris said, crossing her arms. "It's unnatural and too dangerous. What were you thinking? It was irresponsible."

Gemma's hands were shaking, looking nervous. Ian was the one to stand up for her. "Hey, Gemma just wanted to help a friend."

"And now she might've turned the whole city against us," Iris spat. "Nice going."

Before Gemma and Ian could respond, Iris walked to the far side of the bar, glancing out the window. Police cars, military trucks, and unidentified vehicles sped past. They had to be looking for them. Iris ducked beneath the window, trying not to be seen.

"Iris is right," Gemma whispered to Ian. "I might've ruined the potential for relations between our peoples. For good."

"We can fix this," Ian whispered. "I believe that."

As they consoled each other, Iris walked over to check on her fellow guards. Only a handful were left—those who had been taken to the surface with Princess Esme and King Tedros —and they all looked confused, angry, and afraid. With no home to return to, everyone was lost.

Iris glanced around at the other guards. "You all doing okay?"

"Definitely not," Sapphira Xen said. Iris's fellow soldier had red hair up in a bun, dark skin, and a shiny guard uniform. "Couldn't stop thinking about Fairhaven last night. About how I would've died if I was still down there."

"Tell me about it," Kyler Bram said. He had short, dark hair with freckles, pale skin, and a slightly dirtier guard uniform. "Maybe that would've been better. To die with the others, I mean. Because things are going to be tough now that the humans know about us. Who knows what they'll do? One of them was already killing and stealing with our magic."

Sapphira shook her head, leaning against one of the pool tables. "This is all wrong—like some kind of bad dream. And I can't help but feel angry at King Tedros."

The other guards murmured, then Iris spoke up. "Why? I'm angrier at myself. For not stopping Senator Remus before he had a chance to concoct this plan with the traitors that escaped to the surface."

"Well, yeah. We should've known something was up. But Tedros is the king," Sapphira said. "He should be smarter than all of us—he should've done something more. Even killed Senator Remus before he had a chance to do this. If you ask me, King Tedros has blood on his hands. I'm disappointed in his leadership."

"And he didn't lose anyone in his family," Kyler muttered. "His daughter, son-in-law, and fairy godmother are fine. It's us, the common people, who suffered. Awfully convenient for him."

Sapphira nodded. "Exactly. Maybe we should just do away with royalty altogether. Let this be a fresh start for our people— if Gemma hasn't messed it up already by using a potion on a human. What an idiot ..."

As the guards muttered, Iris said nothing, staring down at the floor. Tempers were rising, resentment was brewing, and so much uncertainty was on the horizon. She didn't know what any of them were going to do.

As she mulled it over, three quiet knocks echoed against the back door, and she feared the humans had finally found them.

And that their greeting *wasn't* going to be warm or welcoming. But if they wanted to make Earth their permanent home now after Fairhaven's destruction, Iris would need to find a way forward—or die trying.

CHAPTER 2

Everyone in the bar froze, glancing around at each other with wide eyes. Iris was the one to cross the bar and head toward the back door. She wasn't afraid—not since her home had been lost.

At this point, she had nothing left to lose. She kept one hand on the sword in her scabbard though. Just in case.

She pulled the door open, coming face-to-face with Princess Esme. Noah, King Tedros, and Fairy Godmother Odelia were waiting behind her. Iris bowed, then opened the door a little wider for the royal family to enter.

"Thanks. Sorry if we scared you." Princess Esme stepped inside with her family. Iris quickly shut and locked the door behind them. "But police are roaming the street, searching for us. We thought it'd be best to enter through the back way."

"Maybe we should give ourselves up to the police," Gemma said from behind the bar, standing next to Ian. "Tell them we mean no harm and that the senator wasn't with us."

"Soon, we will. But first thing's first," King Tedros said, walking toward the bar to reach Gemma. He seemed mostly recovered from the poison attack from Gemma's friend. "I saw the news at Noah's apartment. What were you thinking? Drugging a secretary with magic to get her to do your bidding?"

Gemma sighed. "I know. I shouldn't have done that. Princess Esme warned me not to use magic before I left for the surface—"

"And she was right! It's an unfair advantage. Just look at that human scum using it," King Tedros snarled, leaning against the bar. "You should've known better. And now, the humans that oppose us are using it as leverage. They think we're too dangerous to let us stay on the surface."

Gemma gawked. "They want us to leave? But ... where would we go?"

"I don't know. But plenty are angry and afraid of us. And my daughter was the one who encouraged you to head to the surface." King Tedros shook his head. "Perhaps you're both to blame."

When Princess Esme and Gemma said nothing, both looking down, Ian cleared his throat. "Hey, come on—that's enough. Gemma feels bad about this already. And with everything going on in this world, you all should have each other's backs."

"Maybe you're right. For now. Our numbers are too few to punish Gemma." King Tedros narrowed his eyes at Ian. "I don't believe we met."

"Ian. Ian Whitman. Gemma's boyfriend." He placed an arm around her shoulder. "And I'm going to help you all get used to life on the surface. This will blow over—trust me. I've seen my fair share of scandals, coming from a rich family. People will forgive Gemma, and you can work on relations between your people and the humans. You'll need to really work at it, though. Prove you aren't a threat. After all, humans have seen the worst of you, thanks to the senator. You'll have to do something to show them the best."

Ian was optimistic, Iris realized, much like Gemma—but she was the complete opposite. She had a feeling that things would get even worse.

"I appreciate the thought, human, and hope you're right. For all our sakes. I *have* heard about you, and I hope the rest of your kind will be as welcoming." King Tedros shook his head. "My goodness, what a position to be in. Fairhaven's gone, the humans know about us, and now, they mistrust us. Because our fairy godmothers have magic and make potions for us. And you know, Senator Remus tried to enslave humanity and all. My goodness, no wonder they see us as a threat. I would too."

"Not all hope is lost," Gemma said softly. "We can fix this."

"Maybe we can," Princess Esme said with a nod. "I can't believe I really did it. I killed the senator."

"If you ask me, it wasn't enough. All his family should die too," Kyler muttered. "Especially that evil daughter of his."

"No. There's been enough bloodshed," King Tedros said. "The humans have them in their custody, where they'll stay for now. They should never get out of prison again."

Iris stole a glance at Kyler and knew he wanted more done. Sapphira was glaring at King Tedros, likely still blaming him for everything that happened, while the other guards didn't know what to think.

They were in a sad state. Fairhaven was gone in the blink of an eye, destroyed by magical bombs. And there was nothing anyone could do about it.

Ian prepared tea and breakfast for everyone, using whatever he had in the backroom. They ate and drank in silence. No one dared to turn on the television and hear more of the humans questioning and despising their existence.

"Now that we've rested and eaten, I have a proposal for Iris," Princess Esme said to everyone, glancing at her father. "If you approve, of course."

King Tedros sighed. "Go ahead, Esme. Without a kingdom anymore, I'm not even sure I can still be a king. Or that you're even a princess."

"You still are to us," Iris said. "That won't change. Besides, we need leadership at this time."

The group glanced around at each other, then Princess Esme nodded. "Guardswoman Ambrose is right. We should keep our titles. For now, at least."

"Very good, Your Majesties. And since we're on the topic of titles," Iris said, wincing at the taste of human tea but still drinking it down, "I must speak with you in private. I know you said you have an idea, but can we have a word first?"

Princess Esme rose to her feet, her poufy dress getting caught on a nearby chair. "Of course. Follow me into the back room. Everyone else, please wait for us, I'll tell you about my proposal when we return."

The others nodded, chatting amongst themselves. Gemma and Ian continued to sit with each other, holding hands before Noah gave Esme's shoulder an affectionate squeeze. Iris hung around for a second and watched them, wishing she had someone to lean on right now.

But her job came first—always. Her duty. She had pushed away all potential love interests for the sake of it, and now, those possibilities were all gone.

Iris wished she had experienced more that life had to offer before Fairhaven went up in flames.

With her regrets weighing on her mind, she followed Princess Esme into the back room. She shut the door noticing all the boxes and crates that filled the room around them. The princess fluffed her dress, then turned to Iris.

"Yes, Guardswoman?" she asked. "Do you have an idea?"

"Uh, yes, Your Majesty. Sort of." Iris breathed out. "I want you to fire me."

Princess Esme raised an eyebrow. "I beg your pardon? And please, just call me Esme. As I told Gemma before, I never really liked titles. Even before Fairhaven was destroyed."

Iris didn't like the sound of that—she had been raised in those barracks, training to become a guard ever since she was a little girl. She always loved combat, swords, and protecting people. Titles and roles were ingrained in her brain.

"Right, okay. Well, Esme, the truth is ... I failed. Fairhaven, you, the human world." Iris sat on a nearby crate, sighing. "We guards are supposed to protect Fairhaven, and now, it's gone. Senator Remus had a coup planned right under our noses, and we couldn't stop him. And for my failings, I think you should fire me. Even condemn me if you must—send me to jail with the other traitors."

Princess Esme took a moment to think as Iris held her breath, then she shook her head. "I'm sorry, Guardswoman, but I won't be doing that."

"What? But why? We both know I don't deserve to be a guard anymore. Not after what the senator did."

"We were all blindsided by Senator Remus—from day one when he first tried to take over the human world. It was a failure, yes, one we all paid for. But I don't think it's your fault in particular. And you're certainly *not* a traitor." Princess Esme placed a hand on her shoulder. "Besides, our numbers are too thin to fire people who haven't done anything wrong. Please, Iris, we really need you. You must stay."

Iris wanted to argue, but she knew better in the presence of royalty. "I still think you're being too lenient with me ... but all right. I'll remain as a guard."

Princess Esme removed her hand, nodding. "Good, thank you. I think you're being too hard on yourself. Putting the weight of the world on your shoulders. And that's too heavy for one person to bear. I know, I made that mistake once too.

You must learn to forgive yourself, Iris. Only you alone can do that."

Easier said than done.

"I'll try," Iris said. "It may take a while, of course."

"Of course. You lost people in Fairhaven, didn't you?"

Memories flashed through Iris's mind like a slideshow. The Miracle Flower felt hot in her pocket. Iris looked anywhere but Esme's eyes. "Yes. My parents."

Both were gone, along with so many others. Iris would never see them again—would never hug them again. They had been so loving, so supportive of her career, and then they were wiped off the face of the Earth forever.

"I'm sorry," Princess Esme said softly. "Everyone lost something down there. My best friend, Alva ... she's gone as well. I miss her so much already. But instead of wallowing in my grief, I'm going to try to make things right. To fix relations between humans and our people and make a home for us up here."

"Good luck," Iris scoffed, then remembered she was speaking to a princess. "Uh, I mean that in the best way, of course."

"Yes—we'll need all the luck on our side. Now, before we head back to the others, I have just one question."

Iris hopped off the crates. "What is it?"

"We haven't had a general since Alva's father turned traitor by supporting the senator. Iris, tell me ... you're, what? Twenty-six? Serving as a guard since you were eighteen?"

Iris stood up straighter. "That's right, ma'am. Enrolled proudly out of high school."

"Which, if I'm not mistaken, makes you the senior guard out of all the rest. The other surviving guards don't have nearly as many years of experience as you do."

Iris frowned. "Yes, that's right. But what are you—"

"I'd like you to be our new general. To lead us. With no one else and your years of experience, you're the logical choice."

Iris wanted to scream. Become the new general? Was the princess out of her mind? Iris felt like a failure, like she had let all her people down, and now she was being promoted. While she didn't usually question royalty, she couldn't let this one slide.

"No. No, absolutely not," Iris replied. "I don't deserve the rank. Why not give it to someone else? One of the other guards?"

"I already told you—you have the most experience. Look, I know you aren't happy with your service right now, but we need you. I wouldn't ask if it wasn't urgent." Princess Esme paused, searching Iris's eyes. "So, can I count on you?"

Everything in Iris wanted to say no. But maybe, just maybe, this was a chance to redeem herself. To create a new world for her people and prevent more lives from being lost.

She eventually sighed, making her decision. "All right—I accept. But I still don't think I'm right for the job."

"I hope that will change in time. Because from where I'm standing, your service record is impressive. Skilled fighter, strategist, loyal. I think you're going to do amazing. And we need you more than ever right now." Princess Esme reached for the door. "Now, let's head back out there. And introduce you to everyone, *General*."

Iris winced at the title but followed Princess Esme anyway, heading back into the main area of the bar. The whispering from her fellow guards died down when they saw the two of them. King Tedros looked confused, then Princess Esme whispered in his ear.

"Good idea," he whispered back, loud enough for Iris to hear. "We need a new general, especially as we move into a new era for our people. One where we must rebuild."

"Glad you approve." Princess Esme turned to the guards. "After much discussion, Iris Ambrose will be your new general. She just accepted the promotion."

The guards looked shocked, then congratulated Iris on her new position. She still felt like a traitor to her own people.

"Good for you," Sapphira whispered. "Maybe you can get King Tedros to step down."

"That's not on my to-do list," Iris whispered back, making Sapphira frown. "Survival is what matters right now. Making sure these humans don't kill us."

Fortunately, the royal family hadn't heard them. Gemma's former fairy godmother, Blanche, approached the king. She cleared her throat and looked nervous.

"Um, your Royalness?" she asked. "Before all this crap happened, me and Gemma had come to an arrangement. I wanted to leave my post as a fairy godmother, and she gave me her blessing. I know a lot is going on, but I'd still like to honor our deal since my feelings haven't changed—"

"But why, dear?" Fairy Godmother Odelia asked. "You're so good at it. Such an excellent potion maker and student. And Gemma needs a fairy godmother, no?"

"It's all right," Gemma said. "Blanche doesn't want this life anymore. I won't force her to do something she doesn't want to do."

Blanche smiled at her. "Thank you, Gemma. So, what do you say?"

"This is trivial. We have other concerns," King Tedros said. "I'm sorry, Blanche, but as of right now, we can't afford to lose anyone else. You'll have to remain as a fairy godmother."

Blanche looked disappointed, sitting down at the bar. "Then I'm going to need one hell of a drink to get through this. Bartender?"

Ian gave Blanche a drink, all right—another tea, much to

her disappointment. Gemma placed a consoling hand on her fairy godmother's shoulder.

"Well, with that settled, we need to think about our strategy," Princess Esme said. "For now, though, I think we should head back down to Fairhaven."

"What? Why?" Gemma asked, holding Ian close. "Our kingdom ... it's gone."

"It is. But I think our first step is to see the damage for ourselves and honor the ones who lost their lives. Say goodbye to our home before moving on." Princess Esme glanced at her father, then everyone else. "What do you all say?"

King Tedros sighed. "It's a nice thought, Esme. A chance to say goodbye since we didn't have the opportunity before. If Fairy Godmother Odelia believes it's safe, that is."

Fairy Godmother Odelia nodded. "For a little while, yes. But if we stay too long, the poison in the air from the bombs will invade our bodies and make us very sick. I sent a potion down there a little while ago to confirm this. We must be quick about our trip."

Iris gripped the side of the bar hard. What gave Senator Remus the right to destroy their only home like that? If he wasn't already dead, she'd kill him.

"I can't believe I get to see Fairhaven," Ian whispered to Gemma, following them all to the back door. "I just wish I could've seen it in its heyday. Without all this tragedy."

"Me too, Ian," Gemma whispered back, sadly. "Me too."

They stepped out through the back of the bar, then walked toward the nearby storm drain. It was the exact place where Gemma told Iris she had confronted Bobby Blevins, the human who somehow got magic in his bloodstream and used it for theft and murder. Now he had escaped, adding another problem to their growing list.

Iris pulled the grate open. The other guards went through

first, then she stood guard as the royal family, Gemma, and Ian trailed behind. Finally, she went in last. Instead of the normal sounds and smells—chatter, magical flowers, and baked goods—there was nothing, only an acrid, charred smell.

And silence and darkness.

They finished climbing down the ladder, standing on a pile of rubble. Ian pulled out a flashlight, illuminating their surroundings as Fairy Godmother Odelia did the same with her wand. They glanced around, and Iris realized they were standing on the remains of the castle—now burned to the ground. Corpses were scattered everywhere, charred and ashy. Not a single house stood. In the distance, far above their heads back on Earth, human construction crews were investigating, trying to repair the storm drains while searching for survivors.

But there were none. Those powerful magical bombs had wiped out all of Fairhaven, leaving nothing behind.

"Wow. This is ... awful," Ian muttered. "Again, I'm really sorry."

There wasn't a dry eye among those from Fairhaven. King Tedros cleared his throat. "Yes, it's truly a tragedy. To see our beloved home like this ... it's just unimaginable."

"Forgive me if this sounds ignorant," Ian began, "and I'm sure it'll take a long time ... but can't you just rebuild one day? Start over? I've had to do that. Rebuild my life after everything went wrong. And it led me to something wonderful."

As Ian and Gemma shared a smile, Fairy Godmother Odelia shook her head. "Sadly, no. The bombs that Senator Remus used make that impossible. There was magical poison in them that infected Fairhaven's air. As I mentioned before, if we stay down here for too long, we'll be consumed by it. There's no hope for rebuilding, I'm afraid. Everything down here has been tainted."

That was it, then. The surface world was their new home now. If those pesky humans would let them stay.

As the others took the time to grieve, Iris wanted to do something. Anything at all to make her feel like she had some kind of control.

"Let's spread out," Iris said. "Maybe we can find something that survived—something of use to our people. Potions, books, anything. We'll meet back up in twenty minutes."

Iris didn't wait for approval, heading south down a row of townhomes that had blown up, surrounded by darkness, death, and misery. And the resounding voice in her head repeated how much of a failed soldier she was.

CHAPTER 3

Using the flashlight on her belt, it didn't take Iris long to find the remains of her old home—a small townhouse on the edge of Fairhaven, close to the barracks and castle. She had many fond memories of her parents from over the years. Gardening with her mother, learning how to use magical tools with her father, eating the food they had grown together.

It had been her safe place. And now, it was nothing more than a heaping pile of rubble.

She bent down, noticing two blackened skeletons on the ground. Her parents. Then she said a silent prayer, rose to her feet, and turned around so she wouldn't cry. When she did, she saw Gemma standing there, looking at the house behind her.

"Sorry, didn't mean to sneak up on you," Gemma whispered. "I came to find my old house. I take it … this one was yours?"

Iris swallowed the lump in her throat. "That's right. Those bodies belong to my parents."

Gemma closed her eyes. "This is so, so awful. I'm very sorry, Iris."

"Yes, well ... I suppose this is what I deserve for not keeping a closer eye on Senator Remus. And the traitors on the surface."

Gemma opened her eyes, frowning. "What, you blame yourself for this? That's crazy, Iris. You didn't know—"

Before Iris could insist that she should've tried harder, King Tedros' voice carried through the darkness. "Everyone, come here. I've found something."

Concerned, Iris and Gemma took off along with Gemma's father, following the sound of King Tedros' voice. He stood with the others, a few feet away from the destroyed castle. A cellar beneath the ground had been opened to reveal a crypt.

"Whoa," Gemma said, heading back to Ian. "What is this? I didn't know this was here."

"Neither did I," Princess Esme said, turning to her father. "Are you going to explain?"

King Tedros stared blankly into the crypt, then shook his head. "I ... can't. But this isn't good—trust me. Did any of you see anything suspicious? A man wandering around, perhaps?"

"I didn't see anything. Your Majesty?" Iris asked. "Is there something we should know?"

But King Tedros wasn't even looking their way. He continued staring down into the darkness. "The magical explosion ... it must've opened it and let him out."

Unease skittered up Iris's spine, and she put her hand on the hilt of her sword, ready to draw it if necessary.

"Let who out, Father?" Princess Esme asked. "Who are you talking about?"

But he wouldn't say. "Come—let's get back to the surface. And stay close, everyone."

In confusion, everyone followed King Tedros back to the ladder that led to the surface. There was no point in staying in Fairhaven—there was nothing left. As they followed the king over the ash-filled roads, Iris heard everyone else whispering.

"Do you know what's going on?" Ian asked Gemma, trailing behind. "Why is your king is being so weird?"

"I really don't know," Gemma whispered back. "I didn't even know there *was* a crypt there."

"Neither did I," Princess Esme said to Noah. "I've never seen my father this spooked before. Something isn't right."

Noah's eyes widened, though he said nothing. Fairy Godmother Odelia was the only one who seemed to have an idea of what was going on. She eyed the opened crypt over her shoulder, then reached toward the ladder.

"Wait," Princess Esme said. "We came down here to honor the lives lost. Can I say a prayer for the departed souls?"

King Tedros nodded. "Very well."

Esme looked around Fairhaven, then shut her eyes. "There aren't any words for what happened down here other than 'tragedy.' This shouldn't have happened—all these innocent people should still be here. What the senator did was inexcusable."

"At least he's dead," Kyler muttered, bowing his head in prayer. "The rest of his family should follow suit."

"Hear, hear," Sapphira whispered.

"I pray you are now in a better place, free of suffering," Princess Esme continued, not hearing their whispers. "And we will do all we can to make the surface world a home for the ones who survived."

"A lovely speech, Esme," King Tedros said with a nod. "You've learned so much since you were exiled to the surface. I'm proud of you."

"Thank you, Father. I just hope Alva rests in peace." Princess Esme took one last look at Fairhaven, tears making her vision blurry, then she reached for the ladder. "We should get out of here. Come on, everyone."

The royal family went first, then the guards and regular

civilians as they climbed the ladder. It led them into the back alley behind the bar. As Iris pulled the storm drain back over the hole, she couldn't stop thinking about the crypt.

And she had a sinking feeling something wasn't right.

"Well, we ought to get back inside and discuss our next move," Princess Esme said. "For now, we're fortunate we have a place to stay—"

The back door of the bar crashed down into the alley, and Iris reeled, stunned, as several human soldiers in military gear burst from inside the bar, guns and flashlights in their hands. They must have broken in to look for the Fairhaveners. They aimed their weapons at Princess Esme and her people, descending on them like a flock of angry birds.

"Hands where we can see them," one of the soldiers demanded. "No sudden movements. Any hint of magic and we'll fire."

"What's going on here?" Iris asked, feeling the hilt of her sword on her belt. She was prepared to use it if she had to. "Who are you people?"

"The Canadian military. And someone wishes to speak with you," another soldier replied. "All of your people. Come with us, please."

When everyone looked at King Tedros, he nodded. "Very well—we don't want to cause any trouble. Let's go with these soldiers, everyone."

They stepped through the bar's back door, following the soldiers through the bar. Ian shook his head when he looked at the damage the soldiers had caused by breaking in. When they reached the front door, several military trucks waited on the street. The roads were mostly deserted except for some curious and brave humans who wanted to see what was going on.

The royal family hopped into one military truck, then the others divided themselves up. Gemma and Ian stayed together, holding hands as Princess Esme and Noah did the same. Iris stayed with her soldiers and kept a close eye on the human soldiers. She made sure the royal family's military truck was in view at all times.

The soldiers drove them to an office building downtown. They hopped out first, then gestured for Princess Esme's people to follow them. Esme and her people were led inside, through what looked like a conference room for a local politician. When they entered the small adjoining office, a middle-aged, dark-haired human woman in a maroon pantsuit was waiting for them near the desk. Dozens of security guards and soldiers stood with her to keep her safe.

"Ah, there they all are," the woman said. "We really need to talk."

"We have no problem with that," King Tedros said. "We want to live peacefully alongside the humans. My name is King Tedros, the reigning monarch of Fairhaven. Or, what's left of it. Allow me to introduce everyone. This is my daughter, Princess Esme, and her husband, Noah Crawford."

"I've heard of you two," the woman said, shaking their hands. "You, Mr. Crawford, worked for The Human Connection, a charitable organization. Then Esme joined, and you busted the owner for embezzlement and theft. Not to mention all the good you did for the community. Nice work, you two."

"Oh, thank you," Princess Esme replied. "I enjoyed my time there. Who are you, if I might ask?"

"Prime Minister Teresa Lin," the woman said, standing up taller. "I'm responsible for Canada as a whole. I happened to be in Toronto when your world exploded. And I've received a lot of calls from Canadians concerned about your people. But first, let's finish with the introductions."

Iris was surprised at the prime minister's respect. She was a lot friendlier than her soldiers. They kept a close eye on Princess

Esme's people, one hand on their guns at all times as King Tedros finished introducing everyone.

"... and that's my fairy godmother, Odelia. Plus, all our soldiers, including our new general, Iris Ambrose," King Tedros said, then Iris bowed. "We also have some humans with us. Noah, of course, Gemma's father, and Ian Whitman, Gemma's boyfriend."

"I've heard of you too, Mr. Whitman," Prime Minister Lin said. "Your father is a billionaire oil company owner and your mother is a Hollywood actress."

"True," Ian said, "but I'm trying to distance myself from them completely. I much prefer the company of my new friends."

When he glanced at Gemma, she blushed. Prime Minister Lin smiled. "Well, isn't that sweet? I'm glad some humans have accepted you. Anyway, please have a seat, everyone. We have much to discuss."

Iris let the royal family sit down as she remained standing at attention, guarding them. She didn't cower even when the human soldiers glared at her. Prime Minister Lin sat, then removed the smartphone from her pocket.

"The news stations are going wild," she said, showing them a live feed. "Everyone is talking about the discovery of Fairhaven. And not just in Canada, but around the world."

"And we apologize for that," King Tedros said. "This isn't the way we wanted to introduce ourselves. Or at all, really. We managed to keep our home and our people a secret for centuries."

"And bravo for that. My people never suspected anyone lived below the storm drains. Your magic kept you safely hidden —until now. We didn't even know a few of your own were living among us." The prime minister put her phone away. "I've received thousands of emails and phone calls in the last twenty-four hours from my Canadian citizens. They're concerned about your people—and the magical power you possess. Something about one of your own using it to manipulate someone's mind?"

Gemma winced, sinking further into her seat.

"Yes, that's correct," King Tedros said with a sigh. "But it won't happen again. The guilty party has been dealt with."

"Good, good. And, of course, your own senator blew up your home and tried to take all of humanity hostage. What do you have to say about that?"

"He acted of his own accord. He was a traitor against our people in search of power," Princess Esme said. "And he's dead now—I took care of him myself."

"Yes, I heard the report from the local officers. There are other criminals from Fairhaven still in our custody. Some co-conspirators, a woman named Lady Nyssa and her mother, and Duke Cullen. Among others."

"My mother and former best friend are among them. Trust me—never let them out," Gemma said, anger blazing behind her eyes. "Lock them up and throw away the key."

"We'll try our best. We may need your help to keep them locked up, of course. You're more familiar with their crimes and power than we are."

Iris said nothing, shaking her head. They should've kept them locked up in the first place. If the senator had still been behind bars, this tragedy wouldn't have happened. But he had inside help that destroyed all their lives and their home.

"Of course, whatever you need. My fairy godmother will send you a potion to disable their magic. Please don't be afraid to use it—it won't hurt you," King Tedros said. "In the meantime, what do you plan to do with us?"

Prime Minister Lin sighed, rising to her feet. She stared out the window as a large crowd of protestors formed with signs and megaphones. "They found us—word travels fast. They've already started protesting against you, but I'm going to give you a chance. My parents were immigrants to Canada—they know what it's like to lose your home and to have nowhere else to turn. I won't imprison you all for the crime of simply existing."

King Tedros sighed in relief. "Thank you, Prime Minister. That's kind of you."

She nodded, her back still turned. "You're welcome. You'll, of course, have to win over the people on your own. Show them you don't mean them any harm. Much like politicians do, you'll have to go on your own campaign trail of sorts. Being honest and friendly is the only way to win them over."

"We'll try our best," Princess Esme said.

"Good. I'll need you all to register, disclose exactly how your magic works, and give me updates on your progress. Your king can handle this." Prime Minister Lin turned back to face them. "And before I let you all go, I must ask you something. Will you promise to remain non-violent? I can't have you using magic and causing trouble. If I'm going to set you free, you must be on your best behavior."

"We promise," King Tedros said without hesitation. "But only our fairy godmothers have magic. They create potions for us, and in turn, we use them for many different reasons. We aren't a threat without—"

President Lin held up a hand. "Do you think my people will accept that answer? They see you as dangerous magic users. No amount of explaining will likely change that."

King Tedros sighed. "Too bad—because it's the truth. And trust me, we want nothing more than to blend in here and get along with the humans. We have nowhere else to turn now."

"Right. For that, I'm very sorry. It couldn't have been easy losing your families and your homes. Fairhaven, was it?"

"That's right." King Tedros looked down. "So many lives

taken. The traitors led by Senator Remus have been a thorn in our side for ages, but we never thought he would destroy our home. He did it all for power, of course. He knew I'd never support enslaving humanity."

"It's a good thing he's gone, then. We'll keep a close eye on them. There's also the issue of Bobby Blevins—the human who was able to ingest magic and was using it to kill and steal. He escaped custody, as you know. Turns out he had a secret potion in his pocket that the officers missed. It helped him escape. We don't know where he is now or what he has planned. He's on the lam, as we humans call it."

"We'll watch out for him," Princess Esme said. "And once we find him, we'll give him to you and he'll go to jail where he belongs. He shouldn't have had that magic in the first place."

"Agreed. No one should—it's far too dangerous. Anyway, in the spirit of cooperation, I'm providing a place for you all to stay. There's an abandoned church in town. It's got everything you'll need—private rooms, a kitchen, bathrooms. It's still in good condition. We trust it'll serve you well."

Everyone looked at each other. The same surprise Iris felt was reflected in her companions' eyes. The prime minister was being generous. King Tedros was the first one to speak. "Really? My goodness, that's kind of you. Thank you very much."

"Of course. We process immigrants all the time—we help them seek asylum and start new lives. You aren't too different from them. Other than the magic and unusual clothing, of course. Anyway, I'll show you to the abandoned church. And I wish you all luck. Hopefully, in time, the humans will accept you, and you can all have a fresh start. But please, don't make me regret this. I'm risking a lot to help you."

While everyone else was thankful, Iris closed her eyes. How could they have fresh starts knowing their homes were gone forever? And their families along with it? That would always haunt her, distracting her from keeping her people safe. As the new general, that was her focus right now.

Prime Minister Lin led them out of the office, heading toward the doors. "Follow me and keep your heads down, everyone. We don't think the protestors are violent but you should be prepared."

"Allow me to go first," Iris said, stepping ahead of the royal family. "I'll protect you."

King Tedros nodded, then the prime minister opened the doors. The large crowd began screaming and chanting when they saw Princess Esme's people. The soldiers surrounded the royal family, pushing through the swarm. It was clear the humans had no love for them.

"These people are dangerous!" the familiar secretary from the news said. "One of them mind-controlled me. Look, there she is now!"

"If they can blow up their own home, what does that mean for us?" another protestor shouted. "They could kill us all with those magical powers of theirs!"

"Send them packing!" a man shouted. "Get rid of them all. They don't belong in our city!"

Others shouted more obscene things as Princess Esme and their people kept their heads down, trying to get to the military trucks parked on the road. Iris, her soldiers and the military did their best to repel the crowd. But one determined protestor began pushing, sending waves of others that knocked King Tedros down.

"Father!" Princess Esme cried, reaching down to help him up. "Come on, everyone—we need to get out of here."

As she helped him to his feet, Iris shoved a screaming man back so he wouldn't get through to them. When the military trucks were only a few feet away, Iris felt someone strong reach out and shove her down. Legs appeared on all sides, trampling her. If it weren't for her armor, she would've been seriously hurt.

The crowd began pushing even more, separating Iris from the others. She dodged the trampling legs and thrown fists as she tried to pull herself to her feet. When an angry man pinned her down, screaming about them all being terrorists, she felt a hand reach through the crowd and grab her leg, yanking her to safety.

"I'm a friend," he said when Iris reached for the dagger hidden in her boot.

The man dragged her into the nearby bushes, giving her a moment to breathe. The crowd was still irate behind her as they tried to trample the others. She took a deep breath, then rose to her feet. She finally saw the man who had saved her from the crowd.

He was handsome—muscles underneath his t-shirt, dressed casually in jeans and sandals. His dark, curly hair fell to just above his brown eyes. The way he looked at Iris wasn't like the other protestors in the mob. This man was genuinely concerned.

"Are you okay?" he asked. "That crowd … it was pretty violent."

"I'll say," Iris muttered, brushing dirt off her armor. "I'm fine, thank you. But I should get back to my people. Goodbye."

The man looked like he had more to say, but Iris took off, heading back toward the crowd. She elbowed through the screaming protestors to reach King Tedros and their people. Once she had caught up with the help of the soldiers, they clambered into the military trucks, then the prime minister gestured for the drivers to take off. They sped far away from the office and left those rude protestors in the dust—along with that kind man who had saved Iris.

CHAPTER 4

I ris chastised herself the entire car ride for letting the crowd knock her down. What was wrong with her? She was losing her edge. She needed to stay strong, to stay alert. Or she feared another awful incident would happen.

It was hard to imagine anything worse than Fairhaven blowing up, but she didn't want to give fate the chance.

"Hey, you all right?" Gemma asked in the seat next to her, nudging her shoulder. "You look distracted."

Iris nodded. "I'm fine, thank you. I just shouldn't have let the crowd knock me down."

"They were pretty vicious—I almost fell a few times. Ian saved me, though." She reached for his hand, squeezing it with a smile. "You did fine, Iris. This level of hatred is new for all of us."

"I am trained to do better than fine," Iris said, a little harsher than intended. "I need to be stronger."

Gemma's smile faded. "Give yourself a little grace. We're all confused and out of our element. When I reached the truck, I saw someone pulling you to safety. Who was that?"

"I don't know. Some human in the crowd. He had kind eyes."

Had she said that out loud? Iris wanted to hit herself.

"Hmm," Gemma said. "Whoever he was, it was nice of him to rescue you."

It was—and Iris figured she should thank him at some point. But for the most part, she didn't trust these humans. And she didn't understand how Gemma and Princess Esme could fall in love with them so easily.

It was almost like they were spellbound—under a different form of magic. Iris shook her head, swearing that would never be her. Her work as a soldier was too important—especially now that she was the general. Love was just a waste of time and energy.

A few minutes later, the trucks pulled down a residential street in Toronto. Houses in bright colors were built on both sides of the street with a run-down church at the end of the block. When the trucks came to a stop, Princess Esme's people stepped out and looked on in dismay.

Prime Minister Lin joined them, noticing their faces. "I know it isn't the best location—and I do apologize for that. But for now, it's all we have. Our shelters and community houses are full of immigrants and asylum seekers. We have a responsibility to them as well."

"Yes, of course. It's all right, Prime Minister. We know you're doing your best," King Tedros said. "We thank you for finding a place for us on such short notice."

"Of course. Make yourselves at home—maybe consider wearing more discreet clothing, getting a job or helping out around the community. If people will let you, of course. That might change some of my people's opinions." Prime Minister Lin checked her watch, hidden beneath the blazer's sleeve. "I need to go—I'm late for a meeting. But let me know if you need anything. We'll definitely be in touch. Take care, everyone."

After she tucked the key to the church into Princess Esme's hand, the prime minister walked back to the lead truck and hopped inside. The soldiers accompanying her followed, not as trusting as Prime Minister Lin.

As the trucks drove off, the street turned silent. Everyone stared up at the dilapidated church. The windows were broken out, the blue paint on the outside was chipping, and a broken sign still had the words SUNDAY MASS AT NOON written across it. The Catholic cross on top of the roof had fallen off a long time ago and crashed on the browned grass. Princess Esme was the first one to climb the rickety steps, heading toward the dusty double doors.

"Well, it's not a castle, but it'll do. Better than being homeless," she said, unlocking the door and opening it with a squeak. "Come on, everyone."

With murmurs of concern, everyone followed Princess Esme inside the abandoned church. Iris made sure the place was clear first, then she locked the doors behind them. She began boarding up the windows with spare pieces of wood that were lying around, trying to ensure no one could break in and hurt them. Without a fight, at least.

As Gemma and Ian glanced around the pews and checked out the altar, Princess Esme and Noah went inside the kitchen. The fridge was empty but still running, and at least the church had electricity and heat. Casual clothes in different sizes and colors laid on the table for everyone. They changed into them, but Iris kept her armor on. Just in case. The princess opened the back door to reveal a small back yard with a growing garden.

"Ah, wonderful! We'll be able to plant seeds out here and grow our own food," she called out as she stepped through the door into the back yard. "It'll keep us fed, at least. And with the new clothes, we'll fit in a lot better. We really need to work on being independent. Everyone, choose your beds down the hall. I think I spotted the quarters for the priests and nuns."

Everyone nodded, heading down the long hallway. There were bathrooms with multiple stalls, a prayer room, and sleeping quarters with bunkbeds. The guards took their beds, then Fairy Godmother Odelia and Blanche did the same. Blanche was still trying to convince Fairy Godmother Odelia to let her leave the fairy godmother order as Iris walked down the hall.

"… and if anything, the senator blowing up Fairhaven proves how short and unpredictable life is," Blanche was saying to her. "Please. Gemma has already accepted my request. I don't want to be a fairy godmother anymore, damn it."

"I know, my dear, but like King Tedros told you, our numbers are too small for anyone to leave their post. Now, will you help me brew a potion? I know the prime minister said no magic, but as long as we don't use it outside the church, I don't see a problem. Especially with harmless spells."

Blanche sighed and nodded, getting to work as Iris entered the sleeping quarters and chose a bunk. She stared out the nearby window, hearing voices in the distance. She needed to make sure everything was all right and wanted to walk and secure the perimeter of the church. After leaving the church, she walked down the sidewalk, noticing an elementary school in the distance. A large group of kids and their teachers were outside for recess. Other than not having magical potion classes, it didn't look too different from the schools back in Fairhaven.

When Iris noticed a familiar face in the crowd, she paused. It was him—the man with the kind eyes who had pulled her from the dangerous crowd. He was chatting with the teachers, watching over the students. He must work at the school.

Iris was intrigued. She had her duties that took up all her time, but there was something about that man—something that made her want to get to know him. He had already proven he was different by not joining the angry mob. For that, Iris was grateful—and curious.

After she completed walking the perimeter, she turned and headed back inside the church. When Iris heard voices down the hallway, she walked back toward the pews where Princess Esme and King Tedros were doling out orders to their small group. It was depressing to realize how much their numbers had dwindled.

"... and you, Guardswoman Sapphira, will be in charge of growing vegetables and fruit outside," Princess Esme said. "I found some tomato seeds in the kitchen. Get started right away. Guardsman Kyler, you'll be in charge of cleaning up. The rest of you, please—work together. We can make this our new home, but it'll take some work."

The guards nodded, scurrying away to complete their tasks. Gemma and Ian were cleaning up some of the debris in the main hall as the two fairy godmothers stirred potions down the corridor.

Iris crept closer as Princess Esme turned to Noah and her father. "In the meantime, I'm going to contact the local news station. We'll try to give an interview tonight—this time, without using magic."

"Good idea. Which Gemma should apologize for," King Tedros said, eyeing her. "This could be a chance to show the public we don't mean them any harm. Hopefully, they'll stop protesting soon."

"And I'll call work—ask The Human Connection for help," Noah added, reaching for the smartphone in his pocket. "It's what they do, after all. Be right back."

As he went into the corner, calling his work, Iris cleared her throat. "Is it really a good idea to go on the news? What if we make things worse?"

"I don't see how," Princess Esme replied. "The public's eager to hear from us, and we want to ease their fears. The prime minister is hoping for that too. We'll be careful; don't worry. These humans should hear from us directly."

"All right then. You seem to have everything under control here. Anything you need me to do?"

Princess Esme shrugged. "There's plenty, yes. Why don't you scope out the area, General? Give us a detailed report of the neighborhood? For security reasons."

"Will do. I'll see if anyone suspicious is out there," Iris replied. "You can never be too careful."

"Exactly. Just try not to irritate the humans any more than we already have. We haven't got off on the best of terms." Princess Esme shook her head. "And thanks again for accepting the position as general. I know you don't think you're fit for it, but we really needed someone. You're doing a great job so far."

Iris didn't agree. They had no home, no money or prospects, and she had already gotten trampled by an angry crowd. Why didn't Princess Esme realize how bleak things were, like Iris did?

"You're welcome," Iris simply said, then turned toward the doors. "I will return shortly."

"Be careful, General!" King Tedros called.

Iris promised she would, then stepped outside the church. As she looked around, much would need to be done to make it a safer living environment—including some maintenance, painting, and defensive measures. Maybe they could even build a barracks and a watchtower.

"Getting ahead of myself," Iris muttered.

For now, she was focused on scouting the area, securing the perimeter, and strengthening the fence in the back yard. As she walked down the street, people glanced out their windows. Judging by their wide-eyed expressions, some of them recognized Iris, probably from the news. She certainly stuck out in her armor, but she didn't want to take it off. She needed it for protection. She kept one hand on her sword's scabbard, keeping her head swiveling for any threats. So far, no one approached or tried anything.

She didn't want to stab a human—she knew that wouldn't help relations—but she'd do anything to keep her people safe. Now more than ever.

As she completed her survey of the block, she spotted a few stores where one of their people could try to get a job or buy ingredients. The humans didn't have a bustling marketplace like the one back in Fairhaven, complete with dragons flying overhead, but the little shops looked well-stocked. As she window-shopped, staring inside a small grocery store, the owner came over and pulled the curtains down with a glare.

It was clear they hadn't won anyone over. Not yet, at least.

When she turned, the bell had rung at the elementary school. The kids playing in the field rushed inside to head back to class. The rest of the teachers joined them, but the kind man who had saved her from the crowd hung back. When he spotted Iris, he recognized her and smiled before waving.

Iris didn't know what to do, so she waved back at him, awkwardly flailing her arms. She dropped them a second later when she realized how uncomfortable she must've looked. The man who saved her certainly didn't feel the same way as that angry shopkeeper or the crowd of protestors. Why was he so different?

When he vanished inside the school, Iris turned around and headed back toward the church. She entered, finding Noah sitting on one of the pews. He ran a hand through his hair with his mouth pinched.

"... and I'm really sorry," Princess Esme was saying to him. She and King Tedros stood over him, looking down at his face with pity. "This is all my fault."

"No—it's all right. I should've expected this." Noah sighed. "I don't blame you, Esme. Not at all."

"What's going on?" Iris asked, walking closer.

"Ah, you're back safely. Good," King Tedros said. "Unfortunately, Noah just found out he was fired from The Human Connection. Esme as well."

"Turns out the shareholders are worried that my obvious connection to Princess Esme is bad for business," Noah muttered. "Something about their image. So, Esme and I are out of a job. "

"I'm sorry," Iris said. "What will you do now?"

Noah shrugged. "I don't know—I'll have to find another job. If anyone will hire me now that they know I'm with your people. They don't seem to trust you *or* me by association. Even after all the good work I've done for The Human Connection. It's bullshit."

"Definitely," Princess Esme replied, rubbing his back. "Don't worry—we'll find something. I'd say we could disguise ourselves but everyone will recognize us now. Hey, maybe your father could help?"

"I don't know. I've been thinking about it and ... maybe we should keep our distance from my family and our human friends. Just so they're not caught in the crossfire of anyone's rage."

"That's a good idea," Gemma said, coming around the corner with Ian and a broom. "I made some good friends up here on the surface, and I don't want to put them in jeopardy. We'll stay away from them until the public's opinion has turned in our favor."

Noah nodded. "Exactly. In the meantime, I'll probably lose

my apartment. Won't have enough money to pay rent. I guess I'll have to stay here with you all. The church *is* pretty cozy. Or it will be, once we fix it up, of course."

Princess Esme walked toward the altar. "We could throw a rug down here, make it real romantic. It'll feel like home soon enough."

As the others went over their design ideas for the church, Iris knew it would never feel like home. It would never come close to Fairhaven—not if those protestors had anything to say about it.

"At least I still have my bar, though I wonder if it'll suffer when people find out I'm dating Gemma," Ian said, tapping his fingers against his chin. "I'll try to help as much as I can—pass along any money I make. Enough for some food, at least. Maybe clean clothes."

Gemma nodded, kissing his cheek. Gemma's father watched them proudly. "You're the best. How did I get so lucky?"

As Iris watched them kiss and the others bicker over where to position furniture, a knock sounded on the door. Iris walked toward the window and peered through the wooden boards she had put up.

"Who is it?" Princess Esme asked behind her.

"A family, I think," Iris said, her eyes focusing on the people on the step. "With ... a basket? Let me see. Be on your guard, everyone."

Everyone nodded, and Iris put a hand on her sword. She opened the front door quickly. A family of three stood there—a middle-aged man and woman, then what looked like their teenage daughter. They dressed casually, had dewy brown skin, and carried a basket of fruit, bread, and some instant microwave meals.

"Can I help you?" Iris asked gruffly.

"Actually, we were hoping to help *you*," the woman said with a smile. She spoke with an Indian accent, one Iris recognized from watching a human movie set in Bollywood. "May we come in?"

Iris shrugged, stepping aside. "All right. But I *am* armed with a sword—just in case you try anything."

"We wouldn't hurt a fly, trust me," the man said, stepping inside the church with the large basket. "Thank you. My, we never thought this church would ever see people inside it again. It closed down years ago—low attendance. It's nice to see some life in it."

The woman and the teenage girl nodded, entering the church. The teenager looked less than thrilled to be there, on her phone and texting the entire time. Iris didn't know how these humans could waste so much of their lives on their silly cellular devices. The parents were more present, glancing around at the state of the church.

"Just needs a fresh coat of paint and it'll look beautiful," the woman said with a smile, then held out a hand toward Iris. "I'm sorry—we're being rude. We haven't even made introductions. My name is Ayesha Bhatia. This is my husband, Ramesh, and our daughter, Maya."

The girl barely made a sound, still glued to her phone, but her husband waved and nodded. "We live across from the church. When we heard the prime minister had given it to you, we wanted to welcome you to the neighborhood. Your discovery is all over the news."

"We know. Lots of people don't trust us," King Tedros said, walking toward them. His robe trailed along the old wooden floor. "My name is King Tedros. This is my daughter, Princess Esme, and her husband, Noah Crawford ..."

Once the introductions were over, Ramesh set the basket

down. "Nice to meet you all. This is for you—some food to get you settled. We hope you can eat our food, at least."

"We can, thank you," Gemma said. "That's very kind."

Iris doubted this family had pure intentions. Was this some kind of prank—or something darker?

Iris leaned against the wall, crossing her arms. "*Too* kind. What do you want in return?"

Ayesha frowned. "I beg your pardon?"

"You must want something. The majority of people in this city don't trust us. So, why are you here? Is the food poisoned or something?"

"What? Of course not!" Ramesh cried as he and his wife eyes' widened. "We'd never poison anyone. Look, I'll even try some of it."

He reached into the basket, grabbing a cracker. He placed it into his mouth, chewed, and then swallowed. Iris waited for any physical reaction—his throat closing up, magical warts growing across his face—but nothing happened. He was perfectly fine.

"See?" Ramesh asked. "It's safe to eat. We do this for all our neighbors, no matter where they're from. We just like to be welcoming."

"And we know what it's like to be outsiders," Ayesha said. "We come from a different country—moved here for better jobs in finance—and people haven't always treated us with kindness. So, we just want to say you're not alone. Our physiology may be different, but we have similar backgrounds. And if you need anything, you can come find us, day or night. We live just across the street."

"That won't be necessary," Iris said. "But thank you."

The family looked disappointed, then Maya looked up from her phone and sighed. "Can I go back to school now? My lunch break is almost over, and I wasted it here instead of hanging with my friends. Ugh."

Ayesha nodded. "Yes, of course. We just thought you might want to tag along to meet our new neighbors. Anyway, take care, everyone—and enjoy the snacks."

The three of them left the church, heading down the steps. Iris closed the door and watched them enter their house across the street. When she turned around, Princess Esme, King Tedros, and Noah were looking at her with frowns.

"What?" she asked.

"You didn't have to be so rude. They seem like nice, genuine people," Princess Esme said, looking through the basket. "This food will help us for a while. So kind of them."

As they sorted through the basket, Iris frowned. They might have trusted that human family, but she didn't. Although that man had saved her from the crowd and other humans had brought them food, it was going to take more than that to earn her trust.

Almost as long as it would take to win over the humans.

CHAPTER 5

For the rest of the day, Princess Esme and her people worked on cleaning and sprucing up the church and making it a safer place to live. When most of the glass was cleaned up, then the windows were repaired, they ate the food that the Bhatia family had brought over, sitting on pews and chatting.

Noah turned on the local news with his phone, letting them all watch the livestream. The reporter had driven to the penitentiary to interview Giselle McMillan—and that name jogged Iris's memory.

"Isn't she the one you two put away?" Iris asked, pointing at Noah and Esme as she sat next to them on the pews. "The former CEO of The Human Connection?"

"That's the one," Noah replied with the phone in his hand. "I can't believe the news would care what a convict has to say."

"They're desperate for any scoop on us, especially if it's negative," Princess Esme said. "Anyone who's ever interacted with us will be a target."

And maybe, a target for their enemies too.

"I had no idea my former employee was one of them, no,"

Giselle said to the reporter behind bars. She was wearing an orange jumpsuit, her hair messy with bags under her eyes. She looked much different than when she was their boss. "She seemed perfectly normal—and polite. If I knew then what I know now, I would've turned her over to the police."

"But why?" Gemma asked. "She just admitted you were polite. You've done nothing wrong."

Iris glanced out the window. "It's just like the Bhatias said —they mistrust us because we're outsiders. These humans have some real problems." She flicked a glance at Noah who was, technically, her new prince. "Um, apologies, Your Majesty. No offense meant."

"None taken," he replied, flipping through the news livestreams. "Some humans are racist, yeah. That can't be changed. But hopefully, we'll win over enough of them. Look, another broadcast."

A reporter interviewed Ian's parents—Mr. and Mrs. Whitman. They sat in their mansion, sipping wine as the reporter asked them questions. They dressed glamorously and looked like they had money.

"Oh my God. Not my parents," Ian muttered, hiding his face in his hands. He could barely watch the livestream. "They're interviewing them, too?"

"So much for keeping our families out of the spotlight," Noah muttered.

"... and no, we had no idea that our son's girlfriend was a witch. Or whatever they are," Mrs. Whitman said, her nose scrunched up. "But I knew she wasn't good enough for my son. That much was clear when that tart walked through the front door, especially in that God-awful gown."

His father nodded, staring into the camera. "And Ian, if you're watching this—come home, son. We miss you. And we're worried about your safety hanging out with those ...

magical people. Leave Gemma and this foolishness behind and come back where you belong."

Ian shook his head, reaching for Gemma's hand. "I *am* where I belong, right now. And that'll never change."

As she smiled at Ian, their attention was drawn back to the livestream on Noah's phone when someone crashed the Whitman's interview. Ian said it was his brother, Marcus, only a few years younger than him. He approached the camera behind his parents, glaring at them as he crossed his arms.

"What are you two doing?" Marcus asked. "We all know that Ian's girlfriend was kind and sweet. She even saved that nice lady's bookstore. Who cares if she comes from somewhere else? Or that they have magic? I trust her. More importantly, Ian loves her. You have no right to—"

The camera cut off, just as Ian's parents began to chastise Marcus for interrupting them. Noah shook his head. "Anyone who defends us will be silenced, I guess. The news only wants to highlight people who hate your kind. It makes for better TV, after all."

"Despicable," Iris muttered.

She rose to her feet, hearing enough as Noah continued playing the broadcasts. She couldn't listen to those humans and their hatred anymore. As she stared out the window, her eyes fell on the elementary school down the street. The bell had rung and all the kids were heading home for the evening.

When she saw that kind man again, chatting and laughing with some students, she wondered if he was truly human after all. None of them—except for a small handful—had shown their people compassion.

"Be right back," Iris called over her shoulder, her eyes on the kind man. "Just going to check something out."

"Okay, be careful," Princess Esme replied, then went back to watching the interviews on Noah's phone.

Iris promised she would, then left the church. She locked the doors behind her as kids and parents headed down the sidewalk. They noticed her, clutching their children a little closer. Iris rolled her eyes at their fear. She would never hurt them and thought they were being a little ridiculous for treating the refugees from Fairhaven like monsters.

She walked down the path, ignoring the stares and murmurs as she headed toward the school. The kind man stood there, a briefcase at his side as he said goodbye to the other teachers. When he turned toward the gate, he saw Iris and stopped.

"Oh," he began. "It's you. Hello again."

When he smiled at her, Iris didn't return the gesture. "Hello."

"Um, is there something I can do for you?" The man motioned at the school. "We have a break room inside. Are you hungry? Thirsty? You can relax on our couch if you'd like."

Again, he was being kind. Iris wasn't used to that. "Is that even allowed? I don't think these humans would want me around their kids."

He nodded. "Yes, you're probably right. I forget not everyone is as comfortable as I am to be around people from other cultures. But my offer still stands. I could grab you some food or coffee and bring it to you."

She shook her head. "No, thanks. A family brought over a basket of food, actually. So at least we won't starve in the meantime."

The man looked relieved. "Ah, that's good to hear. Glad some people support you. If you ask me, those constant negative news stories are unfair and misleading."

"You think so?"

He nodded. "Yes—there's so much more the news could be

talking about. So what if there's an underground society? I say you have the right to live as much as we do."

Iris was surprised. "That's ... a refreshing view to have. Thanks."

"No problem." The man leaned closer, holding out a hand. "My name is Grant. Grant Thatcher. I teach grade four here."

"I figured you worked here." Iris shook his hand, a strange feeling coursing through her. A tingle that spread through her body. "Guardswoman—uh, General now. General Iris Ambrose."

When he dropped her hand, the sensation disappeared. What happened? Were those tingles dangerous, proof that he had done something bad to her body?

"General? Wow. That's awesome. Well, nice to meet you, General Ambrose."

Iris winced. "Please, call me Iris. Becoming general ... it wasn't a title I wanted. But I had no choice but to accept since our numbers are so few."

"Yeah, I heard your home was destroyed. By some madman senator?" Grant shook his head. "I'm really sorry, Iris. This must be overwhelming for you and your people."

Completely, Iris wanted to say. "We'll survive—we always have. Anyway, I just wanted to come over here and say ... thank you for pulling me from the crowd. I wasn't expecting a human to save me."

"Hey, we're not all bad. Don't let those TV interviews fool you." Grant smiled at her. "You needed help, and I happened to be there. That angry mob shouldn't have been there in the first place."

Iris nodded. "Agreed. Still, I appreciate it."

"Of course. Are you sure I can't get you anything? I can drive to the store, pick up some basic necessities. Soap, snacks, toiletries—"

When Iris heard a click in the distance, she pounced on Grant, slamming him to the ground. "Get down!"

On top of him, Iris realized how muscular he was. That long sleeve t-shirt did a good job of hiding his athleticism. He looked up at her, pinned beneath her armor before he glanced around.

"What?" he asked. "What is it?"

Iris scanned the area, then noticed the source of the sound. It wasn't a human assassin like she thought—but someone with a camera. They were snapping pictures of Iris and Grant together, still lying on the ground. Iris blushed and quickly rose to her feet.

"I'm so sorry," she began, holding out a hand to help him up. "I heard a sound and thought it was someone dangerous."

Grant took her hand, pulling himself to his feet. He glanced around the school and noticed the man with the camera. "Ah, it's just paparazzi. Probably hoping to sell your pictures to the news or something. I'd get used to that—more people will probably be after you for a quick buck. It's despicable if you ask me."

"I think so too." Iris's eyes were still on the photographer before turning to Grant. "I'm sorry, I didn't mean to hurt you. Are you all right?"

As she checked him over for any bruises, he nodded with a smile. "Don't worry—I can take a fall. I've been tackled plenty of times by my fourth graders. But thanks for protecting me. If that had *really* been someone dangerous, you would've saved my life."

"That's my job. To protect." Iris glanced at the church down the street. "Anyway, I should get back. Thanks again."

When she tried to turn, Grant reached for her arm. "Wait— let me give you my number. Just in case you need anything. A grocery store run, a shoulder to cry on, someone to vent to. I'm your guy."

He pulled a piece of paper out of his briefcase, then wrote his information down and handed it over. Iris looked at his number with a frown. "But ... why? You don't have to do that."

He shrugged. "Let's just say ... I know what it's like to be different. See you around, Iris. And take care."

He headed down the street, carrying his briefcase full of school reports as he walked home. Iris watched him go before realizing the photographer was still snapping pictures of her. Rolling her eyes, she stashed the paper deep in her pocket and headed back to the church. She was relieved to get inside as she closed and locked the door.

No more concerned eyes or people snapping pictures. The church was a welcome respite from the insanity of the outside world. Of the *human* world, one Iris found too judgmental, violent, and strange.

When she turned around, everyone was still watching the news. But Gemma stood and walked over to Iris. "There you are. Everything okay? You just took off all of a sudden."

Iris nodded. "I'm fine. Just wanted to thank the human who pulled me from the crowd. His name is Grant—he's a teacher at an elementary school down the street. He gave me his number and offered to pick us up some stuff if we ever needed it. Toiletries, food, that sort of thing."

"Really? Good to know. He seems like a nice man." Gemma paused, studying Iris's face. "Are you sure you're all right? Your cheeks are all flushed."

"Are they?" Iris placed a hand against her cheek, realizing she did have a bit of a fever. "Oh, it's probably nothing. Just hot under all this armor. Excuse me."

Leaving Gemma in the main hall, Iris scurried down the corridor to her bunk room. None of the soldiers were inside— they were standing guard around the church, making sure no human got past them. Iris climbed into her bunk, lying down for a moment. She still felt warm and sweaty.

Had Grant done something to her? He seemed so nice, so normal. She pushed him out of her mind, trying to rest, though he seemed to wiggle his way back into her thoughts for some strange reason.

When dinner rolled around, Iris joined everyone else for more snacks. It wasn't anything like the stew back in Fairhaven, but it was food. Mostly crackers, granola bars, and microwave meals. Once dinner was over, Noah got a call, then nodded and hung up before turning to Princess Esme.

"Your interview request on the news was accepted," he said. "They're eager to get you on TV to talk about your people."

"Good, good. Maybe we can change people's minds about us. Or, at least have a voice for ourselves." Princess Esme turned to her father. "We should talk about strategy. Anything you want me to say?"

As King Tedros went over their speech, an hour passed quickly before it was time to head to the news station. Iris decided to accompany them, offering the royal family her protection while her other guards remained at the church to watch over it. Without a vehicle, they had to walk to the news studio in town, passing more concerned people on the sidewalk. Iris would've killed for a unicorn like the old days on patrol, the saddle broken-in and comfortable. She kept one hand on her sword, carefully scanning the crowd for assassins.

Real ones, this time—and not just photographers. She cringed when she thought of how she had tackled Grant to the ground. Surely, he must've thought she was strange.

She was still wondering what he meant by feeling like an outsider when they reached the back doors of the news station. The bodyguard at the door glared at them, then let them inside when Princess Esme said they had an interview. Gemma glanced around as they walked through the news station.

"The last time I was here, I was fighting to save a friend's bookstore," she muttered. "It's when I used a potion on that secretary."

"Which is why you're going to apologize for that on live television," King Tedros scolded, making her nod. "Come, I think I see the reporter."

They followed the king down the hallway, then Iris noticed they were being watched. Assistants and security stayed close, apparently ready to act in case they tried anything. Did they really think they were a threat?

The TV reporter was wrapping up her conversation at a plain white desk, chatting with a scientist about magical people living under the city and how they avoided discovery for so long. When the interview was over, the reporter turned to face the camera.

"Well, it's the news story that's consumed every station around the globe for the last twenty-four hours. The discovery of a magical kingdom called Fairhaven below Toronto," she said, arranging her papers on the desk. "And right now, I have an interview with the people in question. We thank them for agreeing to an interview. Princess Esme?"

On her cue, Princess Esme walked toward the desk, sitting across from the reporter. Gemma, Noah, and King Tedros joined her in their own chairs while the others stayed back. Iris glanced outside, noticing a crowd had formed when news of their live interview had spread. She feared it would be another mob situation like before—and Grant wasn't around to save her this time.

"Hello again," the reporter said to Gemma. "You were just on my station not that long ago, asking for help to save a friend's bookstore."

"That's right." Gemma sighed. "And I used a magical potion to manipulate the secretary at the front desk to let me by. First off, I just want to say how sorry I am. I know it was wrong—but I was desperate to help a friend. Barbara, if you're out there, just know how much I care about you. And I hope finding out who I really am won't change our friendship at all."

"A sweet sentiment," the reporter said, "but surely you can understand how frightened it's made everyone. People in the city are wondering if they've been mind-controlled into things that they can't remember."

"Absolutely not," Princess Esme said, looking into the camera. "That was an isolated incident. I've been on the surface for a year now and never did anything."

"That worries people too. How you all stayed under the radar for so long. The people who have written to us have concerns about our military and police dropping the ball," the reporter replied. "They're also concerned about the human with magic, a man named Bobby Blevins, who escaped custody, and your own senator who blew up your home."

"More isolated incidents," King Tedros said. "We want the human to be caught like anyone else, and the senator is dead. His co-conspirators were handed over to the police. They're behind bars now. The danger is over."

Was it really? The empty crypt's discovery weighed on Iris's mind, along with what the humans might do next. The danger being over was a blissfully ignorant viewpoint—but she knew the king was probably just trying to calm the public.

"My father's right," Princess Esme added. "We know you don't trust our people, but we really don't mean you any harm. Not all of us are like Senator Remus. I thought coming on tonight would be a good way to tell you a little about our people and our history. To help you realize we're not a threat."

"Only time will tell." The reporter glanced down at her

papers. "Onto another matter. Rumors swirl about Bobby Blevins—a human who escaped police custody. We've learned he had magical abilities and was using them to steal and kill. Can you comment on that? Because he has magic, is he part of your kind? Fairhaveners?"

"No, definitely not. And for the record, we don't know where he could be," Gemma answered. She had more experience with Bobby Blevins than any of the others. "We know he shouldn't have that magic. That his powers are a fluke, something only our fairy godmothers should possess. It doesn't make sense to us either."

"I see. He sounds dangerous, and I sincerely hope the police find him soon. Oh, before we continue, there have been speculations that you're aliens or some sort of mole people. The world would like to know—myself included—what are you? What's your species called? Because you're certainly not human."

Princess Esme paused. "We've never been asked that before. We don't really have a name for our people. We just ... are, you know? But if you really need a label, I guess you could call us Fae. Fae from Fairhaven."

"Fae. Thank you, I'll write that down."

Princess Esme nodded. "Great. Now, Gemma, would you like to tell them something about yourself?"

Gemma looked nervous as she fidgeted with her hands. "Uh, okay. Well, I have anxiety like a lot of humans do. I came to the surface at the request of the princess and my father to live a little. I love romantic fantasy books, good food, and helping people. Both Princess Esme and I fell in love with humans, and they can swear that we don't mean you any harm—"

"That's all well and good," the reporter interrupted, "but the people in town have questions. What are your plans going forward? What do you have to say to people who think you're too dangerous to let roam free?"

As Princess Esme tried to answer all the questions calmly and diplomatically, Iris just shook her head, watching from the sidelines. The reporter didn't care about getting to know them —she just wanted views and clicks. Grant and the Bhatia family aside, plus Noah and Ian, Iris really didn't care for these humans.

As she scanned the perimeter for threats, she noticed the back door open. The same secretary who had been on the news —who Gemma had used a potion on—entered the studio, then nodded at someone outside.

The next thing Iris knew, someone threw something inside the studio. Iris dove for it but missed, then a smoke bomb hissed into the studio, clouding their vision mid-interview.

CHAPTER 6

I ris wasted no time. Although she couldn't see very well through the smoke, she still ran through it anyway, heading in the direction of the news desk. She reached through, pulling out Princess Esme, King Tedros, and Noah.

Once they were free to breathe clean air in the hallway, Iris went back for Gemma and the reporter. Some of the employees opened the windows, trying to air out the smoke bomb before they ran into the back alley for some fresh air.

"You all right?" Iris asked them, looking at her people. She let out a cough before taking a deep breath.

Princess Esme nodded, rising to her feet as she helped her father and Noah up. "I am. Everyone else?"

The others agreed, bringing in fans to clear out the smoke and taking deep breaths. The film crew was wondering what had happened as Ian held Gemma close. But Iris knew the truth —that the secretary and an unknown partner had thrown the smoke bomb inside the room.

They wanted to ruin the interview.

Iris stared down the alley behind the news station. But no one was there. When she heard the screech of tires in the distance, she knew they had gotten away. And the fact that they had gone from screaming in protest to throwing smoke bombs made her nervous.

What if someone tried something else? Something a little deadlier?

After waiting around for a little while, the reporter eventually gave them the green light to re-enter the studio. Most of the smoke had been removed by the crew.

"We apologize for that," King Tedros was telling the reporter, watching as she drank water to get the smoke out of her lungs. "Are you all right?"

The reporter nodded. "I'm fine, yes. I'm used to dealing with threats as a journalist, sadly. But someone out there really doesn't like you."

"Seems that way, yes." Princess Esme glanced at the ceiling. "Do you have camera footage? We'd like to see for ourselves who did this."

"Of course." The reporter gestured at the door. "Let's give the smoke some time to clear before heading back in."

Iris and the others went with the reporter inside the studio, then to a far door at the end of the hall. It led into a surveillance room with video screens and a security guard at a desk. He was playing on his smartphone, clearly not paying attention.

The reporter crossed her arms. "You didn't even see that, did you?"

The security guard looked up. "See what? Whoa, what's all that smoke in the air?"

"Pathetic." The reporter pushed past the guard, replaying the footage. "Here it is—they came from the back door."

Iris knew that already and wasn't as shocked as the others as the secretary appeared in the doorway, opening it for someone in the alley. They watched as the other person threw the smoke bomb inside before they ran off and vanished in a car. Sadly, there were no cameras in the back alley, and no footage caught the other assailant. Only their arm had been visible on camera.

"That secretary again," Gemma muttered, turning to King Tedros. "I'm so sorry—this is all my fault. If I hadn't used that potion on her, she wouldn't be so opposed to us."

King Tedros sighed. "It does make things more difficult, yes, but there's no point in blaming yourself. It happened—and now we must deal with it. Surely this secretary has a name?"

The reporter nodded, stopping the footage. "She sure does. Sheila Bond. A good secretary—she's worked here for a few years now. Today was her day off. Never had any trouble with her. She certainly has never acted like this before."

"Well, our people were never discovered before this," Princess Esme replied. "Any idea who the arm belonged to that threw the smoke bomb?"

"No clue, sorry. But rest assured, the secretary will be fired. This was an attack on the station, and I don't intend to let it slide."

"Good. Neither would I," Iris said. "Can you forward this video to the police, at least?"

The reporter nodded, pressing a few buttons on the computer. "I can, yes. Are you planning to press charges?"

Princess Esme glanced at her father, then shook her head. "No, in the interest of peace, we're going to be lenient. We don't want any more trouble with the humans. As long as this is an isolated incident, then we'll just forget about it."

But Iris had a feeling it wasn't going to be isolated—that the people who opposed them were ticking time bombs waiting to strike.

"That's kind of you. But I won't be so lenient. That woman is *so* fired," the reporter muttered. "Anyway, thanks for coming in. You ever want another interview, let me know. People are eager to find out everything they can about you."

Princess Esme thanked the reporter, then gestured for her people to follow her. The employees whispered to each other and pointed at the Fairhaveners as they left the news station. Iris glanced down the street, looking for the secretary and her partner in crime, but they had fled.

"Well, that was interesting." Noah lifted his arm and sniffed his sleeve. His nose wrinkled and he jerked away from the offending scent. "Gah, I still smell like smoke."

"There are showers back at the church along with fresh clothes. We can all wash off," Princess Esme said. "Speaking of which, we should get back. Just in case someone tries something else."

They headed down the street to take the path back to the church. As they passed a barber shop, they noticed a television hanging from the wall inside, playing their interview with the smoke bomb. All the people getting their hair cut in the shop had their eyes glued to the screen. Even the barbers.

"I hope these humans will realize we're not the ones causing the violence," Gemma said, walking hand-in-hand with Ian. "It was one of their own this time."

"Some probably condone the violence," Ian replied. "They're scared—you have to remember that. Scared of what your fairy godmothers could do with those potions. And scared people do stupid things."

As they headed down the street that led to the church, Iris noticed the Bhatia family outside on their front lawn. Ayesha and her husband were wiping something off the side of their house with soap and water from a nearby bucket.

"What's going on over there?" Gemma asked, pointing.

"Head inside the church," Iris ordered. "I'll check it out."

The others nodded, walking inside the church as Iris

crossed the street. She cleared her throat as she approached the Bhatia family. When they turned around, smiling at her, she finally saw what they were scrubbing off the side of their house.

Someone had sprayed the words "GO BACK TO YOUR COUNTRY" in red paint across their garage. Ayesha had managed to get some of it off, though the red paint was tough.

"Ah, Iris, was it?" Ramesh asked. "Good to see you again."

Iris nodded. "And you. I ... apologize if I was rude yesterday. When I asked about your motives. I'm sure you can understand that I'm only being cautious."

"We do understand, yes. We don't trust many people either." Ayesha pointed at the red paint, her cloth covered in it. "I'm sure you can see why."

"I do. What happened?"

Ramesh sighed as his wife continued scrubbing the side of the house. "We just got home from work and found this ugly message. We're trying to wipe it off before our daughter gets back from studying at a friend's house. We don't want her to see it—don't want her to get upset."

Iris could understand that. She wasn't a parent—and probably wouldn't be after taking an oath to be a soldier—but she wanted to protect those who depended on her just the same.

"I see. That's too bad. Do you need a hand?"

"If you'd like," Ayesha said, pointing at her porch. "There's an extra scrub brush with soap over there."

Iris nodded, climbing the steps onto their porch. A Siamese cat blinked at her from the window—she had only seen those on TV. They were much cuter than their snobby cartoon counterparts. She reached for the brush, then headed down the steps and began scrubbing the red paint off the garage door. She used all her strength to get the last bits of it washed away.

Sweaty, Iris pulled back from the wall and nodded. "I think we did it. The hateful message is gone."

"Thank you so much. We would've been out here for hours," Ayesha said, taking the cloth from Iris. "You're very strong."

"Soldiers need to be. Did you see who wrote the message?"

"Some teenage punks, actually. They drove past and spray-painted it before taking off. We caught them on our surveillance footage when we checked our computer." Ramesh shook his head. "It's sad to see young people so full of hate, but they must learn it from somewhere. Most likely their parents."

"Hatred is definitely taught." Ayesha stepped back from the wall. "Anyway, we saw your princess's interview on television. We thought she handled herself well—before the smoke bomb. Are you all right?"

Iris nodded. "We're fine, thank you. Just being a little more cautious."

Ayesha gestured at the wall, squeaky clean and smelling of soap. "We understand that. And we meant what we said before. If you need anything, come get us. We must stand against hate together. It's the only way we'll defeat it."

"Agreed." Iris paused, thinking. "But I don't understand. These humans mistrust us for obvious reasons—we're not like them at all. And our fairy godmothers have magic. But you ... you're human. You may come from a different part of the world, but you're still one of them. How can they be so awful to you?"

Ramesh looked down. "It's been constant since we moved to Canada—our very presence irritates these hateful people. We've tried to kill them with kindness, but they've been getting worse. And it seems your arrival has made them hate all outsiders even more. We're just as scary to them as you are."

Iris shook her head. "It's just ... unbelievable. And wrong. You shouldn't have to deal with this."

"But we do." Ayesha's lip quivered, then she gestured at her front door. "We should head back inside and make dinner before our daughter gets home. Thanks again for your help."

Iris nodded, then turned and crossed the street. When she entered the church doors and shut and locked them behind her, she found her people talking in the pews. And it looked serious.

"There you are," King Tedros said. "Is the Bhatia family all right?"

Iris nodded. "They're fine—just the victim of a hateful spray-painted message. It seems the people who want us to leave also want them to leave. All outsiders, really."

"Awful." A muscle ticked in Noah's jaw and he clenched his fists. "They've been kind to us. If they ever need our help, we should give it."

"Agreed," King Tedros said. "We have few friends these days. We must hold onto them—especially if we have things in common. Oh, Iris, something was left for you on the doorstep. The guards took it into the kitchen. They think it's safe."

With a raised eyebrow, Iris headed for the kitchen. The appliances in there were old and dusty but Kyler and the other soldiers were still doing their best to use them for cooking. They needed to learn how to be more self-sufficient. When she heard whispering coming from the utility closet, full of brooms and cleaning supplies the priests had left, she snuck over to listen.

"... and you're talking about a coup d'etat. I think that's what the humans call it. I've been reading some of their books on my breaks," Kyler whispered. "That's crazy. And a lot of trouble."

Iris peered through the closet's door, spotting Kyler with Sapphira when they were supposed to be working. What were they talking about?

"Oh, come on," Sapphira hissed, crossing her arms. "Even you said you were upset with King Tedros for doing nothing to stop the senator."

"Yeah, I am. And I wish the senator's family had been killed too. But overthrowing the king because you're mad at him ... I don't know. That might be a step too far."

Sapphira had said something similar to Iris at Ian's bar. She'd just assumed the soldier was letting off steam—getting out the rage she felt at the senator slipping through their fingers. But why did Iris have a bad feeling something was going to happen?

"Just think about it. We've been friends for ages, Kyler—and I need your support. Maybe a change in leadership is what we need. Being on the surface means Fairhaven's rules don't apply anymore. Times are different, and we need to usher in a new era."

Kyler said something too low to hear, then they came out of the closet. Iris crossed her arms before they finally noticed her. And judging by the guilty looks on their faces, they knew they had gotten caught.

"Uh, General. Hello," Kyler said. "We were just ..."

"Taking a break. Working the garden gets tiring. Boy, do I miss those Fairhaven patrols," Sapphira said, sighing. "I loved staring at the magical lake. I think I miss it the most. Anyway, we've got stuff to do. Kyler, want to join me in the garden? I could use some help with the weeds."

After he nodded, they brushed past, heading outside to the garden. Iris watched them from the window but they didn't whisper again. She made a mental note to keep an eye on them, hoping to stop any infighting before it started.

The humans were already against them—they didn't need to stand against each other.

Iris turned, then noticed a giant basket on the table. Had the Bhatias left something else? She checked the note nestled in between toilet paper, toothpaste and toothbrushes, and sanitary pads, realizing it was handwritten in perfect cursive.

Dear Iris,

I'm not sure how different your people are, so I just got a bunch of generic stuff, the note read. *I hope this helps. I know you didn't ask me to bring anything, but I thought I should. Let me know if there's anything else I can do.*

Yours,
Grant.

And he had signed his name so elegantly. Iris reached for the note, bringing it up to her nose before she could stop herself. It smelled like cologne—like warm wood on a summer's day. For some reason, she couldn't stop herself from inhaling it.

"What are you doing?"

Iris spun around. Gemma stood just behind her, staring at the note in her hands. Iris stuttered before finding the words. "Uh, just checking on the supplies Grant left. That teacher who saved me from the crowd. Some toiletries and other things."

"How nice." Gemma walked toward the table, inspecting the basket. "We'll put this to good use, just like the stuff the Bhatias left. But I meant, why were you smelling the card?"

"For … for protection purposes, of course. To make sure it wasn't laced with poison." Iris sniffed it again, then set it down. "All clean. I think we can trust this human."

"Good. We can add another friend to the list, I guess."

Iris nodded. "Anyway, excuse me. I'm going to patrol the perimeter."

"Iris, wait."

Just as she reached the door, Iris froze, then spun around. "Yes, Gemma? Something I can do for you?"

"I was just curious. Have you ever been in love?"

Iris cleared her throat. "That's ... an awfully personal question."

"I know—I'm sorry. But I'd never been in love until I met Ian. And I'm glad I took the risk. Now that Fairhaven's gone, I'm just so glad to have someone."

Iris felt a twinge of jealousy rip through her stomach. That was new. "Well ... that's nice."

"It is." Gemma stepped closer. "I know you're married to your job—that soldiers are expected to serve for life and never marry or have children. You don't even have fairy godmothers, for crying out loud. That's quite a devotion to your duty."

"Which I accepted proudly. The day I was made a guardswoman by King Tedros was the best day of my life."

"But things have changed," Gemma urged. "We aren't in Fairhaven anymore. And given how tough things are now ... I'm just saying, finding a friend, or partner, and falling in love could be just what you need. I find Ian's scent very comforting to me too."

Iris blushed as red as a Fairhaven tomato. Gemma *had* seen her sniffing that note *and* interpreted what she was doing correctly—she'd been caught red-handed.

"It's all right," Gemma said with a smile. "I won't tell anyone. You've got a little crush on that Grant guy, don't you? When you were smelling that note, you looked ... I don't know. Almost spellbound."

Iris crossed her arms. "I was not. It was a moment of weakness—it won't happen again."

Gemma shook her head, walking toward the door. "That's what I thought when I came to the surface. That I'd never find love. But when I met Ian for the first time ... something changed inside me. The energy between us was almost magical. And now that we're together, I'm glad I took a chance on him. I don't know what I'd do without Ian. So, I'm just saying— maybe give love a chance. Even if it doesn't work out, it sure is fun to be spellbound."

Gemma left her with that, walking out of the kitchen. Iris wanted to laugh. A guardswoman of Fairhaven did *not* get spellbound for anyone—only her job. She couldn't focus on love, not when her people were in trouble and humans were out to get them. If she got distracted, then her people would have no one to protect them and nowhere to go.

Now if only she could stop thinking about how good one of those humans smelled.

CHAPTER 7

As Iris walked back into the main hall, Ian came through the double doors. He shut and locked them before heading over to Gemma. He sighed, sitting next to her with a paper in his hands.

"Back so soon from the bar?" Gemma glanced at the paper. "What do you have there?"

"A threatening letter, taped to my bar's front door." Ian set the paper down on the pew. "See for yourselves."

Everyone crowded around, trying to see the note. It read, in messy handwriting, "GO TO HELL, MAGIC LOVERS."

"Someone just left that for you?" Princess Esme winced.

Ian nodded. "That's right. I opened my bar and no one came in—I think word has spread that I'm associated with you all. And they aren't happy."

"Oh, Ian." Gemma frowned, reaching for his hand. "I'm so sorry. We'll fix this and get your bar back up and running—I promise."

Ian nodded, though Iris wasn't quite sure how that would happen. Some of the humans had made their opinions clear. It didn't seem like they would change their minds.

Noah turned his phone back on, watching the replay of their interview. The throwing of the smoke bomb made them all cringe. Iris could still feel a bit of it in her lungs, and she tried not to cough around the others and show weakness. Noah read through the comments of the livestream while shaking his head.

"These comments are awful," he muttered. "So many people hate your kind. And it *is* a reasonable response—considering what Senator Remus did. Trying to enslave people and blowing up Fairhaven. But why blame you all for it?"

"Some people are just hateful, that's all," Fairy Godmother Odelia said, glancing at the king. "They lump us all together instead of seeing us as individuals. Just like them. I understand their concerns, but it's still hurtful."

The king nodded, saying nothing. But Iris got the feeling there was a deeper meaning to their conversation. Just what was going on? Did it have anything to do with that strange open crypt?

"Well, I thought the interview would help. I guess it didn't." Princess Esme rose to her feet, pacing. "So much for that."

"It's a good start, at least. Don't be discouraged," Gemma said. "There are still more things we can try."

As Noah read through the nasty comments, the words "breaking news" appeared on the app. He clicked it and it took him to a live interview with Prime Minister Teresa Lin. She stood in front of a microphone, addressing the camera and all the photographers there.

"Thank you for joining me tonight," she said. "I know you're all still worried about the discovery of Fairhaven. Like you, I watched the interview they gave and thought they came across as good people. I detected no violence from any of them. It's unfortunate someone threw a smoke bomb into the middle of the interview, something I want to discourage at all costs. I urge restraint and peace ..."

Iris just shook her head, knowing that would never happen. Not with people like Sheila Bond using Senator Remus' evil actions to encourage their fears.

Over the next few hours, some of their people headed to bed while others stayed awake to patrol. Noah eventually turned off his phone with the constant news cycle about Fairhaven's people. He walked down the hallway, grabbing a bed with Princess Esme as Gemma and Ian did the same.

Iris didn't have anyone to sleep next to, so she stayed awake, keeping an eye on the perimeter after everyone had gone to bed. When she felt her eyes growing tired, she yawned and headed down the hall.

Just as she turned into the sleeping quarters, hearing the snores of her guards, a slight tremor broke out beneath her feet. Iris's heart raced. Was it something left over from what the senator had done? Was Fairhaven being bombed again?

She ran into the main hall and flung the front doors open. The sky was dark and everyone on the street was asleep. Not even a car drove past. When the ground trembled again, so lightly she thought she almost didn't feel it, she started running down the street to check it out.

She came across a graveyard—where the rumbling seemed to be more pronounced. She looked over her shoulder to make sure no one was watching, then headed past the cemetery's gate. The tremors increased in there, rattling the headstones. Iris ran her hands along a gravestone that looked like it was springing out of the ground.

"What the hell?" she muttered.

When she heard an eerie laugh, chills spread down her arms; she spun around, seeing nobody there. The cemetery was empty. The tremors stopped a moment later, making her wonder if she had imagined the whole thing. She hadn't gotten much sleep since Fairhaven was destroyed—maybe her mind was playing tricks on her.

But when she looked back, noticing the gravestone had actually moved a little to the right, she knew it had been real. The tremors, the hair-raising laugh. And the dark feeling in the pit of her stomach?

Fear.

She looked around for a while but couldn't find anything. Eventually, she started on the path back to the church. When she arrived, everyone inside appeared to still be sleeping except for whoever is whispering down the hall. She paused to listen after walking down the corridor.

"... and you know what this means," King Tedros whispered. "Those tremors. If Icarus is back, the whole world is in danger. And this won't win us any favor with the humans."

"Perhaps we should tell someone," Fairy Godmother Odelia replied. Iris peered into the room. They each huddled beneath their own blankets in their own beds, and King Tedros's hands trembled. "Like the General. Perhaps we can send her on a mission to handle this."

"That's just the problem, Odelia." King Tedros sat on his bed and sighed. "I've never known how to handle Icarus. And if he's escaped, there's no telling what he's capable of."

Fairy Godmother Odelia didn't say anything to that, but she clutched the blanket to her chest and shivered. Iris could tell she was concerned. Icarus—that name didn't ring any bells. But Iris had a feeling it related to the open crypt back in Fairhaven.

Not wanting to get caught, she hurried to the sleeping quarters, quickly slipped out of her armor, then jumped onto her bunk. She got under the covers and forced her eyes closed. All the drama with the tremors and the hateful humans could wait until the morning.

When she awoke, Iris was alone in the sleeping quarters. A delicious smell wafted down the hallway. She jumped up, realizing she had slept longer than she wanted. Her body was still tired, finding it difficult to sleep in a place so foreign.

After heading down the hall, she was relieved to see everyone sitting on the pews, eating bread and cheese for breakfast with some coffee and whatever else Grant and the Bhatias had brought over. She followed her nose to a container labeled BUTTER CHICKEN. Iris's soldiers joined them for a few minutes to hurriedly eat their breakfast, then returned to their assignments. Sapphira handed her a breakfast plate with a smile before heading into the garden.

"Good morning, General," Princess Esme said, sitting with her father, fairy godmother, and Noah. "How did you sleep?"

Awful, Iris wanted to say.

"Fine," she muttered instead, then sat on the pew next to Gemma and Ian. She nodded at them before taking a bite of her bread. "Bah, human food. It has a strange smell to it. The only thing I can stomach is their coffee."

"Coffee is pretty amazing. As for everything else, you'll get used to it, don't worry," Gemma said with a smile. "Me and Esme did."

When Princess Esme nodded, then began sharing stories about their time on the surface, Iris choked her food down. It was nothing like the cuisine they had back in Fairhaven—just another thing she missed about her homeland.

"I think we should tell you what was on the news this morning, Iris," Noah said. "They were talking about you."

She swallowed a grape. "Me? Why?"

Had they seen her run off to the cemetery, she wondered? Did the humans think they were responsible for the tremors?

"Someone spotted you at an elementary school," Gemma said. "A photographer snapped some photos of you with Grant. Some photos of you on top of him, to be specific."

Iris rolled her eyes. "Oh, yes—that. I heard a click and thought there was an assassin, so I lunged on the human to protect him. It was only a photographer, though. Nothing to worry about."

Gemma just smiled, returning to her food. Iris found it irritating how giddy Gemma was about Iris's imaginary love life.

Iris cleared her throat. "What are they saying about me?"

"That you were creeping around young children. Maybe even planning something dangerous at the school," Princess Esme said. "Unfortunately, it hasn't improved our image."

Iris wanted to curse. She had only gone over there to thank Grant for rescuing her—not to cause more trouble. She had even declined to enter the school. If the humans were going to blow everything out of proportion, then she'd never see him again.

"I know it wasn't your intention, but we must be more careful," King Tedros said, eating a piece of fruit. "We have to be on our best behavior. We don't want to give the humans any more ammunition against us."

Iris nodded, though it was easier said than done. Especially when the humans were looking for any reason to mistrust them.

Once Iris had finished breakfast, her soldiers returned to collect their plates. She glanced around and heard no one gossiping about the tremors. Had they really not felt it?

"So, is anyone going to mention what happened last night?" she asked.

Princess Esme glanced over. "What do you mean? What happened last night?"

"You ... didn't feel it? The tremors?"

Everyone gave her a blank stare.

"Okay, then," Iris muttered. "I guess you were all asleep. But before I went to bed, I felt tremors beneath the ground. They were soft—maybe you all didn't hear it. Nor did the humans."

"If they had, I'm sure it would've been on the news. There's been nothing," Noah said. "Go on, General."

"I followed the tremors to the local cemetery. The gravestones ... they were shaking. Then I heard an evil laugh behind me, like nothing I'd heard before. When the tremors stopped, I came back. Everything seemed fine, so I went to bed, but ... I don't know. It was alarming."

When everyone frowned, it was clear they had no idea what Iris was talking about. But from the corner of her eye, she saw King Tedros and Fairy Godmother Odelia share a look, and she knew there was something they weren't telling them.

"Sorry, I didn't feel anything," Ian said. "I think I passed out hard. These past few days have been difficult."

"Absolutely," King Tedros said, his eyes landing on Iris. "Perhaps it was just a small earthquake and nothing more. I'm sure it's nothing to worry about, General."

Iris said nothing as the chit-chat continued. What was he hiding? As their general, didn't she deserve to know if there was a threat? She was only trying to keep them safe, after all, and she couldn't do that while in the dark about important things.

Princess Esme rose to her feet, grabbing paper and a pen out of a nearby drawer. "Okay, I think I have a few ideas in mind on how we can win over the humans. Just like our Human Connection days, Noah, we're going to do as many good deeds as we can to prove that we just want to live alongside them. I was thinking ... a car wash?"

"Ooh, good idea," Noah said, watching as Princess Esme scribbled it down. "Humans love their cars. Trust me."

"Good, good. Now ... what about something with Ian's bar?"

Princess Esme glanced at him and Gemma. "A fun game—something we could play with the humans?"

"Ian used to do trivia nights," Gemma said. "Of course, that was before he started receiving threatening notes."

"Can't say I like it," Ian huffed. "But yeah, I'd be onboard. Just need to find a way to get people to come back to my bar. Maybe ... free beer?"

As they went over their ideas, Iris kept her eyes glued to King Tedros and Fairy Godmother Odelia. They weren't saying anything, sitting in silence, staring into space. Was it possible they were thinking of the tremors?

Iris knew she had to ask them what they had been whispering about last night. As she rose to her feet, she changed out of her new clothes and into her armor, the steel sword clunking against her body. A knock sounded on the door and everyone quieted, wondering who it could be.

"Allow me," Iris said, reaching for her sword.

She approached the door, then swung it open with her sword in hand. Grant stood there on the step with a smile. It faded when he saw the sword, holding his hands up defensively.

"No need to start stabbing—it's only me," he began. "Good morning to you."

"Sorry," Iris grumbled, putting the sword away. "We're being more cautious these days. What are you doing here? Don't you have a class to teach?"

It came out a little harsher than intended. Just as Grant went to respond, the others walked over to the door to meet their guest. Gemma smiled and held out a hand.

"Grant, was it?" she asked. "Nice to meet you. Iris has told us a lot about you."

Grant smiled again, glancing at Iris. "Has she? Only good things, I hope."

"*Very* good things," Gemma said with a giggle.

Iris elbowed Gemma, trying to get her to quiet down. "This is Gemma Solace, one of my people. And this is Princess Esme and her husband, Noah ..."

After going through the entire crowd, Grant greeted them all with a nod. "I'm Grant, Grant Thatcher. I teach at the local elementary school. Nice to meet you all. It's kind of exciting, actually. I've never met a different species before."

"First time for everything," Gemma said, her eyes twinkling as she glanced back and forth between Grant and Iris. "We'll leave you two alone. Excuse us. We're thinking of ideas to win over the humans."

Gemma gestured for everyone to head back inside the church. Iris stepped outside and shut the double doors behind her.

"So, what are you doing here, Grant?" she asked. "You didn't have a chance to tell me before my people ambushed you."

"I don't mind—it was nice meeting them. And I came to check on you. Did you get the basket?"

"I did. Kind of you, but not necessary."

"I know, but I hope you can put it all to good use. I saw that interview your princess gave last night. Sorry about the whole smoke bomb incident."

"Thanks. We're fine, though."

"Good. That's good." Grant paused. "Anyway, I came with a proposal. You deserved a better introduction than what you got last night."

"What are you getting at?"

Grant gestured down the street. "Well, I'm heading to work now. I thought maybe, for our show and tell today, you could introduce yourself to my students. Maybe show them you're nothing to be feared. Then, hopefully, they'll go home and tell their parents how nice you were, and it will help some people to get over their prejudices."

Iris mulled over his suggestion. "It's a nice idea, but I'm not so sure. Did you see the news this morning? The photographer sold pictures of us. People are concerned I was hanging around an elementary school. They might think I'm trying to hurt their children."

Grant sighed. "Yes, I saw that and thought it was unfair. But like I said, this is a chance to set the record straight. My students are lovely, you know. They'll accept you. And maybe ... I wanted to know more about you too."

Iris raised an eyebrow. Had he meant that to come out sounding so flirty?

"You do?" she asked. "Why?"

Grant stuttered, searching for an answer. "All of you, really. Your people in general. So, what do you say? Are you up for a little show and tell?"

"Speaking ... really isn't my forte. I'm a fighter, not a talker. You should invite the princess instead, or maybe the king—"

But Grant shook his head. "No, I think you're perfect. People will want to get to know a regular person, not a royal. They might relate better to you. Come on. Don't leave a teacher hanging. Just say yes. I'll even throw in some free coffee from the break room for you."

Iris *did* love coffee—maybe it was the only thing she liked about the human world.

"You drive a hard bargain," she said, making Grant smile. "I do love coffee. All right, I'll come to your show and tell."

Grant's eyes lit up. "Perfect! All right, follow me—I'll take you to the school. Class is almost starting."

Iris gawked. "Now? You want me to come with you ... now?"

"No time like the present." He smiled and gestured at the path. "After you, my lady in shining armor."

CHAPTER 8

Iris left her people behind at the church, giving them time to strategize their next move as she walked down the stairs. Grant led her down the street where he ignored the stares of the curious and concerned people out for walks. While Iris noticed, Grant didn't mention it.

"I'm sure those humans are wondering why you're out with me," Iris said, sticking close to Grant. Her eyes scanned their surroundings like a hawk. "It doesn't look like they approve."

Grant shrugged and glanced back at her with a smile. "Let them stare. I don't need their approval."

"Hmm. It truly doesn't bother you?"

"Not in the slightest. Like I said before, I'm used to being different."

There it was again. Intrigued, Iris intended to ask him what he meant, but he quickly changed the subject.

"So, how long have you been a guard for?" he asked. "Have you always wanted to watch over your people?"

She nodded, catching up with him on the sidewalk. If he didn't care about the humans staring at them, then she wouldn't either. Or she'd try not to. "Yes, even when I was a child. I always enjoyed protecting people and sword fighting."

Grant glanced at the sword on her hip. "You'll have to teach me how to sword fight sometime. Just promise you'll go easy on a puny human, okay? I don't have any experience."

"I can teach you, sure."

"I can't wait." He paused. "But speaking of that sword, maybe you oughta check it in at the school's office. So none of the teachers freak out. Because it's technically a weapon, after all, and it's still a school."

"Right, I can do that." Iris figured she'd better ask him something about himself so she didn't seem rude. "Have you ... always been a teacher?"

"I got my teaching degree about five years ago. I enrolled right out of high school. Best decision I ever made." When Grant looked toward the school, he smiled. "I love my students. They make my life complete."

As they approached the front gates of the elementary school, teachers and students were arriving for another busy day. When parents dropping off their kids saw Iris approaching with Grant, they gave them a second glance before murmuring. Still, Grant didn't seem bothered.

After he opened the gate, he gestured for her to follow. "Follow me—my classroom is pretty close to the doors."

"Okay. Are you sure I won't get in trouble for being here?"

"Don't worry," he said, giving her a half-smile. "I'll protect you."

For some strange reason, Iris believed him. She had spent her whole life protecting others—and felt like a failure. For once, maybe she wanted someone to protect *her*.

After Grant had led Iris into the school, they left her sword in the office. The secretary—wide-eyed at both Iris *and* the weapon—promised she'd keep it safe, then gave Iris a visitor's pass. She taped it to her belt as the two glanced around. It was different from Fairhaven academies—there were no magic potions or spellcasting classrooms. Instead of fairy godmothers and guards, they had teachers and young students. They all stopped and gave Iris a funny look before walking past. The walls were painted a dull white, matching the dirty floors. Students' sneakers squeaked, and chatter filled the hallways as they headed to their classes.

"All eyes are on you. It's the armor, I bet," Grant whispered. "It makes you stand out like a sore thumb. But other than that, I wouldn't be able to tell you're not from our world."

Before Iris could respond, a short, blonde-haired woman in a pencil skirt and a blazer walked over. She looked to be in her late twenties. She glanced between Iris and Grant, then crossed her arms.

"Who is this?" she asked. "A new girlfriend?"

"No," Grant replied. "This is Iris. Iris Ambrose. She's a guardswoman—for the people of Fairhaven."

The woman stared at her. "I knew she didn't belong here. I've heard about your people on the news. What are you doing here? Come to hurt our children?"

"That's absurd," Iris replied. "I was invited by Grant. To do a show and tell."

The woman scoffed. "Seriously? You're bringing this ... this witch woman into our school?"

"Technically, I don't use magic at all. I'm just a guardswoman. Now a general."

That didn't make the woman any friendlier.

"It's all right, Lisa," Grant said. "She's here at my request. She won't hurt anyone—and I certainly wouldn't invite someone who I thought would jeopardize my students' safety."

Lisa looked Iris up and down again. "I'll have to tell Principal Hannigan about this. You really should've cleared this little visit with her first, you know."

Grant nodded. "Maybe I should have, yes. But I wanted to give these people a chance to introduce themselves. It's only fair. Now, if you don't mind, I'm going to head to my classroom. Excuse us."

Grant gestured for Iris to follow, then he began heading down the corridor. Iris looked back at Lisa as she sneered at them. She scurried down the hall toward a door marked "Principal," her high heels clicking on the tile.

"Sorry about her," Grant said, glancing over her shoulder as the woman vanished. "That's Lisa Keplum, another teacher here. She teaches grade two. She's been in a bad mood ever since we broke up."

Iris raised an eyebrow. "You two ... were dating?"

"Yeah, for a short time. Just didn't work out." Grant stopped at a classroom door. "Anyway, this is me. Are you ready?"

"I am. Lead the way."

Grant opened the door, then entered the small classroom. It had twenty desks for the students who shuffled in behind them. They hung their backpacks and coats on closet hangers, then took their seats at their desks. After they pulled out their binders, homework, and pencils, they looked up and noticed their teacher.

Grant put his briefcase down on the desk, then walked toward the chalkboard. Iris waited awkwardly by the door for instructions. When the students looked at her, she remained still, not wanting to scare them.

"Good morning, everyone," Grant said with a smile.

"Good morning, Mr. Thatcher," all the students said in unison. They couldn't have been older than nine or ten.

"I hope you all had a good sleep last night. Please, hand in your homework," Grant said, approaching their desks and taking their notebooks. "Good, good. Now, today is show and tell. I hope you all brought something to share about yourselves."

His students nodded, pulling objects out from under their desks. One boy had a turtle, another girl had brought a princess gown, and another student had a book. They all had something that described their personalities.

"Wonderful. I brought something as well," Grant said, putting the homework on his desk before turning to Iris. "This is General Iris Ambrose. I'm sure you've heard from your parents or guardians about the discovery of Fairhaven, yes? It's been all over the news."

Some students nodded, others began murmuring. Grant gently shushed them. To Iris's surprise, they listened immediately and hushed. They clearly respected their teacher a lot.

One dark-haired boy raised his hand. "My dad says their people are dangerous with all their magic and stuff. That we don't know anything about them and they shouldn't be allowed to stay here. He said maybe the prime minister should kill them all."

"Justin!" Grant cried, crossing his arms. "That's an awful thing to say."

Justin shrugged. "What? That's just what my dad told me."

"Well, what do you think?" Grant gestured at Iris. "Does Iris look like a threat?"

Justin paused, scanning her up and down. "Um ... no. Not really."

"Exactly. If you go through life thinking everyone is an enemy, you might miss the chance at finding a new friend." Grant smiled. "Anyway, I'll have to have a chat with your father. Wishing death on anyone is terrible. We just don't know these people, that's all." Grant walked toward the chalkboard, writing the words "SHOW AND TELL" on the board. "Everyone's a stranger before they're a friend. And, in the interest of peace and unity, I brought Iris here to talk about her people a little. Iris, would you like to take over?"

Grant turned to her, wiping the chalk on his pants. It left a white handprint across his brown slacks. Iris glanced toward the kids, noticing all their eyes on her. She had never addressed people like this—especially children—and suddenly felt self-conscious.

"Very well," Iris said, approaching the chalkboard. Grant stepped toward his desk to give her space. "As your teacher said, my name is Iris. General Iris Ambrose. I come from Fairhaven, a magical city below your storm drains that was recently destroyed by a greedy senator who wanted to enslave your people."

A girl's hand shot up. "What does enslave mean?"

"He wanted to control us," Grant explained. "We're very glad he didn't have a chance."

Iris nodded. "I am too. Trust me—not all of us are like the senator and his family. They had been questioning our king for too long. And, unfortunately, the senator's fairy godmother made magic compatible on the surface, which one of your kind exploited."

"Fairy godmothers?" a boy in overalls asked, wearing large glasses. His eyes widened. "That's cool, actually. Like something out of a fairy tale."

"Dork," the boy named Justin sneered.

The other students laughed at the insult, making the other boy sink in his seat. Grant sighed. "Justin, what I have told you about name-calling? Say sorry to Ronan right now, please."

Justin rolled his eyes. "Sorry."

Iris knew he hadn't meant that at all. Ronan hung his head, not asking any more questions. She felt bad for that boy.

"Moving on," Grant said, leaning against his desk. He

glanced at Iris with a smile. "Give us three fun facts about Fairhaven or yourself. Go ahead."

Iris thought for a moment. "Very well. We had dragons, griffins, and phoenixes down in Fairhaven. Our princess and her new husband flew on a dragon after their wedding."

Some of the students oohed and aahed, though Justin didn't look too impressed. What was that kid's problem? Iris continued, ignoring him for now.

"We have fairy godmothers, as I said. They're usually good at spellcasting and must attend a college. They make potions and are all given a charge—someone to watch over. Guards like me don't have one, of course. We're expected to protect Fairhaven and give up our normal lives."

"Sounds tough," Grant said gently. "Almost like … a monk. Or a samurai. Sorry, you probably don't know those terms."

When Iris shook her head, the boy named Ronan walked toward the bookshelf, looking for something. He found a book on Japanese culture and walked to the front of the class to hand it to Iris. He then opened the book, finding the page with samurai. It had a picture of an ancient Japanese samurai with similar armor.

"Like that," Ronan said. "Mr. Thatcher's right—you look like one of them."

Grant smiled as Iris looked through the book. "Aw, that's sweet of you to teach her, Ronan. They have as much to learn about us as we do about them."

"Teacher's pet," Justin muttered, trying to hide it with a cough.

Iris and Ronan heard him but Grant hadn't. Ronan let her keep the book, heading back to his desk where he put his head down. Iris closed the book and put it on the table.

"I guess I have some reading to do. Your samurai sound interesting. Thank you, Ronan," Iris said, making the boy half-smile. "And the last fact. Let's see ... well, my father was a locksmith, and my mother was a gardener. I enjoyed tending our garden with them when I was a child. Now that they're gone—taken by the senator's wicked plan—I miss them very much. Tell your parents that you love them while you still can, children. Before it's too late."

When the kids looked sad, Grant glanced at them. "Iris is right—we need to cherish every moment we get. And we're sorry to hear about your parents."

"Thank you. Fortunately, the senator is dead and his co-conspirators are in jail. They shouldn't hurt anyone ever again." Iris gestured at her empty scabbard. "Normally, I have my sword in here. I left it with your front office for safety reasons. If necessary, I'd use it to protect my people."

"Can I see your sword? And hold it?" Ronan asked. "I bet it's super cool."

Grant shook his head. "Maybe another time. I don't want any of you to accidentally get hurt—I don't think your parents would ever forgive me. Anyway, thanks for sharing all that, Iris. I hope it helped teach my kids something about your people. If anything, the more I learn about you, the more I realize how similar we are."

Iris paused, thinking. "I suppose we are. Similar and different at the same time."

"Which makes our world that much more interesting and exciting to live in," Grant said with a smile. "My students are going to show off their presentations now. Would you care to watch?"

"Sure, I don't have any pressing matters to attend to." Iris stepped toward the desk, still keeping an eye out for any potential danger. "Go ahead."

As Grant nodded, glancing around the classroom to choose which student would go first, two people approached his door.

One of them was Lisa—his ex—with a scowl. Iris didn't like her but forced herself to keep calm. She was with another woman, much older with white hair. That woman carried a walkie-talkie and a set of keys.

Lisa cleared her throat. "Sorry to interrupt, but Principal Hannigan wanted to speak to you. Both of you."

Grant glanced over, noticing them standing there. "Oh ... all right. Students, I'll be right back. You can get your presentations ready in the meantime."

The kids nodded, organizing their things and chatting as Grant headed to the door. Iris followed closely. When she and Grant had stepped out into the hallway, Lisa closed the door, peering in at the children through the glass. The principal was already staring at Iris with worried eyes.

Grant cleared his throat. "Principal Hannigan, hello. I assume you're here about my choice of guests?"

"That's right." Principal Hannigan turned to Iris. "Lisa told me you're ... one of them."

"I am." Iris thought back to her king's order, wanting to keep the peace. "I apologize if I offended anyone. Grant asked me to come to show and tell to introduce my people, and I didn't see the harm."

"He really should've checked with me first," Principal Hannigan muttered, "but I can see his intentions were good."

"You can?" Grant asked, surprised.

The principal nodded. "Yes—and I admit, I'm curious about their people too. But like I said, inform me next time."

"Will do. Thank you, Principal Hannigan."

"What?" Lisa demanded, glancing between them. "Grant brought this outsider here and put this entire school at risk. What if she's dangerous? Just like the rest of them?"

"Her name is Iris," Grant began, sounding a little annoyed, "and I don't think she's dangerous. If anything, her people can say the same about us. Humans are just as unpredictable. Like the one who threw that smoke bomb during the interview."

"That was completely different." Lisa shook her head. "We don't know anything about these Fairhaveners. Or Fae. Whatever the hell they're called—"

"And we won't if we keep shunning them. We need to talk, to work out our differences," Grant interrupted. "At least, that's what I'm all about. What I teach my students. Obviously, you don't understand, Lisa, and that's disappointing."

Lisa looked offended, flinching as if she had gotten slapped. Principal Hannigan cleared her throat. "Yes, well ... as I said, warn me next time. I'd like to tell our students' parents in advance so they won't be afraid. For now, you may return to your show and tell."

When Grant nodded, the principal walked away, her keys jingling down the hall. Lisa glanced between them and shook her head before following. She was almost like a lost puppy, chasing the principal down.

"They have people like Lisa where I'm from too," Iris said once they were alone.

"People like what?"

"Shit disturbers and brown-nosers."

Grant laughed. "Yeah, Lisa can be a bit of both. When I first started dating her, she seemed great. But as time went on ... I saw her true colors."

"Will she be a problem?"

Grant shrugged. "Nah, probably not. Best to just ignore her. Like I said, she's upset I broke up with her, so she's looking for any little reason to get me in trouble."

"I see. I'm glad the principal isn't upset with you, at least."

"Me too. I thought I'd get in more trouble, but Donna's a sweet woman. I've known her my entire teaching career. She knows I'd never put my students' lives in danger. Ever." Grant shook his head. "Anyway, sorry about all that. Again. Let's head back to the show and tell, shall we? You can get to know more of my students and love them the way I do."

Iris nodded, letting Grant enter the classroom first before she followed. The way he spoke about his students—and genuinely cared for them—was incredibly attractive.

Uh oh, Iris thought as she followed Grant to his desk. *I'm catching feelings for one of these humans. I'm no better than Gemma or Princess Esme.*

And maybe, just maybe, she started to understand why they had both fallen for a human.

CHAPTER 9

T he show and tell continued as Iris and Grant watched from his desk. Each student went up to the chalkboard, then talked a little about their lives and what they had brought. Everything from pets to food to books and video games were brought up, and Grant encouraged them all.

"Great job!" he said. "You're all doing well. Who wants to go next? Maybe ... Justin Bond?"

Bond? Where had Iris heard that name before? She racked her brain, but she couldn't remember.

"Fine," Justin said, rising to his feet. He carried a notepad to the chalkboard. "I brought a notepad. 'Cause my mom works at a news station and all. She and my dad tell me everything that's going on in town. Anyway, that's it."

It finally hit Iris. Justin was the son of the secretary who Gemma had tricked into getting on television—and it seemed like her husband was just as hateful. What were they teaching their son?

Grant nodded. "Thank you, Justin. I have a soft spot in my heart for journalists. They do important work. Now, Ronan? Would you like to go next? You're the last one."

Some of the other kids snickered, making Ronan blush in embarrassment. He sat up straighter when he realized Grant's eyes were on him. With a sigh, he grabbed something from inside his desk and walked toward the chalkboard.

"I, um, brought a lightsaber," Ronan said, showing the toy to everyone. It lit up blue when he pressed the button. "I really like Star Wars."

"Nerd," Justin called out, making the kids laugh around him.

"Justin! That isn't nice," Grant scolded, leaning against his desk. "One more outburst and I'll be sending you to detention."

Justin rolled his eyes, but thankfully, kept his mouth shut for the rest of Ronan's presentation. The shy boy talked a little bit about Star Wars—having to explain the movies to Iris who had no idea—and showed off the lightsaber.

"Thank you, Ronan. I'm a fan of Star Wars too," Grant said as Ronan took his seat, putting his lightsaber back in his desk. "Now, if Iris would like to stick around, we're just about to begin our history lesson. Maybe you could learn something?"

Iris nodded, choosing an empty desk near the back of the room. "I'd like that. Please, go on."

Grant smiled as he reached for a piece of chalk, then began talking about the history of the world. They went over fast facts about ancient history first—Egypt, Greece, and Rome—and Iris listened intently, finding it fascinating. Maybe there was much to learn on Earth after all. And as luck would have it, Grant was already a teacher and could help Iris learn.

When the bell rang forty-five minutes later, Grant set his chalk down as all the kids rose to their feet. "All right, there's the first recess bell. When you come back in, we'll be going over the math homework. I hope everyone's done it!"

All the kids groaned, grabbing their things before clamoring into the hallway. They followed the long halls out the doors where they played outside on the slide and swings. Iris rose to her feet just as Grant began to erase what he had written off the chalkboard.

"Well, I hope you enjoyed that little history lesson," Grant said. "The kids seemed interested in you at least, so that's a start."

Iris nodded. "It went well. Thanks again for inviting me."

He smiled, wiping his chalk on the side of his pants. "Of course, you're welcome. I won't ask you to stay any longer—I'm sure you have other things to do."

"I should get back to the church, yes. But I had a few questions first."

Grant leaned against the chalkboard, his sleeves riding up. Iris could see the outline of his muscles underneath. "Sure, go ahead."

Iris cleared her throat, trying not to think of his muscles. And what he might look like under that shirt. "It's about one of your students. Justin Bond?"

"Oh. What about him? I know he can be a bit rude, but we're working on that. I hope he'll learn some compassion in my class."

"I hope so too. His mother … I think I know her. I've seen her, I mean." Iris had flashbacks of the smoke bomb. "His mother used to be the secretary at the news station. The reporter promised she'd be fired for being involved in throwing a smoke bomb at my people."

"Yikes. Why would she do that?"

"Well, it's sort of complicated, but one of my people used a potion on her to get an interview. She's been a staunch critic of my people ever since."

Grant's eyes widened. "Wow, that's quite the connection. I had no idea. No wonder Justin has been so vocal about how he doesn't like your people. He must be learning that at home. And kids are so impressionable."

"Definitely. I just wanted to make you aware—to ask you to watch that boy. His mother already helped to ruin Princess Esme's interview. I don't want any other trouble."

"I'll watch him, I promise. I could call his parents in for a meeting? Have you all meet face to face?"

"No, I think that would make it worse. Just keep an eye on that family and let me know if you see anything suspicious."

"Okay, will do. I'm really sorry about all that—I don't know why people can't be civil." Grant sighed. "Takes me right back to my childhood."

"You mentioned that before," Iris said, stepping closer. "That you knew what it felt like to be different. I didn't have a chance to ask. What did you mean?"

Grant reached into his pocket, pulling out his smartphone. He held up a picture of two elderly men hugging. "These are my parents. I have two dads."

Iris blinked. "Okay. And?"

"That's ... not strange to you? That two men can be in love and even raise children?"

"Why would it be? I don't understand." Iris frowned. "In Fairhaven, that was quite common. One of Princess Esme's closest friends was a lesbian. Sadly, she was one of many lost when Fairhaven exploded."

"Oh, I'm sorry to hear that. Give your princess my condolences." Grant put his phone back into his pocket. "Well, in case you didn't know, lots of people have issues with that up here. Gay rights. It's been legal in Canada for decades, but some still don't support it. And there are countries where people will be put to death for being gay."

And there it was again, Iris thought—humanity's violence. Did it ever end?

Iris shook her head. "Beyond awful."

"It is. Growing up with two dads, I was bullied a lot. Kids said lots of cruel things to me." Grant paused, looking like he was reliving some of the old memories. "Those wounds never really fade. Anyway, that's what I meant by being different. That I was bullied and ostracized and know what it's like to not be accepted."

"So, you do. Is that why you became a teacher?"

"Part of it, yeah. Also, because I love teaching and learning," Grant said, a smile growing on his face, "and because I wanted to teach kids about kindness and compassion. I try to make all my students feel like they belong here."

"Well, that's a beautiful sentiment. I appreciate what you're trying to do. I just hope some kids—like Justin—can come around to believe it."

Grant nodded. "Fingers crossed. Now, let's get you that coffee I promised before you go. The teacher's lounge is just down the hall."

Iris followed him out of the classroom, heading down the corridor to a cozy teacher's lounge. It had a few couches, televisions, and a mini-fridge beside a coffee maker. Grant put a pot on, waiting for the coffee to brew.

As Iris took a seat on one of the couches, Grant sat across from her. "So, you know a little bit about my family. You mentioned something about yours too. A locksmith father and a gardener for a mother?"

Iris swallowed the lump in her throat, blinking back tears when she thought of her parents. "That's right. They were the best mother and father a child could ask for, and I miss them every day."

Grant turned silent for a moment, then he leaned over and placed a hand on hers. "Really, Iris, I'm so sorry about your home's destruction. If there's anything I can do, let me know."

Iris felt butterflies from his touch as she nodded. "Thank you, but you've already done more than enough. Sending us that basket and inviting me here was a gift."

Grant smiled, removing his hand. Iris already missed his touch. "Good, glad I could make a difference. It's what I hope to do as a teacher. Maybe ... maybe you could even meet my dads one day? I know they're curious about your people. And they're very nice people. I think you'd get along well."

Meeting his family? That sounded like a big step.

Before Iris could respond, the coffee maker made a noise. Grant rose to his feet and walked toward the machine. He fetched two cups of coffee, bringing it over to the couch. He handed a mug to her as their fingers brushed again, sending more electricity up and down Iris's arms. No magic necessary.

"Here you are. One fresh cup of coffee," Grant said, sitting down and taking a long sip. "One of the many reasons I get up in the morning."

Iris took a sip and nodded. "Coffee is one of the few human things I like. It's wonderful."

"You love coffee too?" Grant smiled. "A woman after my own heart, then. Coffee is my soulmate."

When the door squeaked open, several teachers entered the lounge. They froze when they noticed Iris and then quickly fled the room. Lisa was the only one who stayed, grabbing a cup of coffee and walking toward Grant.

"She's still here," Lisa muttered. "I thought your little show and tell was over?"

"It is. Just wanted to give Iris a cup of coffee to say thank you for coming in," Grant said, setting his coffee down. It left a brown ring on the table when he picked it up again. "One more thing, Iris. We have a school field trip tomorrow afternoon to the local zoo. Every grade is coming along. Now, I might get in trouble if I invite you directly, but if we both happen to be there at the same time, in a public place ..."

Iris saw where he was going with that. "Then it's not as bad. Good idea."

Grant smiled. "I have those every now and then."

"What?" Lisa demanded. "Why? You can't keep inviting this ... this strange woman to all these school events—"

"And why not?" Grant asked. "There will be plenty of staff and teachers there to make sure everyone's safe. And Iris is just teaching the kids about her culture. I thought our school board was all about diversity and love?"

Lisa shook her head. "Parents aren't going to be happy to hear about this, Grant. Trust me. You're going to jeopardize your job."

"If that's the price for being kind and including people, then so be it. Besides, the zoo is a public place. Iris has every right to be there." Grant turned back to Iris. "So, what do you say? You've never been to our zoo before, have you?"

Iris shook her head. "I haven't. You wouldn't have animals like we do back home, would you?"

Grant laughed. "Dragons? Unfortunately, not—only in movies and books. But we *do* have some pretty cool animals of our own. Penguins, lions, flamingos. And it would be a good chance for you to learn more about us too while also showing my students who you are."

"Then I'll be there tomorrow afternoon."

"Perfect!" Grant smiled. "Looking forward to it."

Iris nodded, then glanced over at Lisa. The woman looked like she might explode. Her cheeks were red like tomatoes. She set her coffee down, then stormed out of the teacher's lounge before slamming the door.

"I guess not everyone supports our zoo field trip," Iris said quietly.

"Lisa just needs some time to come around to the idea, that's all." Grant set his coffee down again. "Well, I'll show you out. Thanks again for coming today. My students learned a lot."

Iris finished her coffee, then followed Grant out of the teacher's lounge. She made sure to give back her visitor's pass and pick up her sword in the front office. Smiling as she took it from the desk, it was a welcomed sight. Grant then led her toward the doors before opening one for her like a perfect gentleman. After walking outside, he waved goodbye, then Iris headed to the path.

As she turned, she looked over her shoulder, noticing Ronan sitting by himself on the swing. He had his lightsaber on his lap but wasn't playing with it. He looked sad, his head down while he sat quietly. Then Justin and a bunch of other boys approached him.

Iris couldn't hear what they were saying, but judging by the wicked smirks across their faces, it wasn't anything good. Justin pulled out some blank paper from his pocket, breaking off small pieces. Then he wadded it into a ball and flung it at Ronan. The boy put a hand up, begging him to stop. But Justin just laughed before his friends joined in.

Unable to watch anymore, Iris hopped over the fence and approached the swings. "Hey, stop that! Leave Ronan alone."

Justin and his friends stopped throwing the paper balls. He glanced at Iris, sneering. "Oh, it's you. My mom says your people are dangerous. I don't think you should be here."

"I was invited by your teacher. I mean no harm." Iris crossed her arms. "I can understand your mother's apprehension, but she's wrong."

"Yeah, sure. Whatever." Justin turned to his friends. "Come on, let's go find something else to do. I'm tired of looking at these dorks."

He and his friends left, heading to the other side of the playground with the rest of the kids. Ronan watched them go before lifting his head to look at Iris.

"Thanks." He wiped bits of paper from his clothes. "I didn't think Justin would ever leave me alone."

"I'm sorry he treats you that way. It isn't right." Iris sat on the swing next to him, trying not to fall off and embarrass herself. "How long has he been bothering you?"

"Since the start of the school year. I didn't do anything to him. I don't know why he can't leave me alone." Ronan sighed. "It really sucks."

"I bet. Have you told Grant? Mr. Thatcher, I mean?"

"No. What's the point? It'll only make it worse. I just gotta hold out until school is over."

Iris frowned, feeling sorry for the boy. Was there anything she could do to cheer him up?

She noticed the lightsaber, then rose to her feet. "That's an interesting weapon. A lightsaber, was it? From your Star War?"

"It's Star *Wars*," Ronan corrected, "and it's not real, it's totally fake. I wish it was real though. Then I could have cool lightsaber battles."

"Why can't you?" Iris removed her sword from its sheath, stepping back from Ronan. "We can battle for fun right here. Don't worry—I won't hurt you."

Ronan perked up at that. "Really? Okay. No one ever wants to have lightsaber battles with me."

He rose to his feet, holding up his lightsaber. Iris smiled and held up her weapon in defense. "That's a shame. It'd be an honor to duel you, Ronan. One, two, three ... strike!"

For the next ten minutes, they pretended to battle. Iris was careful not to strike her sword too hard and hurt Ronan. When he held up his light saber, Iris dramatically fell to the ground, pretending to hold her chest wound.

"You beat me," she cried, acting like she was bleeding out. "Well done, Ronan."

He looked triumphant as he set his lightsaber down. "Thanks. It was fun dueling you."

"You were a worthy opponent," Iris said as she rose to her feet. "I hope that cheered you up a bit."

Ronan nodded. "Yeah, it did. Maybe we can have more lightsaber battles? Or ... maybe you can even teach me how to use a real sword?"

"If your teacher and parents agree, then sure. Until then, farewell, Ronan. And remember that you are a strong champion, capable of defeating great evil. Never underestimate yourself."

That made Ronan smile. When he sat back down on the swing, looking at his lightsaber, he didn't seem as sad. Iris hoped she had done something good that day.

As she walked toward the fence, heading to the road, the bell rang behind her. All the kids ran back to the school for their next class. She heard a throat clear behind her, then she turned around and noticed Lisa standing there.

"That field trip tomorrow?" she asked. "I wouldn't go if I were you."

Iris raised an eyebrow. "And why not?"

"Because you don't belong here. What they've been saying about you on the news is true—you're too dangerous. I don't trust all that magic your people have. I don't like it, either."

"I don't have magic. Our fairy godmothers do. And I don't like how violent you humans can be, so I suppose we're even," Iris shot back. "Grant invited me to the zoo, and I said I would go. I intend to keep my promise."

"Uh-huh. He doesn't like you that way, you know. He's just curious since your people are different," Lisa sneered. "I wouldn't get too excited."

So that was what this was about—she was jealous of how close Iris and Grant were becoming. Iris turned her back, refusing to stoop to her level.

"Goodbye, Lisa," she called out. "See you tomorrow for the field trip."

The woman scoffed before heading back inside the school. It wasn't going to be easy to win over people like her—like Lisa and Justin's parents—but if Iris could get through to at least one person, just like Ronan, then maybe it was all worth it. Grant sure seemed to think so.

And the more time she spent with Grant, the more she came to care for him. It was unexpected, but sometimes, that was how the best things happened.

CHAPTER 10

Iris reached the church a little while later, locking the door behind her. Princess Esme and their people were still planning their next moves and seemed relieved she was back. The altar was covered in pages of notes that mentioned fundraiser ideas and parties to win over the humans.

"You're back. Where did you go?" Gemma asked. "We were getting a bit worried."

"Grant asked me to give a show and tell at his school," Iris explained, sitting next to them on the pews. "It went well, I think. Some of his students are nice."

Princess Esme raised an eyebrow. "Just some?"

"Just some. One of his students, Ronan, is being bullied. He's a nice boy. I sat with him on the swings before we had a lightsaber battle. All pretend, of course. It put a smile on his face."

Gemma smiled. "That's lovely."

"Yes, but what's a ... lightsaber?" King Tedros asked with a frown.

Princess Esme laughed. "I'll have to show you those movies sometime, Father." She turned to Iris and Gemma. "It's always nice when you can make a difference in someone's life, even if it's small, isn't it?"

When Gemma nodded, Iris realized it did. She hadn't guessed helping the humans would bring her so much satisfaction.

"Anyway, we're having a car wash early tomorrow morning," Princess Esme continued. "We'll need to put signs around the neighborhood announcing it. We thought it was a low-effort way to reach out—to chat with the humans and make them see we aren't dangerous."

Noah kissed her cheek. "It's a great idea, babe. We'll all be there."

"I have a field trip to go to in the afternoon. It was Grant's idea," Iris said, "but I'll be there tomorrow morning."

Gemma raised an eyebrow. "This Grant is spending a lot of time with you, isn't he?"

When Iris didn't say anything, King Tedros spoke up. "I say the more the merrier. We can't change people's minds alone—we'll need the support of humans for that. Now, is anyone hungry?"

After eating lunch, Iris and the others returned to their tasks around the church. Studying, cleaning, gardening, and patrolling the grounds were twenty-four-seven jobs. Iris didn't complain once, helping out her soldiers as much as she could.

When a knock sounded on the door after dinnertime, Iris found Maya standing on the step. It looked like she had just come home from school with a backpack on her shoulders. She had her smartphone in her hand, as always, and was popping her gum.

"Oh, it's you," Iris began. "The Bhatias daughter. How can we—"

"Stay away from my parents," Maya spat. "I mean it."

"What? Why?"

Gemma walked toward the doors, peering over Iris's shoulder. "Who is it? Oh, Maya, it's you. Hello! How are your parents?"

"They're not good. They keep getting harassed. Everywhere," Maya said. "Outside our house, on the way to work, the subway. It's not cool."

"Harassed how?" Iris asked, raising an eyebrow.

"Yelled at on the street and made fun of. All for being immigrants. Even kids at school are looking at me funny, but I fit in a lot better than my parents. The lack of an accent, mostly." Maya shook her head. "You being here has made everyone afraid of outsiders and immigrants, including my parents. My family's abuse has gotten ten times worse since you arrived."

"Oh, we're terribly sorry," Gemma said. "It wasn't our intention to—"

"Yeah, well, it's happening. And I'm sick of it. I'm really worried about my parents' safety," Maya interrupted. "So just stay away from them. If they come around, send them away. They're too nice to tell you this, so it'll have to be me. Stop making our lives more dangerous by hanging around. We've got enough problems, okay?"

Before they could respond, Maya turned and walked down the church steps, then headed to her house across the street. Iris only shook her head and closed the door. Gemma had more sympathy, still staring out the window at the house.

"Poor girl," she murmured. "She's right—we're putting other humans in jeopardy. Other outsiders like us."

"We didn't plan on it," Iris shot back. "If I had a choice, I'd leave this place and head home. But that isn't possible—thanks to Senator Remus. Whatever magical bombs he set off permanently polluted our home. We're stuck here."

Just his name sent pangs of anger through her body. Iris would ring his neck if he wasn't already dead.

"Even if it means leaving Grant?" Gemma asked.

Iris thought for a moment. "Yes, even if it meant that. There's no place like home."

Gemma sighed, sitting on a nearby pew. "You're right about that. I miss Fairhaven a lot too. I wish we could undo the senator's destruction, but ... it's too late."

Far too late, Iris thought. And she still felt guilty about it.

"But maybe this is a good thing," Gemma said, perking up. "Maybe ... maybe it was all meant to happen for a reason. That's usually the theme of all those romantic fantasy novels I read."

Iris cocked an eyebrow. "And what reason could there be for our home going up in flames? For all our people dying? And for us, the survivors, to lose everything we've ever known?"

The faces of Iris's parents flashed across her mind. No matter how well-meaning Gemma was, Iris would *never* believe they were taken for a good reason.

Gemma hesitated. "Well, when you put it like that ... yeah, it sounds awful. And I'm sad we lost so many. But this is a chance —to maybe teach these humans to accept others. To bring people together. I don't know, Iris. I'm just trying to find a positive spin here."

"Well, I'm not," Iris grumbled. "Everything is hard and difficult and I don't see it getting any better. People like Grant are refreshing, yes, but it doesn't change how bleak everything is. We just have to accept that. Real life isn't a fairy tale, Gemma, and it never will be."

As Iris turned, Gemma shook her head. "I won't stop hoping, Iris. I'll keep believing that things will get better for everyone—human and otherwise. I have to."

Iris just rolled her eyes, leaving to continue her patrols around the church. Gemma was too much of an idealist, too much of a romantic. And Iris was far too realistic to accept her views.

After they finished their tasks, everyone gathered in the pews to watch the news on Noah's phone. It was the same old story—humans afraid of Princess Esme's people, voicing their concerns. It had completely overshadowed every other news story across the world.

After everyone retired to bed, Iris stayed up a little later as usual. When she heard those familiar tremors outside again, she opened the church doors, realizing they were still coming from the graveyard. But when she headed toward the cemetery, she found nothing. Again.

Just as she reached the doors, a streak of magic light spat across the sky and vanished, leaving a purple mist behind. Iris wasn't sure exactly what was going on, but she knew one thing.

It wasn't good.

When she found King Tedros and Fairy Godmother Odelia still awake, chatting in the kitchen and drinking tea, Iris entered and cleared her throat. "My patrols are done, Your Majesty. No humans have breached our walls."

"Good," King Tedros said, looking up at her from the table. "Maybe one day we'll allow them to enter our home, but for now, it's probably best we keep the doors closed. For our own safety."

"Agreed. Before I head to bed, Your Majesty ... I need to ask you a question."

Fairy Godmother Odelia's alarmed gaze cut to King Tedros. King Tedros nodded. "Go ahead, General."

"Have you felt those tremors? I haven't seen anyone mention it on the news. It's happened two nights in a row now."

King Tedros paused, staring at Fairy Godmother Odelia. Then he shook his head. "No ... no, I haven't. Like I said before, they're probably just minor earthquakes."

In the old days, Iris would've accepted that answer and

been done with it like a good soldier. But things had changed—her people were in danger more than ever. What kind of general would she be if she didn't take charge to figure it out?

"See, I don't think it is," Iris said as she stepped closer. "I think you're lying."

Fairy Godmother Odelia scoffed. "Why ever would we lie, dear? We have nothing to hide."

Iris crossed her arms. "Oh, no? Does the crypt in Fairhaven jog your memory? What about the name Icarus and how he might be a threat?"

The only sounds in the kitchen were the leaky faucet and the clanking of teacups on saucers. Then King Tedros rose, setting his cup down. "You weren't supposed to hear that, General. Were you spying on us?"

"No—I was on patrol and happened to overhear. But I'm getting concerned. Since it seems so serious, I must insist that you tell me everything you know, Your Majesty." Iris knew she was out of line but persisted anyway. "Or I'm going to wake everyone up and let them know you two are hiding something. I don't think they would be happy to hear that, now, would they? Especially Princess Esme?"

King Tedros thought for a moment, then he sighed. "Very well. If you must know, come with me. We'll speak outside—in private."

"Why? Why can't the others know?"

"Because, dear," Fairy Godmother Odelia said, rising to her feet, "they have suffered enough. And to learn something awful may be coming our way ... it might be too much for them to take."

When Odelia said that, Iris's heart began to race. Just who was this Icarus?

She followed them out of the kitchen, heading into the garden. The sky was dark and full of stars, but the tremors had stopped. It seemed like a calm night—as far as everyone else knew.

Iris stopped by a potted plant that smelled like basil. "Okay, we're outside now. What's going on, your Majesty?"

King Tedros closed the kitchen door behind him. "That empty crypt? It belonged to Icarus. One of my ancestors, a former king, sealed Icarus in that crypt centuries ago. He could not be killed. Ancient soldiers tried, of course, letting the fairy godmothers design every potion they could think of. Nothing worked to kill him. He was invulnerable."

"How is that possible?"

"It's a long story, but Icarus was the first and only fairy godfather," Odelia explained. "He was so strong in potion-making and spellcasting that the Fairy Godmother Council granted him a position. He watched over the royal family because of his skill, much like I do. But then he became obsessed with death."

"A human's fault," King Tedros said quietly. "One of them found us below the city. This was before we took greater precautions using magic to hide our kingdom. She found the ladder, then went down out of curiosity and slipped. Anyway, she was a young woman. Someone who might have gone on to change the human world for the better. We'll never know, I suppose."

"Because she slipped off the ladder into Fairhaven and smacked her head on the pavement and lost her life," Fairy Godmother Odelia said. "We tried our best to heal her, but she was gone. Icarus was the one who watched her fall to her death. He felt guilty when she was declared dead, but there was nothing he could do. We returned her body to the surface to her family where they buried her."

"And rumor has it," King Tedros added, "her mother's

shrieks of grief could be heard for miles, even deep below in Fairhaven."

Iris sat on a nearby bench. "A tragedy for sure. But maybe it's best the human died. If she survived, she might've told everyone about our kingdom. Our ancestors might've been in greater trouble than we are now."

"Or she could've been a great ally, one who could've helped our two peoples live in harmony. We'll never know now. With either outcome, a life lost is always terrible." King Tedros shook his head. "Anyway, Icarus became obsessed with death after that. With trying to bring her back to life to make amends. He did some atrocious, forbidden things like animal sacrifices, using dragon blood for despicable rituals. To bring the dead back to life."

Iris thought about it for a moment. No wonder the grave-stones shook—maybe Icarus was performing magic on the surface and that was also the reason for the purple mist. It could've all been related in some horrible, sacrificial necro-mancy spell. The worst and most-dangerous kind of magic.

"And then?" Iris asked. "He figured it out, yes?"

King Tedros sighed. "Unfortunately. That dragon blood was the key. He made himself immortal, but then it drove him mad. He started off with good intentions but ended up corrupted. He quickly forgot the human woman who lost her life and went down a dark path, using his magic for evil and necromancy."

"And he could not be killed," Fairy Godmother Odelia added, "so King Tedros' ancestor sealed him away, deep below the castle. He stayed in that crypt for centuries, never causing trouble again."

"Until Senator Remus set off those magical bombs," Iris realized out loud, making them nod. "He didn't know, did he? What he was bringing back?"

"No. No one knew about Icarus except for us two." King

Tedros gestured between him and Odelia. "And now you. My ancestor feared others would panic. Or worse, try to follow in Icarus' footsteps. So, they locked him away, never to be spoken of again, which worked for a very long time. Eventually, when my daughter takes over the kingdom, she will learn the truth. But ..."

"But?"

Fairy Godmother Odelia said it since the king was too afraid. "*But* with Icarus on the loose, another problem caused by our senator, our future is in jeopardy. With his freedom, he could do anything. To us, to the humans. Nothing is impossible for such a powerful, immortal wielder of magic."

Iris's mind spun. So, immortality *was* possible—she had no idea. Even with all their magic, her people never could beat death before. But this Fairy Godfather Icarus had, and it made him a threat to everyone everywhere.

Especially now that he was free.

Iris gulped. "If Icarus does something to the humans ... they might never trust us again. They'll think they were right about us all along."

King Tedros stared at the dark sky. "I know. The implications ... are grave. No pun intended, of course."

"Do you have any idea where Icarus could be now? What he's planning?"

"We have no theories, only fears," Fairy Godmother Odelia said. "Remember—he's a madman. He won't act logically. But since you saw those gravestones shake, we fear he might try to do something with human corpses. Playing with death is his specialty, after all."

Could Icarus bring her family back? And all the ones they lost? Maybe that was wrong, unnatural. But the idea still floated around in the back of her mind anyway.

"What if ... what if we found him and used him for good?"

Even though she knew the answer, she asked anyway. "To bring back all our people? Like my parents? It's worth a shot."

"Absolutely not. To do so would be to mess with the natural orders of things," Fairy Godmother Odelia chastised. "Death is sad, but it's a normal part of life—even for us Fairhaveners. We must not be tempted to use forbidden magic. Or it could corrupt us too, much like it did with Icarus."

Iris knew the fairy godmother had a point. Still, she wished she could see her parents again and restore Fairhaven to what it once was.

"Anyway, I'm sorry we kept this from you, General," King Tedros said, looking back at Iris. "But such heavy secrets are not shared lightly."

"I understand. Do you have any kind of plan for dealing with him if he strikes? *When* he strikes, I guess?"

King Tedros glanced at his fairy godmother, then shook his head. "None, I'm afraid. Our ancestors had no idea either. For now, he's probably disoriented and weak, having been let out for the first time in centuries. Everything will be new to him. But when he regains full power ... I'm still not sure how to defeat him."

That's just great, Iris thought. No plan, no help, no other information. Just a powerful immortal hellbent on causing destruction.

"Since I saw that crypt open, it's weighed on my mind for days. Our next move," King Tedros said softly. "I knew he had escaped. But I'm just as helpless as everyone else to stop him. And since our lives are already so difficult, I didn't want to tell everyone and worsen morale."

"Well, there must be a way. There's *always* a way. At least, if Gemma and Princess Esme are to be believed," Iris said, standing up straight. "If this Icarus attacks beyond causing tremors and magical streaks in the sky, as your general, I vow to stop him. Whatever it takes."

Even if it cost her life. What was the point of living when her homeland and parents were gone?

"We appreciate that, General. We're lucky to have you looking out for us." King Tedros opened the back door. "Now, we should all get to bed—it's very late. And please, let's keep this revelation a secret for now. While telling the police about Icarus might seem like the next logical step, these humans hate us enough already. We'll wait to inform them until we have a better plan or we know what Icarus intends to do."

Iris nodded, fearing the worst for her people—and Grant and the humans—as she entered the church. She said good-night to the king and his fairy godmother, then headed to the sleeping quarters where everyone snored soundly.

She would not get such a restful sleep—not when they had so many enemies. Between Icarus and the mistrustful humans, life on the surface wasn't going to get easier anytime soon.

Or maybe ever.

CHAPTER 11

It was a long night.

Still reeling from the revelation of Icarus—and what it would mean for everyone on the surface—Iris tossed and turned. She eventually went into the garden to meditate, trying to quiet her mind.

It didn't work.

When the morning sun appeared in the sky, Iris went into the kitchen, devouring as much coffee as she could. Iris sat on one of the pews while sipping her coffee cup as the rest of her people woke up.

Princess Esme, Gemma and her father, Noah, Ian, and the others looked well-rested, smiling at Iris as they entered the kitchen to grab a plate of whatever the guards had made for breakfast. It looked like oatmeal with strawberries the Bhatia's had brought over. As they ate it, making chit-chat, Iris didn't know whether to pity or envy them.

They had no idea about Icarus—they were blissfully ignorant. At one point, Iris had been too. Now it felt like the weight of the world sat on her shoulders.

The truth could be a heavy burden.

King Tedros and Fairy Godmother Odelia joined them for breakfast, bringing Iris a bowl. They smiled at her and didn't mention anything of what they talked about last night. While it looked like they could handle keeping a secret as big as Icarus quiet, Iris was having a hard time.

"So, the time for the car wash is almost here," Princess Esme said to the room, interrupting Iris's thoughts. "Noah and I put up some flyers last night to announce it around the neighborhood."

"And then we had to put up more," Noah added, "because someone tore them down. Left them on the side of the road, all ripped up and stepped on."

Gemma shook her head. "How awful."

"Indeed," Princess Esme said, "but we can't let it stop us, or those nasty people will have won. Whenever you're finished eating, please join us outside. We'll start setting up for the car wash. Noah was kind enough to teach me how to use the hose from the garden."

"And I supplied the soap," Ian said with a smile. "I'm ready to wash some cars and raise money for charity."

Once breakfast was finished, Iris's guards washed their bowls before joining them outside on the front lawn. Noah hammered a sign into the ground, one that read "CAR WASH FOR CHARITY HERE." Ian brought the hose, soap, and buckets around to begin before pulling out his smartphone.

"Just wanted to check the news real quick," Ian said. "See what people are saying about us this morning."

They all huddled around Ian as he turned on a news livestream. The same reporter they had spoken to at the news station was sitting behind her desk, recapping the weather and local events. Much of the news was still about their people.

"When are they going to give it a rest?" Iris muttered. "Find something else to talk about?"

"Possibly never," Gemma said with a sigh. "But maybe we can do enough good to change the news stories in our favor."

Everyone nodded, though Iris wasn't so sure.

"... and construction crews and seismologists are looking into the tremors that rumbled through the streets of Toronto last night," the reporter said. "They were faint, but some people across the city still heard and felt them. Many are asking if it was a minor earthquake or the use of Fairhaven's magic wreaking havoc on our city ..."

So, the humans finally felt the tremors. Iris knew why—it was Icarus, back to cause chaos. When she glanced at King Tedros and Fairy Godmother Odelia, they both looked worried, avoiding her eyes.

"These humans are blaming everything on us," Mr. Solace said. "Haven't they ever heard of earthquakes? Maybe it has nothing to do with our people."

How wrong you are, Iris thought.

As the reporter switched to the local sports news, someone interrupted the live broadcast. They ran in front of the camera with a sign that read "PROTECT OUR KIDS—TELL THESE FAIRHAVEN FREAKS TO LEAVE." Sheila Bond's face peeked from behind the poster.

"Not this woman again," Iris muttered.

"People of Toronto, hear me!" Sheila cried to the camera. "I risked everything to tell you this. These people from Fairhaven are dangerous, and our prime minister isn't doing anything about it. What happens when they resort to violence? What about our children and most vulnerable—"

A security guard rushed in, grabbing Sheila and dragging her away. She screamed as she dropped her sign on the ground. And the channel cut to a commercial break.

Ian shook his head. "Well, seems like that woman is back to

cause trouble," he said. "Helping to throw that smoke bomb at us wasn't enough, apparently."

Gemma sighed. "I get that she's afraid of us, but she's going about it in the wrong way. If they just spent time with us—talking and getting to know us all—they'd realize we aren't a threat."

"They have no intention of doing that," Iris said. "They've decided we're guilty. And they aren't backing off anytime soon."

No one said anything, realizing Iris was right. Ian eventually turned off his phone when a Jeep pulled up toward the sidewalk. Gemma and Princess Esme both smiled, looking excited when they saw Maya in the backseat. Two teenage boys were sitting in the front seat and looked like they were on their way to school.

"Hi there!" Princess Esme called out, walking toward the Jeep. "Welcome to our car wash. All proceeds will go to the local children's hospital—"

"Get out of our city, you freaks!" the teenage boy driving the Jeep cried. "None of us want you here."

Before Princess Esme and Gemma could respond, the two teenage boys reached below their legs, grabbing a basket of something. When they began to throw them at Princess Esme's people, Iris realized they were eggs. Definitely not griffin eggs—those would've been much larger and heavier.

One egg hit Gemma in the face, causing her to gasp. The egg streaked down her neck and onto her dress. As Princess Esme tried to help Gemma wipe the egg off her face, she was hit in the head, her hair covered with the slimy substance. Noah, Ian, Mr. Solace, and King Tedros rushed toward the Jeep.

"Hey, stop that!" Noah cried. "You can't just throw eggs at people. That's assault!"

"Yeah, what happened to common decency?" Ian demanded.

The boys just laughed, then the driver stepped on the gas and sped off. Maya stared out the back window while looking at them in pity. Iris's guards rushed inside, grabbing a few towels so Princess Esme and Gemma could wipe off the egg.

"Ugh, these eggs are so sticky," Gemma said. "I think I'll need to take a shower."

Princess Esme nodded. "Me too. You go ahead first, Gemma —I'll wait."

As Gemma thanked her and headed inside to use the shower, Iris kept her eyes on the Jeep, watching it fade down the street. She couldn't believe Maya had been in the backseat. She didn't like it when her parents were the targets of bullies, so why would she just sit by while her friends bullied them? It wasn't too different.

"Mean boys," King Tedros muttered. "I just don't understand why they would be so rude."

"They're ignorant—plain and simple," Iris replied. "And Maya was in the backseat. Maya Bhatia. Though she didn't throw the eggs, she was still complicit. I think I'll speak with her parents later. Despite her warning us to stay away."

King Tedros nodded. "Good idea. Maybe you can persuade them to get those boys to leave us alone, at least. All right, while we wait for Princess Esme and Gemma to wash off, let's continue setting up the car wash. Maybe our next customer will be friendlier."

For the next hour, they waited around outside, hoping someone would park their car to be washed and donate. How else could they win over the humans? Plenty of cars drove past, having seen the signs Noah and Princess Esme had hung up, but they didn't stop. They just stared, murmured, and drove away.

Iris was getting bored waiting outside. It was starting to get hot under her armor, but she kept it on in case there was trouble. She counted the clouds in the sky while waiting for people to show up. Eventually, some of Gemma and Princess Esme's human friends showed up to show their support—leaving donations—and Iris was introduced to them all.

"General, meet Barbara Danvers and her grandson, Jacob. They own a bookstore," Gemma explained. "And this is Carly Brenton and her daughter, Abby. They live in the same apartment building that Noah did. I met them when I moved in and we became great friends."

"Nice to meet you," Iris said politely, greeting them all.

"My new boyfriend is on his way too. He's a firefighter," Carly said with a smile. "We all just wanted to come out and support you."

"Even Luigi is supposed to show up, a local pizza owner," Barbara said. "My grandson's been working at his shop."

"How has that been going?" Gemma asked, leading them away to chat privately.

As they talked, Iris met Princess Esme and Noah's friends—Tanya and her three kids, then Gina, an older lady. Iris let them catch up privately as she scanned the perimeter. To their relief, Gemma and Princess Esme's friends left donations, or they wouldn't have raised any money at all.

Iris's people got to work on lathering up the cars, scrubbing them with soap and water as an unmarked police car pulled up beside the church. They exchanged fearful glances after Iris noticed a detective badge dangling from the rear-view mirror. Had they done something wrong? But it was only Noah's father, Detective Crawford, who stepped out of the vehicle.

He caught up with Noah and they looked relieved to see each other. Iris crossed the lawn, heading toward them. "What's going on?"

"Your mother and best friend wanted to see you too, but I

told them to stay away," Detective Crawford said. "For their own safety."

Noah nodded. "I understand. We tried to do the same, but our friends still showed up today to support us anyway. They're too kind."

Detective Crawford leaned over, putting some paper bills into their donation box. "There. I'll show my support too."

"Aw, thanks, Dad. I know you don't quite understand Princess Esme's people, but that's nice of you. So, why are you really here? Not that it isn't nice to see you."

"We identified the person who threw the smoke bomb at you during your interview," Detective Crawford called, making them all gather around to hear the news. "Surveillance footage from a nearby building finally caught them. We know the woman who let him inside was Sheila Bond, the secretary at the news station. And the man who threw the smoke bomb was her husband, Michael."

"I should've expected that," Iris muttered. "I know their son, Justin. He's in Grant's class. He mentioned his parents have been saying rude things about us in private."

"In public too," Noah said. "Now it makes sense."

"But that's not all," Detective Crawford continued. "This Michael Bond? Maybe you've heard of this lunatic. He's a proud racist, hating everyone who wasn't born here. The discovery of your people has made his hatred worse. He's got some followers who support him. A little supremacy group that harasses immigrants and outsiders and anyone not like them. Unfortunately, that includes all of you."

Gemma shook her head. "Other people support that kind of hatred? That's disappointing."

"Very. We're keeping an eye on him, don't worry. This isn't the first time he's caused trouble. But he *has* been getting worse since you all got here. Now, since your king didn't want to press charges, there ain't nothing we can do right now. But let me know if someone messes with you, all right?"

"We will. Thanks, Dad," Noah said, placing a hand on his shoulder. "Come on, I'll walk you back to your car. How's Mom doing?"

As Noah led his father away, the car wash went on, despite everyone's fears. The secretary and her husband didn't seem like they would give up harassing them any time soon. What else were they planning?

As Iris considered it, still thinking about Icarus too, she heard a bicycle horn beep behind her. She turned around, watching as Grant approached on a blue bicycle with a smile.

A perfect, handsome smile that almost made Iris melt.

"Hey, Iris," Grant began. "Almost time for the field trip. You still coming? I was just on my way there. My students should be arriving any minute now."

Iris nodded. "Of course, I'll grab one of those strange taxi things and meet you at the zoo. I was just helping Princess Esme with her car wash."

"You've got some people here at least," Grant said, glancing around. "Not a bad start."

"Actually, these humans are all old friends of Princess Esme and Gemma Solace. Before they knew they were from Fairhaven. We haven't won over anyone new yet. Maybe we never will."

"Well, you won me over," Grant said with a smile, making Iris blush. "That's an accomplishment. Here—for your fundraiser. I want to help."

He placed a few paper bills into their donation basket, making Iris nod. "Thanks. The proceeds go toward the children's hospital, I hear."

"A good cause. Hopefully, more people will show up to get

their cars washed and leave a donation. I don't have a car—just this bicycle. Or I walk. Better for the environment that way."

As he beeped his bicycle horn again, Iris glanced down at it. "Did you want me to wash it for you? Since you donated?"

Grant laughed. "No, that's not necessary. Hey, have you ever been on a bicycle before?"

"Never. We had other means of transportation in Fairhaven, like dragons, unicorns, griffins. Unfortunately, all were lost in the explosion."

She felt a pang of sadness for all the animal lives stolen too. Senator Remus had taken everything from them, and she wished they could've saved a few of their magical creatures.

But she had a feeling it would've scared humans on the surface to see a dragon flying around. And they were trying to win them over, not push them away even more.

"Right. Again, I'm really sorry," Grant said. "I would've liked to see them. Anyway, maybe I can take you bike riding sometime? Show you the ropes? It's not difficult once you get the hang of it. It's all about balance. And I know a great bike path through a forest not far from here."

"If there's time, then sure. I know Princess Esme has other fundraising events in mind."

"Of course. And let me know about them—I'd like to come," Grant said, smiling again. "Anyway, I'll find you at the zoo. I know Ronan is excited to see you again."

"Aw. Really?"

"Yes, he said you sat with him on the swings. Something about a lightsaber battle?"

A smile tugged at Iris's lips. "There might've been one, yes. He was a strong, worthy opponent. I made sure he knew it too."

"Well, it was kind of you to spend time with him. He really appreciated it." Grant sighed. "I know Ronan's been getting bullied by the other kids—Justin Bond in particular. I try to break it up, but I just can't get through to Justin."

Look at his parents, Iris wanted to say. *They've made him as hateful as they are.*

"I'm glad Ronan has your support. I don't think he has much at home. Just thought you should know that you made a difference."

"Glad to hear it. Ronan is a sweet boy." Iris gestured at Princess Esme in the crowd. "I'm just going to tell the others where I'm heading. Give me one minute."

Grant nodded, waiting by the curb with his bicycle. He made chit-chat with some of Iris's guards as she headed toward Princess Esme. She was still chatting with her old friends and Iris didn't want to bother her. Gemma was alone, washing a friend's car.

"I'm going on a zoo field trip," Iris explained. "Just in case you all wonder where I ran off to. I'm meeting Grant there, just in case some of the students' parents have an issue. Everything seems calm for now and the other soldiers will be on duty as usual. Will you be okay without me?"

Gemma looked up, her hands full of soap and water. "We'll be fine, Iris. Go ahead with Grant and have a good time. Ooh, he's already looking at you."

When Iris turned around, Grant was still waiting by the curb, staring at them both. He gave them a wave and a smile when he saw they were looking over. Gemma waved back, then giggled.

"He's very handsome. Don't tell Ian I said that," Gemma whispered. "I'm happy for you, Iris. You deserve someone great."

"Grant and I aren't together," Iris said quickly. "He's just someone kind who's been trying to help us get used to the human world. And make friends. That's all. I'm sure he's just trying to be a good person."

Gemma laughed. "Agree to disagree. I think someone's got feelings for you. Anyway, don't let me keep you. Have a great time at the zoo."

Iris thanked her, then crossed the field to head back to Grant. Once she caught up with him, he walked his bike beside her as they headed to the school, chit-chatting about the news and the weather.

And although Iris had a million other things to worry about, deep down, she hoped Gemma was right that feelings were growing between her and Grant—at least on her end—something exciting and new.

Maybe it was the change of pace Iris needed.

CHAPTER 12

When Iris arrived at the school with Grant, watching him lock up his bicycle outside the front gate, the students and their parent chaperones showed up. It seemed like they had already learned about Iris's presence there the day before. When they saw her, they stood around and gossiped.

"Sorry about the looky-loos. Again," Grant said, glancing at the crowd before turning to Iris. "Principal Hannigan sent out a newsletter telling everyone you were here yesterday. She had to —parental rights and all that."

Iris nodded. "I have no problem with that. If any of them wishes to speak with me, they can do so anytime."

"Good. They'll probably keep their distance, though. So many people are afraid of what they don't understand." Grant sighed, looking like he was reliving some tough memories. "Anyway, our school bus is parked down here. It'll take us to the zoo."

"Great. Let me just grab a taxi." Iris paused. "Erm...I'm actually not quite sure what to do. Back home, we'd just wave our arms in the air and a griffin would pick us up and fly us where we needed to go."

Grant laughed, pulling out his smartphone. "Now *that* I'd like to see. Hang on, let me call you a taxi and give you some money for the ride. It should be here soon."

As Iris nodded, Grant talked into the phone, ordering one taxi to the school. As they waited around, chit-chatting, a rowdy crowd of school-aged children stood nearby, lining up at the school busses. Justin and his mother stood at the bus doors.

"... and your father and I ought to pull you out of this school," she was muttering, fixing her son's hair. "Now that we know what kind of deranged company they keep. What was your stupid teacher thinking?"

"Hey, I don't like those freaks either," Justin replied, swatting his mother's hand away, "but I have friends here, Mom. Switching schools in the middle of the year sucks. And stop messing with my hair! It looks fine."

Sheila looked like she had something else to say before she noticed Iris and Grant. "Oh. It's you."

Grant cleared his throat. "Hello, Mrs. Bond. How are you doing today?"

Sheila narrowed her eyes, glaring at Grant. "How do you think? You should've gotten parental permission before letting one of these ... creatures ... attend a show and tell. I didn't appreciate learning about it after the fact from my son. Parents have rights too."

"And so does Iris. I wanted to teach my kids about her culture," Grant replied. "Is something wrong with that, Mrs. Bond?"

"Where do I start?" she huffed. "For obvious reasons, I'm going on the field trip today. To make sure my son stays safe since you obviously don't care about your students anymore."

As Iris stood by silently, Justin said nothing, looking

between his teacher and his mother. Were any of his hateful thoughts his own? Or had he been programmed that way by his parents? She pitied him for being born into a family like that.

Grant looked offended. "Mrs. Bond, trust me, I take their safety very seriously. I'd never put them in danger. I love my kids more than anything—"

"Then stop inviting dangerous people to their classroom," Sheila interrupted. "My husband wishes he could be here today, but he's doing important work."

Iris wondered what it was. More work being hateful?

"And since I was recently fired from my job as a secretary at the news station," Sheila continued, "we're relying on his salary and donations from concerned people in town to stay afloat. Can you believe the news station fired me? I thought it was outrageous."

"I saw the news. You burst in front of the camera and interrupted the reporter to protest," Grant said. "The smoke bomb you were part of really scared everyone. It was inappropriate and dangerous."

Sheila rolled her eyes. "I was only speaking the truth. I didn't hurt anyone with the smoke bomb, now, did I? It was only to get people to pay attention. Anyway, losing my job means I'll have all the time in the world to make sure my son stays safe and avoids these dangerous Fae creatures while I look for another job. Maybe one in journalism where I can warn everyone about your kind."

"We're not dangerous," Iris said. "We don't want to hurt anyone. If you gave us a chance, you'd see that."

"I've seen enough, thank you very much," Sheila spat. "Excuse us, we're going to get on the bus now."

Sheila pushed past them, bumping into Iris's shoulder. She grimaced and it looked like it hurt Sheila more as she groaned after knocking into Iris's armor. She glared at Iris, then shoved her son onto the bus, and they took their seats near the back. The kids already on the bus continued to talk and play games. Lisa joined them on the bus a few moments later, yet another face Iris didn't want to see. Fortunately, they didn't speak.

"Sorry about that," Grant whispered, watching Sheila and Lisa through the window. "I had no idea Sheila was going to chaperone the field trip today. Or that Lisa was going to ride on my bus. She must've gotten another teacher to supervise her class."

All so she could sit with Grant and try to turn him against Iris, she would bet. That sounded right up Lisa's alley.

"Anyway, maybe when we get to the zoo, this could be your chance to talk to Sheila? To try to convince her your people can be trusted?"

"No thanks," Iris whispered back. "I don't think it'll change much. She and her husband seem intent on kicking us out of Toronto. Did you know her husband, Michael Bond, is a racist? That he's known to police for being an extremist?"

Grant's face went pale. "I ... had no idea, no. No wonder Justin says such awful things. His father is a bad influence. His mother is too, apparently."

"Agreed. And they're making our lives more difficult." Iris shook her head. "I think it's best if I stay away from them for now."

"Oh, there's your taxi. Tell them you want them to drive you to the Toronto Zoo. Here, some cash for the ride."

Iris took the paper bills from his hand. "That's kind of you, Grant. I'll have to find some way to repay you."

"Don't worry about it." His eyes twinkled. "See you soon."

As Iris swooned at Grant's kindness, he boarded the bus. He took a seat behind the driver next to a student in his class. Iris turned, heading to the taxi that had pulled into the school's courtyard. She gave the driver the address and they drove behind the bus the whole way. Ronan sat near the back of the bus, staring out the back window, and noticed Iris in the taxi with a smile. He waved and started drawing smiley faces on the window for her.

At least someone's happy to see me, Iris thought.

The school became smaller behind them as the driver took them to the Toronto Zoo. When they arrived, Iris paid the driver and stepped out. She kept a distance from the school busses as Grant helped the children off. As soon as Ronan had stepped off the bus, he ran over to Iris.

"Hi, Iris!" he cried with a big smile. "I didn't know you were coming too."

"I just happened to be heading to the zoo on the same day you were," Iris said, loud enough so the parent chaperones could hear. They glanced over at her and murmured. "Funny coincidence."

"Yeah, it is! Do you have zoos where you come from?" Ronan asked. "With dragons and stuff?"

"We did," Iris said sadly. "Before it was destroyed."

Ronan looked sad. "Oh. That sucks."

"Indeed."

He paused, then pulled out his lightsaber from his bag. "Do you want to have another lightsaber battle?"

"That would be fun, Ronan, but perhaps not here? The parents might object."

Ronan's eyebrows fell, looking disappointed. But he nodded anyway, slipping his lightsaber back into his bag. "Okay, I get it. I always bring my lightsaber with me. It makes me feel like a superhero."

"You are already a superhero, Ronan. Whether or not you bring a lightsaber."

That made him smile. "Thanks. You know, my mom didn't want me to come on this field trip."

"Oh, no? Does she have something against zoos?"

"No—she was scared of sending me to school after she heard you were there yesterday. She's afraid of your people."

Iris sighed. "Most humans are, unfortunately. I'm glad she let you come anyway."

"Me too. I really had to beg her." Ronan looked down. "I wanted her to come too—to chaperone the field trip and meet you. But she couldn't. She was too busy."

"With work?"

"No, with my younger siblings. I have two brothers and two sisters," Ronan explained. "She's stressed out and tired a lot. I miss when it was just the two of us. We hung out a lot more. And Dad's too busy with work to come too."

Iris felt bad for the boy. She had been an only child, never having to compete for her parents' affection, but she knew it must be difficult.

"I'm sorry, Ronan," Iris finally said. "If you'd like, I can be your chaperone. We can walk the zoo together. You can even teach me about your Earth animals."

Ronan's eyes lit up. "Okay! That sounds fun. Have you ever heard of a hippopotamus?"

As they entered the zoo, Ronan taught Iris everything he knew about the animals there. Then Iris told him a little about the animals back in Fairhaven. What it was like to travel on a dragon, what griffins ate, and how phoenixes laid their eggs. The little boy listened with wide eyes the whole time.

"Come on, everyone," Grant called out, gesturing at the group of kids. "We've got a tour guide waiting for us, so please, stick close to them. There's going to be a test on what you learned today so pay attention!"

The students nodded, following Grant and the other teachers. Iris tried to trail behind so no one would think she was on the school trip with them. The employee working at the zoo's entrance stamped the back of their hands and gave them each a map of the park.

"Um, ma'am?" the zoo employee asked, eyeing Iris' scabbard. "We don't allow weapons on zoo property. Safety reasons, you see. You'll either need to leave it with me or leave the zoo."

With Ronan staring at her, Iris didn't want to disappoint him. She handed the sword over. "All right, I understand. Please keep it safe."

The employee nodded, promising he would. He tagged along with the group. Grant stopped along a sidewalk, counting all his students. "Good—everyone's here. The park is a large place so stick close to your parent or chaperone. Whatever you do, don't stick food or your hands into the cages. We'll get lunch when we're almost done. Oh, look—there's our tour guide."

A beautiful blonde woman walked over, wearing the logo of the zoo on her green shirt. She smiled and shook Grant's hand. Her eyes lingered on him a little too long, a sickening feeling knotting in Iris's stomach.

Was it … jealousy? She had only felt it once—when a guard back home got a promotion over her, but never in a romantic situation. She shook her head and tried to ignore the feeling like a knife on her spine.

Grant wasn't hers, so what right did she have to be jealous?

"Nice to meet you, Mr. Thatcher. So glad you could be here," the woman said with a big grin, then she turned to the students. "My name is Kelsey and I'll be your tour guide today. We'll start with our aquatic animals first. Follow me, please, and stay close!"

Iris trailed behind the group of kids and parents, hearing their whispered gossip about her up ahead. She tried to keep her distance so she wouldn't freak anyone out. But Ronan was determined to stay close to her, even pulling on her arm a few times to point out some animals.

"Look—fish!" Ronan cried as they walked into the aquarium exhibit. The blue tank lights illuminated the fish inside and the sound of trickling water echoed around the room. People filled the dark room, tapping on the glass and pointing out the colorful fish.

"I love fish," Ronan said, pressing his face against a tank of koi. "I wish I could breathe underwater."

Iris stood back, watching Ronan play with the fish through the glass as the tour went on around them. "We probably have a potion for that. Our fairy godmothers—down to only two now, unfortunately—could most likely whip something up."

"Really?" Ronan spun around, his eyes wide. "That would be so cool!"

Iris bit back a laugh. "I wish other humans found us as interesting as you do, kid. They mostly just hate and fear us."

"Yeah. I don't get it," Ronan said as he and Iris caught up with the tour. "Even my mom is scared. I think being different is cool. And I wish other kids would think the same."

So did Iris. As she listened to him ramble on about fish, the tour guide summed up the exhibit and took them out a back door. It led into a colder section of the zoo—separate exhibits where the penguins, polar bears, and seals lounged on thick pieces of ice. Ronan whispered the names of the animals as they stopped outside the enclosures' glass.

"Look—one of our employees is feeding that seal," the tour guide said, pointing at a man in zoo uniform feeding the seal with fish from a bucket. The seal ate it up without chewing. "Sally the Seal was very hungry today! Did you know gray seals eat four to six percent of their body weight in food each day?"

"That's a lot of fish," Grant said, stepping closer to Iris and Ronan. "I guess you could say fish have the *seal* of approval."

Kelsey the tour guide laughed so hard it was almost obnoxious. From Lisa's expression, it looked like the teacher was getting as sick of that woman as Iris was—something they had in common. Grant smiled as his students finally understood the joke.

"I never tire of hearing animal puns," Kelsey said with a giggle. "Especially from a teacher so handsome. Now, come on —we'll head to the bird exhibit next ..."

Iris and Ronan trailed behind, staying far away from Justin, Sheila, and Lisa. After Grant checked on his students, making sure they were all safe and enjoying themselves, he walked over to Iris.

"I see you found a zoo buddy," Grant said, patting Ronan's head. "You two having a good time?"

"The best!" Ronan cried. "The fish are still my favorite. I love their fins and scales."

"Yes, they're marvelous creatures. Maybe we should get a pet fish for the classroom."

"Ooh, can I name him?"

Grant laughed. "We'll see, Ronan. We'll probably take a vote to decide. Anyway, Iris! What a surprise to see you here."

With all the parents staring at her, Iris played along. "Oh, hello, Grant. It seems we had the same idea today. A little trip to the zoo."

"That we did. So, what about you? Are you learning a bit about our Earth animals?"

Iris nodded, stepping into the bird enclosure. "I am. The seals were adorable."

"Agreed. Just wait until you see the giraffes—"

"Ooh, a peacock!" Ronan cried, reaching for Iris's hand. "Let's go see!"

Iris tried to stifle a laugh as Ronan pulled her forward, heading for the peacock's enclosure. He didn't release her hand as they quietly watched the peacock groom itself and then eat some food off the ground. Justin snickered, elbowing a nearby student.

"Hey, look—Ronan's holding hands with the freak," he muttered loud enough for people to hear. "What a loser."

"What, does he think she's his mommy?" Sheila shook her head. "That poor child. Don't his parents care that he's hanging around a danger to our society?"

Iris felt relieved when Ronan didn't hear that, continuing to stare at the peacock. He made funny noises to try to get the animal to look over at them. While Iris felt disappointed that she couldn't spend more time with Grant, she was having a great day with Ronan.

As Grant walked off, pointing out a flamingo to a student in his class, the tour guide headed toward Iris. She cleared her throat as Ronan continued to make funny noises at the peacock. He wasn't listening, too distracted by the animals which gave Iris and the woman a chance to talk.

"So, you're one of them, aren't you?" the tour guide whispered. "One of the magical people they found underground?"

Iris nodded. "That's right. I am."

"Hmm. You're not as scary in person," Kelsey replied, looking Iris up and down. "The way the media made you out, you'd think you were monsters."

"The media can't always be trusted. More often than not, people are just looking to cause outrage and sensationalize things. For their own benefit."

Iris stole a glance over at Sheila, watching her whisper with Justin while staring in their direction. Just what were they doing? They should've been looking around the exhibit, not gossiping about her.

"Maybe you're right," Kelsey replied, then gestured at Grant. "Anyway, I came over to ask a question. You and that handsome teacher ... I saw you talking. You seemed close. Are you dating him? Can your people even date humans?"

"We can, yes. Two of our kind already have. And no, we're not dating. We're only friends."

For some reason, sadness tugged at Iris's heart when she said that out loud. Maybe she wanted more. But did Grant want that?

"Oh, that's good. Do you know if he's single? Should I ask him out?"

Iris had two options—she could tell the tour guide the truth that yes, Grant was single. And that he was a good person, worthy of dating. Or she could lie in the hopes of dating him eventually.

Although Iris wasn't proud of it, she chose the latter.

"Sorry, he's engaged to someone," Iris lied. "And madly in love, I hear. They're getting married next month."

"Darn. The good ones are always taken." Kelsey sighed. "Anyway, thanks for letting me know. I guess my search for the perfect man isn't over yet. Oh, kids—please don't lean on the fence. You'll scare the birds!"

As the tour guide rushed to scold the kids for taunting the animals, Sheila and Justin had vanished, worrying Iris. Were they planning something? At least Ronan was still there, the one kid she was supposed to keep an eye on. As a chaperone, losing him would've made her look even worse.

Iris glanced around, looking for Grant, but found him wandering off with Lisa. She was leading him through a garden of animal sculptures and statues. She had managed to get rid of the flirty tour guide, but his ex?

Something told Iris she was going to continue to be a problem.

CHAPTER 13

"Stay here," Iris told Ronan, watching as he continued to make funny faces at the peacocks. "I'll be right back, okay?"

Ronan was barely listening, too enamored by the birds. "Okay!"

Checking on him once more, Iris followed Lisa and Grant into the garden of sculptures. A maze was set up for the kids to play in. As she approached the corner of a shrub, she heard Lisa and Grant whispering. Iris kept her distance to listen in.

"... and we were good together. You know we were," Lisa was saying. "Come on, Grant. What do you say? Let's give us another try."

Iris poked her head around the shrub, noticing Grant and Lisa standing next to a lion sculpture. Lisa was trying to hold hands with Grant. For a moment, Iris feared he would go back to her. But then he stepped away and shook his head.

"No, Lisa. I *thought* we were good together," Grant began, "but then I saw who you really are. Needy, backstabbing, cruel. And I don't like the way you've treated Iris."

Lisa rolled her eyes. "Oh, please. It's no different from how other people are treating those freaks."

"See? Calling them that is unacceptable. And downright mean," Grant spat. "Canada is better than that. *Humans* are better than that. And it's why I can't be with you again. Or ever."

Lisa narrowed her eyes at him. "There's something else, isn't there? Or *someone* else, I should say?"

Grant said nothing.

"Ah hah!" Lisa cried, pointing her finger in his face. "I knew it. Is it that Iris woman? I didn't think you were attracted to witches. Or Fae. Whatever the hell they are."

Iris's cheeks burned as they gossiped about her. Did Grant really have feelings for her?

"She shouldn't even be here," Lisa continued. "The zoo should've denied her entry!"

"They can't do that. She has the right to go wherever she wants, just like everyone else. And you know what? It's none of your business," Grant said as he crossed his arms. "Stay out of it. And leave Iris alone. Now, if you'll excuse me, I need to get back to my students. You should too."

As Grant walked away, Iris hid behind a shrub, trying not to be seen. Lisa chased after him. "You'll regret this, Grant. Don't say I didn't warn you!"

Grant waved her off, walking back to the bird enclosure. Lisa was still fuming. She pulled out her smartphone, then began talking into it too low for Iris to hear before walking away. Iris figured she'd better get back to the group before Grant realized she was gone.

Following the path out of the maze, Iris headed back to the bird enclosure, finding them all still there. Grant was chatting with a concerned parent who was ranting and raving about Iris.

"... and I'm not sure I want those people around my children," the mother was saying. "Are you sure they're safe?"

Grant nodded. "I trust Iris and her people, Mrs. Burnham. I know better than to think an entire group of people act and think the same way. I won't condemn Iris for the crimes of another, and I wouldn't bring her around if I thought she was dangerous. Now, aren't the colors on that bird so beautiful?"

Grant tried to defend her people and change the subject, but the parents didn't look too convinced. Iris shook her head and walked back to the peacock exhibit where she left Ronan. But when she glanced around, the boy wasn't there.

"Ronan?" she whispered. "Where did you go?"

Panicking, Iris walked around the side of the enclosure, then peeked over the gate. Ronan wouldn't have jumped in to spend time with the peacocks, would he? The boy was sweet but oblivious to danger.

After not finding him in the enclosure, Iris began to worry. She dreaded having to tell Grant that she lost a child. She'd have to admit she had walked away to spy on him and Lisa.

That wasn't going to win her any points with the humans.

But she had no choice. Taking a deep breath, Iris approached Grant. He had just finished pointing out some more colorful birds to his students. He turned to Iris when he saw her approaching, a big smile on his face.

"Hey, Iris!" he began. "Just teaching my students about the birds here. Hey, are you all right? You don't look so good."

Iris played with her hands. "Well, I'm really sorry to tell you this, but—"

She paused when she felt someone tugging on her arm. When she turned around, it was Ronan, carrying a big fluff of pink cotton candy. The food coloring had stained his lips as he pulled off pieces to eat.

"This cotton candy is so good," he said. "Do you want some?"

"Ronan!" Iris cried, bending down to his level. "There you are. Where did you go?"

"One of the zoo employees was selling cotton candy. I really wanted some, so I used my allowance money. Do you want a piece?"

Iris shook her head. "No, thank you. You really shouldn't wander off like that, though. I was worried when I couldn't find you."

"Oh. Sorry."

"It's all right, Ronan. I'm just glad you're safe." Iris rose, taking a deep breath before turning to Grant. "Sorry, false alarm. Ronan is all right."

"Good thing." Grant leaned in closer, his minty breath tickling Iris's ear. Goosebumps raised on her skin. "Don't beat yourself up over it. Kids like to run off without thinking. You wouldn't believe how many students I've lost, but fortunately, they've all been okay. They can slip away pretty quickly though."

When he pulled back, Iris nodded. "Yeah, I see that. I'll pay more attention next time."

As Grant smiled at her, Iris realized he wasn't nearly as angry as she thought he would be. Maybe he was just that kind —or maybe he liked her enough to overlook her flaws. Iris hoped it was a little of both.

"All right, everyone, let's move on to the final area, then grab some food," Kelsey the tour guide said. "We're heading to the safari animals' enclosure now. Did you know that lions can reach speeds up to eighty kilometers an hour?"

As the kids oohed and aahed, Ronan finished his cotton candy. Iris kept a closer eye on him. She wasn't going to lose him twice—not even if Lisa pulled Grant away to gossip again.

Lisa returned, putting her smartphone away while sneering in Iris's direction. She ignored the woman and walked with Ronan behind the tour guide.

The two people she didn't see were Sheila and her son, Justin. Where had they disappeared to?

When they entered the safari part of the zoo, Iris saw long fields of grass for the different animals. Ronan pointed out the lions, tigers, giraffes, and zebras, then they paused to listen to the tour guide explain them all. Iris finally spotted Sheila and her son milling around one of the lion cages.

When they noticed she was staring, they looked guilty as sin. Iris had a bad feeling about them—again.

"... and here we have our lion exhibit," Kelsey said, pointing at the large cats. "They live together except for one. Jabari, our oldest lion, has his own cage. He can be a bit ornery and stubborn sometimes. Even violent, so we keep him away from the other animals."

Ronan raised his hand. "Which one is he? This cage is empty."

When Ronan pointed at a large, vacant cage off to the side, filled with food troughs and rocks to climb, Kelsey frowned. "Weird. He definitely should be inside that cage. Maybe one of the employees took him out for some reason—"

When Iris heard a roar behind her, she spun around, then finally understood where the lion had disappeared to. He was out of the cage—and licking his lips like they were his next meal. She knew it was only a matter of time until he pounced.

"Be very quiet," Iris whispered. "Slowly, head to the exit. Don't make any sudden movements or the lion might attack—"

Naturally, no one listened to her.

The kids screamed, fleeing to the exit gate. Grant and the other teachers tried to corral the students and get them out of the area first. The rest of the visitors at the zoo noticed what had happened and started screaming and running too. When Iris glanced around, Sheila and her son were missing again.

She had an awful thought. Were they responsible for letting this big, angry cat out of his exhibit?

Iris didn't have time to think about it. As the lion barred its teeth, Ronan held out a hand. "Good kitty. You wouldn't hurt us, would you?"

"Ronan, no!" Iris cried. "Get away from that animal!"

The lion pounced toward Ronan just as Iris dove in front of him, taking the blow herself. Ronan screamed and backed away. The lion attached its massive jaw to Iris's arm, her skin only protected by her armor. But she still felt a crushing kind of pressure.

She thanked the fairy godmothers for putting enough magic inside the guards' uniform to protect her. And the Miracle Flower her mother had given her was still a good luck charm after all this time.

The zookeepers looked paralyzed by fear, wondering what to do. Grant pulled Ronan out of the enclosure and left him with the other students and teachers—all of them wide-eyed and watching Iris wrestle with the lion—before running to her side.

"My God, Iris!" Grant cried. "Are you all right?"

"Never better," Iris grunted, trying to get the lion to remove its jaw from her arm. "Let go of me, creature. I command you!"

When Iris began making wild animal sounds, the lion listened. It removed its jaw from her arm, leaving the armor scratched underneath.

"Get back in your cage. Right now," she demanded, making eye contact with the animal. She puffed out her chest in an attempt to look menacing. "Attack me again and it'll be the last mistake you make."

The lion roared one last time, trying to intimidate her, but Iris stood tall, shielding Grant and the others from the animal.

After a tense stare down, the lion eventually growled and headed back inside the enclosure. Kelsey the zookeeper quickly closed the cage and locked it behind them.

"Holy hell, are you all right?" Grant asked, reaching for Iris's arm. "Your armor is dented."

"Better than my arm," Iris said as she glanced down at herself. "I think I'm fine. The armor saved my life—just as it was meant to." Though she'd be bruised tomorrow, for sure.

"Thank goodness for that. You saved Ronan's life, you know," Grant said, nodding at the boy over their shoulder. "Probably everyone else's too. You were brave to take on that animal."

Iris glanced behind her, the students, teachers, and parents stared at her in amazement. They still murmured about her, but this time, it was out of relief instead of concern.

"It was nothing. I'm trained to protect others with my life," Iris replied, turning back to Grant. "Plus, I was Ronan's unofficial chaperone. I had to keep him safe."

"Well, you went above and beyond. You were amazing." Grant smiled. "I've never seen anyone get a lion to back down like that. You could've been a zookeeper, you know. How did you do it?"

"I had plenty of training back home. Granted, it was with magical animals, but the principle is still the same. Make eye contact to establish dominance, talk in a deeper register, and don't back down. Animals are all about power and authority. Once you establish yourself as being fearless and in charge, they'll listen to you."

"You did it flawlessly. I'm so glad you were here—or that might've ended up differently. You'll have to teach me more about all the lessons you learned back home sometime."

As Iris nodded, Kelsey rushed over. "My goodness, that was intense. Are you all right? Do your people even feel pain?"

"We most certainly do. We're not too different from humans. And yes, I'm fine. My armor saved me."

"Good, good. If you hadn't gotten Jabari to back down, I was just about to summon an employee with a tranquilizer gun. But it's better this way. He doesn't listen to anyone—and he's been a problem before. You were lucky to survive."

"And very skilled," Grant added. "I wish I had that power."

Kelsey nodded. "Yes, you definitely could work here. Anyway, I'm glad everyone's all right. I still don't understand how Jabari escaped his cage though. The lock is very secure."

Iris walked toward the cage, watching the lion drinking water inside. He looked at Iris before rolling over and showing his belly. The animal respected her now—he was docile. She just wished humans could be dealt with the same way.

As Iris looked at the lock on the cage, she realized there were tool marks in the form of sharp lines. Someone had hacked away at the lock—they wanted the lion to escape. But who would do something so reckless and dangerous?

When Iris turned around, Sheila and Justin had pushed through the crowd. Sheila approached Grant while keeping a hand on her son's shoulder. "What's going on?"

"I think you know," Iris said, walking over to the group. "You and your son vanished just before the lion was let out of its cage. Did you open it? Were you hoping it would attack and kill me?"

When the others turned to look at Sheila, she scoffed. "That's ridiculous. I didn't do anything!"

Grant glanced at the zookeeper. "Do you have security footage for this part of the zoo? We can see if anyone manipulated the cage."

"We do," Kelsey said. "I'll go check right now—"

"That isn't necessary," Lisa said, walking toward them. "We're not going to treat a parent like a common criminal without any proof. Iris, Grant, did you physically see Sheila and her son open the lion's cage?"

The group of parents, students, and teachers watched on as Grant shook his head. "I didn't, no."

"Me either," Iris huffed, "but I saw them in the vicinity of the cage, then they did disappear beforehand—"

"My son needed to use the bathroom. I went with him," Sheila interrupted. "When we came back, we were just looking at the cage. That isn't a crime, is it?"

Iris glanced at Justin. He wouldn't meet anyone's eyes, he just kept staring at the ground. Iris thought it more than obvious that Sheila was behind this and using her son as an excuse. What kind of mother would do that? To unlock a lion's cage and risk it attacking a group of innocent children was just psychotic. Iris finally saw the dangerous woman she was dealing with.

"Definitely not," Lisa said. "I'm so sorry for the accusations, Mrs. Bond. Clearly Mr. Thatcher isn't thinking straight. He's spent too much time with these Fairhaveners."

"A pity," Sheila spat.

"Definitely. Maybe one of the zookeeper's made a mistake and the animal got out on its own." Lisa put a hand on Sheila's shoulder. "Come—I'll buy you and your son a free lunch from the cafeteria. As an apology."

"That's more like it. We can talk about my concerns about these Fairhaveners in private."

As they walked away, gossiping about Iris, she turned to Grant. "I'm telling you—Sheila and her son were responsible. Or mostly Sheila. They disappeared before the incident."

"I believe you," Grant said. "Be careful, Iris. If they're capable of doing that, who knows what else they have planned."

"I could say the same to you. I don't trust that family."

Kelsey cleared her throat. "Well, I'm very sorry all this happened. Come on—I'll show you all to the cafeteria."

Iris and Grant nodded, following Kelsey to the crowd. The parents and teachers kept their distance, but the kids thought Iris was cool after they calmed down from the lion attack. No one was more impressed than Ronan, clinging to her side and asking questions.

"You were so brave taking on that lion!" he cried. "How did you know it would listen to you?"

"I didn't," Iris replied, walking with him to the cafeteria. The students walked behind her to listen in. "But someone had to do something. You were in danger, Ronan. I couldn't let any harm come to you."

Ronan smiled. "Thanks. I was too scared to stand up to the animal. I screamed and ran away like a coward."

"No, you did the right thing. You let an adult handle the situation." Iris bent down to his eye level. "Remember, having courage doesn't always mean leaping into danger and acting recklessly. Sometimes, it's about doing the best thing for everyone in that moment. And self-preservation is never a bad thing."

"Yeah, okay. I see what you mean." Then Ronan's eyes lit up. "Did you do stuff like that back home? Get animals to back down?"

"I did. Let's get lunch and I'll tell you all about it." Iris glanced over her shoulder, noticing the students looking up at her with wide-eyed curiosity. "And our audience too, apparently."

After grabbing some free sandwiches and juice from the cafeteria, Iris took a seat at a table with Ronan. Some of the other kids joined them, pulling over chairs to listen. The parents weren't too happy, but their kids wouldn't listen when they asked them to leave Iris alone.

Even Grant walked over, plopping his sandwich and soda down while taking a seat across from Iris. "Don't start without me. I want to hear all about your magical adventures."

With Grant's eyes on her, Iris suddenly felt nervous. She didn't know if the butterflies in her stomach were for him or just leftover anxiety from fighting a lion. "Um, all right. One time, a dragon got away from its rider and was in a bad mood. Animals have mood swings too, you know. Well, when it started pecking at the castle, huffing and blowing fire, me and the other guards were assigned to get it down. I looked the dragon right in the eyes, lifted my sword, and screamed, 'enough!' I was terrified, though, and trying not to let it show. I was an ant on the ground compared to that creature. After a while, it came down and returned to its owner. We're trained to deal with animal threats like those."

"Cool!" one kid in the audience cried.

"You're a natural hero, then," Grant said with a smile. "That's impressive."

Iris blushed again. "Thank you. I don't do it for the glory, though—that's not my style. I do it to protect people. Because it's my duty."

"Well, I think you're pretty fantastic. Not many would risk their lives like that." Grant thought for a moment. "We should give you a title. Maybe ... the Hero of the Zoo?"

"The great animal tamer!" Ronan yelled, making everyone around Iris nod.

She smiled and thanked them, though it didn't feel right. The more people called her a hero, the more she thought about how she had failed to save Fairhaven from Senator Remus.

She felt like a fraud, a loser. But she didn't want to tell the others that and ruin the mood. For once, they were finally starting to like her.

"Do you have any more stories?" Ronan asked, munching on his sandwich.

Iris cleared her throat, not used to all the attention. "I sure do. Let me tell you about the time I stopped a griffin. It had gotten its maw on a fairy godmother's unattended laughing potion and set it loose. Suddenly, everyone in Fairhaven broke out in unstoppable giggles, even me …"

CHAPTER 14

After finishing lunch and telling all the heroic stories she could remember, Iris and the kids moved on. They checked out the monkey enclosure next—with Ronan doing an impression and making Iris laugh. Then the field trip was over, and they all headed outside to leave.

Sheila and Justin had taken off, getting picked up by Michael Bond. As Iris watched, making sure he didn't try anything, he glared at her from the driver's seat before speeding off down the road. His tires left muddy marks on the street. His bumper sticker read PROTECT THIS CITY—KICK OUT THE OUTSIDERS, letting everyone know where he stood on the matter.

Grant stood by the first school bus's steps, counting Ronan and all the other kids. "Okay, I think we have everyone. Except Sheila and Justin Bond. Where did they go?"

"That awful husband of hers picked them up. And I need to do something first before we go. Will you wait for me?"

Grant smiled. "Of course. The kids and I will sing road trip songs in the meantime."

Iris nodded, watching as Grant climbed onto one of the

busses and thanked the kids for their good behavior. They began singing songs about zoo animals as Iris entered the zoo again, following the signs on the wall. Next to the bathroom sign was one that read SECURITY THIS WAY, directing Iris down the long hall.

When she reached the security office, the sign ON LUNCH BREAK hung on the door. She reached for the doorknob, finding it unlocked before she headed inside. She noticed a small desk with a security guard's things sitting there, then several screens of security footage for the zoo.

Iris sat down, rerolling the footage. It took her a few minutes to figure out how to use the computer. She went back to the footage before lunch when the lion had broken out. And lo and behold, Sheila had been the one to break into the lion's cage, using a tool she found in the maintenance closet to break the lock. Justin was her lookout before they ran off and the students came in to see the lion.

When the lion eventually broke out, then attacked Iris, she turned off the video. She had lived it once—she didn't need to see it again. She still had the bite marks along her armor.

The door to the security office opened behind her, then a burly guard entered. He looked angry when he saw her sitting at the desk. "Hey, who are you? I wasn't aware another guard was coming to fill my shift. Wait a minute ... you aren't wearing the zoo's uniform."

"No, I'm not." Iris rose to her feet. "I'll just be going now."

As she moved around him, the security guard took a closer look. "I know you. You're one of those Fairhaven freaks, aren't you?"

Iris was getting tired of being called that. She turned back to the man, sighing. "And if I am?"

"Your people aren't going to stay in Toronto for long, you know. Concerned citizens are writing to the prime minister every day, trying to get her to throw you all out. And I think it's working," the security guard sneered. "People like you don't belong in our city."

"Well, where do you propose we go? Our home was destroyed. How would you feel if that happened to Toronto?"

The guard shrugged. "Not my problem. I don't really care where you go—just get out of here. And if I catch you in my security office again, we're going to have a real problem."

I just fought a lion and won, Iris wanted to say. *You really think you could take me?*

But she didn't—she knew better than to cause more problems. The guard was angry enough and she had gotten what she wanted from the security footage. And with his bad attitude toward her people, no wonder Sheila was able to open the lion's enclosure without anyone coming around to stop her. Maybe some of the zoo's guards were even in on it, maybe they weren't.

With so many enemies, it was hard to know who to trust.

Iris just shook her head, then left the office. The guard slammed the door behind her. She remembered to head to the office, getting her sword back. As she headed down the hallway, Grant was coming around the corner. The two banged into each other before realizing who it was.

"Oh, sorry," Grant said. "Didn't see you there."

"It's all right—I wasn't looking. My fault." Iris tried to hide her blush as their bodies collided, then cleared her throat. "What are you doing?"

"Looking for you, actually. The kids are getting rowdy—we should get them back to school. Are you coming?"

"I am. Just checked out the security footage," Iris said, walking down the hall with Grant toward the front gate. "Sheila was indeed the one who let out the lion. The footage confirmed it."

"Shit," Grant cursed. "Glad my students weren't around to hear me say that. Do you want to alert the police?"

"Yes, but I'll do it anonymously. I don't want more hatred of my people. Setting a lion loose around a bunch of kids is attempted murder, if you ask me. If anyone set a dragon loose back home, there would be serious consequences."

Grant nodded, pausing near the zoo's gates. "It's disturbing for sure. Oh, you've got a little something there …"

He reached up a hand, wiping off dirt from the side of Iris's face. She noticed what it was as he brushed it off his hands. "That was probably from when the lion attacked me. Thanks."

"No problem. You definitely won points with my students for that, you know. They'll be talking about you fearlessly defending them from a lion for a long time. I will be too. It was amazing."

Iris shook her head. "Not amazing, just what's expected of me—"

"No," Grant interrupted. "It's definitely amazing. *You're* amazing. And I wish you would see that about yourself."

Iris didn't know what to say. She had never gotten such an earnest compliment before. "Well … thank you. I'm glad you think so."

"I *know* so. And I was wondering if—"

When the school bus's horn beeped, both Iris and Grant turned around. The bus driver looked apologetic as Lisa leaned over his shoulder, beeping the horn. She stuck her head out the window as she continued to sound it.

"Come on!" she cried. "We'd like to get back to school sometime this century. Hurry up!"

Grant sighed. "I guess we'd better go. Come on—we'll talk back at the school. When we have a private moment."

A private moment? Iris liked the sound of that.

She nodded, heading to the road. Grant called her another

taxi and gave her more money for it like a perfect gentleman. As the taxi arrived, Iris got in and gave the address to the school, her eyes on the line of busses the whole way. When Grant sat down, Lisa immediately sat next to him, talking his ear off. But he seemed to be barely listening as he gazed out the window.

When the busses arrived back at the school, Iris stepped out, paying the taxi. The driver sped off as Ronan rushed off the bus to reach her.

"Hi again," Ronan said with a big smile. "I had a fun time at the zoo today. Did you?"

Iris nodded. "I did. Which animal was your favorite?"

She let Ronan ramble on for a few minutes. As the boy became more comfortable around her, the more he shared things about himself. He told her all about his love of Disney movies, superheroes, and nerdy things.

"It doesn't make me very popular," Ronan said, "but I still love them anyway. Like my lightsaber. I'll never forget the battle we had. It was so cool!"

Iris smiled. "Good, I'm glad."

"Maybe you can come on more field trips? And more show and tells? Oh, and have I shown you my new Pokémon cards?"

Ronan clearly needed a friend, and Iris was more than happy to listen to him. When Grant directed all the kids back into the school with only one class left for the day, Ronan sighed and headed inside. But not before waving at Iris from the hall window as she and Grant stood around to chat.

"I wanted to thank you for coming today. You handled the kids well," Grant said, leaning against the wall. "I don't know what we would've done if you weren't there to stop that lion. Thinking of that animal hurting one of my kids ... it makes my insides twist into a knot."

"I think Sheila only released the lion because I was there

and she wanted to protest. She may have even hoped it would hurt me or be blamed on me."

"Yes, most likely." Grant shook his head. "Awful. My poor kids will be traumatized about that for a while."

"Anyone would. You know, I was thinking in the taxi, that maybe I shouldn't go on these trips anymore. To protect your students."

"And let the naysayers win? Forget that," Grant said passionately. "Sheila should be the one to back off, not you. I'm going to speak with my principal and make sure she tells the parents that no violence is allowed. Whether or not they agree with your people."

Iris's mouth curved upward into a smile. "I appreciate that. Anyway, I should get back to the church and check on my people."

"Of course. But hey," Grant said, awkwardly scratching the back of his neck, "I was going to ask you something. Before Lisa so rudely sounded the horn. Maybe we ... actually, never mind."

Iris playfully nudged his arm, feeling his muscled bicep. "Go on. Tell me."

Grant was actually blushing—Iris couldn't believe it. A faint redness appeared on his ivory cheeks. "Well, all right. I don't know why I got nervous there for a second. But like I said before, I go bike riding a lot. And I'm planning another ride tomorrow. I'm heading out into the woods on a popular trail. Would you ... like to come with me?"

"I would," Iris said without hesitation, "but I'll need a bicycle. Even though I can't really ride one."

"Hey, no worries. I can teach you. I *am* a teacher, after all."

Iris blushed at the thought of Grant putting his hands on her to guide her on the bike. "Right, okay. And I'll need to check with my people to make sure they don't need me."

"Of course. I'll rent you a bicycle and come by tomorrow

morning. If you can't go, no worries. But I just thought I'd ask."
Grant hesitated. "If you can't tell ... I like talking with you, Iris.
And I hope the feeling is mutual."

Iris nodded. "It definitely is. You're not like the other
humans I've met."

"I'm taking that as a compliment," Grant said with a shy
smile.

"It is. Believe me."

"Good. Anyway, I should get back to class. Last one of the
day before the weekend comes. I'm teaching ... God, what *am* I
teaching?" Grant pulled out his school planner from his pocket,
reading it over. "Right, geography. Sorry—talking with you
makes my head spin. In a good way, I promise."

"You feel it too then? I thought it was only me. Good luck
with your next class, Grant. I'll see you tomorrow morning."

He waved goodbye with a smile, and she could feel him
watching her leave the school. To her relief, no protestors
stopped her outside, and she was able to head back to the
church. On the way down the sidewalk, she came across Maya
coming home early from school.

The same boys who had crashed their car wash were dropping her off. She kissed the one in the front seat, then waved at
them before they drove away. Iris knew now was her chance to
confront Maya for her behavior.

When Maya saw Iris coming, her smile faded. "Oh. It's you."

"It's me," Iris said, pausing on her front lawn. She crossed
her arms. "I can't believe you're friends with those boys who
told us to leave Toronto. I thought you'd be more sympathetic
to outsiders. Considering your family isn't from this country."

"Hey, it's not the same," Maya snarled. "Don't compare the
two."

"I see no difference. Your parents preach love and accep-
tance, and I thought you did too. But then you're hanging out

with boys who are petty and rude. And kissing one of them as well. Do your parents know about that?"

Maya blushed. "No, they don't. And I'd appreciate it if you didn't tell them. They might get upset with me, and I don't want them to be. They're having a hard enough time fitting into this country. And those boys ... Jack, in the driver's seat? He's my boyfriend. He's a nice guy. His brother is too. They're just scared of your people, that's all."

Iris shook her head. "Fear is no excuse. I fear these spiders of yours on the surface, but I have no intention of harassing and killing them all. I think you should encourage your boyfriend and his brother to reconsider the way they treat others. Today it's us, but tomorrow, it could be your family. That's the thing about hate, Maya. It never ends—it just moves on to harass someone else. Unless you take a stand and stop it."

When a car came around the corner, Iris realized it was Maya's parents returning from work. Maya looked nervous as she turned back to Iris. "Look, maybe Jack and his brother did something stupid, but I can't change their minds. I don't have that power. And they've never done that stuff to me. Now, would you get out of here? I meant what I said before. I don't want you hanging around my parents anymore."

"Aren't you afraid your boyfriend might turn on you? I hope he won't." Iris stepped back, shaking her head. "But, if that's the company you keep, then I'm disappointed in your character, Maya. I know your parents would be too. Tell your boyfriend and his brother to leave us alone, at least. My people don't need more enemies."

Before Maya could respond, Iris turned, crossing the street to head toward the church. The Bhatias pulled into their driveway and waved at Iris. She waved back only to be polite, watching them enter the house with their daughter. Maya looked nervous—and they had no idea who she was hanging around with behind their backs.

As Iris walked up the steps to the church, another tremor rattled the ground. She froze and looked around. She had never felt these tremors in the day—only at nighttime when everyone was asleep.

Icarus was getting stronger.

Iris took off running, following the tremors. People poked their heads out of their houses to see what was going on. She found herself at the nearest cemetery again, watching a woman in all black cry in the arms of another woman. Judging by the open empty casket behind them, a funeral was taking place— but the body was missing.

"... what is going on?" she was asking. "This can't be possible!"

"Fan out. Find that corpse," Iris heard someone in the funeral party say, issuing orders to the employees of the cemetery. "Find where Mrs. Richter's husband went. Corpses can't just get up and walk away, so get whatever that thing is back to us."

Iris understood it now—the dead man had come back to life, getting out of the casket and walking away from his own funeral. Almost like a braindead zombie Iris had read about in human fiction. The employees nodded, then took off down the sidewalk. Iris didn't see any walking corpses, but the news was alarming. Was this Icarus' doing? Did he have something in mind for the cemetery? And possibly the world?

She wanted to give her condolences to the widow but paused, fearing the woman might blame Iris for this. So, she just turned and headed back to the church. When she entered, she found her people in the pews as usual, waiting on dinner and planning their next move. Iris didn't see Princess Esme anywhere.

"Hello," Iris said, closing the door behind her. "I'm back. Where's the princess?"

"Throwing up," Gemma said sadly, standing over a paper with a lot of things written down. "She wasn't feeling well. Noah's with her, holding back her hair. Poor thing."

Ian nodded. "It's probably stress. The car wash ... well, it didn't go quite to plan."

"What do you mean? What happened?"

"More people came by after you left. Humans," King Tedros explained, stepping forward. "They threw things at us and called us names. We had to head inside and cancel. We made some money, though. Mostly from Esme and Gemma's friends."

"Which we're going to donate to the children's hospital as soon as Princess Esme is feeling better," Gemma added. "It's a start, at least. She's got more plans and things to try."

Iris sat down. "The princess doesn't give up, does she?"

"Never. It's admirable." Gemma walked over, sitting next to Iris with a smile. "So, how did the field trip go with Grant? And why is your armor all scuffed up?"

When everyone else looked at her, Iris figured she'd better come clean. "It went well ... up until Sheila Bond unlocked the lion's cage. I fought the creature off and won, saving the children."

The church was dead silent.

"Jesus," Ian finally muttered. "That's awful. But well done on stopping that lion. Not an easy thing to do."

"All the guards are trained in animal handling, as I explained. It was nothing. But I fear what else Sheila may do."

"Point taken," King Tedros said, glancing at Fairy Godmother Odelia. "We'll put more of our soldiers on perimeter watch. Just in case. It's not exactly a secret that the prime minister gave us this church. Perhaps Sheila and her husband are working their way up to more dramatic measures."

Something more dramatic than a lion? Iris was afraid to see that. And whatever Icarus was cooking up had to be even worse. Like a corpse walking away at its own funeral.

"Will do. I'll need a fairy godmother to repair my armor. And one more thing," Iris said. "Walking past a funeral today ... the family was in distress. But it wasn't just regular mourning. The man who had died ... got up out of his own casket and left. Walked away like a zombie—and it's my understanding they've only existed in human fiction up until now. The dead shouldn't come back to life."

King Tedros went pale as the others murmured behind him. "That's most concerning. We'll need to look into that as well. With that discovery and the Bond's ... we have our hands full, don't we?"

"Don't we ever," Iris muttered.

CHAPTER 15

With the vanishing dead man still on their minds, Gemma showed Iris all the money they had raised, looking proud over the donation box. Iris didn't think there was a lot of cash there—but making anything at all was a miracle. As Gemma closed the donation box, then Fairy Godmother Odelia whipped up a potion and fixed Iris' dented armor, Princess Esme and Noah came out of the bathroom.

Princess Esme wiped the sweat off her brow. "Well, throwing up coffee sure isn't pleasant."

Noah patted her back. "I'll say. Are you sure you don't want your fairy godmother to look at you?"

"Because I can," Fairy Godmother Odelia said, rising from her feet. "A simple spell can check and see if you've got an illness—"

"No, it's all right. No need for all the fuss," Princess Esme said, sitting down on one of the pews. "It's just anxiety, I'm sure. From everything going on. I bet Gemma knows what I mean."

Gemma nodded. "I definitely do. Anxiety can cause nausea, migraines, joint aches. The list goes on. And coming up to the surface has been stressful for us all. Even my anxiety is bad these days."

As Ian comforted Gemma, Noah did the same for Princess Esme. Iris briefly thought back to Grant. Would he comfort her the same way? Would he hold her, love her, and promise everything would be all right?

It sounded lovely when Iris pictured it in her mind.

"Well, I'm glad you're all right," King Tedros said, patting his daughter's shoulder. "Now, Gemma counted all the money. It's not a lot, but we did get some donations."

Princess Esme rose to her feet. "Good—it's a start. Maybe once the humans see us donating it, they'll come to our next event."

"Next one?" Iris raised an eyebrow. "Having the first one was risky enough. And you want to do it again?"

"Of course I do—it's nice to help people. And it'll help us win over the humans. I just know it will." Princess Esme reached for the donation box. "Come on—the children's hospital is only a few blocks from here. Let's deliver it tonight so no one has a chance to steal it."

The others nodded, thinking it was a good idea. But Iris knew nothing was quite that cut and dried.

She didn't bother arguing with the princess, following her outside the church. Some of the guards stayed behind to protect their home. Iris walked down the sidewalk first, one hand on her sword as usual. She had to with the growing number of threats.

When they reached the children's hospital, Gemma ran into her human friend, Carly. She was with her daughter, Abigail, who was receiving treatments for lupus among other autoimmune disorders. They entered the hospital together, walking toward the front desk as Princess Esme's people followed. Iris quickly used one of the payphones to send the anonymous tip of Lisa letting out the lion at the zoo to the police.

She doubted the police would take it seriously, but she had to try. And there was video proof after all.

"Hello there," Princess Esme said, setting the donations down on the front desk. The nurse hung up the phone and looked down at the box and then Iris walked over. "We're here to make a donation to your hospital. It's not a lot, but hopefully it'll help some kids."

The nurse hesitated, glancing around at them. "You ... you people are from Fairhaven, aren't you?"

"Yes, we are," Iris said. "Is that a problem?"

"I, uh, need to talk to my supervisor. Be right back."

The nurse scurried away, heading into a side office. She had pulled out her smartphone and was sending a text message to someone. Then they heard her murmuring in the office. People sitting in the waiting room noticed them and stared. Carly shook her head, apologizing for their bad behavior. She and Abby had no fears being around Gemma and Ian at all.

"I wish more of your people were like you," Iris muttered, making the others nod.

When the nurse returned, she had a tall supervisor with her in blue scrubs. They walked back toward the desk. "I'm told you'd like to make a donation?"

"That's right," Princess Esme said, stepping back. "No strings attached—just take it. And hopefully, we'll have more to donate soon. I plan to hold more fundraisers."

"I'm sorry, but we can't accept this," the supervisor said, pushing the box back toward Princess Esme. "For safety reasons."

"Safety reasons?" Iris demanded. "Like what? This money could help kids get treatments."

The supervisor looked apologetic. "I know—and I'm thankful you thought of us. While I'd like to accept your donation, it's too risky. There are a lot of concerns about your people, you know. So many are afraid of you. And I'm worried that if they see us taking your donations, the public will get angry at us and remove their support. So, it's just better if we don't accept this."

"Oh, come on," Carly huffed. "I've known Gemma for a while now—she's no danger to anyone. Why not just let them help? It's for a good cause."

The supervisor frowned. "I'm really sorry, but I'm afraid my mind is made up. And if there's nothing else, we'd like you to leave. You're scaring our patients."

Iris noticed the patients were afraid, murmuring about them. Then she scoffed. "Really, this is ridiculous—"

"No, it's all right. We don't want to cause any problems." Princess Esme sighed, reaching for the donation box. "I see your point. We'll just be going, then."

The supervisor and nurse nodded, watching them walk out of the hospital. As they left through the sliding doors, a large crowd had formed outside. And quickly—some people were still showing up in their cars, carrying large signs. Most of their signs were obscene and cruel. Through the window, Carly and Abby watched. She blocked her daughter's eyes from reading those signs.

"How did all these people get here so fast?" Princess Esme called out, watching them surround the doors. "How did they even know we were here?"

"That damn nurse must've called someone. I saw her playing with her phone," Iris huffed. "Tipping off people must be worth something. Anyway, come on—I'll try to get us safely through this crowd. Move it, people! Out of the way!"

Princess Esme's people hid behind Iris, using her as a human shield. She gently pushed humans back as she led everyone toward the sidewalk. Carly and Abby were separated from them in the struggle, making Gemma look back in concern, but the crowd wasn't focused on them. They only wanted to let Princess Esme's people know they weren't wanted.

It was like the office meeting with the prime minister all over again.

"Get out of here, you freaks!" one man in the crowd yelled. "No one wants you here. The Exterminators will deal with you!"

The Exterminators? Iris had never heard that term before. Shoving the angry crowd back, she heard tires screeching in the distance. When Gemma screamed, Iris turned around, noticing a black sedan coming right at them.

Iris wasn't an expert on cars, but she knew it would hurt on impact.

Just as she prepared for the pain, shielding her people from the accident, the car came to a screeching halt. She stood only inches away from the hood. When she looked in the driver's seat, wondering who had tried to run them over, she noticed a middle-aged man with a bald head and tattoos wearing a shirt and jeans.

He leaned out his window, smoking a cigarette. "I heard you freaks were here at the hospital. Look at this crowd—no one wants you here. Our prime minister's too much of a coward to say it so I will. Leave Toronto. Or else. And stay the hell away from my son. I don't want you corrupting him. Or next time, I won't stop my car."

Before Iris could ask any questions, the man backed up,

then sped away, leaving them in his dust. The others coughed before the dust faded. Fortunately, the speeding car scared the crowd, making them disperse out of fear of getting hit.

"Who the hell was that?" Noah demanded. "Which son was he talking about?"

"I believe that was Michael Bond," Iris said, watching his tail lights fade. "The same guy who threw the smoke bomb at us. Sheila's husband and Justin's father."

"Nasty piece of work," Ian muttered. "He almost hit us. And threatened to next time."

"All the more reason to get back to the church. We're too exposed out here." Iris gestured at the sidewalk. "Move it, everyone."

The others nodded, picking up the pace as they headed down the sidewalk. To their relief, the crowd didn't follow. When Iris spotted the church in the distance, she hurried over and opened the doors, ushering everyone inside. She was the last one in and locked the door tightly behind her.

When she turned around, everyone had huddled near the pews. "Everyone all right?"

"Yeah, we're all fine." Princess Esme sniffled. "Just disappointed. We tried to do a good thing and it failed. I can't believe this."

When she sat down, gently crying, Noah comforted her as the church turned silent. No one knew what to say.

"I'm sorry, dear," King Tedros finally said. "Nothing on the surface has gone to plan. It's been difficult on us all."

"I know it has. I'm sorry, I don't know why I'm crying." Princess Esme wiped a tear away. "I've just been feeling a bit more emotional lately."

"It's all right. Never apologize for having emotions," Gemma said, patting her shoulder. "We'll make it through this.

I know we will. Maybe ... maybe we can try something else? Anyone have any ideas?"

As they brainstormed ideas, Princess Esme put her hand over her mouth, then stood up and ran to the bathroom. Noah followed before King Tedros and Fairy Godmother Odelia did the same. When everyone began murmuring in concern about Princess Esme, Iris thought she'd better follow.

She headed to the bathroom, finding Princess Esme throwing up into the toilet. Noah was holding her hair back as King Tedros and Fairy Godmother Odelia watched with worried eyes. When Princess Esme finished, she flushed the toilet and brushed her teeth in the nearby sink.

"So sorry you all had to see that," she said, turning to them while smelling minty fresh. "Probably stress again."

"Are you sure?" Fairy Godmother Odelia stepped toward her, reaching for her wand. "Because Blanche and I could whip something up—"

"Really, like I said—no need to fuss over me. I'm fine. And there are more important things to do." When Princess Esme's stomach growled, she sighed. "Like making dinner. Let's go help the guards make something. Maybe a nice meal will settle my stomach."

Fairy Godmother Odelia nodded, watching Esme and Noah head to the kitchen. She stayed back to murmur with King Tedros. They both looked worried about Princess Esme's health. Iris was too, though she was more concerned about Icarus and the dead man vanishing from his own funeral. Iris knew she would've been devastated if that had happened to her parents.

King Tedros turned to her, almost reading her mind. "We're alone now, so we should talk. About the dead human getting up from his casket and leaving. I just didn't want to say it in front of the others and worry them. But Icarus—this has to be his doing.

When his power strengthened in Fairhaven all those centuries ago, this is what he did. Raised the dead because he could, then attempted to build his own army before being locked inside that crypt. It seems he's doing the same with these poor humans. And this time, I don't think our people will be able to cover it up."

"I figured that," Iris said with a nod. "What do we do? I fear he's getting stronger. We need to take action."

"That we do. After dark, I want you to go on patrol and look for him. Take some guards with you but don't tell them what's going on. This is still a need-to-know situation—we don't want to frighten everyone. But we can't allow him to bring any more humans back to life as his soldiers. And that may be the least terrifying part of his plan."

Iris shivered at that, wondering what else he would do.

"And if I remember correctly," Fairy Godmother Odelia began, "Icarus was always drawn to dark, dingy places. Check out caves, warehouses, abandoned buildings. He will most likely use one as a lair. A headquarters of sorts. He must be staying somewhere local, thinking up his next plan there."

Iris nodded. "Will do. The sooner I find this Icarus, the sooner I can stop him and prevent more resurrections. Any idea on how to kill an immortal? Does he have any weaknesses?"

"None that our people ever found," King Tedros said sadly. "I'm sorry I don't have a better plan for you. In the old days, when we had more guards and fairy godmothers, maybe we would've found a solution somehow. But with so few of our own still alive ... stopping Icarus will be even more difficult. I pray you'll discover something that will help."

Iris did too.

As she walked back into the main hall, waiting for dinner to finishing cooking, she found Gemma and Ian talking. Iris cleared her throat and walked over. "Hey, Ian, can I ask a favor?"

Ian looked up and nodded. "Of course. What is it?"

"You have a ... what is it? A smartphone? Where you can watch the local news and access the internet?"

"Sure do." Ian pulled it out of his pocket, handing it to Iris. "You need to look for something?"

"I do. I need to search for the Exterminators. I've never heard of such a thing before." Iris passed the phone back. "Maybe you'd better look it up. I'm no good at technology."

Ian nodded, taking the phone back. When he searched for exterminators, he got a lot of websites for pest removal services in the city. Iris had a feeling that wasn't it, so she made him keep looking. After scrolling through the results, Ian found something with the name MICHAEL BOND attached.

"That has to be it," Iris said. "Click it, please."

Ian nodded, opening the website. He read a few paragraphs and his eyes widened. "This is ... whoa."

"What is it?" Gemma asked, peering over her shoulder. Then her eyes widened too. "Oh my gosh. This website ... it's like a manifesto of what Michael Bond wants to do. His 'Exterminators,' as they call themselves, are really just racist thugs. They want to remove all outsiders from Canada. That includes immigrants like the Bhatias and of course, us, which are his main focus. And he's got supporters. They see him as some kind of leader."

"I knew it wasn't anything good," Iris muttered. "They sound like a terrorist group. The police and prime minister need to be aware of this. For everyone's safety."

"Good idea. Ugh, I can't read this anymore." Ian went into his contacts folder. "I'll find the number the prime minister gave us. Maybe we can invite her over—figure out what to do. Or warn her at least."

As Iris nodded, Princess Esme walked into the main hall. "Dinner's ready, everyone! Fresh stew from the garden. The fairy godmothers whipped up a potion that made the vegetables grow faster in the garden, so do remember to thank them. The butternut squash looks amazing, doesn't it?"

They entered the kitchen, quickly eating their dinner. Ian contacted the prime minister's number and was told she would drop by from a staff member after finishing a few meetings. Iris glanced at the clock, eagerly awaiting her patrol.

Maybe they would have some answers on Icarus soon. But then again, he seemed to be good at evading capture.

"Big surprise—the news is talking about us again," Noah said, setting his phone down on the table. It was set to the news livestream website. "Some teacher this time."

Iris's ears perked up, then she glanced down at the phone. Lisa was on the news—and badmouthing her people.

"... and a fellow teacher of mine that attends Viola Desmond Elementary, Grant Thatcher," Lisa began, "is allowing one of those dangerous Fairhaven creatures around his students. Can you believe that? Principal Hannigan and my fellow teachers are too scared to speak up against it. But you know what? I'm not. If you ask me, Grant should be fired for this."

The reporter nodded. "That does sound serious. Why would he do this?"

Lisa rolled her eyes. "He believes in equality and kindness, which is all fine and dandy to an extent, but this is just reckless. He clearly doesn't care about his students' safety ..."

"That's a lie!" Iris cried, smashing her fist down on the table. She made everyone around her jump. "Grant loves those kids. Lisa's just angry he won't get back together with her."

"You know this teacher woman?" King Tedros asked.

"Unfortunately," Iris grumbled. "She's a menace. Hated me from the moment I met her. And now, she's a liar looking for revenge. Grant was only trying to do a good thing and now he's being villainized for it. It's sickening."

"Poor Grant," Gemma said. "I hope his job isn't in jeopardy. This is going to create even more outrage."

"We just can't avoid bad press, can we?" Princess Esme said with a sigh as she finished her stew.

Everyone agreed. When a knock sounded on the church doors, Iris hoped it would be the prime minister. They needed a solution to deal with all these threats—especially as they grew worse.

CHAPTER 16

When Iris opened the door, Grant stood on the front steps. He had wheeled over his bicycle while pushing another in his hands. When he saw Iris, he smiled, giving her a look that always made her swoon.

"Grant," Iris said, surprised. "What are you doing here? I thought our bicycle date wasn't until tomorrow."

Grant sighed. "It was, but I could use an escape. Have you seen the news?"

"With Lisa? Yes, I have. I'm sorry. It's awful that she's going after your teaching career. You only wanted to help introduce my people to yours, and now she's trying to use that against you."

"I knew she was a petty, petty woman, but this is a new low. Even for her. Principal Hannigan has been calling and calling, wanting me to talk about this latest crisis, but I don't want to deal with that right now. I know the school board and parents will have something to say. I'll call tomorrow and deal with it, but not now." Grant beeped the horn on the other bicycle. "So, what do you say we go somewhere and forget about all our problems?"

Iris gawked. "You still want to spend time with me? My connection to Fairhaven might've just cost you your job, Grant. I know how much your students mean to you. If you want to distance yourself from us—from *me* specifically—I would understand."

"And that would make me a hypocrite. Something I teach my kids not to be. So, no, I don't intend to stop seeing you." Grant paused. "If that's all right with you, of course. I just don't want the bullies to win."

"Me either. Only if you're sure. Let me just tell everyone where I'm going so they don't worry." When Iris spun around, Gemma was standing there, spying on them with a big smile. "Gemma! Were you there the entire time?"

"I was," she said with a giggle. "And you two are so cute together. Hi, Grant."

He waved, still holding onto the bikes. "Hello, Gemma. I saw that crowd swarm you on the news. So sorry about that."

"Thank you. But don't worry about that for now—like you said, just go and find an escape." Gemma winked at Iris, lowering her voice. "Just be safe. Make sure to use protection."

Protection? Did she think they were going to be intimate together? When they still barely knew one another? Iris was still a virgin, dedicating her life to being a guardswoman, and she wasn't even thinking about anything physical right now, even if she did find Grant attractive. A million other things were more important.

Iris blushed. "I can assure you that we're not going to have—"

"For bike riding, silly," Gemma interrupted. "Wear a helmet at least. We don't want our general falling off and getting hurt."

"Oh. That's what you meant." Iris blushed even harder, then patted her breastplate. "This is what I wear armor for. I'll be fine. You all stay safe, okay? Lock the doors and don't let anyone inside."

"We will. I'll tell the others where you're going. Have a good time, you two."

Gemma waved at Iris and Grant, then shut the doors to the church. Iris only walked away once she heard Gemma lock them. Grant handed the other bicycle to Iris, one painted yellow with a little bell, then gestured at the path near the road.

"Follow me," Grant said. "I know the path that'll take us into the forest. And before we go, I have to ask—I know you all went to the hospital. Are you all right?"

Iris accepted his spare helmet, strapping it around her head. "Yes, we're fine. We tried to make a donation after our car wash. But the hospital turned us away. I guess they don't want to be associated with us—they fear it'll attract enemies."

"Sadly, they're probably right. I'm sorry. For everything." Grant put his own helmet on. "Maybe getting out is something we both need. Are you ready?"

Iris sat on the bicycle. "I think so. Though, I have to warn you—I've never ridden on one of these before. Dragons, yes. Bicycles? No."

"That's all right. First time for everything. We'll practice first, of course, before I take you to my favorite place." Grant sat down on his bicycle, painted blue. "Just follow my lead."

He rode around the street, showing her how to peddle and balance. Iris tried to copy but fell off a few times. When she feared he would judge her for not knowing how to ride a bike, he didn't. He turned his bicycle around and helped her up.

"There you go," he said, pulling her to her feet. "You okay?"

Iris sighed. "Yeah, I am. Just embarrassed. Maybe bike riding isn't for me."

"Sure it is! But you won't be good at something the first

time you try." He gestured at her bike. "Go ahead, sit down. I'll give you a push. Take it slow, okay? There's no rush to learn."

Iris nodded, sitting back down on the bike. If it had been anyone else, she would've quit. But it was Grant. And something about him was hard to walk away from.

He gently pushed her forward, then let go when she began to peddle on her own. He stood back with a proud smile. "There you go, Iris. You got it!"

"I'm doing it," Iris said with a smile. "It's really no different from riding a dragon. Takes the same amount of balance and coordination. You really are a great teacher, you know."

He smiled. "I try. It's nice to see you so happy on that bike."

Iris blushed again, more than she ever had in her life. "It's pretty fun. Come on, Grant—keep up!"

Grant laughed, getting back onto his bike. Iris was doing much better and was able to ride beside him. With people watching them on the street, whispering and murmuring while pointing at them, Iris ignored them and stayed close to Grant, the wind blowing through her braided hair through the holes of the helmet. She felt fearless after her lesson with him.

When he smiled at her, she did the same. And genuinely meant it for the first time in a while.

"Look at you go—after some trial and error, you're a natural. You just needed some practice. It feels nice, doesn't it? Riding a bike?" Grant asked beside her. "The breeze, being outside, feeling free. I love it."

Iris nodded. "I wish we had bicycles back home. All we had were dragons and unicorns."

Grant laughed. "Hey, those don't sound too bad to me. Come on—the path is this way."

Iris nodded, following Grant down the street. They cut through a field that led into a large forest. It had paths for hikers and cyclists, hidden behind trees where no one would see them. It was the most privacy that Iris had in a while. With everyone inside eating dinner, the bike path was quiet and clear, only the birds chirping in the trees around them.

"I bike a lot for my mental health too," Grant said beside her, pulling Iris out of her thoughts. They rode along the quiet dirt trail. "It brings me a sense of peace. Being in nature does that too. Do you have a place that brings you peace?"

Iris thought for a moment, keeping up the pace that Grant had set. "I used to. In my bunk in the barracks back home. That's gone now. All of Fairhaven, just ... gone. Destroyed in the blink of an eye."

Grant turned quiet for a moment. "I'm sorry. This can't be easy, trying to get used to Earth while still grieving your home and your family. I wish things could be easier for you."

"Yeah, you and me both." Iris shook her head. "But we came out here to escape, remember? Let's not talk about these things for now."

"Good point. All right, we'll talk about something else. Are you ... are you single?"

Iris nearly fell off her bicycle. "Yes ... yes, I am. Guards don't usually date. They take vows of celibacy and focus completely on guarding the castle and defending the lives of their people."

Grant looked disappointed, his face dropping. "Oh. That's too bad."

"But those rules don't really apply anymore," Iris said, glancing at Grant out of the corner of her eye. She was mostly focused on not falling off her bike and making a fool of herself in front of him. "None of our former laws do. In fact, Gemma keeps encouraging me to date. To see what life has to offer."

"I agree with her." Grant smiled. "There's some shade up ahead—and a little cliff. We should take a break. Come on, I'll show you."

Iris nodded, peddling after him. Grant led her to a cliff that overlooked a small ravine. He got off his bike, staring out at the water as the sun began to set. It cast an orange glow over the town.

"Sunset. My favorite time of day," Grant said, laying his bicycle on the grass. "Isn't it beautiful?"

"Very." Iris followed his lead, laying her bicycle down too. "I can see why you love this place so much. It's gorgeous."

"It really is. It's a bit embarrassing to admit, but ..." Grant turned to her, his cheeks red. "I call this place 'The Screaming Cliff.'"

Iris raised an eyebrow. "Oh? Does the cliff have a mouth?"

"Ha, no. Maybe where you're from they do, but not here. It's just a normal cliff." Grant gazed out at the sunrise again. "I'm the one who comes here to do the screaming. Sometimes, you just need to let it all out. All your emotions—sadness, anxiety, fear. I thought maybe you could use it too."

Iris paused. "You ... want me to scream? To vent my frustrations?"

"If you'd like. I know it's silly, but it does help. Might be good for you to—"

Iris opened her mouth, screaming as loud as she could. The birds got spooked in the nearby tree and flew away. Their wings flapped into the sky and the birds vanished for someplace quieter. Iris was glad no one else was in the forest or they might've been afraid.

"Oops," Iris said. "Guess I scared the birds off."

Grant laughed. "It was a good scream. Sounded like you really needed it."

"I did. You want to go?"

"Don't mind if I do."

When Grant screamed, more animals took off in fear. The squirrels flocked from their tree to the bushes where it was safer. After Grant finished, his voice was hoarse.

"That was a good session," Grant said, turning to Iris. "Thanks for indulging me. And not calling me weird."

"It wasn't weird at all. In fact, I thought it was a good idea. That scream … I've been holding it in since Fairhaven was blown up." Iris walked to the edge of the cliff, gazing down at the serene water. "I feel like a failure, you know. Like I should've seen the warning signs about Senator Remus and his traitorous sympathizers. We should've stopped them from escaping to the surface—we should've kept a closer eye on all of them. *I* should have. And innocent lives paid for my mistakes."

Grant stepped closer, placing a hand on her shoulder. "Iris, I think you're being too hard on yourself. I wasn't there and didn't know this Remus fellow, but I'm sure you did all you could. None of your other people predicted what he would do, did they?"

"No," Iris said, softly. "But—"

"No buts," Grant interrupted. "Nothing that happened was your fault, okay? Not. Your. Fault. And for what it's worth, I think you're doing great with what you've been given. Not many people would be strong enough to survive this long on Earth with as many enemies as you have."

"Tell me about it." Iris glanced at Grant. "Thank you. For taking me here, for that pep talk. I don't often like to discuss emotions, but … with you, it's easy. And I needed it."

Grant smiled. "Just happy to help."

"So, what do you come here to scream about? If you wouldn't mind sharing."

"With you? Not at all. It might seem small compared to what you're going through, though." Grant stared out at the sunset again. "I come here to scream about Lisa and how our relationship didn't work out. Because … well, you've met her. Sometimes I come here because my students drive me crazy. I love them, but they're not always easy to handle. And, of course, I come here to scream about when I was bullied as a kid. Some scars never heal."

"Because you had two fathers?"

"That's right. Who you still have to meet." Grant turned his head to hold her gaze, smiling at her. "I think they'd love you, by the way. I'd still like for you to meet them."

"I'd like that too. They must be incredible people if they raised a man like you."

Grant smiled again. "Why, thank you."

When a group of teenagers walked by, giggling, Iris startled. She reached for her hilt but, when she saw they meant them no harm, released it. The teenagers noticed them, then quickened their pace with worried glances over their shoulders.

"Hope they didn't hear us screaming," Grant said. "That'd be embarrassing."

"Definitely. Well, thanks for taking me out here. I had a great time. We should probably head back though. I don't like being away from my people for too long."

"I understand." As Iris picked up her bike, Grant rushed over, standing in front of her. "There's just one thing I wanted to ask you. Which I'm incredibly nervous about now."

"It's all right. What is it?"

Grant hesitated. "Well ... I had another motive for bringing you out here. I've been trying to work up the courage to ask you out on a date."

"A date?" Iris paused. "As in, a romantic date?"

"That's right. Do they have different dates where you come from?"

"No, it's pretty much the same back in Fairhaven."

"Good, good. At least we're on the same page with that." Grant laughed. "So ... what do you say? I mean, I think I've been pretty obvious about my interest. I think you're beautiful and funny. And unique. We just get along well. I want to see if there could be something more between us."

"I think those same things about you," Iris whispered, "but ... you know we can't be together."

Grant frowned. "Why not?"

"You don't know? You've been watching the news. You've seen all the hatred. We come from two different worlds, Grant. No one trusts my people. If you were to be with me publicly, it could ruin your life. It's already started to threaten your teaching career."

"So? I won't hide." He stepped closer. "I like you, Iris. And I know you like me too or you wouldn't be here. Why complicate things?"

"Because the world we live in is complicated. *Your* world. That's why."

"Haven't some of your people found love with humans, though? Your princess? And your friend, Gemma?"

Iris sighed. "Yes, they have. But that was unusual. And way before the world found out about our people and began to hate and mistrust us. Look at Noah and Ian now—they're staying with us at the church. Noah lost his job and Ian's bar is empty these days. Their lives are in danger just by being around us." Iris shook her head. "I won't let that happen to you. It's because I care about you so much, Grant, that I'm saying no. Let me protect you."

"I don't want to be protected, Iris. I want to love and be loved. My parents taught me to say how I feel and go for it. And that's what I'm going to do right now."

Iris paused. "What are you talking about—"

Grant leaned in, cupping her face in his soft hands and planting a kiss on her lips. Iris felt herself giving in and kissing back. Her stomach was doing somersaults. They stayed like that for a few seconds, his lips warm and soft, his hands gentle before Grant pulled away. They were both breathless, and Iris wished it had never ended.

"If you tell me you felt nothing from that," Grant began, still panting, "then I'll leave you alone."

Iris opened her mouth to speak.

Grant cut her off. "And don't lie. Say how you feel, Iris. Seize every moment and live life to the fullest. You're not just a guard anymore—you can have a real life on Earth. And that's more important than ever with all the threats surrounding us."

Grant was right about that. And little did he know that with Icarus still on the loose, their days might be numbered. Maybe it wasn't a bad thing after all to pursue a relationship with him. Iris really did like him, and that kiss had sent fireworks through her entire body.

"All right. You win," Iris said with a sigh. "I felt it. That connection between us. I've never felt something like that before."

Grant's eyes lit up. "Neither have I. So, does that mean ...?"

"I'll go on a date with you, yes. But if things get more dangerous, especially with Lisa and everyone else poking around, then we'll need to take a step back. Reassess the situation."

That was her guard training talking. Deep down, Iris hoped nothing bad would happen to Grant for being with her. She'd never forgive herself if it did.

"Okay. I can get onboard with that. Tomorrow morning, you and me—breakfast together at a nice restaurant. I know a place. My treat." Grant smiled, gesturing at the bikes. "I'll pick you up tomorrow. For now, let's get you back to the church. And, uh, if you don't mind ... I'd like to walk the bikes and hold your hand on the way back."

"What if people see?"

"Let them see," Grant said, reaching for Iris's hand and squeezing it. She liked the way it felt. "Let *everyone* see. I don't care at all."

CHAPTER 17

Hand in hand, Grant and Iris walked their bicycles back to the church, not caring who was watching them. And people were—they always did when they spotted a Fairhavener on the street. But Grant's calmness kept Iris calm too.

"See you tomorrow for breakfast," Grant said, kissing Iris's cheek. "Thanks again for coming with me today. I hope you sleep well."

Iris blushed, wondering how Grant could always make her feel that way. "You too. Looking forward to tomorrow."

He grinned from ear to ear, taking the two bicycles with him as he walked down the street. Iris was still blushing as she headed inside the church. Still thinking about Grant, it took her a moment to even notice the prime minister and her bodyguards sitting on the pews with Princess Esme's people.

"Ah, there you are, General," King Tedros said. "Prime Minister Lin just arrived. You're right on time."

"Good," Iris said, walking over and sitting on one of the pews. She hoped her flushed cheeks weren't obvious. "Good evening, Prime Minister. What did I miss?"

"Well, we were just talking about your people. And the reaction Toronto has had." Prime Minister Lin sighed. "I was hoping everyone would've moved on by now—or at least, become more accepting. But it seems it's heading in the opposite direction."

Gemma nodded. "Did you see us on the news, trying to donate to the children's hospital?"

"I did. And while it was a sweet idea, I don't think you should leave this church anymore. It's clear my citizens are enraged by your presence."

"So ... what does that mean?" Princess Esme asked, rubbing her stomach. She looked pale and nauseous again.

"It means you should lay low. Keep away from people—for now. At least, until the violence has passed." The prime minister glanced around at them all, noticing their concerned faces. "I'm sorry. I know that probably wasn't the answer you wanted to hear."

"Definitely not," Princess Esme said, grabbing the donation box. "I still hope people will come around to accept us. In the meantime, do you think you could deliver our donation to the children's hospital? I'm sure they'd accept it from the prime minister."

"Of course." Prime Minister Lin took the donation box, setting it on her lap. "Again, I'm sorry you're all going through this. As I mentioned before, I come from a family of immigrants —I know what it's like to be a stranger in a strange land. Just hold out a little bit longer, all right? Keep to yourselves and stay calm. This might pass one day."

"And if it doesn't?" Iris asked. "If the humans hate us forever?"

Prime Minister Lin paused. "I just don't know, General. I've tried to calm them down with several press conferences, but they won't even listen to me. Supporting your people will no doubt affect me in the next election. I'm sure I'll lose points with constituents who think you're too dangerous to let stay here."

"Well, we thank you for your hospitality," King Tedros said. "I'm sorry we've put you through so much."

"Don't mention it. I really do want the best for you, even if it takes a while." Prime Minister Lin rose to her feet, holding the donation box. "I should get going. I have a few more meetings tonight before I can head home."

"One last thing," Iris said, following the prime minister to the door. "Does the name Michael Bond ring any bells?"

Prime Minister Lin paused near the door, sighing. "Oh, yes it does. He's part of a radical and racist group called the Exterminators. They hate immigrants and outsiders—they want them all gone. Or exterminated, as they call it. The police told me he was the one who threw the smoke bomb during your TV interview?"

"That's right. I just saw him earlier—he was hanging around the hospital when we tried to donate. Can't you do something about him?"

"I'm trying to get his organization classified as a hate group in Parliament. But my opponents are arguing that it's free speech." Prime Minister Lin shook her head. "Politics is a tough battleground. Anyway, as I said, the best thing to do is stay inside. That will keep you safe from Mr. Bond and anyone else who hopes to catch you on the street."

Would it? The man seemed unpredictable. What if they attacked their church? Were they even allowed to defend themselves?

"You take care now," Prime Minister Lin said as the bodyguards opened the door for her. "I hope the public's opinion of you changes soon. And for the better."

Iris nodded, watching the prime minister and her guards

leave the church. They got into their black SUVs that were nearby and sped away. Iris sighed, closing the door to the church.

Laying low meant not going out and seeing Grant anymore. And that just wasn't a promise Iris could make.

As she headed back toward the pews, everyone was discussing the situation. Princess Esme and Noah were gone—and judging by the throwing-up sounds coming from the bathroom, Iris knew why. Again.

"Poor girl," Fairy Godmother Odelia said. "She won't let me examine her. Stubborn—just like her father."

"That stubbornness has kept us alive," King Tedros joked. "It can be used for good too. Anyway, I suppose we ought to listen to what the prime minister said. No more going out—for now, at least."

"No way," Princess Esme said, appearing in the doorway to the bathroom. "I still have plans to win over the people. I know we can do it, Father."

King Tedros sighed, glancing over his shoulder at her. "But Michael Bond and his group are dangerous, and the prime minister was clear—"

"I know what the prime minister said," Princess Esme interrupted as she walked over. "But I respectfully disagree. We have to keep pushing—keep showing everyone who we are. We're kind and peaceful and compassionate and good. We're not cowards who hide in the face of danger. Or hatred."

"Princess Esme has a point," Gemma said. "If we disappear now, we'll look weak. We need to stand up to these bullies. What do you think, General?"

Everyone stared at Iris. "I think we should be careful, no matter what we do."

"Wise advice," King Tedros said, bowing. "All right, everyone—it's getting late. Let's clean up and head to bed.

We'll continue this discussion in the morning after we've all gotten some sleep."

The others nodded, heading to their rooms down the hall. King Tedros and Iris shared a look. Tonight was the night—the beginning of her patrol into finding Icarus. Iris hoped she would have good luck.

As she helped the guards clean up in the kitchen, Sapphira and Kyler pulled her aside. When they glanced at each other for a little too long, Iris thought they looked like they were up to something. Something big.

"I think now is the time," Sapphira said, glancing over her shoulder to make sure no one was listening. The other guards were too busy or had gone to bed. "We should ask King Tedros to step down. He's clearly failed us—he let our kingdom be destroyed by Senator Remus. And now, he's doomed us to a life on the surface where humans hate us."

"And the senator's family needs to pay," Kyler added. "With blood. We should get the police to release them into our custody and make them all suffer. Nyssa, Cullen, Gemma's mother—Mrs. Solace. All of them."

Iris wondered if they had a point for a moment. King Tedros had been keeping secrets—and Icarus was the biggest, worst one of them all. What if he was hiding something else? What if there *was* cause to replace him?

But then her sensible guard training got back into her head, telling her to respect King Tedros' authority. He was king for a reason. And right now, they had bigger problems.

Iris frowned. "What has gotten into you two? We're trying to avoid violence, not cause more of it. And torturing the senator's family while overthrowing the king won't help."

"In the name of justice, it will," Sapphira argued, crossing her arms. "Come on, Iris. We thought you were with us."

"I'm your *general*," Iris hissed, "and you'll address me as such. No, I don't support this insane plan. King Tedros is our monarch—and Princess Esme will be one day, when he passes away. As for the senator's family, they can rot in prison for the rest of their lives. We've got enough problems already without causing more."

But Sapphira and Kyler didn't look satisfied. They glanced at each other, almost communicating wordlessly. That made Iris nervous.

"Promise me you two won't do anything," Iris urged. "That you won't usurp the royal family and that you'll leave the senator's co-conspirators alone. Can I trust you two to remain peaceful?"

"For now," Sapphira said. "But things need to change. Fairhaven is gone—it's a different world now. We need new leaders with new plans instead of the same old ones."

Kyler nodded. "Yeah, agreed. And killing the senator's family would ensure we could start fresh. No longer would they be a threat to the world."

"We're not murderers. Besides, what would the humans think if we replaced our king and killed our enemies? They would fear us even more." Iris sighed. "No more of these discussions, you two. I mean it. Or I'll tell the king."

Sapphira scoffed. "Threatening to snitch on us? I thought you understood and wanted change too. But I guess not."

As they turned to walk away, Iris followed. "Wait a minute—we're not done. I'm assembling the guards for a patrol tonight."

Sapphira and Kyler turned back to Iris, glancing at each other. Kyler was the first one to speak. "What? Why?"

"Yeah, you heard the prime minister," Sapphira said. "We're supposed to lie low, remember?"

"I know that. But this is important." Iris paused in the doorway of the kitchen. "It's a need-to-know mission, so I'm afraid I can't tell you. But get the other guards—we're moving out soon. After dark."

Sapphira and Kyler looked hesitant, but they still told the other guards the plan. Iris heard them murmuring in confusion about the patrol in the kitchen. She suited up, making sure her sword was snugly in her scabbard as she waited by the door. When darkness overtook the sky, the other guards approached her, wearing their armor and ready for patrol.

"Ah, good. You're all here. Thank you," Iris said to Sapphira and Kyler, then turned to the other guards. "I know doing this goes against the prime minister's orders, and I'm sure you're all confused why I won't tell you what's going on. But trust me— this patrol is necessary. We're looking for any signs of magic or dangerous individuals."

Sapphira raised a hand. "Anyone in particular?"

Icarus' name was on the tip of her tongue, but Iris shook her head. "No. Just keep an eye out."

The guards nodded, not asking any questions as they left the church. After Iris locked the double doors, ensuring their people were safe inside, they began walking down the street under the cover of darkness. When Iris saw people milling around the Bhatia's house, she crossed the street and ran over.

"Hey, stop!" she called out. "Leave that house alone!"

When the people vandalizing the house saw them, they took off down the sidewalk. The street lamps helped to illuminate some of their faces. They were teenagers—and one of them looked very familiar.

It was Maya's boyfriend; the same one who had been driving the Jeep at the car wash.

When Iris stepped closer, analyzing the house, she saw more streaks of paint across the wall. One of those teenagers had written "GO BACK TO YOUR OWN COUNTRY" with a bunch of hateful symbols. Iris shook her head, wondering why Maya's boyfriend would do such a thing.

Surely, he knew she wasn't from this country. Did Maya know what her boyfriend was up to?

When a light flicked on inside the house, Iris walked around and knocked on the door. Her guards waited for her on the sidewalk. When she glanced over her shoulder, and saw Sapphira and Kyler murmuring and hoped they weren't planning something again.

She had enough to deal with these days.

When the door opened, Ayesha stood there in her robe and slippers. Her husband and Maya came down the stairs behind her. "Oh, hello, Iris. I thought I heard a noise outside. Is everything all right?"

"I'm afraid not, Mrs. Bhatia. Some teenagers were vandalizing the side of your house again with more hateful messages. I chased them off."

Ayesha shook her head. "I don't understand how kids can be so hateful these days. Thanks for scaring them away. I'm heading back to bed, but in the morning, I'll wash it off. Again."

"Okay, sounds good. I'm very sorry you're going through all this."

"I could say the same to you, Iris. Be well."

Iris nodded, turning around as the Bhatias went back to bed. She headed toward the sidewalk just as Maya came running out of the back door in her pajamas. She read the hateful message before shaking her head and rushing after Iris.

"Wait!" Maya cried. "You said the people who did this were teenagers. Do you know who they are? Maybe I know them."

Iris spun around. "You definitely do." She didn't want to upset the girl, but she deserved the truth. "One of them was your boyfriend. I saw his face."

Maya turned silent for a moment. "No ... Jack wouldn't do this. He's too sweet. Besides, he loves me!"

"Does he? I don't believe someone who loves you would do such a thing to your house, but that's just me." Iris shook her head. "I told you that hanging around those boys would blow up in your face, Maya. They hate us for being outsiders. You can keep telling yourself that you're not like my people, but you are."

Tears welled in Maya's eyes. "I just ... I can't believe he would do this."

"I know—I'm sorry. If I were you, I'd confront him. Find out why he's doing this to you if he claims to love you. And then break up with him for good."

Maya rubbed her temples. "I guess I have to do something. For now, though, I'm just going to head to bed. Got some studying to do tomorrow. And hey ... I'm sorry I told you to stay away from my parents. I was just scared, you know? Of something like this happening. But I guess I can't stop it."

"It's all right. I understand your fear and anger—I feel it too." Iris glanced at the side of the house again. "Especially when these foul humans won't leave us alone. Take care of yourself, Maya. Let us know if you need our help. And just so you know ... someone who truly loves you would love every part of you. They wouldn't hide, they'd be proud to be seen with you. You deserve better than Jack."

And Iris had gotten better—she had Grant. His admiration for her was inspiring. Maybe one day, it would be love. That was where it felt like things were going—on her end, at least.

Maya considered her words and nodded, then headed inside. She didn't bother to look at the hateful message again. Iris turned, walking back to the sidewalk. Sapphira and Kyler hushed as she approached.

"Sorry about that," Iris began. "Let's head out. Now, I want you all to spread out and stay in groups. Call for help if you see anything suspicious and the rest of us will come running. Look for dark, secluded places in particular—caves, abandoned warehouses, that sort of thing."

"All right. Though we still aren't comfortable with being in the dark about this," Sapphira grumbled. "Literally. I'm heading with Kyler."

Iris didn't like the two of them together—especially when they came up with dangerous plans. They took off into the night, checking out the nearby back alley as the other guards divided themselves into groups.

Iris stayed alone as always, working better on her own. She kept one hand on her sword as she headed deeper into the city. Downtown was dark but not completely empty, with homeless and drug addicts walking around. Iris avoided them, looking for one target in particular.

Icarus. Where was he hiding?

There were no tremors tonight, making Iris wonder if that was a good thing or not. The infamous immortal might have just been planning something worse.

Just as she turned down a back alley, she heard the roar of a motorcycle. When she spun around, she realized that several motorcycles had followed her down the alley, trapping her inside. Their headlights were almost like spotlights, too bright to see who the riders were. And their engines roared, drowning out her call for backup.

"Who are you?" Iris demanded, removing her sword from its scabbard. "What are you doing here?"

The person on the lead motorcycle stepped off first, wearing all leather with a gun at his side. He stepped into the headlights of the motorcycles and Iris finally saw his face. It was Bobby Blevins—the human who had gotten magic in his bloodstream and was caught by Gemma, then escaped from the police.

"I know you," Iris muttered. "I've seen that face before. You're that human who stole our magic, aren't you?"

"That's right," Bobby said, keeping his distance. "I thought my days were over when I got arrested, but I managed to escape the police. They've been looking for me ever since. And now, I hear you magic folk are in our city. How fast things have changed."

Iris nodded. "You're telling me. What are you doing here? What do you want? I ought to contact the police and have them arrest you again. You're too dangerous to let wander the streets."

Bobby laughed, a low, deep rumble. "People are saying the same about you, you know. Ever since I left, I found some friends to help me. Other people just like me—in and out of jail, suffering in the system. And they want a taste of that magic."

"Well, they're not getting it," Iris sneered. "Surrender yourselves to the police. And stop using magic for evil. That's not its intention."

"No? I sure seem to think it is. It's been working well so far. We've just been waiting to get one of your kind alone. And now's our chance. You have no idea how much you're going to help us." Bobby gestured at something over Iris's shoulder. "Get her."

Iris reached for her sword, cutting down one of Bobby's men who tried to attack her. The man cried out and fell to the ground, bleeding. When the other men hesitated, Bobby sighed.

"Do I have to do everything?" he demanded. "Fine."

He snapped his fingers, muttering an incantation under his breath. A magical bubble appeared around Iris like a multi-colored shield. She tried to stab it with her sword but it bounced right off.

"What have you done to me?" Iris demanded. "You

shouldn't even have this magic. Let me out, Blevins. Right now!"

"No can do," Bobby said, approaching her. Then he gestured at his bleeding goon. "Get him cleaned up. As for you, you're coming with me."

Iris sneered. "I don't think so—"

But Bobby snapped his fingers and muttered something again, then Iris felt the bubble fill with gas. She coughed and gagged as she breathed it in before her vision went dark.

CHAPTER 18

When Iris woke up, she glanced around and realized she was lying on a surgical table. Her arms and legs were strapped down, so she couldn't move. An IV was connected to her arm, leading to a machine that showed her vital signs. A long line of medical tools sat next to her head.

She wondered if she was at the hospital, then remembered what had happened. Running into Bobby and his gang. The gas. And now, she was here. Wherever that was.

She lifted her head, the only part of her body that she could move, and saw nothing but trees and forest outside the window. It was clear she wasn't in downtown Toronto anymore. The room she was in looked like a hospital room but inside a house, the walls painted brown with comfortable furniture. And to her disappointment, she wasn't wearing her armor anymore, just her underclothes. Her sword was gone as well, sitting on a nearby chair.

Iris felt naked without her armor and weapon to protect her. How was she going to get out of this?

"Ah, good," someone with a German accent said. Iris only

recognized it from human television. "You're awake now. I'll go tell the others."

"What's going on?" Iris demanded, but the man had walked out of the room.

Iris knew she had to escape—to get back to her people and warn them. So, she started shaking back and forth, trying to pry the bindings loose, but they were strapped tightly against her skin. The surgical bed shook but didn't set her free.

The door opened, then Bobby and his followers entered. Iris took a better look at them all—including the man with the German accent. He wore a white lab coat, and messy gray hair covered his head. He had to be older—much older than Bobby and the rest of his thugs.

"Wakey, wakey," Bobby said as he entered the room. "Did you have a good nap, Sleeping Beauty?"

"Where am I?" Iris demanded. "What's going on?"

"You're our little test subject. That's what's going on," Bobby said, glancing at her vital signs on the monitor. "Have you learned anything yet, Dr. Koch?"

The scientist shook his head, then reached for his medical tools. "Not yet, Bobby. But my experiments have only just begun."

"What kind of experiments?" Iris asked, wide-eyed at the medical instruments. "What are you doing to me?"

"My men here want some of my power," Bobby explained. "I got my magic from being in the warehouse the day that Fairy Godmother Zamira made magic possible on the surface. It was a fluke, really—a stroke of good luck. But now, I'm hoping we can find a way to steal your magic and give it to my men."

"And that's when Bobby contacted me," Dr. Koch explained. "You see, I come from a long line of scientists. My ancestors studied science for the Nazis once upon a time. And this magic of yours intrigues me, so I agreed to help."

"Foolish," Iris muttered. "Humans shouldn't have magic. Dissecting and experimenting on me won't teach you anything. That isn't how it works. I don't have magic anyway, you fool—only our fairy godmothers do."

"Perhaps," Dr. Koch said, loading a syringe with some liquid, "but it'll be fun to try. Hold still now—or I'll make it hurt worse."

As Dr. Koch approached Iris with the syringe, she tried to squirm away, but she couldn't get the bindings loose. She refused to scream or cry and give them the satisfaction. Instead, she closed her eyes, hoping whatever was in that syringe wouldn't hurt.

But then a loud boom echoed in the distance, making Dr. Koch, Bobby, and the other men pause. Iris opened her eyes, watching as they crowded around the window to look outside. Then Bobby turned to his men.

"They've found us. God, I hate those guys," Bobby muttered, grabbing a pistol from his pocket. "Move out—get rid of them. Dr. Koch, get back to experimenting on the guard. We need to learn Fairhaven's secrets."

Dr. Koch nodded, approaching Iris again. But as soon as Bobby and his men walked toward the door, someone kicked it down, then threw a smoke bomb inside the room. It made everyone cough, including Iris, as smoke filled the air.

She knew it had to be Michael Bond. Smoke bombs were his signature.

When people started shooting—and the smoke bomb was still too thick to tell who—Iris knew she really needed to get out of there. She rocked again on the table, feeling the bindings around her foot coming loose. Once it broke, she kicked off the other one, then worked on her hands.

It took a minute but she managed to get free, then slowly rose from the table. She was dizzy and weak—and the smoke bomb wasn't helping—but Iris was determined to get out. She fell to her knees, crawling through the smoky room as bullets zinged around her. She reached up, finding the chair where her armor and sword sat, then grabbed them and crawled to the window.

Just as she reached it, she felt a hand grab her ankle. Looking over her shoulder, she saw Dr. Koch—he wasn't about to let her escape. She kicked him in the face as hard as she could, making him groan in pain, then reached toward the window.

As she struggled to get it open, the shooting became sporadic. Then she heard Bobby's voice ring out through the smoke. "How did you even find us? Why do you keep hounding us like this?"

"Because of that foul magic you got," Michael's voice called out, his body shrouded by the smoke. "You're no better than those magical freaks. We've been following you for a while now —figured out one of your men had a house in the country. Was dumb luck we found you, really."

There was no doubt about it—Michael and his Exterminators were here. And judging by his tone, he didn't like Bobby and his men any more than Iris and her people did. Between each volley of bullets, the men shouted at each other.

"Why don't you just give it up?" Bobby called out, taking cover behind a nearby chair. "Join us. You know we could bring this world to its knees if we worked together."

"Never going to happen," Michael sneered, then popped out of hiding. "Die, scum!"

Just as Iris opened the window, the breeze blew in, clearing some of the smoke. She turned her head and watched as Michael fired his gun and the bullet hit Bobby right in the chest. He collapsed, not even having time to use his magic in the fight. He spasmed before going still.

He was dead. Checking his pulse, she confirmed it.

He was evil, Iris thought, *but even he didn't deserve to be brutally murdered. Though, I am glad he's off the streets.*

But many more enemies remained.

As the fight continued, with Michael shooting at more of Bobby's allies, Iris lunged through the window, falling to the ground behind the house. Michael had been right—they were deep in the country. Iris could barely see through the trees, obscured by darkness.

She ran through the forest and didn't look back. She was hoping for someone—anyone—who could drive her to safety as gunshots rang out behind her. But no one was around, so she quickened her pace, then stopped for a moment to put on her armor and sword.

It took her about an hour to make it back to the city. When she saw buildings and familiar streets, she eventually hailed a taxi and asked the driver to take her to the church. She looked so frantic and anxious that the driver dropped her off for free. Surprised by his kindness, Iris thanked him, her head still woozy. By the time she had arrived at the church, it was in the early hours of the morning, dawn's first glow decorating the sky. Iris was even weaker as she climbed up the stairs and tapped on the door. She couldn't even muster up a knock.

A minute later, Gemma opened it, looking out in her pajamas. Iris groaned to let her know she was there. Gemma gasped and reached down for Iris.

"Iris, oh my gosh!" she cried. "What happened to you? Come on, get inside."

Iris let Gemma pull her inside, then they shut and locked the door behind them. The rest of her people came out into the main hall to see what the commotion was. When they noticed Iris, they began murmuring as Gemma eased her down on one of the pews.

"I'll go get Fairy Godmothers Odelia and Blanche," Gemma said. "They'll patch you up. Wait right here."

Iris nodded, not planning to go anywhere. She was just relieved she had made it back home. Or the only place in the world that felt like it.

Fairy Godmothers Odelia and Blanche came around the corner, then immediately got to work examining Iris. They used potions to check her blood pressure and internal temperature. She eventually pushed them away, shaking her head.

"I'll be fine," Iris said. "I think they used something like chloroform on me."

Noah balled his fists. "Who did this to you? What happened?"

Iris sat back, trying to get some of her strength to return. "Well, I was on patrol and went down a dark alley. The next thing I knew, Bobby Blevins was there, following me. He has a group of men now—and they all want to use magic just like him ..."

When Iris finished telling the story, King Tedros shook his head. "This is just evil! This German Nazi doctor was going to experiment on you?"

Iris nodded. "That's right. One of Bobby's men must've had a home in the country. That's their base of operations."

"God, I hate the Nazis," Ian muttered. "And Bobby's people aren't any better. Neither are the Exterminators. Michael shot him, you said?"

"Yes. We know now that Michael Bond is capable of murder," Iris said, noticing the concerned looks of her people. "His wife and son weren't there, just his followers. And I'm pretty sure he killed Bobby. When I left, Bobby wasn't moving. He was lying still in a pool of his own blood. There may be others."

"Just awful," Princess Esme muttered. "I despise Bobby for

using magic for evil and killing innocent people, but even he didn't deserve to die. It would've been better for him to rot in a jail cell for the rest of his miserable life. But more importantly, Iris, we're all very glad you made it back."

"I am too. I used their battle as a chance to escape." Iris rose to her feet. "I'm slowly starting to feel better, thanks to the fairy godmothers. Did all my guards make it back safely?"

"All but two," King Tedros said. "Sapphira and Kyler. When the others returned, they told us that you three were missing. They decided to head back to the church when they couldn't find you. We were going to send out a search team in the morning."

Iris had a bad feeling in the pit of her stomach. Sapphira and Kyler were missing, her two guards who had a problem with King Tedros' leadership? That didn't sit right with her. She knew she should've done something about them from the start. But what? Send them away? Their numbers were too few to banish their own kind.

"Hopefully, they'll turn up too," Gemma said, interrupting her thoughts. "Just like Iris did. Could they have been taken by Bobby? Or someone else?"

"I didn't see anyone else at the house—just me. But then again, I didn't stay to look around," Iris muttered. "We should tell the prime minister and police about this. I'm pretty sure that a man has been murdered, and his killers are on the loose."

"On it," Noah said, pulling out his smartphone. "I knew Michael was bad news when my father told me he'd been terrorizing immigrants. What kind of lowlife does that? Anyway, I'll call the police."

As Noah walked away, Iris took a moment to breathe. She was glad she had escaped—that the Exterminators had given her an opening, though she doubted they did it on purpose. But she was still worried about Sapphira and Kyler. And what they would do next.

Just when they got rid of one enemy, another popped up. Would it ever end? She was keeping Sapphira and Kyler's worries to herself, not wanting to upset the king, but if they did something, she'd have to warn the others.

"What do we do now?" Gemma asked, looking at the princess. "Things have gotten serious. Really fast."

"Well, calling the police is a good first step." Then Princess Esme sighed. "Maybe the prime minister was right—that we shouldn't leave the church. Something happens every time we do. And this time, it almost cost Iris her life."

They all patted Iris's shoulder and expressed their gratitude that she had survived and made it back. Iris only wanted one person to hold her—and that was Grant. But she also risked his life every time she saw him.

"Okay, cops are on the way. My dad too," Noah said, slipping his smartphone into his pocket as he walked over. "Told them two of our people are missing, possibly kidnapped by Bobby Blevins but we aren't entirely sure. My dad said he'd look into it."

"Good," Princess Esme said, staring out the window. "Hopefully they'll find them and stop Michael Bond's men. That would be a big relief for us."

Iris nodded. "Especially if Bond intends to murder us at some point. We know he's capable now. We aren't out of the woods yet."

Everyone turned silent. The sounds of nervousness—sighing, people biting their nails, and murmuring—filled the room next. Noah comforted Princess Esme as Gemma and Ian stayed close together, waiting for the police to arrive. Iris walked over to King Tedros and Fairy Godmother Odelia and cleared her throat.

"Can we talk in private?" Iris asked.

"Of course." King Tedros gestured at the kitchen. "Follow us."

Iris nodded, heading into the kitchen with King Tedros and Fairy Godmother Odelia. The others continued to look out for the police as they closed the door for some privacy. Iris sighed, sitting down at the coffee table.

"No signs of Icarus," she said. "None that I could see before I was kidnapped, anyway. I failed you. Again."

Fairy Godmother Odelia shook her head. "There are no failures here, General. You were kidnapped. And thank goodness you made it back safely."

"But I couldn't find the one person I set out to look for. And I lost two of my soldiers in one night—"

"Still not your fault," King Tedros interrupted. "We don't blame you. And you shouldn't blame yourself either, you know. Things are very difficult right now. It's a miracle we're all still alive."

Iris still blamed herself but dropped it for the moment. "Okay. What's our next move? Icarus is still out there, though I haven't felt his tremors again."

"Neither have I. And it worries me," King Tedros said, making the other two nod. "Let's put a our search for Icarus on hold. The situation with Blevins' men and Bond's Exterminators needs our focus right now."

"Agreed," Fairy Godmother Odelia said with a nod. "I'm sure the prime minister won't want us going anywhere after this kidnapping."

Iris scoffed. "We can't just give up entirely! Icarus is still out there. And from what you've told me, he sounds like a massive threat—"

When the door swung open into the kitchen, all their heads shot in its direction. Gemma stood there while pointing over her shoulder. "The police are here—with the prime minister. They want to talk to you, Iris. I'm not interrupting anything, am I?"

"Not at all." King Tedros faked a smile. "We were just telling Iris how glad we are that she's safe. Come, let's go speak with the police."

Iris nodded, standing up and following the three of them out of the kitchen. When she entered the main hall, the prime minister was sitting there with her bodyguards, chatting with Princess Esme, Noah, and the rest of their people. Dozens of officers had shown up with Detective Crawford, their cars parked along the road outside.

"... and this is a very serious accusation," Prime Minister Lin was saying. "I'll have officers scour the countryside for any sign of this house. And Mr. Blevins' body. Ah, Iris—there you are. Are you all right?"

"As right as I can be after getting kidnapped and drugged," Iris muttered. "Michael Bond murdered Bobby Blevins in cold blood, Prime Minister. Bobby wanted to experiment on me to gain magic for the rest of his men. But Michael had been following him, wanting to kill him for using magic."

"Do you know where we could find this country home where it all happened?"

Iris frowned. "Sorry, but no. I was transported there while unconscious. And it was dark—I can't even remember the path I took to get home, especially while dazed and confused. I ran for a while, then eventually found a taxi and asked the driver to take me back to the church."

"I see. I'll have officers conduct searches, then, and hope we get lucky. We're all very glad you made it, though we worry for two of your guards. Detective Crawford's looking into this matter since it involves murder. And he claims to know you all personally." Then the prime minister's face turned somber. "But I told you all to lie low at the church. What happened?"

Iris couldn't very well tell her about Icarus. Society already mistrusted her people—they didn't need another reason.

As she searched for an answer, King Tedros stepped forward. "That was my fault, Prime Minister Lin. I organized a patrol party—just as a precaution. But with this kidnapping and two of our own still missing, it won't happen again. We're going to stay confined to this church."

"I hope you will," Prime Minister Lin said. "It's for your own safety. Now, Detective Crawford, where would you like to start your search?"

As they went over their ideas and search tactics, Iris said nothing, shaking her head. She couldn't give up the search now —no matter how many humans with guns stood in her way.

Icarus was dangerous—and still out there. And Iris was going to find him and make up for all her failings.

She had to.

CHAPTER 19

P rime Minister Lin and all the officers, including Noah's father, left shortly after that to search for Iris's guards. She didn't like sending other people out on what should've been her patrol—since they were *her* guards—but it didn't seem like she had a choice. Maybe it was safer that way.

Iris excused herself, heading to the bathroom to wash up. She washed her face in the mirror and took several deep breaths. Although guard training covered a lot, they hadn't taught her what to do in the event of a kidnapping—or how to deal with the trauma afterward.

Just another sacrifice she had made in the line of duty.

As she finished washing her face and looked in the mirror, she gasped, seeing the wrinkled face of an old man. Icarus's face —she was sure it was him. Who else would it be? And then the screaming faces of her parents as they burned to death in Fairhaven's explosion. But when she spun around, no one was there.

"Just an illusion," she muttered to herself. "A stress response. You're fine."

As she came out of the bathroom, she found Gemma waiting for her in the hall. "Hey, Iris. You feeling okay?"

"I think so. Just needed to take a minute. Everything all right?"

"Oh, yes—everything's fine. Sorry to worry you. No word on our missing guards yet, but I'm staying hopeful." Then Gemma smiled. "I came to get you. Someone's at the door to see you—someone I think you're going to like."

Iris knew Gemma had to be talking about Grant. Besides Noah and Ian, he was the only other human she could stand.

She walked through the main hall, politely saying hello to everyone she passed as she headed for the door. Gemma went back to sitting with Ian and Princess Esme. When Iris opened the door, Grant stood on the step, holding wildflowers in his hand.

"Good morning, Iris," he began, holding out the flowers. "Picked these just for you. Near the cliff where we had our screaming session."

Iris had never been given flowers before. She took them from his hands, sniffing them. "They're lovely, thank you. I guess I should put them in water?"

"If you want them to live, yes," Grant said with a laugh. "I'll talk to some of your people while I wait for you. I have a breakfast place in mind whenever you're ready."

Right—the breakfast date. Iris had nearly forgotten with the stress of the kidnapping, the insane doctor, and watching Bobby die.

She walked into the kitchen, passing the remaining guards as she put the flowers in a vase. They looked beautiful as she set them out on the table in front of the sun. Then she frowned, noticing a small note sitting there.

"Hey, did anyone leave this behind?" Iris called out.

All the other guards in the kitchen shook their heads, then

one of them wearing a chef's apron gestured at the table. "We didn't open it. Saw it there yesterday and assumed it was yours."

"No, it's not mine." Iris reached for the note. "But I should see who it belongs to."

When she unfolded the note, it only said a few words. "I'M SORRY. WE HAD TO." And it was Sapphira's familiar handwriting.

And wherever she went, Kyler was quick to follow. Those two were best friends and inseparable. It was at that moment that Iris knew the truth—Sapphira and Kyler weren't kidnapped.

They had chosen to run off. And whatever they had planned next, knowing how much they disagreed with King Tedros, really worried Iris.

She placed the note deep in her pocket, intending to speak to the king later about it. Grant was standing in the main hall as he chatted with everyone, and she didn't want to keep him waiting. Despite everything, she was truly happy to see him again.

He looked over and smiled when he saw her. "Hey, Iris— there you are. I was just chatting with your friends. You ready to go?"

Iris doubted they had told him about the kidnapping—or he would've been a lot more concerned. She wasn't sure she wanted him to know that she had been kidnapped by Bobby Blevins. Although she had fallen hard for Grant, just being around him was dangerous, and the less he knew, the better.

"Ready," Iris said, faking a smile. "I'll be back everyone. Be safe in the meantime."

"The prime minister doesn't want us to leave, you know," King Tedros said. "Is this really necessary?"

Iris glanced at Grant. "I think it is. Don't worry—we'll be fine."

"Are you sure?" Grant raised an eyebrow. "Because I wouldn't want to go against the prime minister ..."

But Iris really needed to get out. She shook her head, reaching for Grant's hand as butterflies coursed through her bloodstream. "Really, it's okay. And we won't be long."

King Tedros allowed it, walking Iris and Grant outside. He quickly locked the door behind them. Just being outside under the hot sun made Iris feel like a target—like Michael Bond or Icarus or anyone else could've attacked her at any moment. She kept her head swiveling around, looking for enemies and remaining on high alert.

"You sure you're okay?" Grant asked. "You just seem ... anxious. More than usual. Is it because the prime minister doesn't want you to leave?"

"Yes and no. I'm fine, Grant. Just being cautious," Iris lied. "Which way to the restaurant?"

Grant pointed the way, then they walked there, chatting along the sidewalk. Cars driving past stared but no one confronted them. Iris kept an eye on all the vehicles, ensuring they weren't Bond coming back to finish the job.

They reached the sandwich shop downtown a short while later. Grant opened the door for Iris before they walked inside the air-conditioned shop. There was a board with a list of breakfast sandwiches, cookies, and drinks to order.

When the diners saw them enter, they began to murmur and stare, noticing Iris's armor and her large sword poking out of her scabbard. Iris nudged Grant, drawing his eyes away from the board.

"Maybe we ought to take our food and go," she whispered. "We've got an audience."

Grant looked around, noticing everyone staring. He reached

for Iris's hand and squeezed it. "All right, if you're more comfortable with that, then we can leave. Let's just get our food and find a spot in the shade to eat it. Have you ever had poutine?"

Iris shook her head. Grant smiled, stepping forward as he placed an order for two egg sandwiches, two sodas, and two poutines. The young girl scanned Iris up and down, her hands trembling for a moment before accepting Grant's money. As she handed over the bag of food a few minutes later, she sighed in relief when she saw them leaving.

"Down here," Grant said, leaving the restaurant with Iris. "There's a nice spot for a picnic not too far from the shop."

"Okay, sounds good." Iris followed Grant down the sidewalk. "You know, they saw us holding hands in there."

Grant shrugged. "And? Like I said before, I don't care who looks. Their issue with your people is their problem—not yours or mine. Ooh, look, a shady spot. Here should be perfect."

Grant found a large tree, then sat underneath it in the shade. He passed Iris her sandwich, poutine, and drink as she sat across from him with her legs tucked in. As they ate their food—and Iris discovered she did love the Canadian poutine after all, much like coffee—they chit-chatted about everyday things. The breeze blew through the trees, birds chirping above their heads.

"So, what happened between you and your principal?" Iris asked, taking another bite of her sandwich. "Did you get in trouble?"

"Fortunately, no. Donna's a sweetheart. Without her support, I definitely would've been sacked." Grant wiped his mouth with a napkin, removing some of the poutine gravy that had gotten on his face. "Lisa and a few other teachers definitely wanted me fired, though. And some angry parents who came in."

"Yikes. How long can your principal hold them off?"

Grant shrugged, sipping his soda. "I don't know. Hopefully their opinions will change soon, and I won't have to fight so hard for my job. In the meantime, Lisa was fired. Donna said she couldn't trust her not to blab to the media again."

Iris's eyes widened. "Wow. Didn't see that one coming. I thought you'd be fired for letting me come to the school. Was Lisa upset?"

"Very. She threatened me when she came back to clear out her desk." Grant finished his sandwich, laying his head back against the tree. "Just be careful, all right? Now that Lisa doesn't have a job, she'll have more time on her hands to harass you."

"Just great." Iris sighed. "Well, despite everything that's going on, I appreciate you taking me here. It was a lovely date."

"It was. But I don't intend for it to be over just yet." Grant rose to his feet, holding out his hand. "Come on—there's more to see in Toronto. You ever been skating?"

Iris shook her head, then she threw out their food scraps in a nearby garbage can. The few people on the street stared at them as Grant tugged Iris's hand along. She swore she saw Michael Bond watching them from a few feet away in a car, but when she turned back, it was only a man who looked like him.

She was just being paranoid—and for good reason. But if Bond wasn't following them, then what was he doing? What was his next big plan after shooting Bobby Blevins and his magical-obsessed gang?

Grant continued to tug Iris down the street, making her forget about her troubles for a little while. She even found herself smiling—and smiling hard—for the first time in a while. Grant turned, entering a large building that had a skating rink inside. Flashing lights and pop music were playing overhead as people skated on the ice.

"Hockey and ice skating are popular in Canada," Grant explained as they stood back, watching people glide on the rink. "By winter, you'll see what I mean. For now, though, until the weather gets chillier, we'll have to skate inside. What do you say?"

Iris knew she shouldn't have lingered—that staying inside the church was much safer. But Grant looked so excited, almost in a childlike way, that made Iris feel the same way.

"All right," she said with a grin. "Let's do it."

"Good. But you'll need something better to skate in than that armor and sword. It would be too difficult. And maybe a disguise to help you blend in is just what you need." Grant paused. "Wait here—I'll be right back."

Iris nodded, watching as Grant fled the skating rink. He returned a few minutes later with an oversized sweater and leggings he had bought from a store down the block. He reached her with a smile, holding the clothes up.

"I guessed your size," he began. "Thought you could change into this. I hope it's okay."

Iris smiled, taking the clothes. "They're more than okay. Thanks, Grant. I'll be right back."

He nodded as she headed into the bathroom, changing into the clothes. She felt a lot more human when she looked at herself in the mirror. She left the bathroom while carrying her armor and sword, hiding them underneath a bench for later.

"So?" Iris asked, twirling in front of him. "How do I look?"

"Just perfect," he said, beaming. "Come on, let's get skates."

Arm-in-arm, Grant and Iris walked to the other side of the skating rink where they rented skates in their size. Grant helped Iris sit down and tie her laces since she had no experience. To their relief, no one bothered them, but maybe that was because the skating rink was dark and loud. As soon as they stepped onto the ice, Iris nearly fell.

"Got you," Grant said, holding her upright. "Much like bike riding, skating takes balance. Hold onto me—I'll protect you."

That sent butterflies shooting through Iris's stomach. With a blush, she held onto Grant's arm for dear life, slowly skating on the ice with him. He was much better than she was—no doubt due to years of practice.

"My sister and I used to come here a lot as kids. We were pretty good skaters," Grant said, gliding around while holding Iris upright. "Those were fun times. When we weren't being bullied at school."

"I'm sorry. Judging by what I've seen, kids can be cruel. But you didn't tell me you had a sister."

"No, I suppose I didn't. I don't see her a lot—she's got two kids and works a busy job. But yes, Marissa and I were both adopted as babies by our fathers. Our real mother was a teen mom, the father was her high school teacher. We're twins."

Iris raised an eyebrow. "Her teacher? That's inappropriate."

Grant nodded, gliding Iris in a perfect circle. "And illegal. He went to jail, I think. Maybe he's out now. I don't know much about my birth parents—I never looked them up. Despite all the awful bullying we endured for having gay fathers, Marissa and I wouldn't have traded them in for the world. They were—and still are—amazing parents."

"That's good to hear. Your father is the man who raises you, not one who's related by blood. Or *fathers,* in your case."

Grant smiled. "Exactly—I knew you'd understand."

A couple skated by, then the woman jumped into the man's arms. He swung her around as they both laughed. When he set her down, they kissed passionately on the ice, then Grant turned to Iris.

"Hey, we should do that," he whispered. "Could be fun."

Iris had her doubts that she could pull it off, but looking at Grant, she felt invincible. So, she nodded. "All right. I'm in."

"Yeah? Okay, awesome. Now, I'm going to pick you up and spin you around on the count of three. Ready? One, two ... three!"

When Grant reached for Iris, he only got her halfway up in the air before he lost his grip. He slipped on the ice, then crashed beside her as she fell too. The other skaters glided over to make sure they were all right. And it still didn't seem that they knew Iris wasn't from Earth.

She had to admit, she preferred keeping a low profile. The gossip and frequent stares got on her nerves after a while.

"I'm okay, thank you," Grant said, then turned to Iris. "You all right? I didn't hurt you, did I?"

Iris shook her head. "No, Grant—you didn't. I'm a lot tougher than I look."

He smiled, holding her gaze. "I know. That's why I like you so much. Strong is sexy."

As she blushed, Grant held out a hand, then helped them both to their feet. It was a miracle neither of them had gotten hurt.

"It was a good effort," Grant said, "and you did well for your first skating experience. I think we'll need a bit more practice before we try that move again, though."

I'll practice with you any day of the week.

"Okay, sounds good," she said. "Now, I'm not usually one to complain, but these skates are killing my feet. Can we take them off now?"

Grant nodded, gently leading Iris to the edge of the skating rink. They stepped off carefully and removed their skates. Iris felt much better, preferring to be on solid ground than ice. She had to always be at her best—with Icarus and so many other enemies out there.

After paying for their time and skates, then carrying her armor and sword, Grant led Iris out of the skating rink, checking his watch. "Well, I should probably get you back to the church where it's safer for you. I've got some papers to grade and tests to plan. You can keep the clothes, by the way. In case you need a disguise in the future. But I had a lovely time—as always."

Iris smiled. "I did too."

"And if you don't mind," Grant said with a blush, "I'd like to kiss you. Again."

Iris grinned. "Okay." She reached out her hands and Grant pulled her flush against him, then wrapped his arms around her waist. Her stomach flipped as she watched as his tongue glided across his bottom lip.

He gave that sexy half smile and slowly, torturously, brought his lips to hers. This kiss was more methodical than the first one they'd shared. Like each brush of their lips, each soft sigh, each touch of his hands was meant to break down her defenses. When they finally broke apart, Iris's lips were swollen, and she couldn't stop smiling.

Grant tucked a strand of her dark hair behind her ear, then placed another gentle kiss on her forehead.

"I really like you, Iris," Grant said against her temple.

A thrill zipped through her body, and she snuggled into his arms. "I really like you too."

"I'd love to see you again. How about ... you come to my apartment tomorrow night for dinner? I can cook you up something special. If you think the prime minister will allow it."

They broke apart and she looked up at his hopeful face. "If we stay inside and avoid trouble, I don't see the harm. I'd like that, Grant. Can't wait."

Grant grinned and tugged on her hand. "Perfect. Come on— I'll walk you back so I know you got home safe."

Iris nodded, heading down the street with Grant while holding his hand. Out in public again. On the way to the church, people began to notice them, murmuring and staring. She much preferred the anonymity of the dark skating rink.

As they passed a little blue townhouse with kids' furniture and toys out on the front lawn, Iris spotted someone familiar. Ronan was out there—sitting on the swings by himself, holding his lightsaber. He looked so sad, so lonely. Iris hated seeing him that way.

She waved, getting his attention. "Hello, Ronan."

When Ronan saw Iris, he sprang up from the swing, then sprinted over. "Hi, Iris! And hi, Mr. Thatcher. Are you two getting married?"

Married? Iris nearly laughed. That was a bit soon.

Grant laughed. "No, we're not, buddy. What makes you think that?"

"Well, you're holding hands. I've only ever seen Mom and Dad hold hands like that."

"Oh. Yes, we are." Grant looked down at Iris's hand, not pulling away. "Well, we're not getting married. You don't have to be husband and wife to hold hands. But ... I would like to take things to the next step if you don't mind, Iris?"

She turned to him, almost forgetting Ronan was even there, just watching them. Grant had a way of making the whole world disappear. "What do you mean?"

"Well, I was waiting to ask this question, but things have been going great. And life's short so I don't want to wait any longer." Grant cleared his throat. "Iris ... do you want to be my girlfriend?"

CHAPTER 20

Iris had never been asked to be anyone's girlfriend before.

She had lived a life of servitude, a life of duty and honor. Her work came before everything else—Fairhaven was always more important. But with Fairhaven gone, the answer seemed obvious. And so right in her heart.

"I will," Iris said with a smile. "I'll be your girlfriend."

"All right!" Grant said, beaming as he kissed her cheek. "Whew, glad to get that off my chest. I was scared you might say no. Man, I feel like the happiest guy alive."

"Can I come to the wedding when you get married?" Ronan asked, reminding Iris that he was still there. "Can I have a lightsaber battle with you on the dance floor?"

Grant laughed. "Ronan, like I said—there aren't any wedding plans. It's a bit too soon for that, buddy. But one day ... yes, you can come to the wedding."

Grant was already thinking of marriage? The more Iris thought about it, the more she liked the sound of that. Of starting a new life, one filled with love and companionship. Her parents would've wanted that for her too. Her heart ached, wishing she could've introduced Grant to them.

Ronan smiled. "Okay, cool! Since you're here, can I show you my room? Mom made me clean it this morning so it looks really nice."

Grant gestured down the street. "We'd love to, but we really should get going. As I'm sure you've heard, it's dangerous for Iris to be on these streets—"

"I'll be quick!" Ronan cried, tugging on both Iris and Grant's arms. "It's just this way. I can't wait to show you!"

Grant gave Iris an apologetic look, but she just smiled. Ronan led them across the front yard before opening the door into the small bungalow. As Iris and Grant followed him inside, they noticed the house was messy. Old diapers and baby bottles coated the floor, the rooms needed a good dusting, and a pile of dishes sat on the kitchen counter.

"Are your mom and dad home?" Grant asked, glancing around.

Ronan nodded. "Yeah, Mom's in her room. She's getting my baby sister ready for her swimming lesson. Dad's at work—like always. Come on, my room's just down here."

Ronan gestured down the hall, then headed to a small room. The sign on the door read "RONAN'S SECRET ROOM— DO NOT ENTER." After he opened the door, he gestured for them to follow, then Grant and Iris followed him in. They looked around and noticed all the Star Wars posters, superhero comics, and figurines lined up neatly on a shelf. His homework was half-finished and tossed over his bed.

"Look, I have more lightsabers!" Ronan cried, pulling another one from under the bed. This one was bright red and glowing. "Iris promised me she'd teach me how to use a real sword one day, Mr. Thatcher. Like a warrior."

"Did she?" Grant laughed. "Well, that's nice. Just be careful. I can't have one of my favorite students getting hurt."

As he ruffled Ronan's hair affectionately, the boy beamed. "One of your favorite students? Really?"

"Why, of course, Ronan. All my students are my favorite students. And you have a very nice room."

Iris nodded, looking closer at a figurine. "A room fit for a warrior."

"Thanks. I just wish I could get Justin and his friends to stop bullying me." Ronan slid his lightsaber back under the bed, then sat down and sighed. "It really hurts."

Grant frowned. "I'm sorry, Ronan. I was bullied when I was younger too, so I understand. Do you want me to talk to him? Or his parents?"

"No. I told Iris that'll just make it worse." Ronan kicked his feet over the side of the bed. "I need to handle it on my own. Like a true warrior. What would you do back home if someone was bullying you, Iris?"

Iris paused. "Well ... most likely I would engage in combat with them. And the winner would get bragging rights."

Ronan's eyes lit up. "Then that's what I'll do! I'll challenge Justin to a duel."

"Whoa, not so fast." Grant kneeled beside Ronan. "Maybe that's how they do it in Fairhaven, but here on Earth, we should use our words to solve our problems. Try talking with Justin— ask him to stop. Show compassion and kindness. Too often, these bullies only hurt other people because they're hurt on the inside."

"Huh," Ronan murmured. "I never thought of it like that."

"It's true." Grant rose to his feet. "And we can't control how other people treat us, but we *can* control our response to it. We can rise above it and do better. *Be* better people. That's what I try to teach all my students."

As Ronan thought about it, footsteps echoed down the hallway, then they stopped at the door. "Ronan, I'm heading out with—who are these people?"

When Iris spun around, she saw a middle-aged blonde woman standing in the doorway. She wore an old pair of sweatpants and a stained t-shirt. And she carried a toddler, a girl who looked similar to Ronan. Three other younger kids clung to her legs.

"Oh, I'm sorry, Mrs. Padwell," Grant said, stepping toward her. "It's me—Mr. Thatcher, Ronan's teacher. My girlfriend and I happened to be walking by when Ronan saw us. He wanted to show us his room."

Ronan jumped off his bed, walking toward Iris. "This is who I was telling you about, Mom! It's Iris. We had a lightsaber battle together."

Mrs. Padwell narrowed her eyes at Iris. "I see. Ronan, could you give us a moment to talk in private, please? Here, take your baby sister to the kitchen with the others. Get them some snacks."

Ronan pouted. "But I wasn't done showing Iris and Mr. Thatcher my toys—"

"Now, Ronan," Mrs. Padwell said, a little firmer. "Please and thank you."

Ronan sighed, nodding as he approached his mother. He took his baby sister from her arms and gestured for his other siblings to follow. They stumbled after him, heading down the hallway to the kitchen. It left Iris and Grant alone with Ronan's mother—and Iris could feel the tension in the air.

"Really, I apologize for dropping by unannounced like this," Grant began. "It won't happen again—"

"I hope not," Mrs. Padwell interrupted. "My son told me all about you, Iris, and I'm concerned. I don't want you around Ronan—or any of my kids. I think your people are dangerous, just like the news says you are."

"A lot of it is exaggerated, Mrs. Padwell," Iris began. "The truth is, I care for Ronan. He's a wonderful boy, but he's lonely and getting bullied at school. I want to help him. For starters, I think you need to be there for Ronan a lot more."

Mrs. Padwell scoffed. "First you come to my son's school, now you're giving me parenting advice? Oh, that's rich. I spend a lot of time with Ronan, you know. He isn't neglected at all."

"Of course, Mrs. Padwell," Grant said. "We apologize if we offended you—"

"What offends me, Mr. Thatcher, is that you allow these outsiders around our children. I can't believe you're dating one of them." Mrs. Padwell shook her head. "The other parents have been talking about you, you know. About your lack of judgment lately. I got off the phone not that long ago with Mrs. Bond. She really wants you fired."

"I know," Grant said, "and I'm sorry you all feel that way. I hope you can understand that I just want everyone to get along. That my intention was never to hurt your kids, but to teach them that other people exist, those who are different than them. And they deserve our respect and understanding."

"Which sounds great in a perfect world, but our world is far from perfect, Mr. Thatcher. Safety must come first over diversity. If you don't stop bringing this woman around, I'll pull Ronan from your school. I know the other parents are considering the same."

Iris frowned. "That's a bit extreme. Grant is a good teacher and an even better man—"

Mrs. Padwell shook her head, clearly not convinced. "Please, just leave. And stay away from my son. I don't want him mixed up in all this and getting hurt."

Iris could understand his mother's apprehension. Everyone close to Iris and her people—Grant included—were targets for their enemies. And since Ronan was a child, they had an obligation to protect him. Iris didn't want to see anyone hurt, but especially a sweet little boy.

"Okay, Mrs. Padwell. You win," Iris said with a sigh. "We'll be leaving now. Take care."

She watched Iris walk out of the room, then Grant followed. They walked the hallway to the front door where Ronan was giving his younger siblings some snacks. When he saw them, he smiled widely and waved.

"Goodbye, Iris and Mr. Thatcher!" he called out. "Can't wait to see you again!"

Iris just smiled, not having the heart to tell him that his mother didn't approve. Iris opened the front door and walked outside with Grant, letting the door close gently behind them. She shook her head as they stopped on the sidewalk outside the house.

"Poor Ronan," Iris whispered. "He just wants a friend. He'll be so devastated when his mother tells him to stay away from me."

"I know. I'm sorry." Grant sighed. "I really wish people would be more tolerant and respectful in this day and age. I've tried so hard, but these parents are hard to get through to. At least my kids are coming around to the idea of you. Well, all of them except Justin."

"Because his parents have brainwashed him," Iris muttered. "I'm concerned about your job, Grant. And about the parents threatening to pull their students. Maybe I should stop coming around to the school. For a little while, at least, until things get better. If they ever do."

Grant nodded. "All right, if you think that's best. I still intend to talk to my kids about you. And I fully intend to keep seeing you, those parents' discrimination be damned."

Iris thought it was sweet that Grant was willing to risk his job for her, but she didn't like that. Not when she knew his teaching job meant so much to him. But before she could respond, Grant cleared his throat.

"Anyway, let's get you back to the church where it's safe. If I agree with Mrs. Padwell on anything, it's that these streets are a lot more dangerous now. Best to keep moving so we aren't an easy target."

Iris nodded, walking down the street with Grant. She didn't dare to look back in case it made her sad. Although she wasn't an optimistic person, she hoped she'd get to see Ronan again soon—if his mother would change her mind about people from Fairhaven.

Once they reached the church, Iris climbed the steps to the front door, then turned to Grant. "Well, despite being told to stay away from Ronan, I had a lovely time with you. Thanks for broadening my horizons."

"Anytime. And like I said, I want to cook dinner for you tomorrow night. Show you my apartment."

Iris nodded. "I'd like that too. Want me to give you a tour of the church? It's not fancy, but we call it home."

"Sure, I'd like that. I haven't been to a church in a very long time. Not a religious person."

Iris opened the door, stepping inside. "Oh, no?"

"Nah. My only religion is kindness—I think it's all you need." Grant followed her inside the church, closing the squeaky door behind him. "Do your people have religion? I've never asked."

"Not really. I suppose ... magic is our religion. And kindness to some extent."

Iris's thoughts briefly flitted to Icarus. He was the closest thing they had to a God—an immortal. But Iris wasn't about to worship him.

As Iris led Grant through the main hall, she noticed everyone lingering around outside the sleeping quarters. Gemma and Ian paced while King Tedros and the rest of the guards stood nearby. Fairy Godmother Odelia, Princess Esme, and Noah weren't there.

"I'm back," Iris said as she approached. "What's going on? You all look tense."

"Esme threw up again," Gemma said, turning to her. "Fairy Godmother Odelia finally convinced Esme to let her check her out. We're just waiting on the news. Oh, hi, Grant."

Grant waved at everyone. "Hello. If this is a bad time, I can come back—"

The door to the sleeping quarters opened, then Princess Esme and Noah came out smiling. Fairy Godmother Odelia followed with a similar grin on her face. Iris knew it had to be good news, but what was going on?

"It's all right, everyone. No need to worry yourselves sick," Esme said, glancing around. "We know the reason I've been throwing up. The potion Odelia whipped up showed me the truth."

"What is it, dear?" King Tedros asked. "Food poisoning? Anxiety?"

"No, Father." Esme smiled wider. "I'm pregnant. You're going to be a grandfather."

The room turned silent for a moment before everyone broke out in cheers. They congratulated Princess Esme and Noah, including Grant, and everyone seemed excited about the birth of a new royal.

But Iris wasn't.

The world was a dangerous place—they could barely protect themselves. Not to mention they would need more food, diapers, and toys. How was it all going to work out?

"Oh, I'm so happy for you two," King Tedros said, hugging his daughter. "Your mother would be overjoyed as well."

"And now we've got a new reason to make this world a

better place," Gemma said, beaming. "For the next generation of our people."

"The first half-born," Fairy Godmother Odelia added. "One part Fae, one part human. We had no idea this was possible, so it'll be a learning experience for us all. I can't wait to meet the little bundle of joy."

As they all cheered again, Grant nudged Iris's shoulder. "Hey, you don't seem too excited. You all right?"

Grant seemed to sense when Iris was in a bad mood. Despite their time together being short, he already knew her so well.

"Yeah, I'm fine. It's not that I'm not excited," Iris whispered, not wanting Princess Esme to overhear, "I'm just ... worried. With everything going on, how can we support a child at this time? How can we protect them? And would the people of Earth even accept a half-Fae child? Humans will probably fear them too. That poor child might be the victim of a lifetime of hate and prejudice."

"I hear you," Grant whispered back. "There are a lot of unknowns. But still, I'm happy for your people. Maybe this baby is just what you all need. Might bring some joy around here."

Grant had a point, Iris had to admit—though she was still concerned about the future.

"I'm glad you're okay, Esme," Gemma said. "We were worried about your health for a while. It's nice to finally have answers. Anyway, why don't we go out and celebrate?"

"Where?" Iris crossed her arms. "You know these streets are dangerous. Prime Minister Lin told us to stay inside."

A rule Iris had already broken for Grant. But that was different, she told herself. She was a trained guard and she wasn't pregnant.

"How about my bar?" Ian asked. "It's a safe place. We'll stay inside and lock the doors. No one will get to us."

"I like that idea," King Tedros said. "Let's head out. And hopefully, when we get back, the police will have answers on our two missing guards."

"And I can tell my father the good news," Noah said with a grin, following Princess Esme to the door. "I'm going to be a daddy."

"Correction," Princess Esme said, kissing his cheek, "you're going to be an *amazing* daddy."

"Fingers crossed. I just wish I still had my job at The Human Connection. How am I going to support this family?"

"We'll find a way." Princess Esme reached for his hand, squeezing it. "I believe that."

Iris quickly showed Grant around, then followed the crowd down the street. Ian pointed the way to his bar and they avoided the concerned stares of the passersby. When they arrived at Ian's bar, he unlocked the door and led them inside before shutting it behind them.

"Ah, I love this place. I miss working here," Ian said, walking behind the bar, "but business hasn't been great lately. So, I've decided to keep it closed for now."

Gemma frowned, taking a seat near the bar. "I'm so sorry, Ian."

"Don't be, babe—these peoples' hatred is not your fault. Anyway, free drinks for everyone to celebrate!" Ian called out. "Well, except for Princess Esme. One soda coming up for her."

"Thank you." Princess Esme took a seat at the bar, patting her stomach as Noah sat down next to her. "I know there's already a lot going on, but I'm so excited. Can't wait to meet this baby."

"Me too," Noah said, his hands over Esme's stomach. "It's going to be so loved. And so beautiful, just like their momma."

As Princess Esme and Noah debated over kids' names, Iris and Grant took a seat at the end of the bar. Ian gave them free drinks, then they chatted about her people and their dinner plans for tomorrow night.

"Told my sister all about you, by the way," Grant said, sipping a beer. "Marissa's really excited to meet you—"

Before Grant had the chance to finish, several car engines roared outside the bar.

CHAPTER 21

I ris was the first to get up to investigate the sound, walking toward the window with her sword drawn. Her first fear was that it was Bobby—but he was dead. The second was that it was Icarus, but she hadn't seen any sign of him in a while.

Which she wasn't entirely sure was a good thing.

But instead, it was the third person she feared the most—Michael Bond. He and his men, dressed similarly in dark jeans and handkerchiefs, pulled up in their black vehicles. They parked outside the bar, cornering them inside.

"Who is it?" Ian asked, wiping down the bar. "Customers, I hope? I haven't had any good business in a while. And I need to pay my rent soon."

"No, not customers," Iris said as the others peered out the window over her shoulder. "But enemies. Be on guard, everyone. It's Michael Bond and his Exterminators."

As everyone's eyes widened, three rough knocks sounded on the bar door. Iris put a finger against her lips and urged them all to be quiet. Maybe, if they were silent and lucky, Michael and his racist gang would leave them alone.

But he wasn't the leaving type.

"We know you're in there," Michael called out, pounding on the door again. "I heard rumors your people frequent this bar. That one of you freaks is dating the owner."

"And?" Iris demanded through the door. "What do you want? We have nothing to say to you."

"Oh, but we got a lot to say to you. Open up. We don't want violence—just conversation."

"Not likely," Iris muttered. She took a deep breath, then turned to the others. "Sorry, but our little celebration is over. Out the back door, all of you. We'll go around and leave."

Everyone nodded, setting their drinks aside and heading to the back door. Iris opened the door, thinking it was safe when she saw Sheila standing there with some of Michael's men.

"We've got you surrounded," Sheila snarled. "You're not getting out until we talk."

She pushed past Iris, entering the bar. Everything inside Iris screamed at her to fight Sheila and the gang—but she had to keep the peace. If only for the protection of her people.

Sheila and her men sauntered toward the front door, then unlocked it so Michael and the rest of their group could enter. They strode inside the bar, glancing around at the drinks and décor before closing the door behind them.

"Nice establishment you got here," Michael said, sitting at the bar to look at Ian. "Too bad you let vermin inside. This place reeks now."

"My girlfriend and friends are *not* vermin," Ian spat. "And I'd really appreciate it if you all left. Immediately."

"We will soon. After we finish talking." Michael threw some money onto the bar. "I'm a paying customer, so can I get a beer or what?"

The Fairhaveners turned to look at Iris, waiting for her

approval. She nodded. "Get him his damn beer. We don't want any trouble."

"All you people do is bring trouble," Michael grumbled. "But good. We got something important to say—and it can't wait."

Although he didn't look thrilled, Ian took Michael's money and served him a beer. Michael took a sip and then burped. Iris winced at him as Sheila and his men stood around, almost protecting Michael. And then Iris noticed Lisa in the crowd.

"What are you looking at?" Lisa hissed. "I lost my job because of you, you know."

"No, Lisa. You did that to yourself." Grant rose to his feet, walking over. "You just couldn't let it go."

"Of course, I couldn't! These people are dangerous. And it breaks my heart that you don't see it, Grant." Lisa shook her head. "You're going to get hurt, you know. Seriously hurt. And that hurts *me*."

"So, this is your solution?" Iris asked. "You're with them now? The Exterminators?"

"She is," Sheila replied proudly. "Lisa and I have been good friends for a while now, meeting at school. We're paying her bills for her since she was fired. She's working with us now."

"Doing what, exactly?" Princess Esme asked, one hand on her stomach as Noah stood beside her. "What do you want?"

"Peace on the surface. That's all," Michael said, taking another sip. "Which means we want you people to leave. For good."

"And go where?" Noah asked. "I'm human, just like Ian and Grant. This is our home too. And we believe that they should stay."

The three men nodded, then Grant reached over and grabbed Iris's hand. Lisa noticed with wide eyes. "How far you've fallen, Grant. Now you're *with* one of them?"

"That's right," Grant said. "And I'm the happiest I've ever

been with Iris. Please, stop all this madness and just leave them alone. They don't mean any harm. If you still care about me, you'd back off."

While it looked like Lisa was considering it—much to Iris's surprise—Michael Bond took another long swig of his beer, then slammed it down on the bar. "No can do. We're giving you seventy-two hours to leave this city. Or shit gets real."

"It hasn't already?" Iris asked, still clutching Grant's hand. "I watched you shoot Bobby Blevins and his group and not even flinch. Did you forget about that?"

She swore she saw a hint of a smile on Michael's face before it vanished. "I don't know what you're talking about. I've never even met Bobby before."

Iris couldn't believe it. Was Michael really going to lie about murder when she had seen it with her own eyes?

"That's a lie," Iris spat. "I saw you. After they kidnapped me, you and your group found their little countryside hideout. And you shot and killed them all for wanting to use magic. During the smoke bomb and all the shooting, I managed to escape."

Michael rose to his feet. "You've got quite the imagination. Like I told the police, it's all lies. I never did any of that."

"Yes, that's right. Michael was with me all week," Sheila said, and Iris knew she was lying. "Didn't the police tell you? They found the countryside home but no bodies. Not even any blood. Michael gave his full cooperation and the police stopped hunting for Bobby and his supposedly murdered friends."

"Not supposedly. It definitely happened," Iris said through gritted teeth. "You must've scrubbed that house top to bottom, then. Ditched all the evidence and the bodies. Where did you hide them?"

Michael turned to Sheila. "Delusional—all of them."

At that moment, Iris wished she had proof—pictures, blood evidence, anything at all. But she had nothing. Only the faded bruise from where Bobby had hit her, but that didn't prove Michael and his men had been at the house.

Michael walked to the front door, his people following. "Consider this a favor to all of you—and a warning. Leave this town. Go wherever, find some island in the middle of nowhere. You've got three days. If not ... World War Three is coming."

"What does that mean?" Iris demanded, following him. "What do you have planned?"

Michael said nothing as he opened the door to the bar, then gestured for his gang to follow. After they left the bar, they got into their cars, vanishing down the road. Iris saw an outline of a familiar face in Michael's backseat.

Dr. Koch—the same man who was going to do experiments on Iris to find out how to use magic for Bobby and his group. But how had he ended up with Michael and the Exterminators? Had they kidnapped him? It was a miracle the scientist hadn't died with the rest of Blevin's men.

"God, I hate that guy," Ian muttered as the bar turned quiet.

"Same here. And I'm calling my father." Noah pulled his smartphone out of his pocket. "Not just to tell him the good news, but also to ask about the house in the country."

As he pulled out his phone, dialing his father's number, Grant turned to Iris. "I don't understand. What are you all talking about? What house in the country?"

Iris sat down, taking a deep breath. "I didn't tell you because I didn't want you to worry. But, the other night, I was kidnapped by Bobby Blevins and his men ..."

After Iris went through the story, Grant reached for her hand. "I'm so sorry, Iris. That's beyond awful. But you should've told me—I would've come over and stayed with you. Just to make sure you were all right."

"That's sweet of you, Grant, but I'm fine. And more determined than ever to stop Michael and his Exterminators. He can lie all he wants, but I know the truth. He and his men murdered Bobby Blevins and his group. All because Blevins' men wanted magic. I don't know where they hid the bodies or the evidence, but they did. And the police have no idea."

As everyone turned quiet, Noah hung up, then walked over. "Well, my father's overjoyed about the baby news. That's good at least. Unfortunately, the two missing guards still haven't been found. Anyway, he said he was just about to call and tell us the news. Michael and his group walked into the police station—completely cooperated. My dad said they were confident and cocky, acting innocent."

"But they're not," Iris said. "I know they aren't."

"I believe you. Everyone here does too," Noah said, making the group nod. "And several officers found the house in the countryside they believe you were talking about. Due to the lack of evidence there, they can't do anything. All charges are dropped until if and when the bodies are found. Or any evidence, really."

"Then I'll go back to that country house," Iris said. "I'll find evidence."

"Don't," Gemma urged. "It might not be safe. You heard Michael Bond—he wants us to leave or it's World War Three. I'm already afraid of what that'll be."

As everyone nodded, Iris was still staring out the window. "I am too. And you know that scientist, Dr. Koch, who was going to do experiments on me? He was with Michael in his backseat. I just don't know if he's there willingly or if Bond kidnapped him."

"Hmm. What for?" Princess Esme asked, glancing around. "Why not just kill him like the others?"

"I don't know. Michael must have a plan for that deranged German scientist—he always does. Just like this World War Three plan." Iris shook her head. "Maybe if we kidnap Dr. Koch, he can testify about what he saw at that house. Because right now, all the police have is my word and no one believes us at the moment. Without evidence, I'd need a witness to get justice for Bobby and his men."

"No. That sounds incredibly dangerous," King Tedros said. "All of it—from kidnapping Dr. Koch in the hopes that he'll agree to testify, which he might not, to returning to the home in the countryside where you were taken. I think we should just return to the church and stay out of it."

"And in seventy-two hours, when we haven't left Toronto? When Michael attacks?"

"Let him," King Tedros replied. "Then maybe the cops will see him for how dangerous he really is. Come—we'll celebrate back at the church where it's safer."

Everyone nodded, finishing their drinks and thanking Ian for opening the bar for them. They left together, heading down the street in one large group. Fortunately, no one tried anything, and the Exterminators didn't return. The party of Fairhaveners made it back to the church shortly after it started to rain.

"Well, that was the most intense celebration I've ever been to," Grant said as Iris's people headed inside the church, leaving them on the step to chat. "And I'm really sorry about Lisa. I can't believe she's working with the Exterminators now."

But Iris could. Without her job, Lisa had nothing to lose. Why not go all the way with her hatred?

"I could try to call her?" Grant continued. "Beg her to stop this nonsense? It's a longshot, but maybe she'll listen to me."

"I appreciate the thought, but no thanks. It's probably best if you stay out of it for your own safety." Iris sighed, running a hand through her hair. "Things just get more complicated, don't they?"

"They do. Thank goodness love is easy," Grant said, winking

at Iris. "One thing that isn't complicated is how much I care for you. And I'm really looking forward to seeing you tomorrow night for dinner."

"I am too. Despite everything." Iris leaned in, kissing Grant gently on the lips. "Get home safely. See you tomorrow."

Grant kissed back, then began walking home through the rainy streets. Iris hoped nothing bad would happen to him. With Lisa still wanting to get back with Grant and despising Iris for taking him away, she feared he'd be caught in the crossfire of an ugly battle.

Iris entered the church, locking the door behind her. Everyone had either gotten back to their chores or went to take a nap. Dealing with Michael and his group had a way of exhausting everyone.

Princess Esme was still up and moving around, trying to figure out the best place to install a nursery. She, Noah, and Fairy Godmother Odelia were going through the rooms, moving furniture around. Iris knew they were just using it as a distraction from all their problems.

Just as Iris finished cleaning up, planning to head to bed, Noah walked over with his smartphone in hand. "Hey—you gotta see this. I asked everyone to gather in the main hall."

Iris nodded, joining them all in the main hall where Noah sat down and pressed play on a video. It was from YouTube—and after some explaining, Iris learned it was a video-sharing website. Michael and his Exterminators had released a video, talking directly to the camera in a dark and dingy basement.

"No clue where they are," Noah said, holding up the phone for everyone to see. "But they've got a base somewhere. And this video is getting tons of views—jumping up several thousand every few minutes."

Gemma nodded. "I can see why. Michael has done a great

job of getting people's attention. Of using fear to manipulate them."

Noah agreed, then pressed play on the video. It was like a hateful diary entry—one where Michael, Sheila, Lisa, and the rest of their Exterminators expressed concerns about Iris's people.

"... and when the time comes to kick these people out of our city, which it will," Michael said, staring directly into the camera, "I hope the average citizen will rise up and choose a side. Choose us—choose normalcy and tradition. These dangerous magical freaks don't belong in our town. And if the prime minister won't do anything about it, we will."

The video went black after that, then Noah showed everyone the comments. Most people were afraid—expressing concern—but some sided with Michael, wanting Iris's people out of Toronto. Humans from all over the world had tuned in, expressing their support from other countries.

"This ... this is a threat," Gemma said. "All caught on video, clear as day. Surely the police and prime minister will see that. Should we call and tell them? And try to convince them that Iris was right and Michael really did kill people?"

Iris rose to her feet, scoffing. "What's the point? The prime minister hasn't been able to stop any of this before. Why would things change now?"

"Well, we need to do something," Princess Esme said. "Because it sounds like Michael is encouraging people to riot and take up arms to kill us. And I've got more than just myself to protect now."

When Princess Esme patted her stomach, Noah nodded. "You're right—our baby is counting on us. I'll call the prime minister, see what she wants to do. Everyone, keep your fingers crossed."

As Noah dialed the number the prime minister had given

them, trying to get through, all of Iris's guards began to murmur in between their patrols. Things just seemed to go from bad to worse. She walked toward the window, looking up at the dark, starry sky. She missed everything about Fairhaven —but mostly the safety it provided.

As her eyes landed on the Bhatia house, she saw a figure walking through the dark. It was Maya—and she was coming their way, dressed in a dark hoodie and tights. Iris reached for her sword, hoping there wasn't another battle on their doorstep.

CHAPTER 22

Maya approached the doors of the church, knocking twice. Iris was still peering out the window and noticed she was holding a bag behind her back. Was it something dangerous? Like a weapon?

"Come on, let me in," Maya whispered. "I know you're home—I was looking out the window and saw you all get back. Besides, it's freezing out here."

Iris opened the door an inch, her sword at her side. "What is it, Maya?"

"I wanted you to know I dumped my boyfriend. Oh, and this is for you." Maya pulled a large bag of snacks from behind her back. "For your people, I mean. To eat. I just wanted to help."

Iris took the bag, nodding. "That's kind of you. You broke up with your boyfriend?"

"I did. Can I come inside? It's cold."

Iris stepped aside, letting Maya enter the church. Her people waved at the teenage girl before going back to what they were doing before. Maya stopped shivering as badly, turning to look at Iris as she shut the door.

"There, that's better. Thanks." Maya breathed out. "Well, I had a talk with my boyfriend, just like you said I should. He admitted he was the one graffitiing my house."

"It's always the people closest to you who betray you." Iris shook her head, setting the bag of food down. It looked like chips, popcorn, and candy. "And then?"

"I asked him how he could do this. Vandalize the house of his own girlfriend. He said it was peer pressure—that the boys at school hate outsiders and it's spread from your people to mine. Anyone who's not originally from Canada, I mean."

"Yes, that seems to be the popular ideology these days."

"You have no idea." Maya sat down on the nearby pew, sighing. "Anyway, I said I couldn't be with someone like that. Someone who was writing nasty messages to anyone, but especially my own family. He cried and begged for forgiveness but I broke up with him. Told him to never call me again."

"Good for you, Maya. I don't have much experience with love, but I know someone who supposedly cares about you should never hurt you on purpose." Iris nodded at her. "I'm proud of you."

"Thanks. Just came to tell you the news. I asked my boyfriend to leave your people alone, too, though I'm not sure it clicked." Maya shook her head. "A lot of these teenage boys ... they're like, brainwashed by the Exterminators or something. All their racist messaging is targeting them. Telling them their home is under attack, that invaders are here. That sort of thing. And my stupid boyfriend believes it all. Oh, sorry. *Ex*-boyfriend."

"Younger minds are more impressionable," Iris said, thinking back to Senator Remus and his brainwashing of his sympathizers. "I'm glad you see it for what it is. Propaganda."

Maya rose to her feet. "Yeah, I do. Guess I'm just smarter than other kids my age. Maybe it's because I'm an outsider too.

Anyway, just wanted to warn you to be careful. A lot of people really don't like you. And I don't get why—you haven't done anything wrong."

"So many fear what they don't understand. That's all I know. But I appreciate your warning, Maya. And I hope you find someone who truly cares for you and treats you better."

Maya half-smiled. "Thanks, me too. Hope you can put that food to good use. Mom and Dad say hi, by the way."

"Tell them we said hello as well. They've been supporters of us since day one, something we greatly appreciate."

"Will do." Maya walked to the door, then paused. "And I'm really sorry I told you to leave my family alone. I was just worried about my parents, you know? They're at risk enough without adding more fuel to the fire. But I guess we can't let the bullies win. So, if you want to talk to my parents, go for it. Let's show Toronto that not all humans are scared of your people. If there's any way we can help you, let me know."

"Thank you, that's sweet. But it probably is a good idea to keep our distance." Iris opened the door for Maya. "There are ... lots of dangers out there at the moment. On that note, be safe, Maya. Thanks for the snacks. And take care."

The teenage girl nodded, then rushed across the dark street to head back to her house. Iris made sure she got inside safely before shutting and locking the doors to the church. When Iris turned around, reaching for the goodie bag, Gemma walked over.

"That was Maya, right?" she asked. "What was she doing here?"

"Just being a good neighbor, that's all." Iris held up the goodie bag. "She brought this over as well. And warned us that a lot of teenagers, mostly the males, are being brainwashed by Michael Bond and his Exterminators."

Gemma sighed. "Makes me sad. They're being manipulated to hate and they don't even realize it."

After Iris nodded, then dropped off the goodie bag inside the kitchen, she walked out into the main hall and found Noah off his smartphone. He was telling everyone what the prime minister had said to him.

"... and her hands are tied, really. She said Michael Bond has every right to free speech," Noah was explaining, "and that he can express his concerns. She's going to call him and personally warn him not to do anything violent, though."

"That could make it worse," Princess Esme muttered. "Being told what to do."

Noah shrugged. "Prime Minister Lin's trying, anyway. And she doesn't really want to pick sides. She admitted that while she's an immigrant, she's also a politician trying to win the next election. She wants to hear both sides, all concerns, and try to support everyone moving forward."

"Oh, please," Ian muttered, crossing his arms. "That isn't possible. It's coming down to war—the Exterminators or us. She'll have to choose who to support soon. Did you tell her Michael gave us seventy-two hours to get out of Toronto?"

"I did. She said if he tries anything, to call her immediately and let her know. Besides that, her plan is the same—we should stay inside and not go back to the bar again. She was upset about that, you know. And she's going to hold another press conference to talk about peace and co-existence."

As the others murmured about their future, Iris just shook her head. Peace talks hadn't worked before—what made the prime minister think they would do anything now?

War was coming, whether they all liked it or not. And sides would need to be chosen. Iris knew who she was willing to die for.

"Oh, and she said congratulations about our baby," Noah added, rubbing Princess Esme's shoulder. "She's concerned about the child's safety, though."

"We are too. I'm glad she knows—maybe she can help when the time comes." Princess Esme patted her stomach. "We should probably keep our pregnancy a secret from the other humans, though. Just in case."

"Agreed." King Tedros kissed his daughter's forehead. "Your safety comes first, my dear. Now, what else is on the agenda for today?"

"My dad is stopping by to drop off supplies and give us his congratulations, but that's it," Noah said. "So don't be alarmed when there's a knock on the door."

Everyone nodded, returning to their chores for the rest of the day. An hour later, a knock sounded on the door; it was Detective Crawford, as promised. He stood on the step with grocery bags full of supplies and food—and diapers.

When Iris opened the door, he nodded at her. "Hello, General. Just here to see my son."

"He's right inside, Detective. Go ahead in."

Detective Crawford pushed past her, then Iris locked the door. When she turned around, Detective Crawford was hugging Princess Esme and his son, congratulating them. He had even brought a card from Noah's mother and extended family.

"I brought some baby supplies over. Might seem a bit early for that, but just in case it gets harder to see you, here it is." Detective Crawford set the basket down. "Food for now, plus diapers and toys for when the baby gets here."

Noah grinned, reading the card. "Dad, you're too thoughtful. Thanks. Is Mom excited?"

"Oh, very. She won't shut up about her first grandchild. I'm happy for you too. You all deserve the best." Detective Crawford glanced around. "Besides my best wishes, I came by to pass on the news. The police are trying their best to keep it under wraps to not cause panic, but we've had reports of dead people coming back to life. Humans at their own funerals. Ain't that something?"

Iris gulped. Icarus was back at work—this had to be his doing. But why bring all these people back to life? What was he planning to do with the dead bodies, and where were they now?

"Weird," Gemma said. "Do you have any leads?"

"None," Detective Crawford replied. "We just assumed it was a coroner's error at first, that these people were really still alive, but there have been too many cases now to think it's coincidental. Do your people know anything about this?"

King Tedros and Fairy Godmother Odelia shared a look, then their eyes flitted to Iris. Were they going to tell the detective the truth about Icarus? Everyone else shook their heads, having no idea.

"Sorry, Detective," King Tedros lied. "We're just as stumped as you are."

"Too bad. I thought magic was at work here, but maybe we missed something." Detective Crawford sighed. "And I mean, these people were really dead. The coroner confirmed it at the autopsies. Then, at their own funerals, they came out of their caskets and ambled down the street. The why and how of it all, plus where they are now, is a mystery."

"Those poor families," Princess Esme murmured. "No one should have to see their family member's body come back to life and walk off like that. If we see or hear anything, we'll let you know."

"Thank you, I'd appreciate that. Well, I'm heading home for the evening." Detective Crawford walked to the door. "Be careful, all of you. These streets just keep getting weirder and more dangerous by the day. The Exterminators are still an issue too, one we're keeping an eye on."

"Good," Noah said, walking his father outside. "Because Michael Bond and his men are unstable. I still can't believe you didn't find anything solid at the house ..."

As they chatted about the situation on the step, Iris gestured at King Tedros and Fairy Godmother Odelia. "Can I talk to you both in the kitchen again? Alone?"

They nodded, separating from the group as the others continued to murmur over their shoulders. The kitchen was empty this time of night as the king and his fairy godmother took their seats at the table. Iris stayed standing, crossing her arms.

"Why didn't you tell Detective Crawford about Icarus?" Iris demanded. "This is so obviously his doing. He's bringing these people back to life for some reason."

"Not so loud," King Tedros hissed, glancing over his shoulder. No one was spying on them. "And think about it, General. If the humans find out one of our own is behind this, bringing their loved ones back to life and perverting them, they'd hate us even more."

"I know secrecy isn't ideal, but it's the best thing at the moment," Fairy Godmother Odelia said. "There's a reason Icarus has been hidden for centuries. We can only hope you discover his whereabouts on your patrols and find some way to end him—quickly and quietly—before it escalates."

"That's a lot on my shoulders," Iris muttered. "Asking me to kill an immortal when we have no idea whether he can be killed or not. And I think the situation has already escalated—more dead people have been stolen. We need a better plan, damn it!"

Iris had never taken that tone with her superiors before. She was always dutiful, always loyal and respectful. But this situation was different.

It could end the world.

King Tedros sighed. "I know, Iris. I wish there was a better way. But we have no other options. Please, continue your patrols tonight. Be extra cautious. Icarus still remains a priority, despite the Exterminators ramping up their violence. The immortal must be stopped."

Without giving her a chance to respond, King Tedros and Fairy Godmother Odelia left the kitchen, chatting with the others in the main hall. Iris couldn't ask any more questions in front of them, so she waited a few hours until they all went to bed. When it was past midnight, Iris made sure her armor and sword were ready and left.

After searching the streets for hours, she found no evidence of Icarus—or Sapphira and Kyler. All three of those disappearances bothered her. She hoped that Kyler and Sapphira would come to their senses and return on their own. She neglected to tell King Tedros, hoping it would be true.

Iris headed back shortly after that, making it to the church without incident. The guards were on patrol and let her know that everything was fine. She got into her bed quietly—avoiding waking up her people—and fell asleep. In the morning, her alarm scared her. As she walked into the kitchen, yearning for coffee, she shook her head when she spotted King Tedros and Fairy Godmother Odelia.

They seemed to understand the signal—that neither Icarus nor the lost guards had been found.

As she ate her breakfast, wondering where they all could be, Iris thought back to Michael's warning. They only had two days left now to leave Toronto—the clock was ticking. And she was nervous to see what his version of World War Three included.

After breakfast, Noah turned on the broadcast of Prime

Minister Lin on his phone. Once again, she called for peace, but it seemed to fall on deaf ears. Then Noah went back to the Exterminator's YouTube page, finding another video.

"Hey, General?" he called out, patting the pew next to him. "Come see this. That Lisa woman posted a video on the Exterminator's account."

Iris walked over, leaning over the pew to watch the video. Lisa sat in the same basement—their center of operations— and held up her phone, showing pictures of Lisa and Grant kissing. Just the thought of Lisa and Grant ever being intimate made Iris's blood boil, even if they weren't together anymore.

"... and he's just like those other two. Noah Crawford and Ian Whitman," Lisa was saying. "Grant Thatcher is nothing but a dirty freak lover. He's dating one of them now, their general named Iris. Stay away from them all—they're dangerous."

When the screen turned black, Noah set his phone down. "That's where the video ends. She just wanted to bash your relationship, it seems."

"Figures," Iris muttered. "Now the entire world will know me and Grant are a couple. He didn't seem too concerned about it, which was sweet, but I still am. Whether we like it or not, everyone who associates with us is a target. The Bhatias included."

It wasn't just about their safety—this situation had grown bigger than all of them. They had friends and a city to protect.

Iris felt like she carried the weight of the world on her shoulders as she helped her guards clean and cook the entire day. Princess Esme and Noah tried to keep things light by chatting about the baby, but everyone was still worried.

Wait until they learn about Icarus, Iris thought, dusting and wiping down the kitchen.

When dinnertime rolled around, Grant knocked at the door. Iris was glad to see his face on her doorstep again—even if their relationship put him in danger. It was a nice little break—a beautiful distraction—from the world falling apart all around them.

Almost like Grant was a dazzling ray of light through the darkest thunderstorm.

CHAPTER 23

After a hug and a kiss, Iris said goodbye to her people and left the church with Grant. They walked hand-in-hand. Even on a Sunday around dinnertime, the streets of Toronto bustled with people.

"We'll have to take the subway," Grant said, glancing over at Iris. "My apartment's a bit far, which is why I usually bike. But I wanted to show you the subway. Did you have any underground transportation like that back home?"

"No. Well, just dragons and some other magical animals, like I said. Never any busses or cars."

"I'm really sad I won't get to see that. Anyway, follow me."

Grant took her deeper into the city, then they found the entrance to the subway. It led underground—though not as deep as Fairhaven. Once there, they rode an escalator to reach the tracks. Construction crews were patching up leaky holes and cracks in the flooring.

"The subway really took a hit when Fairhaven was destroyed," Grant said, paying the fare at the gate so they could both get past. "I'm glad we didn't lose the subway. Toronto really needs it."

As Iris listened, more people eventually saw them, pointing and murmuring. Grant pulled Iris closer to him—a sweet gesture. But the staring was still getting on Iris's nerves.

"I assume you've seen the Exterminator's YouTube channel? The group that Michael Bond's in charge of?" Iris whispered. "Lisa posted a video not that long ago. She exposed our relationship to the whole world."

Grant nodded, waiting for the subway. "I saw. Hard not to. Guess that explains the increased number of stares. But the way I see it, people are going to talk anyway. May as well give them something to talk about."

"I just worry about your safety. About you dating me publicly now that Lisa exposed us."

Grant squeezed her hand, giving her a smile. "It's like I said —I chose my side. And one day, I think history will look back on me fondly. It's all these other hateful people who are in the wrong."

Iris agreed, then the subway arrived a minute later. People pushed and shoved, getting onto the train as Grant pulled Iris with him. They found two quiet seats near the back and waited for the train to depart. A few people onboard whispered about them, but fortunately, they were left alone.

The only person who looked happy to see them was a baby, maybe ten months old, being carried on his mother's shoulder. He had short blond hair and dimples that would make anyone swoon. He was staring at Iris, grinning at her with small baby teeth. His mother didn't notice as she continued to stare out the window while rocking her baby.

"Wow, that baby sure seems to love you," Grant whispered. "This is why I became a teacher. Kids are so pure—so sweet. They don't hate like adults do."

"Agreed. I don't have much experience with babies, but it's nice to know I don't scare at least one of them."

Grant laughed. "He's too cute. You want kids one day?"

Iris paused. "I don't know. I've never been asked that question. I suppose, with the right man ... yes, I think I do. That is, if the world gets its act together and stops seeing my people as villains. I don't want to bring a baby into a world where we're still a target. I'm concerned enough about Princess Esme's child."

"I understand that. But good to know." Grant stretched, placing an arm around Iris's shoulder. "I want kids too. But like you said, when the world is a bit more stable."

Iris nodded, grateful her people could have children with humans if they wanted to. It was an option for the future, at least. An opportunity. If they could just take care of the Exterminators and stop Icarus for good.

When the subway arrived at its destination fifteen minutes later—with Grant explaining the stops—they got off, then walked up the stairs to reach the surface again. Grant had taken Iris into a busy part of town, full of apartment skyscrapers and families out for walks.

"My apartment's this way," Grant said, gently guiding Iris down the street. "I think you'll like it—it's real cozy. I've been thinking of getting a cat, but I'm not sure if I have enough time. I'm so busy with my students. And, you know, dating an incredible woman."

Iris blushed. "I've never had a pet myself. A cat or a dog would be wonderful."

And a dog would provide the church with a bit more protection. Iris thought about it, wondering if bringing a pet into their fold was a good idea.

"Maybe we could adopt one together?" Grant asked. "Unless it's too soon. Let me know if it is—I don't want to rush you."

"It doesn't feel too soon at all."

Grant smiled. "Good, it doesn't to me either. It feels ... right. Like this is what I've been waiting for my whole life."

Iris said nothing, though she felt the same. She hadn't known love was something she wanted until it had landed right in front of her. And now, she had no intention of letting go—the danger be damned.

When they reached a tall apartment building, Grant used a key card to gain access to the building. The lobby had several benches, mailboxes, and an elevator to ride to the different floors. Grant led Iris to the closest elevator, then pressed the button for the third level.

"Here we go," Grant said as the elevator ascended. "Your place is bigger than mine, but this is home for me. And I think it's pretty fantastic."

"It's got you in it, so I know it is."

Grant laughed. "Aw, shucks—you'll make a guy blush."

Iris smiled as the elevator arrived on the third floor, then they walked down the corridor. The hall was quiet and deserted—something Iris was grateful for, as Grant led her to a door at the end of the hallway. Reaching into his pocket for his keys, he then unlocked the door with a gentle squeak.

"Here we are," he said. "My home is your home. Please, make yourself comfortable."

Iris nodded, entering the apartment. Grant had been right as he showed her around—it was cozy with one bedroom, a small bathroom, a living room, and a kitchen with an attached dining area. The balcony had the perfect view of Toronto and all its people out on the streets. Grant closed the door behind them, then placed his keys down on the coffee table.

"Sorry about the mess," Grant said, clearing off the couch that had tests he was grading. "Just school stuff. You can have a seat if you'd like. Want a drink?"

Iris nodded, sitting down. She felt comfortable enough to

remove her armor and expose the thin pants and t-shirt she had on underneath. "Just water, please. Thank you."

When she noticed Grant staring at her, she raised an eyebrow, then he laughed. "Sorry, sorry—don't mean to stare. It's just... it's a nice look. To finally see you let your hair down."

Iris sighed as Grant entered the kitchen and grabbed a water bottle out of the refrigerator for her. "I haven't felt like I could since we got here. I've got the armor on constantly in case something bad happens—taking it off only to shower or go skating with you. But ... I don't know. I feel safe here."

Grant handed her the water bottle, smiling. "That's what I like to hear. Now, is pasta all right?"

"Never had it," Iris said, sipping her water, "but I should learn to like human food. As much as I like their coffee, anyway. Do you need my help?"

Grant shook his head as he grabbed a package of pasta from his cupboard. "No, thank you—you're my guest. Let me treat you for once. Feel free to turn on the TV while you wait for dinner."

Iris nodded, reaching for the remote as she heard Grant begin to cook over her shoulder. She flipped through the channels—learning about human sports and sci-fi shows—before landing on the news.

"... and authorities are still investigating the theft of several kegs of gunpowder from a local Toronto warehouse," the reporter said, standing outside the warehouse on the docks. "They haven't found any connection to the Fairhaven outsiders who stole bombs to blow up their magical kingdom underneath our city, though they don't deny the similarities. They want to remind the public that the ones who committed the bombing are dead or still safely in jail. No suspects are being considered at the moment, but police urge anyone with information to come forward ..."

Gunpowder stolen? Iris frowned, wondering what that was about. And if it related to the co-conspirators after all. But they were in jail—the reporter confirmed it. So, who else would want to steal gunpowder?

Iris changed the channel, trying to find something more upbeat when she came across a show about puppies. While she was thinking about adopting a dog, a knock sounded on the door. Grant walked toward it with a towel over his shoulder as the pasta cooked on the stove.

"I have no idea who that could be," Grant said to Iris as he walked by. "I wasn't expecting any visitors, just you."

Iris watched as he looked through the peephole, then smiled. He opened the door and embraced two people who stood on his welcome mat. Iris rose to her feet, then walked over as she noticed two elderly men standing there.

Both men were dressed similarly in jeans, sweaters, and sneakers, carrying shopping bags. One had dark skin with graying hair, while the other was pale and bald. Then Iris noticed the gleam off the wedding rings on their left hands.

"Dads! You're here," Grant said, letting them into the apartment. He shut the door behind them and gestured at Iris. "This is Iris Ambrose, my girlfriend. I invited her over for dinner tonight. Iris, meet my fathers—Stephen and Drew Thatcher. They're both retired teachers. It's easy to see why I chose my career path."

"So nice to finally meet you," Stephen said, the one with graying hair. He shook Iris's hand immediately. "Grant has gushed so much about you."

"And we're sorry to just drop in like this. We had no idea you two were having dinner," Drew said, glancing at Grant. "We were just shopping in the area and wanted to see our lovely son. Really, this wasn't planned at all. Do you want us to come back at another time? To give you two some privacy?"

Grant glanced at Iris. She felt bad turning them away, so she shook her head. "No, it's all right—please stay. Very nice to meet you both."

"Thank you, you too." Drew set his bags down against the door. "What are you cooking? Smells heavenly."

"Pasta," Grant replied. "Want some?"

"Well, we did have a late lunch," Stephen said, stealing a glance at his husband, "but what the heck; we'll both have a little bit. Grant's cooking is amazing, Iris—you're in for a treat. He was always cooking and baking growing up. Why don't we chat for a bit while he makes dinner?"

Iris nodded, leading the two men to the couch. She taught them a little about her culture as Grant continued to cook the pasta behind them. Then it was Iris's turn to ask questions, curious about the men who raised Grant and his sister.

"So, you have another child, yes?" Iris asked. "A daughter named Marissa?"

"That's right," Stephen said. "She and Grant are biologically related—twins, actually. She's blessed us with two beautiful grandchildren. Did Grant tell you about his adoption?"

"He did, yes. That his mother was a teenager who gave her children up for adoption. And the father was her much older high school teacher."

"Creepy, isn't it?" Drew shook his head. "But yes, that's the story. Steve and I weren't even married back then—gay marriage wasn't legal in Canada yet. It was a struggle to adopt both of them, but when we saw their cute faces in the hospital, we knew we wanted a family. Grant and Marissa were worth the fight."

Stephen nodded, placing a hand over his husband's. "Oh, definitely. You see, we were both at the hospital that day because my father was dying of cancer. And then we stumbled across the hospital room where Grant and

Marissa were being born. We found out the teenage mother was giving them up for adoption and things happened from there. A long legal battle, but it turned out for the best. I'd like to think my father had a hand in it all. Somehow."

"Maybe he did. Marissa and I were lucky you adopted us," Grant said with a smile from the kitchen. "Dinner's ready, by the way. Come and get it."

Iris nodded, rising to her feet before she took a seat at the dining room table. Grant plated the food and poured the drinks —pasta primavera with a baguette and wine—and passed it around the dinner table. Grant sat next to Iris as his fathers sat across from them, reaching for their forks.

"Looks amazing," Iris said, taking a bite. They taught her how to twirl it on the fork first. "Tastes that way too. I'll have to tell the others about this. We've been growing our own vegetables and experimenting with human food."

Grant smiled. "I'd be happy to cook it for you all anytime."

"Isn't that sweet?" Stephen asked Drew, then took a sip of his wine. "They're adorable."

Drew nodded, taking another bite of his pasta. "And I'm glad to see all the naysayers haven't kept you apart. We saw that YouTube video of Lisa badmouthing you two. We never liked that woman. And we know parents are upset you brought Iris to school too."

Grant sighed, twirling his pasta around his fork. "It's been tough, yes. I wish Lisa would find someone else and move on. But I love Iris. I wouldn't trade her in for anything."

The table went silent. Iris glanced at Grant, unable to believe he had said the L-word. Stephen and Drew just smiled at each other.

Iris had never been in love before, had never even considered love as an option in her life, but as she explored her own feelings, warmth seeped through her body. "You ... you love me?"

Grant smiled. "That sorta slipped out. Wasn't planning to break the news at an impromptu dinner with my parents, but yes. I love you, Iris. I'm not one to believe in love at first sight, but I'm pretty sure it happened when I first saw you. Now, you don't have to say it back if you don't feel it—"

"I love you too, Grant," Iris said, the words tumbling out of her mouth. More importantly, she meant it, from the deepest corners of her heart. "I really do."

Grant beamed even wider, reaching for her hand. "Then that makes me happy. Best dinner ever."

"I'll say," Stephen said, both he and Drew smiling. "We're happy for you two. Grant hasn't had the easiest life, but it's nice to see him happy."

Grant broke off a piece of baguette. "Dad's talking about me growing up bullied because I had two fathers. That was a hard time, yes, but I like to think it made me a kinder person. And led me right to finding Iris."

"Silver linings, eh?" Drew winked at Grant.

"Definitely," Grant said with a nod. "And since you've met my fathers, Iris, we'll have to set something up with my sister. She works a lot, but I'll send her a text—ask her when the best time is to meet you. If that's okay."

Iris nodded. "I don't mind at all. If she's as lovely as your parents, I'm sure I'll have a good time."

Stephen giggled. "Aw, thank you, Iris. You're lovely as well. I can't understand why so many people have a problem with your kind."

"Ignorance, honey." Drew took another bite of his pasta. "It's been an issue with the human race forever."

Grant made a sound of agreement in his throat. "It has. I try to encourage kindness in my students because of it."

"And we're so proud of you," Stephen said, then turned to Iris. "Well, since you met us, it's only fair to ask. When do we get to meet your parents? We'd love to meet more of your kind."

"If it isn't too soon," Drew said with a little laugh. "My husband's just excited. I am too."

Grant cleared his throat. "Actually, Dads ... that's not possible. When Senator Remus blew up Fairhaven, he killed her parents in the process. Along with everyone else down there, tragically."

Both of Grant's fathers looked shocked, their mouths falling open.

"Oh, you poor dear," Stephen said, leaning across the table to reach for her hand. "I'm so sorry. And sorry that I brought it up."

"It's okay. You didn't know." Iris shifted in her seat. "I miss them a lot."

"Of course you do. Iris, again—I'm so sorry." Grant placed a comforting hand on her shoulder, then reached for his wine. "Uh, Dads, tell Iris how you two met. It's a funny story."

Iris knew Grant was trying to cheer her up. It was sweet, but nothing could make her forget her parents. She forced a smile and tried to have a good time anyway.

Stephen laughed. "It really is. You go ahead, Drew. You tell it better than me."

"All right, all right. It was a sunny day, and I was rollerblading downtown. Rollerblading was popular back then, you know, but I wasn't very good at it. When I tripped and fell on the sidewalk, this handsome young man came over to make sure I was all right. But as he did, a giant seagull pooped on my head! Oh, I was so mortified, but he was kind and made me feel at ease ..."

As Iris listened to the story, holding Grant's hand on the table, she realized she wanted this—a simple life with the man she loved, their friends, and some privacy, laughing over good food and wine. She only wished her parents could be there to enjoy the happier moments.

But when Iris heard the ticking clock on the wall, reminding her of Michael's threat, she had a feeling their enemies weren't going to allow that.

CHAPTER 24

Iris chatted with Grant and his parents over dinner, laughing at their family stories and finally feeling like she belonged somewhere. After Grant served them all dessert —strawberry cheesecake, which Iris tried for the first time and loved—his fathers bid them goodbye and left the apartment.

"I'll call you. Get home safe!" Grant called to his parents down the hall, then shut the door and turned to Iris. "Sorry about that. I swear—I didn't know they were going to drop by tonight. I *did* want you to meet my dads at some point, but I would've rather given you a heads up."

Iris shook her head. "Don't worry about it, Grant—it was fine. And you were right, they were lovely people. They didn't seem to care that I wasn't from your world at all."

"I know. My dads are the best." Grant smiled. "Anyway, just so you know ... I meant what I said before. About loving you. I've felt it growing for a while and then it just slipped out."

"I feel it too." Iris reached for his hand, squeezing it tight. "While I have no experience with love—or humans for that matter—I'm glad I found you. That you're my first love."

"Well, I *do* have experience with love, but I'm very glad I found you. I wish you were my first, but all the former loves led me to you. Which I'm thankful for. Even Lisa." Grant reached for his smartphone. "And like I said, I really want you to meet my sister. Let me text her."

He typed into his phone while Iris waited patiently for his sister to respond. It took her a few minutes but she finally did, agreeing to meet up at a local coffee shop tomorrow morning.

"Perfect, she'll be there. I think she's really going to like you." Grant gestured at the couch. "You have time to stay a little bit? We could watch some movies before I take you home."

"Sounds great. What's your favorite?"

After Grant put on *School of Rock* with actor Jack Black, he explained the story and how it was one of the movies that made him want to be a teacher. They cuddled on the couch. Iris lost track of time at one point, she was so involved in the movie. When she glanced over at Grant during a funny scene, wanting to see if he laughing like her, he was already staring at her.

"What?" Iris asked. "Do I have food on my face?"

Grant laughed. "No, no—you're perfect. I'm just ... really lucky I found you, that's all."

"I'm glad I found you too. After Fairhaven was destroyed ... I never thought I'd feel happiness again, only pain." Iris shook her head. "But you changed that, Grant. Thank you."

"My pleasure. You changed my life too, you know. In the best way possible."

As they stared at each other, Grant's gaze darted to Iris's lips. He captured her mouth with his, exploring. She met him gasp for gasp, and they got lost in the moment. Before she knew it, they were making out on the couch. Iris had never been kissed like that before—with so much passion and love.

Grant pulled away first, breathless. "I'd really like to take this to the bedroom ... but only if you're comfortable with that. I know you've never done anything like this before, so I wanted to make sure."

Him being a perfect gentleman only turned Iris on more. Her whole body felt like it was on fire in the best way as she reached for his hand, pulling him to his feet. "Grant, I've never been more sure of anything."

He grinned, then leaned back in to kiss her. Their hands tangled in each other's hair as they kissed all the way to the bedroom. And for the next hour, they showed each other just how much they cared—over and over again.

When they were spent and exhausted, Grant rolled toward Iris, both their naked bodies covered in the sheets. "That was incredible."

Iris nodded. "Definitely. I couldn't have asked for a better first time."

Grant kissed her again, softly. "I love you, Iris."

"And I love you, Grant. I had no idea all this would happen when I first came to your world."

"Sometimes, life will surprise you." Grant winked, then stood and reached for his clothes that had fallen onto the floor. "Not to kick you out or anything, but I should get you home. The city gets more dangerous after sundown. But I'll be back tomorrow morning so you can meet my sister."

Iris pulled her clothes and armor back on, then kissed his cheek. "Sounds great. Thanks for a perfect evening. And your dads were right—you're an amazing chef. Good at other things too."

It was Grant's turn to blush as he led Iris out of his apartment, locking the door behind them. They took the familiar path down the elevator and out of his building. Still hand-in-hand, they rode the subway back to Iris's part of town. Grant guided her back to the church to make sure she got there safely.

"Tell everyone I said hi," Grant said, kissing her softly on the lips. "Sweet dreams, Iris."

She wished him the same, then entered the church. She found her people planning more fundraisers to help charities, designing the nursery, and playing some board games they had found in the church's closet. Gemma was the first one to approach her, smiling.

"Hey, Iris. You're glowing, you know," she said, looking her up and down. "Did you have a good time with Grant?"

"The perfect time, actually. I'm his girlfriend now. And ... we made love for the first time."

Gemma's eyes widened. "Wow—that's amazing! I'm so happy for you two. See? I knew I was right when I told you that you and Grant would be cute together. I knew you liked him ever since I saw you sniffing that note."

Iris blushed, glancing around to make sure no one heard that. "Please—not so loud. But yes, I'm very happy and so is he. I'm going to meet his sister tomorrow. Accidentally met his parents over dinner. And it went well."

"Really? That's a big step. Glad it was all fine." Gemma gestured over her shoulder. "Want to play some human board games? We just discovered *Sorry*. It's pretty fun! I can even teach you some board games I learned while working at Barbara's bookstore."

When Iris glanced over at her people sitting on the floor, laughing as they played some brightly colored board game, it *did* look fun. But something else was on Iris's mind—something important.

"No thanks. You go ahead," Iris said. "I'm just going to take it easy."

Gemma nodded and returned to the group. Ian kissed her cheek as she joined the board game again. And for once, Iris understood the love they shared. It was the same kind of love she had for Grant.

And she would do anything to keep him safe—which meant she needed to stop the Exterminators for good. Proving they had killed Bobby Blevins and his gang would land them in jail and get them off the streets, something that Iris found very appealing.

She walked down the hallway, finding the two fairy godmothers in a small room. They were chatting and making some magical healing potions. They sprinkled in some of the herbs from the garden, then said a special incantation that made it magical. The pot Fairy Godmother Odelia was stirring lit up in a purple spray of light.

"This should help Esme's morning sickness and provide nutrients to the growing baby," she explained to Blanche. "She shouldn't throw up as much."

Blanche nodded. "That's good. Say ... when the baby is born, you think King Tedros might let me stop being a fairy godmother? Gemma already gave me her blessing, and I think the birth of this child will usher in a new age—"

"We'll talk about it at a later time, Blanche. Right now, every person is needed around here. You know this."

Blanche sighed but dropped the issue, continuing to stir her own magical pot. Iris cleared her throat. "Sorry to bother you ladies, but I need a favor, Fairy Godmother Odelia."

"Not bothering at all." Fairy Godmother Odelia abandoned her pot, stepping toward Iris. "Glad you're back too. Did you enjoy your date with Grant? Gemma mentioned it."

"Yes—it went well. But I need a potion made."

She frowned. "It's not a love spell, is it? We're trying to keep our promise to Prime Minister Lin and not use magic on the surface. The only potions we're making are for our own people, things like cures for nausea and headaches. And the potions we used on the garden to make the plants produce quickly."

"No, no, nothing like that. I definitely didn't need a love potion to fall in love. Anyway, I know you're not making anything else, but I was hoping there would be a potion to find hidden DNA or blood residue after it's been cleaned up?"

"What do you mean, dear?" Fairy Godmother Odelia blinked. "What are you using this for?"

Iris knew no one would ever let her return to that house in the countryside—if she could even find it again. She was lucky to have escaped the first time. But Iris knew the bodies of Bobby Blevins and his crew had to be somewhere, and maybe magic could help. If used for good, Iris didn't see the harm.

"It's for Icarus," Iris lied, making sure Blanche wasn't listening over Odelia's shoulder. "For another patrol. If he's hurt or killed anyone, the potion may be able to find proof."

"Hmm. I suppose I can see how that would be helpful. All right—I think I can whip something up. But don't tell anyone I'm doing this."

Iris nodded as Fairy Godmother Odelia walked back to her pot, stirring in some ingredients while muttering a rhyming incantation. Iris didn't know how it all worked, but it got the job done. A few minutes later, a blue liquid formed and Fairy Godmother Odelia scooped it into a vial. She tightened the lid and passed it to Iris.

"Do be careful, dear," Fairy Godmother Odelia urged. "And let no one see this potion."

Iris took the potion, tucking it into the pocket of her armor. The vial was small enough to fit. "Will do, thank you. I'll let you know if I'm successful."

Fairy Godmother Odelia nodded, then returned to making other harmless potions with Blanche. The other fairy godmother kept trying to find ways to get out of her job.

Minding her own business, Iris walked into the main hall with the potion, then slipped out through the kitchen's back door before anyone could question her.

She rode the subway again, using what little money she had for the ride. Whatever had been left from what Grant had given her for the taxis. Without Grant around, another human, the stares and sneers were even meaner. Iris ignored them, riding at the back of the train as far out of the city as it would take her.

Once she got off at the last stop, she walked out of the subway, then headed for the countryside on foot. She racked her brain, trying to remember the route. Some landmarks and street signs eventually started to look familiar. It took a while to make it there, then she walked down the dirt-covered back roads in search of the house to which she had been taken. Things were much quieter and peaceful in the country, and she appreciated not being stared at.

After traveling a few miles, Iris recognized it—the house where Blevins and his gang had taken her. It sent a chill down her spine. While usually brave, Iris had a sinking feeling of dread in her stomach as she approached the run-down country house. She reached for her sword and searched everywhere but didn't find anyone on the property.

She broke the window to get inside, then glanced around. Michael Bond and his Exterminators must've sanitized the place well. It smelled like lemon cleaner and there were no dead bodies, blood, or surgical tools left behind. Only the bullet holes in the walls and the damaged paint remained.

Except for those bullet holes, it looked like a normal house in the country—far different from the first time Iris had seen it.

"The police couldn't find anything, but they didn't have magic on their side," she muttered to herself, pulling the potion out of her armor's pocket. "Come on—show me something.

Blood, a note, some used clothes. Anything that ties to what really happened here."

She removed the cap from the potion, then poured the blue liquid around the room. It turned to a blue mist before it moved by itself toward the back door. Iris followed, letting the potion lead her out into the large forest behind the house. The blue mist continued to spread through the forest—like it was leading her somewhere. A magical GPS.

Iris kept a hand on her sword, following the mist through the trees. She looked down and noticed drag marks on the ground—as if something, maybe bodies, had been pulled through the woods. Why hadn't the police checked there? She didn't know whether to attribute it to incompetence or their own prejudice.

There had to be officers on the force who hated Iris and her people. Maybe they didn't see the tracks because they didn't want to.

Whatever the reason, Iris continued following the blue mist and drag marks until it led to a small cave. There was nothing inside—not even any animals—but the mist ended there. The cave had to be important somehow.

Falling to her knees and getting dirt on her armor, she touched the ground around the cave and found it disturbed—as if someone had dug it up, buried something, and then covered it again. Using her hands, Iris began digging, looking for anything. Then she found something.

Then the pungent smell hit her nostrils, confirming it was a dead body.

She removed more of the dirt, finding several dead bodies buried deep in the soil around the cave. It was Bobby Blevins and his men—shot to death and already rotting, nothing but a pile of corpses. Iris rose to her feet and plugged her nose.

She had actually found it—the proof she needed to get the

police to charge Michael Bond with murder. And all she needed was a little magic.

Turning back toward the woods, she ran through the trees, then stopped on the road. She waved her hands in the air, flagging down a truck as it passed. The truck driver—a burly middle-aged man—looked afraid of Iris, slowing down so he wouldn't hit her.

"Please, call the police," Iris urged. "I found several bodies."

The man's eyes widened. Although it didn't seem like he trusted her, he called the police quickly. They showed up twenty minutes later, arriving in several police cars. Iris gestured for them to follow her through the woods and toward the cave.

"Over there," Iris pointed at the soil. "The bodies of Bobby Blevins and his men, just like I told you. Michael Bond shot them to death after Bobby kidnapped me and brought me here. My guess? They covered up the blood and buried the bodies themselves far from the house, hoping the police wouldn't find it."

One of the police officers inspected the bodies, then turned to Iris. "And you found them when we couldn't, how? How did you know to look here?"

Iris hesitated, wondering if she should tell them about the magic potion she'd used. Although they weren't supposed to use magic on the surface, she had no choice. She had no other explanation for knowing where to look.

"I used a magic potion," Iris said, figuring honesty was the best policy, "one that could sense death and blood evidence that was cleaned up. I followed it out here."

The police officer crossed his arms. "And how do we know you didn't plant these bodies yourself? Nothing proves Michael Bond did this."

"It proves I wasn't lying about my story. Recover the bodies

—run DNA tests at your lab. Use science instead of magic. Maybe you'll find something."

The officer shook his head. "All this sounds like you're trying to frame Michael Bond. If you ask me, I don't trust your kind. I don't think the prime minister was right to keep you all here."

"Well, I'm sorry you feel that way. But I swear to you— Michael Bond did this. What about all the bullet holes and damaged paint? You must've noticed that. You can clearly see there was a fight here. And since my people have never had guns, it can't be us."

The police officer shrugged. "How do I know it wasn't there before? This house is run-down. Old. Could've been made by the previous owners or something. Or, hell, maybe *you* made those holes to cast suspicion on Michael Bond."

This cop had an answer for everything, the stubborn fool. Iris huffed. "No, those bullet holes are from the gunfight that happened here. After I was kidnapped. Michael Bond murdered Bobby Blevins and his men for wanting magic. He's dangerous and should be behind bars."

The officer rolled his eyes. "We'll just see about that. I'll call my superiors—and the prime minister. They can decide what to do with you."

As the officer walked away, making a few phone calls, Iris knew no one would believe her, especially as the hatred for her people spread through every part of the city. And it was frustrating to have found the bodies but not be able to link Michael Bond to the crime.

As she stared down at the graves, she knew this case was far from over.

CHAPTER 25

More cop cars arrived shortly after, then Detective Crawford and Prime Minister Lin. They chatted with the officers on duty to learn what happened before walking through the home to meet with Iris near the cave. And Prime Minister Lin *did* not look happy.

"I thought I told your people to stay inside?" she asked, crossing her arms. "To lay low? You aren't making my job easy, you know."

Iris sighed. "I know—and I'm sorry, Prime Minister. But I had to come back here. Where Bobby Blevins took me. And using magic, I was able to find the bodies that your officers missed."

"I can tell you right now," Detective Crawford said, peering down at the graves, "that magic of yours ain't gonna hold up in court. I believe your story, but the public definitely won't."

"The detective is right," Prime Minister Lin said, blocking her nose. "My goodness, do those bodies stink. And while finding the bodies definitely helps the police—along with the bullet holes—there's still no firm connection to Michael Bond and his Exterminators. Something you'll need if you want to convict him. The officers will still look for DNA, but I'm not sure it'll help."

Iris nodded, knowing that already. Who would've thought it would be so hard to prove to the world that Michael Bond was a murderer?

"What about his new YouTube channel?" Iris asked. "He and his followers have been spreading lies about us."

"Like I told the detective's son on the phone," Prime Minister Lin began, her gaze everywhere but the pile of decomposing corpses, "he does have free speech rights. He and his group are still on our radar, however, and we're keeping a close eye on them. We just can't act until he does something criminal. *Provably* criminal, of course."

Of course. Iris wanted to scream, feeling like she had missed the chance to get a dangerous man off the streets. Dangerous to her people *and* everyone else.

"The coroner will take the bodies away now. You should return to the church," Prime Minister Lin said. "In the meantime, do be careful around that teacher, will you? Grant something? I heard from the YouTube video that you're dating him. You wouldn't want to put his life in jeopardy."

"I know that—believe me, Prime Minister," Iris said. "I'm trying to keep him safe. But back to Michael Bond. He gave us seventy-two hours to leave Toronto. That was almost two days ago now. Tomorrow will mark the last twenty-four hours. Shouldn't we, I don't know, plan for the worst?"

"Yes, which is why I'm urging you to stay inside. Keep your heads down and don't draw any attention to yourselves. And don't tell members of the public that Princess Esme is pregnant. That may cause even more concern." Prime Minister Lin shook her head. "My job these days just gets more challenging. I'll have an officer drop you off at your church, Iris, where you should stay for the time being. We'll notify you of any progress."

"I'll drive her back," Detective Crawford said. "Then I can say hello to my son too."

"Very well. Get back safely, both of you. We must all be on our guard these days."

On that, they could agree.

"Wait," Iris began. "Shouldn't you change our location, perhaps to a new safehouse? Or put a patrol of officers outside our church? I feel like there's more you could be doing to protect my people—"

"I'm afraid I can't. Resources are stretched thin these days," Prime Minister Lin said. "But I'll let you know if that changes. Take care, Iris."

Detective Crawford gestured for Iris to follow, then they took the long way around the house so they wouldn't contaminate any possible evidence. Police officers were inside, checking the place over again for anything they might've missed the first time before collecting the bodies. But Michael Bond and his men had been thorough—Iris doubted they would find anything useful. The bullet holes weren't enough.

"I'm gonna keep searching for evidence to prove what really happened at that house. I believe you, Iris. And I'm real concerned about this countdown from Michael Bond you were talking about," Detective Crawford said, getting into the driver's seat of his unmarked police car. Iris joined him in the front and shut her door. "What do you think he's gonna do?"

Iris put her seatbelt on just as Detective Crawford pulled away from the house, the officers becoming smaller in their rear-view mirror. "I just don't know, Detective. But if the smoke bomb and murders were any indication, it's not going to be good. Maybe that stolen gunpowder is part of their sick plan too."

"Possibly, yes." Detective Crawford sighed as he drove farther away. "Look, maybe you oughta get out of Toronto—do what he says. I'm sure we can arrange some plane tickets for you all, move you into a safe house outta Canada or something. Just until the Exterminators are caught."

"I'm not sure running away is the answer, either," Iris replied, stealing a glance at Detective Crawford. "The prime minister doesn't think so. Besides, I have ... someone here I don't want to abandon. If we leave, then Michael Bond will have won. We can't have that."

"All right, all right. I see your point." Detective Crawford sighed, both hands on the steering wheel. "I just ... I want you all to be careful. Especially since I'm expecting my first grandchild now. I want to have the opportunity to meet them. I even called Noah, inviting him and Esme to stay with me and my wife, but he refused. Said he loved your people and wanted you all to stick together. He was adamant you'd overcome this by each other's side."

Iris smiled. That had been sweet of Noah—to not want to separate them, despite the dangers. He was a good man.

"Stubborn boy. Just like his old man," Detective Crawford grunted. "So, watch out for my son and his wife, all right?"

"With my life, Detective. You have my word."

That seemed to satisfy the detective, though Iris could tell he was still nervous. When they made it back to the city, he parked on the street, then he and Iris entered the church. The sun was beginning to set and all her people were cleaning up the church while getting ready for bed.

"Iris, hey—there you are," Gemma said, sweeping dust off the floor into a garbage can. "We all wondered where you went. What happened?"

Iris sighed. "I used Fairy Godmother Odelia's potion to find the bodies. You know, of Bobby Blevins and his men? Michael

Bond and his gang buried them near the cave in the woods behind that house in the country."

When the rest of her people heard the story, they came out of their rooms, murmuring. Fairy Godmother Odelia stepped forward. "So ... you lied to me about what the potion was going to be used for? And went to the place we told you to stay away from?"

"I did—and I'm sorry. But I had to go back there, to find the evidence the police missed. It didn't do much good, though. While finding the bodies was a step in the right direction, it still can't prove Michael Bond killed them. Not unless they find DNA by some miracle."

"And I'm telling you, I searched that country house from top to bottom," Detective Crawford said. "He and his men scrubbed that place clean. Not one trace of evidence to prove they were there. Oh, hello, Noah."

Noah came out of the side room and hugged his father. "Hi, Dad. Too bad about the lack of evidence."

"Yeah, I know. Damn it ..."

"Look, General, while we understand what you were trying to do," King Tedros said, "I'm still disappointed you went out there. And alone. If something had happened to you, we wouldn't have even known where you were."

Iris nodded. "I understand that, Your Majesty, but I didn't want to risk your lives. And I needed to find those bodies. It was bothering me."

King Tedros sighed. "Well, you found them. Now it's time to let the police do their jobs. I'm afraid I'll have to agree with what the prime minister has been saying all along—we should stay inside the church and not go out. Especially with Michael Bond's seventy-two-hour threat coming to a close."

"Smart," Detective Crawford said, turning to his son and Princess Esme. "You two stay safe, all right? Your mother and I would be devastated if anything happened to you. That son-of-a-bitch Bond comes around, you call me and I'll be here to defend you. Let me handle him—one human to another. If I have to kill him, at least the public won't blame your people."

"I don't want him dead," Princess Esme said. "That's a bit extreme. Yes, he killed Bobby Blevins, but murder isn't the answer. If we can avoid it, then we should."

"Like you avoided killing Senator Remus?" Iris asked. "Sometimes, murder is necessary. Maybe we should kill Michael Bond before he has a chance to do it to us."

And Icarus while they were at it—if he could even be killed. Iris filled with fury when she thought of all their enemies, making their lives harder on the surface. They needed to be dealt with one way or another. Iris felt like a hypocrite, knowing she had told Sapphira and Kyler that murder wasn't the answer, but these days, they were running out of options.

It was do or die.

"Let's not make any rash decisions tonight," King Tedros said. "Our safety is a priority, which is why we'll be staying inside. General, I don't want you conducting any patrols tonight for your missing guards. It can wait until it's safer to do so."

Iris nodded, not even knowing where to start looking for Sapphira and Kyler—not to mention Icarus. Those three had completely slipped through her fingers. Still hoping her guards would return on their own and right their wrongs, she held off telling the king for a little while again. She figured he had enough on his mind anyway.

"Well, I wish you all luck and safety," Detective Crawford said, hugging his son and Princess Esme. "Take care and we'll be in touch."

Noah walked his father to the door, making sure he got to his car safely. Then he locked the doors to the church again, and everyone got ready for bed. Iris's mind was still racing, worrying about her missing guards, Michael Bond's threat, and Icarus.

Naturally, she didn't get any sleep. She got out of bed the next morning to the sunlight peeking through the curtains of the sleeping quarters. She rubbed her eyes, feeling groggy and tired as she headed into the kitchen for some miracle juice—coffee. Iris glanced at the clock, watching it tick down like a bomb.

Twenty-four hours left for whatever Michael Bond is planning, she thought. It felt like time was ticking down to their execution.

Iris grabbed some cereal, then joined her people for breakfast in the main hall. Noah had his phone out and set on the news livestream again. Iris saw the words "BREAKING NEWS: FORMER PRIME MINISTER GARNEAU DEAD AT 88."

"Oh, shit," Iris muttered. "Is this related to us somehow? Or Michael Bond?"

Noah shook his head, eating toast on one of the pews with Princess Esme. "Nah, the prime minister already called. She said former Prime Minister Jean-Guy Garneau, who served Canada in the nineteen-eighties, died of cancer. Natural causes. His health had been declining for some time, long before your people got here."

"Good," Iris muttered. "I just hope they don't try to pin this on us."

"Me too," Gemma said, eating some yogurt. "Prime Minister Lin also said no DNA evidence was found on Bobby Blevins or his men. The lab rushed the autopsies."

Iris knew that was coming, yet she was still disappointed. It felt like they had missed their last chance to convict Michael Bond. He was a smart, devious man, making Iris wonder if they would ever expose him to the world.

"Apparently, Prime Minister Lin and the former PM were close," Noah said, watching his phone screen. "She'll be speaking at a funeral for him this afternoon. He'll be lying in state all around Canada for people to pay their respects, starting with Toronto today."

"Well, I'm sorry for her loss," Iris replied, finishing her cereal. "But a part of me is just glad we're not the constant news story anymore. For now, at least."

Noah nodded. "Agreed. But I'm sure it'll come back to your people—it always does."

"Maybe we should go pay our respects too?" Princess Esme asked, glancing around the room. "I'm still brainstorming ways to get on humanity's good side. Now that I'm growing another brain inside me, maybe I'll have even better ideas."

As she patted her stomach, King Tedros shook his head, sipping his coffee. "I don't think so—and Prime Minister Lin wouldn't appreciate it. Going out is always a risk, but especially in a crowd that large."

"But this could be our best chance to show how much we care," Princess Esme argued. "We could bring flowers—say a little prayer for the former PM. And give other people our condolences. Come on, Father, I'm really trying to repair relations here."

King Tedros still looked hesitant. "I don't know. Let me think on it."

As the main hall turned quiet, filled with only the chatter from the news station on Noah's phone and their chewing, a knock sounded on the door. Iris put her bowl and coffee down, then crept toward the door and looked through the peephole.

Grant stood on the step, wearing a blue shirt and jeans. He carried a briefcase for another day of work. Iris opened the door, smiling at him. He was like a breath of fresh air.

"Morning, Grant."

"Morning, beautiful." He leaned closer, kissing her cheek. "Ready to meet my sister? Just a quick cup of coffee for now. I have to be at work in about an hour. Monday morning, another school week."

Iris hesitated. "While I would love that ... both King Tedros and Prime Minister Lin are insisting we stay inside. For safety reasons, mostly. And this time, I really think I should listen. Not that sneaking out with you isn't fun, of course."

"I feel the same. Like two teenagers in love. But that seventy-two-hour threat is coming up soon, isn't it? Gah, I can't stand that Michael Bond. I hope you'll be all right." Grant pulled out his smartphone. "And no worries—I'll ask my sister to come here. We can just have coffee in the garden or something. Much safer for us all."

Iris nodded, moving aside to let Grant in. Maya and her parents waved at them from across the street. Iris waved back, grateful to have their friendship at least. Not many humans were offering it these days.

As Grant headed into the main hall, everyone said hello to him, then went back to watching the news. Gemma wiggled her eyebrows and made Iris blush. Iris followed Grant into the kitchen, craving some privacy.

"All right, my sister's on the way here. She completely understands the need for safety right now." Grant set his briefcase down on the table, then pulled Iris close. "How are you doing?"

"I'm okay," Iris said, breathing out. "Better now that you're here."

Grant kissed her sweetly on the lips. "The feeling is mutual. I feel like I don't come alive until you're in the room. As cheesy as that sounds."

"*Very* cheesy as you humans would say, but cute." Iris smiled, loving that Grant could pull out her playful energy. She had been stoic and formal for too long. "We could set up the table and chairs in the garden—make it feel like a coffee shop."

"That sounds like a great idea. I'll grab the table, you take the chairs."

Iris nodded, helping Grant carry everything out into the garden. It was fenced in and quiet, a nice reprieve from the insanity of the world. Iris poured three cups of steaming coffee and set them on the table before bringing out sugar and cream.

When another knock sounded on the door, Gemma came out to tell Iris. She and Grant nodded and walked back inside to open the door, letting his sister in. She was beautiful—long, dark hair, a pencil skirt with a blouse and heels, and a briefcase. Marissa resembled Grant, their nose and eyes identical.

"Sorry I'm late. The kids took forever to get out the door for school and work's hectic," Marissa said, holding up her buzzing phone. "Ah, you must be Iris. My brother has raved so much about you. And trust me, he doesn't talk about a woman unless it's true love."

Grant smiled, squeezing Iris's hand. "My sister is right. Iris, this is Marissa, my sister."

"Nice to meet you," Iris said, shaking her hand. "Thanks for coming here and understanding. We've got some coffee in the garden."

Marissa nodded, waving at all of Iris's people as she shut the door. They led Marissa into the garden where they took their seats at the small table. Her phone continued to go off, but she put it on silent for the time being and pushed it aside.

"Now, I want to know everything," Marissa said, leaning across the table. "About you, your people, how you met my brother. He told me a little but I want to hear it from you."

Iris nodded. "Well, all right. I was a guardswoman back in Fairhaven. It used to be a world below your storm drains where only magic was possible until one of our evil senators changed that ..."

After running through all her history, Marissa looked mesmerized. "Sounds fascinating. What do you think of humans?"

"I wish they would give us a chance." Iris squeezed Grant's hand. "But I'm glad some of them are kind."

Grant smiled. "They'll come around, Iris—don't worry. I still have hope."

"That's so sweet." Marissa beamed at both of them. "You really are adorable. I've been telling my kids about you two. They'd love to meet you. Oh, hang on—got a work call. I can hear it buzzing."

Marissa picked up her phone, then walked to the edge of the garden for some privacy. Grant leaned toward Iris. "I know my sister can be a lot—especially with her millions of questions—but you're doing well. She definitely likes you."

"Good, I'm glad. But I've never asked. What does she do for work?"

Grant sipped his coffee. "Oh, you don't know? I thought it would be obvious from all the questions. Marissa's an independent journalist, always chasing the biggest stories. I'm proud of her for wrangling motherhood *and* a full-time career. She's come a long way ..."

As Grant went on about his sister's strong work ethic, Iris had a pang of doubt in her stomach. What if Grant was only dating her so his sister could get some dirt on their people? He wouldn't do that to her, would he? Fake his feelings for some fame and information?

These days, Iris wasn't sure who to trust.

CHAPTER 26

As Iris thought about every interaction she had with Grant, wondering if he had been using her for fame all this time, Marissa walked back over. "Sorry to cut this short, but I'm needed back at the newspaper. The death of the former prime minister is big-time news right now. But I had a lovely time meeting you, Iris. Let's do it again sometime."

Iris faked a smile. "Sure."

Grant stood and led his sister through the main hall and toward the door. Iris followed, not saying anything—but she knew she'd have to confront Grant about her concerns. Or it would eat away at her.

"Be safe out there, sis. I'll talk to you later," Grant said. "Bye!"

Marissa waved back, then took off down the street toward her car. She vanished around the block as Grant turned to Iris. He kissed her cheek, noticing the look on her face.

"What's wrong?" Grant asked. "You look upset. Did you not like my sister?"

"It's not that, Grant. She was nice. But ... something's bothering me." Iris glanced over her shoulder, noticing everyone in the main hall. "We should talk in private. Follow me."

Grant nodded, heading with Iris down the hallway. He smiled politely at her people before she led him into the empty sleeping quarters and shut the door. Once they were alone, Grant sat on Iris's bunk, his weight causing the bed to shift.

"So, what's up?" Grant asked. "I don't like to see my girl so upset."

Normally, that would've made Iris swoon. But not when so much was on her mind.

She crossed her arms. "I had no idea your sister was a journalist. Were you ever going to tell me?"

"Oh. Is that what this is about?" Grant frowned. "I don't see the problem. Yes, she's a journalist. An independent one, not affiliated with any big corporations. I thought I told you before. I'm sorry."

"It's just ... try to see it from my point of view. You didn't tell me your sister was a journalist all this time. Maybe I'm just paranoid from everything that's going on, but I'm starting to think you only dated me to help her out. To give her the scoop she needs on my people for her job."

Grant's eyes widened, then he rose to his feet. "What? No—absolutely not. I'm genuinely in love with you, Iris, and I've never lied to you or betrayed you. I invited you into my classroom to introduce you to my students and help your people. You know, I'm hurt you'd even suggest I was using you."

"Can you blame me? Traitors are everywhere. And I'm just naturally suspicious and pessimistic—it's how I've survived this long."

He shook his head. "Well, I can't change the way you are. And I guess I can see where you're coming from. But I swear to you—there's nothing sinister about me being here."

Iris wasn't so sure. She had nothing but his word, and she was even starting to doubt that these days.

She just sighed. "Look, it's been a tough week. I think I just need some rest."

Grant frowned as he walked toward the door. "Oh ... all right. You know where I am if you need me."

As he walked off down the hallway, Iris didn't follow. She sat on her bed, wondering if she had made the right decision or not. If he really *was* using her, then it was good riddance. But if he was telling the truth?

Iris might've just lost the love of her life.

She stood, wanting to chase after him; when she ran out into the main hall, she found he had already left. She even looked out the window, but he was gone. Sighing, she took a seat on one of the pews and tried to focus on her duty.

Iris needed to find her guards—and figure out a way to stop Icarus and the Exterminators. A lot of people were counting on her these days.

As Gemma swept the main hall, she looked at Iris, then walked over. "Hey, General? You okay?"

Iris shook her head. "No. No, I'm not. Grant and I just had our first fight."

"Ouch. I remember mine with Ian. It was over something small and petty, but it was pretty devastating." Gemma set her dustpan aside, sitting next to Iris. "You feel like talking about it?"

"I ... accused him of only dating me to get the scoop on my people. Because his sister is a journalist. I just found out today."

Gemma paused. "Hmm. Well, I get why you'd be paranoid. It's hard to trust humans these days. But I don't get that vibe from Grant, you know. I can tell by the way he looks at you— he's genuinely in love. Some things can't be faked."

Was it true? Had Iris made a huge mistake? She didn't know anymore. She didn't know anything.

"Anyway, maybe some time apart is good. You can both clear your heads," Gemma continued, rising to her feet. "Trust me—true love can't be stopped. So, if it's meant to be, it'll be. Have a little faith."

Iris wanted to laugh. She lived her life based on many things, but faith wasn't one of them. Not wanting to be rude, she just nodded as Gemma returned to her chores.

As the day went on, Iris found herself trying to figure out what to say to Grant. To make it up to him. As she helped her remaining guards in the kitchen cook bread, Noah walked in, his smartphone in hand.

"General?" he asked. "Grant just called here looking for you. You don't have a number so he got me instead."

Iris stood up straight. "Why? Is he all right?"

"What? Oh, yeah—he's fine. He just said there was a problem at his school. It's about Ronan. Didn't say anything else other than it was important. He knows you're not supposed to leave the church, but—"

"For Ronan, I will," Iris replied, heading toward the doorway. "If he calls again, tell him I'm on my way. I'll be careful— keep my head down. Tell the others not to worry."

Noah nodded, going to spread the message as Iris entered the main hall and then left the church. She kept her head down as promised, trying not to stick out, but that was a little difficult when her face had been plastered across the news. And the sword and armor didn't help to hide her appearance.

When she made it to the school, she opened the doors, glancing around. The secretary had buzzed her in when she recognized her from before. The students and teachers were in their classrooms, and everything was quiet. She walked to the front office, heading up to the secretary sitting there.

"Hi there. Thanks for letting me in," Iris began. "I got a call from Grant Thatcher?"

The secretary pointed toward the principal's office. "He's in there. I didn't think it was a good idea inviting one of your people here, but he insisted. Go ahead in."

Iris nodded, ignoring the secretary's prejudice as she reached the principal's office and opened the door. When she entered, she found Grant sitting there with Ronan. Donna, his principal, sat across from them. Sheila and Justin Bond were also there; two people Iris didn't want to see.

"What is this *thing* doing here?" Sheila demanded, glaring at Iris. "She's not Ronan's mother. She has no right to be in this meeting!"

"Please calm down, Mrs. Bond. I invited Iris," Grant said, his soft eyes landing on her. "It's good to see you again."

The principal pulled a chair over for Iris, gesturing for her to sit down. She took a seat as her gaze remained on Grant. "I came over as soon as Noah passed along your message. What's going on?"

"What's going on is that Ronan attacked my son," Sheila spat, "and we're getting to the bottom of it with this family meeting. But you're not family—just some tart Grant is dating. So why don't you just go back to your people and leave us all the hell alone?"

Grant slammed his fist onto the table. "Enough, Mrs. Bond. That's no way to speak to anyone."

Donna nodded. "Mr. Thatcher is right. While I don't agree with Iris being here either, I trust Grant. We must all remain civil."

Sheila mumbled under her breath, saying nothing pleasant as Iris reached out to touch Ronan's arm. He stared down at his feet as his lip quivered. "Ronan, is everything all right? Why did you attack Justin?"

Before he could respond, the door opened behind them. Ronan's mother—who Iris and Grant had met at their house—ran into the room, her hair and clothes a mess. She sat and smoothed out her hair.

"Sorry I'm late. Had to scramble to find a babysitter," Ronan's mother said, noticing Iris. "It's you again. One of those … people. What are you doing here?"

"I promise you—it's important," Grant said, nudging Ronan. "Go ahead. Tell everyone what happened."

Ronan sniffled. "Okay. I really wasn't trying to hurt anyone —that's all. But Justin … he was bullying me again. It's been going on for a long time now."

"Impossible," Sheila spat. "My son would never bully anyone."

Iris bit her tongue, but she wanted to tell Sheila that she was setting a poor example for her son. All the hatred that she and Michael Bond preached daily, clearly affected Justin.

"This is the first I've heard about it too," Ronan's mother said, looking at her son. "I'm so sorry, Ronan."

Ronan sniffled. "Thanks. I haven't really told anyone— except for Iris. She's been a good friend."

Both Ronan's mother and Sheila glared at Iris. But Iris was just touched Ronan felt that way about her. She had never been considered anyone's friend before.

"Well, thank you, Ronan," Iris said. "But I still don't understand why you attacked Justin."

"I remember what you said—what your people would do back home if two people had disagreements. They would duel," Ronan said, reaching under the table. He pulled out two lightsabers. "So, I threw one at Justin, thinking he would understand, and charged at him. If I won the duel, he'd have to stop bullying me. But he didn't fight back and … I just hurt him instead. Accidentally."

Justin nodded. "Stabbed me with that stupid thing right on my arm. It really hurt."

"Wait a second, everyone. Back up," Sheila sneered, turning to Iris. "*You* told this boy to attack my son? What the hell is wrong with you?"

"I didn't say those words exactly," Iris muttered. "That is just the way we do it in my culture. But you still haven't addressed the reason Ronan attacked Justin—and that's because your son has been bullying him. I've seen it with my own eyes."

"As if I believe you," Sheila snarled, rising to her feet. "My husband was right about you—your people are animals! If the prime minister had any sense, she'd lock up all your people and throw away the key. Maybe in cages at the circus."

"Mrs. Bond, stop," Donna interjected. "We're here to talk about Ronan and Justin's fight, not Iris's people. To treat them fairly, both boys are suspended for a week."

"A week?" Justin scoffed. "No fair. *I'm* the one who was attacked!"

"You deserved it!" Ronan cried, rising to his feet. "I want the bullying to stop. Just leave me alone!"

When Ronan ran out of the office, tears streaming down his face, Iris felt so bad for him. He was the victim here—despite choosing to fight Justin. But she was also proud he had finally stood up to him.

"Ronan, wait!" Donna cried, but he had already left the office and vanished out the front doors.

Ronan's mother stood. "I'm going to find my son. You, Iris— I meant what I said before. Stay away from him. Can't you see how much harm you've caused already?"

"I just tried to be there for your son, Mrs. Padwell. Someone needs to be." Iris turned to Sheila and Justin. "And you—you need to teach your son that bullying is inappropriate. If you're even capable of that."

Sheila sneered. "I'm not going to sit here and listen to this. And Donna, you can't suspend my son because I'm pulling him from this school. I won't send any child of mine to a place that allows these animals."

When she gestured at Iris, Justin pouted. "But Mom, what about my friends—"

"I don't care," Sheila snapped, grabbing his arm. "We're leaving. Now."

After Sheila and Justin walked out of the office, Ronan's mother did the same. Grant just shook his head.

"Well ... I didn't expect a screaming match," Grant said, turning to his principal. "I invited Iris here to explain what she said to Ronan, but things went sideways."

"Yes, they did." Principal Hannigan sighed. "With Justin removed, maybe Ronan will have an easier time when he returns in a week. Hopefully his mother can find him, and he'll be all right. In the meantime, I can't allow any more bullying to take place here."

"Good luck with that," Iris said, her eyes landing on Grant. "If I see Ronan, I'll let you know. See you around."

Grant looked like he had more to say to Iris—most likely about their spat from earlier—but he had to stay for work. Iris didn't give him a chance to question her, turning on her bootheel and leaving the office. The secretary was gossiping about her on the phone as she passed.

"That's right, Mr. Thatcher invited that strange witch person back here," the secretary whispered into the phone, snapping her gum. "Something needs to be done about these people sooner or later ..."

Iris shook her head, walking back to the church. She didn't see Ronan, his mother, or the Bonds anywhere on the street.

Wherever Ronan was, she hoped he was okay—and that his life would improve soon. He was a sweet boy who deserved better.

When she entered the church and shut the doors, Princess Esme came up to her with a smile. "You're back—and good timing. I finally convinced my father to pay our respects at the former prime minister's funeral. It's just about to start at St. James' Cathedral downtown."

Iris eyed King Tedros over Princess Esme's shoulder. "Are you sure about this, Your Majesties? There will probably be large crowds, and Michael Bond and his people could be there, waiting to cause trouble. Especially as the seventy-two hours come to an end—"

"I'm certain," Princess Esme interrupted. "Now more than ever, we need to show these humans our best qualities. Our kindness, our compassion, our friendship. Prime Minister Lin might be upset, but I'll handle her. I already picked out flowers from the garden to lay on the coffin. See?"

Esme pointed at the side table where a large bouquet of sunflowers sat. They were beautiful, but were they enough to win over the people of Toronto? Iris didn't think so. Still, if she couldn't stop Princess Esme and the others from going, she'd need to protect them.

"All right," Iris said with a sigh. "Let me know when we're moving out. Stay close to me—I'll try to protect you from the crowd if anyone tries anything. We need to be careful."

"We will be. Hopefully—fingers crossed—people will change their minds about us soon. There has to be something we can do." Princess Esme picked up the flowers, then patted her stomach. "My baby deserves a better world. Anyway, are we all ready to go?"

The others nodded, heading to the door. King Tedros and Fairy Godmother Odelia looked just as skeptical as Iris, but she could tell they didn't want to upset Princess Esme. She looked so excited to connect with humanity, so eager to show them her people had only good intentions.

But not everyone did. Princess Esme was too optimistic, too positive—just like Gemma—and Iris worried that would be their downfall soon.

CHAPTER 27

I ris and her guards followed Princess Esme and the other Fairhaveners to St. James' Cathedral where the former prime minister's funeral was being held, feeling like it was a death march. Like they were heading toward a disaster—either from Icarus or Michael Bond.

Clutching her sword, Iris kept turning her head, searching for any threats. Besides the regular stares and gossip, no one approached them. Rain drizzled from the approaching dark clouds, pinging lightly off Iris's armor. As they walked deeper into the city, heading toward the cathedral, they saw long lines of people paying their respects.

"Former Prime Minister Garneau must've been well-respected," Princess Esme said, standing on her tiptoes to see over the crowd. "So many people are here to say goodbye. I think I see Prime Minister Lin over there with her bodyguards."

"Should we say hello?" Gemma asked. "Tell her that we're here?"

"No, not yet," King Tedros replied. "Since we're not supposed to be out and about after all. Come—we'll get in line to pay our respects."

As they walked over to stand in the long line that led into the old cathedral, people around them noticed who they were. And it wasn't long until the reporters filming the funeral began to question them, tearing the focus away from the former prime minister.

"What do you have to say to Michael Bond calling you a liar?" a nearby reporter asked, her cameraman eagerly taping them. "Do you think the Exterminators are a threat?"

Princess Esme stepped up, not missing a beat. "What we want is peace and coexistence. That's all we've wanted since our home blew up and we were forced to stay here. We know people fear us, but there's nothing to be afraid of. We came here today to pay our respects and prove that ..."

As Princess Esme spoke with the reporter, still desperately trying to win humanity's approval, Iris spotted Grant in the crowd. He had arrived with his principal and class of students —all except Ronan and Justin—to also pay their respects, honoring Canada's former prime minister. When he noticed her, he gave her a half smile, and it was then that Iris wanted to apologize.

She had been a fool to doubt him when he had only treated her right. She couldn't believe she had accused him. And as soon as they were done at the cathedral, she was going to visit him and make things right. She had to.

"... and what do you have to say to people who still believe you're dangerous?" the reporter continued asking Princess Esme as Iris started listening again. "Who think you should leave Toronto?"

"I would tell them, please, don't be so narrow-minded. We're willing to talk and get along if they are." Princess Esme pointed at the cathedral. "Now, I believe I've answered enough of your questions. Today is about a former prime minister, and I think we should get back to honoring him."

The reporter agreed, walking away to speak to others in line about the former prime minister as the cameraman followed. While King Tedros complimented Princess Esme for handling herself so well, Iris still scanned the crowd, watching for a threat—especially now that they had been spotted.

When Iris felt something tugging at her hand, she looked down and found Ronan. He wore the same clothes from their school meeting earlier. "Hi, Iris."

"Ronan, there you are." Iris sighed in relief. "I was worried when you ran out of the principal's office. Your mother went looking for you."

"I know. I just haven't wanted to go home yet." Ronan glanced around the big crowd, looking so small and helpless. "Then I got lost and spotted a bunch of people over here. When I saw you, I was glad."

"I'm glad too—that you're all right. Why did you run out of there like that?"

"I was just sad. Mom had no idea what was going on because she never listens, and I don't think Principal Hannigan even believes me that I'm getting bullied." A few tears slipped out of Ronan's eyes. "What am I going to do, Iris?"

Iris bent down to his level, wiping away his tears. "I'm sorry you're going through this, Ronan. The truth is ... not everyone will like you in this life. It's sad, but that's what it is. But you know what? We don't need everyone to like us. We can like ourselves and choose to hang around our friends and family who actually care about us, just as we are. We don't need to stoop to the level of bullies either."

"Okay. I think I understand." Ronan wiped more of his tears away. "I'm sorry I ran off. And tried to playfight with Justin."

"Don't be—you were just trying to settle things. And if it makes you feel better, Justin's mother pulled him out of that school. You won't be seeing him again. Around the playground, at least."

That did seem to make Ronan feel better. He had a half-smile now, looking like he was in better spirits. Iris hoped she had helped him a little bit.

"Can I ... can I stay here with you for a while?" Ronan asked. "I don't want to go home to Mom. Not yet, at least."

Iris sighed. "All right—but stick close to me. The crowd is huge and I don't want you to get trampled. Grant can call your mother and tell her you're safe, at least."

Ronan agreed, sticking to Iris's side like glue. The line moved forward, inching toward the church. Iris spotted a bunch of guards on patrol to watch over the former prime minister's casket that was waiting inside. Prime Minister Lin looked like she was going to give a speech, as she approached a podium on the church steps with papers and a microphone to reach the far edges of the crowd.

"Thank you all for coming today to pay your respects," she said from the podium. "Prime Minister Garneau will be deeply missed ..."

As she went on, with Iris and her people nearing the cathedral's doors, they heard a commotion over their shoulders. Turning around, Iris noticed Michael Bond, Sheila, Lisa, and the rest of their Exterminators arriving. People got out of their way, letting them move to the front of the line as they murmured.

"Former Prime Minister Garneau would never let these Fairhaven freaks stay in our town!" Michael yelled out, then Iris spotted his group handing out flyers to the crowd. Gemma tried to get one to see what all the fuss was about. "He was tough on immigration. If Prime Minister Lin wasn't so weak and woke, she would've kicked them out already. And Toronto would be safe again."

"Weak and woke, weak and woke!" his Exterminators cried.

Some people in the crowd began to agree, then pointed out Iris and her people. Michael Bond sneered at them as he approached. His Exterminators followed, then Prime Minister Lin's gaze landed on them from the stage. Her eyes widened as she signaled for security to handle the issue. Bodyguards spread out, heading toward them from the cathedral's doors.

"What the hell are you doing here?" Michael Bond asked Iris and her people. "This is a funeral for a former prime minister. You know, of Canada? A place you people weren't even born in?"

"We were born close enough," Princess Esme said. "We just wanted to pay our respects. Now, I know we've gotten off on the wrong foot, but we don't want a problem—"

"Yeah? Too bad." Michael moved closer to Princess Esme, getting in her face. "Because you had one the second you came to my city. And I meant what I said before—the clock is ticking. Less than a day now."

"Attack us and it'll be the last mistake you make," Iris said, stepping in front of the princess to shield her from Michael's wrath. "Prime Minister Lin would never let you hurt us."

"She can't stop me. *No one* can stop what's coming. And she'll get hers," Michael spat. "Hope you're ready, freaks. Because I am."

"Hey, leave Iris alone!" Ronan ran over, standing in front of her. "She hasn't done anything to you."

Sheila whispered in her husband's ear, glaring at Iris and Ronan. Then Michael nodded and turned back to them. "It's you—you're that kid who attacked my boy. Figured you'd be close with freaks like these. They put you up to it, didn't they? I bet they want humanity wiped out. So they can have the surface world all to themselves."

Noah shook his head. "That couldn't be further from the truth. I'm a human. I know finding out about their people was overwhelming, but we don't need all this hate. It's not helping anyone."

Before Michael could respond, the bodyguards ran over. "Break it up—all of you. You're allowed to pay your respects but no fighting. And Prime Minister Lin wants to speak with Iris and the rest of the Fae inside."

Michael shook his head, watching them walk toward the cathedral's doors. "Prime Minister Lin's a fool. She'll pay for this—just like you will!"

"That sounded like a threat," Iris muttered as she reached a hand down, making sure Ronan was still there. She walked with her head high next to her people as they reached the cathedral. "Prime Minister Lin really needs to do something about Michael Bond. Before he loses it."

"Agreed," Gemma said, handing over a flyer. "I managed to get one of the papers they were handing out. Look at this."

When Iris took the picture, it was of Prime Minister Lin's face—with a giant X mark through it. Someone, presumably Michael and his people, had written "TRAITOR" across her forehead with images of skulls. Beneath it read, "BAN THE FREAKS FROM OUR CITY."

"They really hate you guys, don't they?" Ian shook his head. "It's depressing."

Iris tucked the flyer into her armor. "Definitely. But let's hear what the prime minister has to say. And Ronan, it was sweet of you to stand up for me but be careful. I don't want you to get hurt."

"Okay, Iris," Ronan said, clinging to her arm. "I just wanted to help."

She ruffled his hair. "I know you did—and I appreciate it.

But your well-being is more important. As soon as we're done here, we need to get you home to your mother. She's probably worried sick."

As Ronan nodded, they entered the cathedral, approaching Prime Minister Lin. She had walked away from the podium and stood to the side. A few feet away, a giant casket with a Canadian flag sat on a table. When Iris peeked over, an elderly man laid inside, wearing an expensive suit. Several priests stood nearby, speaking with each other around an altar with candles and holy books.

Prime Minister Lin sighed as they approached, her bodyguards surrounding her. "Imagine my surprise when one of my men told me you were in the crowd. Was 'stay inside the church and don't come out' not clear enough?"

"This was my fault, Prime Minister," Princess Esme said, one hand on her belly while the other locked with Noah's. "I convinced my people to come here to pay their respects. I haven't given up on extending an olive branch to humanity."

"From what I've seen, the people out there are more likely to set that olive branch on fire rather than accept it," Prime Minister Lin said. "Look, I'll let you pay your respects and show the people your compassion, but then you must get back to your church. Do I have to put you all on house arrest to get you to stay there?"

"No, ma'am," King Tedros replied. "We'll listen this time. We promise."

"Good. Now, go pay your respects and head home. It really is for the best."

"On it. But first, here's a flyer the Exterminators made," Iris said, handing it over. "They're upset with you for the way you've handled this. And Michael Bond reiterated his threats."

Prime Minister Lin took the paper, reading it with a sigh.

"Of course, he did. Leave him to me—I'll have another talk with him. Just get to safety. For the last time, please. Stop trying my patience."

They all agreed, then approached the former prime minister in his casket. A few people stood off to the side who must've been his family—siblings, children, and grandkids, all gathered to say goodbye. They cried into their tissues, watching Iris and her people carefully as they approached.

"Thank you for your service," Princess Esme said, bowing in front of the casket. A cameraman near the altar shot footage of them all. "May you rest in peace."

Everyone copied Princess Esme, bowing and saying a prayer before turning around. Just as Iris was about to lead them to the doors, intending to take them home, a familiar tremor rumbled the floor—even louder than the ones before.

And Iris knew exactly what was coming.

"Earthquake?" Ian asked, glancing around.

"Something worse," Iris said, reaching for Ronan. "Stay close to me. Something evil is on its way—"

Something crashed through the ceiling of the cathedral, landing only a few feet away from the casket. Iris held Ronan tight to protect him from the falling beams as the other guards protected her people. When they turned around, they saw him in all his glory.

Icarus.

His skin was old and wrinkled, falling off in some spots. He wore a tarnished robe with a set of potions attached to his belt —potions he must've used when he was a fairy godfather.

Once a helpful guide to his people, he was now an enemy. He had fallen so far from grace.

"Who the hell is that?" Noah asked, pulling his wife behind him.

"That would be Icarus," King Tedros whispered. "And he still looks the same after all these years."

"Who?" Gemma asked, looking just as confused as the others.

Icarus laughed, a sound so high-pitched and whiny that it hurt their ears. As they winced, Prime Minister Lin's bodyguards opened fire on Icarus, but their bullets just bounced off his robe and pinged onto the floor, increasing his laughter. Prime Minister Lin and her bodyguards were wide-eyed in fear.

"I have been asleep for so long," Icarus said, glancing around the cathedral as people scurried outside in fear, screaming for their lives, "and it feels good to stretch my legs again. To finally get my bearings."

"What are you doing here?" Iris demanded, shielding Ronan. He trembled as he clung to her legs. "What do you want?"

"I used to want justice," Icarus said, "but that was long ago. What I want now is simple—power. And I shall get it."

He threw a potion at the casket, then the former prime minister rose, looking like a zombie. His flesh peeled from his bones and hung in grayish clumps from his hands and face. His mouth moved, but instead of words, he groaned and gurgled. Drool dribbled down his chin.

An older woman, presumably his wife, fainted. A young girl screamed and ran from the building.

The zombie turned to Icarus and inclined his head. He seemed to communicate silently with Icarus, understanding him as he slipped out of the cathedral's back door.

"Where is he going?" Iris demanded. "You can't just take him!"

"I think I can, just like the others. I'm amassing an army. And the time for a showdown is coming," Icarus said, his eyes landing on Princess Esme. "It needs only one final piece. See you all soon."

Icarus threw another potion toward them, making them all scream and jump out of the way. But the potion was only intended for Princess Esme. It exploded in her face, making her clutch her stomach and cry out in pain. Icarus set off another potion and vanished in a gray mist.

CHAPTER 28

I ris rushed forward, looking for any sign of Icarus on the ground or above her, but he was gone. She wondered where he had fled to—and what he had planned with all the dead people he brought back to life.

Whatever it was, it wasn't going to be good.

When Iris turned around, Princess Esme was still clutching her stomach, crying out in pain. "The baby ... I think something's wrong with the baby."

"We need to get back to the church," Iris said, walking closer. "Fairy Godmother Odelia can examine you there. I'll take Ronan home and answer any questions Prime Minister Lin might have. Which I'm sure will be many."

"*How* can you answer any questions?" Gemma asked. "We don't know who that guy was. He's definitely not with us."

Iris glanced at King Tedros, noticing the guilt across his face. "Actually, we *do* know him. King Tedros and Fairy Godmother Odelia didn't want to tell you all and scare you, but ... his name is Icarus."

"Who?" Ian asked, glancing around. "What's going on? This human is lost."

"I am too," Gemma murmured.

"Let's talk about this later," Noah said, holding his wife's hand. "Esme needs help. Now."

"Noah's right. Come on," Fairy Godmother Odelia said, nodding toward the doors. "This way, dear. You're going to be all right …"

As she whispered words of encouragement, they all left the cathedral, and the courtyard stood empty. Everyone had fled when Icarus appeared. The only ones remaining were Prime Minister Lin and her bodyguards, Michael Bond and his group, and Grant's sister—who Iris didn't even know was there. Grant and his classroom of kids had already left, making Iris sigh in relief that they were safe. But they still needed to talk. Or Grant just needed to listen while Iris apologized.

"… and you still can't believe keeping these people here is a good idea," Michael said to the prime minister. "You saw what happened in there. Whoever that freak was, he's even more dangerous than the others!"

While Michael's group nodded in agreement, Prime Minister Lin sighed. "I intend to get to the bottom of this— diplomatically. Let me handle this, all right? Go home where it's safe, please. And stop undermining me."

Michael waved her off, shaking his head in disgust. When he noticed Iris standing in the doorway of the cathedral, he gestured at his watch, reminding her of the remaining twenty-four hours. Just another problem hanging over Iris's head.

Ronan tugged at her armor again, looking afraid. "Who was that guy? Are we in trouble?"

Iris bent down beside him. "I won't let him hurt you, Ronan. That's a promise. We'll get you back home to your mom soon, okay? Let me just talk to the prime minister first."

Ronan nodded, sticking close to Iris as she approached the prime minister. She looked equal parts angry, fed up, and afraid. She noticed the rest of Iris's people walking down the street, heading toward the church as she turned to Iris.

"I think you owe me an explanation," Prime Minister Lin said. "I promised this city that your people were safe—that we should all try to get along in the name of peace. After that ... attack, you're making me look like a liar. Who was that?"

Iris sighed. "I'm sorry, Prime Minister Lin—it wasn't our intention to lie to you. I only found out about Icarus not that long ago. In short, he's an immortal—once a fairy godfather. He went mad, and now he threatens the entire world. And can bring people back from the dead."

Prime Minister's Lin eyes widened, and she remained silent for a few seconds. "That ... is unexpected. I guess it explains all those funeral incidents. How are you planning to deal with him?"

"Well ... that's the tricky part. King Tedros said he doesn't know how to kill him. I mean, how *do* you kill an immortal?"

Ronan tugged at her arm again. "In all the comic books I read, there's always a way. You're going to stop this guy and save the day, Iris. I know you will."

While Iris found it sweet that Ronan believed in her, she wasn't so sure.

"I hope the little boy is right," Prime Minister Lin muttered. "In the meantime, I'm asking all citizens to get off the streets. It isn't safe anymore. I'll be holding another press conference to address the nation about this latest development. What do I tell the public about the former prime minister? Or his family? They're the real victims here, having to see their dead loved one get up and walk away."

"I know—please give them our sympathies. We believe Icarus is building an army of undead. I'm not sure where he's keeping the ones he's bringing back, but I intend to find out. I'm heading back to the church to develop a plan."

"All right. I wish you luck." Prime Minister Lin shook her head, turning to her guards. "Nothing is ever simple, is it? Take me back to my Toronto office, please."

As the bodyguards took Prime Minister Lin away, clearing the streets as they did so, Iris walked over to Grant's sister. Marissa was taking a video of the church on her phone. Ronan followed, clinging to Iris's side.

"It isn't safe to stay here, you know," Iris began. "Icarus could return at any moment."

"Is that his name? Scary guy. I got him on video for my viewers." Marissa turned to Iris, lowering her camera. "Grant called me—he said you were worried he was just using you. Something about helping my career?"

Iris nodded. "That's right, I did. As I'm sure you can imagine, trust is hard to come by these days."

"I bet. But I swear to you, that isn't the truth at all. Grant is in love with you. Truly, madly, deeply. I'm almost jealous of it." She shook her head with a smile. "You have nothing to worry about. My brother is a good man—he'd never use anyone. I hope you two can make up soon."

Iris did too; once all this world-saving stuff was over.

"Fingers crossed. Now, seriously, you need to get off these streets. Icarus is dangerous," Iris urged. "Get home to your kids safely."

Marissa nodded, heading back to the road where her car waited. After she had driven off, Iris gestured for Ronan to follow. She remembered the path to his house and brought him back home safely. After crossing over the many toys lying on the front lawn, she knocked on the door.

Ronan's mother answered a moment later, carrying a toddler in her arms. Her eyes widened when she saw Ronan on her step. "Oh, Ronan, there you are. My baby!"

Ronan ran into his mother's arms, hugging her while she

was still holding onto the toddler. He pulled back to look his mother in the eyes. "I'm sorry I ran away, Mom. I was just upset no one believed me."

"I know. I'm so sorry Justin's been bullying you, sweetie. You should've told me," his mother said, ruffling his hair. "And you know what? Iris was right—we *do* need to spend more time together. Things will be different now, sweetie. I promise."

"Good," Iris said behind them. "Stay inside and don't leave the house. I assume you've heard about the man who attacked St. James' Cathedral?"

"I did," Ronan's mother said, still clutching her children. More toddlers cried out inside the house for her. "It's all over the news—they have live footage. I just ... I can't believe it."

"Iris was so cool, Mom," Ronan said, looking up at her. "She saved me when that scary guy jumped down. She saved me from that lion attack at the zoo too."

"She did, huh?" Ronan's mother looked Iris up and down. "Hmm. My son is a big fan of yours—which is surprising, but maybe I can understand why. I'm starting to think the Exterminators are wrong about you."

"They are. My people have only ever wanted to get along with yours," Iris said. "And once I find a way to stop Icarus, maybe we will. Speaking of which, I need to get going. Take care of yourselves."

"Bye, Iris!" Ronan called out as she turned around and left. "I hope to see you again soon!"

Iris waved at him, then walked down the familiar path that led to the church. No one was out in the streets—too afraid after Icarus' attack—and air raid sirens were going off, usually used in the event of a natural disaster.

Icarus is a disaster all right, Iris thought, *and it's up to me to fix it.*

When she opened the door to the church, Iris heard a baby

crying. Frowning, she walked down the hallway, noticing all her people had gathered in Princess Esme's room. She held a baby swaddled in a pink blanket. Esme looked exhausted and sweaty as she gently rocked the baby, Noah holding her hand.

"What's going on?" Iris asked. "Where did that baby come from?"

Fairy Godmother Odelia turned around. "Princess Esme just gave birth. Meet Princess Alyx, their daughter, and first ever hybrid."

As Iris watched the baby coo, she frowned. "I don't understand. We just found out Princess Esme was pregnant—and I think our pregnancies are a lot like humans. It takes nine months. How did the baby get here so fast?"

"Icarus did something to Esme," King Tedros explained. "That potion he threw at her grew the baby. It's definitely strange, and we aren't sure of anything yet."

"But they're both in good health," Fairy Godmother Odelia said, kissing the baby's head. "I made sure of it myself. And we told the others all about Icarus while you were gone."

"He sounds dangerous," Gemma said, glancing at Fairy Godmother Odelia and King Tedros. "You should've told us about him right away when you saw his crypt empty."

King Tedros sighed, watching his grandchild. "Perhaps, but we were only trying to keep everyone calm. It's too late now—we need action. Iris, we need a plan to stop Icarus."

Noah nodded. "Especially now that we have a new baby in the family. And people are going to be even more afraid of us now that they know about this immortal guy. King Tedros tells us he can't be killed?"

"That's the belief, yes," Iris said, leaning against the doorframe. "But I agree with what Ronan said. I think he's rubbing off on me. There has to be a way—"

When a knock sounded on the door, everyone glanced

around at each other. Reaching for her sword, Iris walked down the hallway and looked out the peephole. It was only the Bhatias on her step—and not Grant like she wanted.

She opened the door, gesturing for them to enter. "Hi. What are you all doing here?"

Maya held up her phone to show Iris. "We wanted to know if you saw Michael Bond's latest YouTube video. It isn't good, Iris."

Iris frowned, taking the phone, and pressed play on Michael's newest video. It had only been uploaded a few minutes ago. The title was enough to send goosebumps down her spine, reading: ENOUGH IS ENOUGH. WE STRIKE NOW.

"Hello citizens of Toronto—and people watching around the world," Michael said to the camera, his group all around him. "I'm sure you've seen the footage of that immortal attacking the cathedral where our dear former prime minister was being honored. His body has been stolen, desecrated. And we've had enough. We tried to warn you that these Fairhaven freaks were dangerous."

"Which is why we're taking action," Sheila said, and Iris noticed Justin hanging around in the background. "Since Prime Minister Lin isn't doing anything, we're overthrowing her and taking the mantle of prime minister. We're going to remove these Fairhaven witches from our world. Permanently."

Iris saw a brief hint of their weapons—mostly guns and knives—before the video cut out. And the worst part was that the comment section was in Michael's favor, mostly everyone agreeing that their people were dangerous. Icarus had *not* helped relations at all.

Iris handed the phone back, shaking her head. "Michael Bond is past threats and petty smoke bombs. He's coming to kill us now."

"He is," Ayesha said, "and we're worried about your people. Maybe you should consider leaving Toronto."

"We can't, Mrs. Bhatia—not with Icarus still out there, the one who attacked St. James' Cathedral. I need to stop him somehow *and* avoid Michael Bond's Exterminators. I'm still trying to figure out a plan."

"Well, we wish you luck," Ramesh said. "We know your people are not like this one you call Icarus. We've seen you all for what you really are—kind and good people, just trying to survive on the surface. If you need our help, you only have to ask."

Iris smiled. "You all have been true friends, but no—this is something we need to do on our own. I won't risk your safety. Head back to your house and stay there. Board the windows and be safe."

The Bhatias nodded, heading back to their house across the street. As Iris watched, she noticed something in the distance—something glowing. When she squinted, she saw a large group of people, at least several hundred, carrying flashlights and other weapons.

It was Michael Bond and his Exterminators. It had to be. They had finally found them somehow.

Iris slammed the door, locking it before running off down the hallway. Her people were still in Princess Esme's room. The baby looked much older now, growing rapidly. "We need to get out of here—now. Michael Bond is coming to kill us all. His latest YouTube video said he's going to overthrow the prime minister and get rid of us."

"What?" Gemma asked, wide-eyed. "He can't do that—"

"He can and will. Now, move!" Iris demanded "Out the back door. There's no time to argue!"

Her people nodded, rising to their feet before following Iris to the kitchen. She gestured for them all to head into the garden before she followed. Princess Esme clung to her daughter tightly, soothing her as she started to cry.

"Is it just me or is she growing again?" Noah asked, looking at his daughter. "Her arms and legs ... they look longer."

"You're right," Princess Esme said, wide-eyed. "What did Icarus do to her?"

"We'll talk about this on the way," Iris said, opening the gate that led out of the garden. "Move it—hurry!"

Just as they fled the garden, heading to the streets behind the church, the angry mob arrived. They kicked open the doors to the church, screaming obscenities and insults as they searched for Iris's people. She and her guards led them down the street, one hand on her sword, and found herself thinking of Grant—even at a time like this.

If she had known what was about to happen, she would've told him she loved him one last time instead of picking a fight. Now she just hoped she'd see him again, in case either Icarus or the Exterminators killed her.

"Where are we going?" Ian asked, holding Gemma's hand as they rushed down the sidewalk. "What's the safest place?"

Iris glanced around nervously. "There *is* no safe place ... but I think I have an idea. Follow me."

CHAPTER 29

Iris took her people to the local school, the same one where Grant worked. She assumed all the kids would've been sent home after Icarus' attack. And when they arrived, finding the school deserted with no cars or school busses outside, she realized she was right.

"I don't think anyone will look for us here," Iris said, walking toward the doors. She frowned when she realized they were unlocked. "Hmm, it's open. Let me check out the school first before we enter—"

When someone opened the door on the other side, Iris reached for her sword, then sighed in relief when it was only Grant. It looked like he was leaving with his briefcase and turning off all the lights behind him. He frowned, pausing when he saw her.

"Iris?" he asked. "What are you doing here?"

"The Exterminators found us, Grant. They're coming to kill us all. I knew it was only a matter of time until our church was discovered," Iris explained, gesturing at her people behind her. "We needed a safe place to lie low, and the school popped into my head."

"Of course," Grant said, opening the door a little wider. "Come on in—before someone sees you. When people started screaming, I brought my class back to school to keep them safe. The kids and teachers were sent home after the attack. I was just locking up before heading home myself."

Iris nodded, gesturing for her people to enter the school. They crowded in the foyer as Grant closed and locked the doors before flicking on a nearby light. When he turned around, noticing the baby in Princess Esme's arms, he looked confused.

"Where did that baby come from?" he asked.

"It's our baby. Princess Alyx is her name," Princess Esme replied, gesturing at Noah. "Icarus did something to me—he made my pregnancy speed up."

"Very strange. Anyway, I'm glad you're all safe," Grant said, turning to Iris, "and that you're here. I wanted to say I'm sorry—"

"*You're* sorry?" Iris frowned. "No, no, no. You have nothing to apologize for. I was in the wrong, accusing you of something you didn't do. You're wonderful, Grant, and I love you. I'm so sorry I ever doubted you."

Grant reached for her hand. "Apology accepted. Seeing that man, Icarus, drop through the cathedral's ceiling … well, it put things into perspective. If the world is ending, I want to spend my last days with you."

Iris smiled. "I feel the same way—"

"Uh, guys?" Gemma asked behind them. "Princess Alyx is growing again."

When Iris and Grant turned around, the baby had grown to a toddler, her baby blanket discarded on the floor. She was already running around and able to babble. Princess Esme, Noah, and the others looked on in shock, not knowing what to say. Fairy Godmother Odelia magically made a new set of clothes under her breath, the kind that would grow with the baby.

"This is ... unnatural," Fairy Godmother Odelia said, dressing the baby. "I've never seen anything like this before, not in all my years of practicing magic. Why on Earth would Icarus do this to you?"

Princess Esme shook her head, on the verge of tears. "I don't know. I just hope our baby will be okay—that nothing's seriously wrong."

Noah nodded, reaching out to pick Alyx up. He bounced her in his arms as she giggled, looking around at everyone with big smiles. She was the perfect blend of her parents and seemed like a normal child.

No one would've been able to guess that she had been magically grown.

"Just like a Chia Pet," Noah muttered. "So weird ..."

When Grant glanced out the window, Iris followed his line of sight, noticing an orange glow in the distance. Flames spewed from the church's windows. Firetrucks sped down the road, heading to the scene.

"Well, I guess our home is gone," Iris muttered. "I don't even have to wonder who burned it down."

"Yeah. Come on, you should all get away from the windows," Grant said, making sure the door was locked, "so no one can see you in here. Head to the gymnasium—you can stay there for a while."

Iris nodded, following Grant down the hallway. Alyx continued to grow a little more every time Iris looked back at her. As they entered the gym, Iris's people sat on the floor, keeping an eye on Alyx and talking about the strange situation.

When Noah's smartphone rang, he put Alyx down and answered it. Iris watched as his eyes widened before he nodded and hung up. "That was my father, Detective Crawford. He said there was an attack at the police station. He's all right, but he said the station is in chaos. Then the line went dead."

Iris's heartbeat quickened. It might have been Icarus—though Iris didn't know why he would attack a police station. But she knew nothing of his plans.

She removed her sword from her scabbard, nodding. "I'll check it out. All of you, stay here—and be quiet. If Michael Bond shows up, run for your lives. I'll find you eventually."

"I'm coming with you," Grant said. "I won't let you do this alone."

Iris sighed. "It's sweet that you want to help, but—"

"No buts," Grant interrupted. "I need to make sure you're safe. Please, let me come with you."

"All right, all right—but stay close. Icarus can't be trusted." She turned to her people. "Stay safe, all of you. We'll be back soon."

As the others nodded, taking seats on the gymnasium floor and keeping an eye on Alyx, Iris and Grant headed down the hallway. Once they were outside, Grant locked the doors behind him before they rushed down the sidewalk. They took the back way around the church, not wanting to get caught, and saw it burning. Michael Bond and the Exterminators were gone and the firefighters had arrived, trying to put out the blaze, but it was strong and spreading.

So much for their home on the surface.

"You can find another place," Grant whispered, trying to comfort her as he placed a hand on her shoulder. "I know it's hard to see, but at least you're all still alive."

"For now," Iris shot back, "until Icarus and the Exterminators catch up with us. Shit, my head is spinning from all this. First things first—the police station. Let's find out what's going on."

Grant nodded, continuing to follow her. The police station

was only a few blocks away. With no one out on the roads, no one got in their way as they approached the building. When Iris heard gunshots echoing from inside, she gestured for Grant to stay behind her, holding her sword up. Then she ran inside the police station and looked around.

The place was worse for wear—emergency lights going off and bullet holes in the walls. When Iris turned down the hallway, heading toward the cells, she noticed that was where the bulk of the officers were. Detective Crawford and the other cops crowded around two people on the floor.

"Hands up!" Detective Crawford yelled out, spinning around and noticing Iris. "Oh, it's only you. The general."

"Hello, Detective," Iris said, her sword still held high as the other officers noticed them. "What's going on?"

The officers parted, letting Iris see who was sitting on the floor. Sapphira was in handcuffs and Kyler was dead—shot in the chest multiple times. He wasn't moving, covered in his own blood.

"Oh my gosh." Iris's hand flew up to her mouth, finding it difficult to see her own guards like that. Even Grant gasped behind her. "What happened?"

"I'm sorry," Sapphira said through tears. "We were only trying to do what was best. We ran away on purpose and planned it out. We thought we were helping our people ..."

When Iris looked behind Sapphira's shoulder, she saw the scene. All of Senator Remus' family members and allies—including Gemma's mother—had been killed, stabbed through the chest through the bars. They were helpless in those cells, awaiting a transfer to jail. And the blood coating Sapphira and Kyler's swords on the ground suggested they had been their killers.

They *had* told Iris they wanted Senator Remus' family dead.

She should've known they were going to do it—and she should've stopped them.

"They entered the police station and fought their way to the cells. Used gunpowder to cause an explosion and distract us all," Detective Crawford explained, and Iris realized that the theft was connected to them. "They wanted your senator's family and friends dead, and they got it. Unfortunately, one of your guards was killed in the struggle. My officer shot him in the chest when he wouldn't back down. Fortunately, the other surrendered."

Iris sighed, putting her sword away. "Then he paid the price. Sapphira, what were you thinking?"

Sapphira teared up as she looked at Kyler's body. "We wanted a fresh start for our people, that's all. To remove the senator's family and force the king to step down. I never thought it would end like this ..."

As she hung her head, crying, the officers took Kyler's body away. Detective Crawford turned back to Iris. "We'll prepare your guard's body for a funeral and take your other one to jail."

Iris nodded. "All right, that sounds reasonable. And Detective? I thought you should know you're a grandfather. Princess Esme had her baby."

The detective looked happy before he thought about it, then frowned. "But ... wasn't she in the early stages of her pregnancy? I thought your people carried for nine months like humans do."

"We do—but long story short, Icarus did something to her with his magic. Your granddaughter, named Alyx, is growing fast."

"Alyx?" Detective Crawford smiled. "What a beautiful name. I can't wait to meet her. Please, Iris—protect my grandbaby. Stop this Icarus monster."

"I'll try my best, Detective. You have my word. We had to

flee our church—the Exterminators found us and wanted us dead. They burned it down." She leaned in closer, lowering her voice. "We're holed up in the elementary school not far from the church. I told everyone to lie low while I work on finding Icarus."

Detective Crawford nodded. "I see. Let me come with you— let me help you stop this immortal. And that way, if you run into Michael Bond, I can take the kill shot. Something tells me that son-of-a-bitch won't come easily."

Iris really didn't want any more bloodshed, but she had enough on her plate with Icarus. "All right, Detective—just let me handle the immortal. Since your officers have everything under control, let's move out."

Iris took one last look at Sapphira, feeling sorry for her. She wanted to ask her more questions but there wasn't any time. Icarus needed her attention.

Shaking her head, Iris left the police station with Grant and Detective Crawford. Just as she wondered where to look for this immortal, hoping to find his base, dozens of people walked toward them from down the road. And while Iris feared it was the Exterminators, it was something worse.

All the dead people Icarus had brought back to life— including the former prime minister—were nothing more than brainless zombies, destroying everything in their path. And they were coming straight at them.

"Looks like Icarus' army has caught up with us," Iris muttered. "They're all heading at us from the east. Does anyone know why?"

Grant thought for a moment, glancing over at them. "Well ... Toronto's largest cemetery is down that way. Mount Pleasant Cemetery. My grandparents are buried there."

"A cemetery?" Detective Crawford turned to Iris. "Could that be where your immortal is hiding?"

"Only one way to find out." Iris held up her sword. "Quick—follow me."

Iris carved a path for Grant and Detective Crawford, slicing down the zombies in her way. Her sword went clean through their chests and they fell to the ground. Fortunately, unlike Icarus, they didn't come back to life. Iris looked down at the former prime minister's dead body with a sigh before gesturing for Grant and Detective Crawford to follow.

When they arrived at the Mount Pleasant Cemetery, moving past the gates, Iris realized Grant had been right. Icarus was there—standing on a tomb, his hands in the air as he summoned more zombies to rise by throwing potions at their graves.

"This is a travesty," Detective Crawford muttered. "The dead should rest—not be used like this."

"All the more reason to stop Icarus, then. Just back me up—and be careful." Iris stepped forward, her sword in hand. "Icarus! This ends here. Stop this madness."

When Icarus saw her approaching, he jumped off the crypt, smiling as his zombies crowded around him. "Ah, the general, is it? You found me."

"Wasn't hard. Just had to follow your abominations." Iris pointed at the dead zombies over her shoulder. "Look, I know all about your story. How you felt bad that a human woman died in Fairhaven, then you tried to save her by experimenting with immortal magic. But it corrupted you—made you blind to all the harm you're causing. The good thing, though? You can end this here. Do the right thing and stop all this insanity."

Icarus thought about it for a moment, then shook his head. "And why should I? I have all this power at my fingertips—and now that I'm free and fully recovered, I plan to use it. No fool, Fairhavener or otherwise, will stop me."

Iris held up her sword. "No, please—"

When Icarus threw the potion, it exploded in a purple mist and sent Iris, Grant, and Detective Crawford flying back. Iris quickly recovered, jumping to her feet as she yelled and ran at Icarus, blade poised to strike. She stabbed her sword right through his chest, hoping she could do it—kill him somehow and end it all here.

But Icarus only laughed, removing the sword from his chest. He reached for Iris's throat and held her up as she struggled. "Foolish! What part of immortal don't you understand? I cheated death centuries ago, and that's why the former king locked me away. If he couldn't kill me, what makes you think you can, some puny little guard?"

Iris struggled against Icarus, gasping for air and punching at his arms, but he was too strong. Detective Crawford began shooting at the immortal, but the bullets bounced off again. When that didn't work, Grant ran at Icarus, trying to stop him from hurting Iris, but a zombie knocked him back.

"Accept it—I've won this game," Icarus told her, increasing his grip on her throat. "I can't be stopped."

"Why ... did you make Princess Esme's child grow?" Iris managed to choke out. "What are you planning to do to them? Leave ... them alone!"

Icarus laughed. "Oh, yes—the fetus. When I sensed her carrying a child, one that was a hybrid, I knew I had to kill it. But I'm not about to murder a baby. Even monsters have ethics, you know."

Both Grant and Detective Crawford were surrounded by zombies and under attack, in trouble themselves. They couldn't get to Iris to save her from the clutches of an evil fairy godfather.

"So I decided to age the child with an old spell. Another forbidden potion," Icarus said, still keeping a firm grip on her windpipe. "When she finally becomes an adult, that's when I'll strike her down. Should be any minute now."

"Why?" Iris choked out. "Why ... not just leave them alone?"

Icarus paused, then shrugged. "I suppose it won't hurt to tell you—since I'm going to kill you all in a minute. That child, the first hybrid? It's the only one who can strike me down. I felt it when I locked eyes with Esme in the church—I knew it in my bones. Their blood will destroy me, so they must be destroyed first."

Only the hybrid could kill Icarus? Iris knew she had to protect that child—that it was their only hope.

Which meant she had to survive just a little while longer.

CHAPTER 30

I carus was a Fairy Godfather, sure. But he still had physiology similar to humans. To escape his grasp, Iris kicked him in the groin as hard as she could. He dropped her on the ground and cried out in pain as she massaged her throat.

"Ouch! You ... you insolent girl!" Icarus sputtered, clutching himself. "Meddling Fairhaven bitch!"

That's me, Iris thought. *Proudly.*

Forcing herself to rise to her feet, Iris ignored Icarus for now, using her sword to cut down the zombies surrounding Grant and Detective Crawford. She helped them both up, then noticed Icarus was watching in amusement. His mouth was upturned in a slight smile, a change from his pained expression.

"It's futile, you know," Icarus said. "I've already won. All that's left to do is to kill you and then I'll rule over this puny world."

"You can kill us right here," Grant said, reaching for Iris's hand, "but you can't kill the love we share. Our kindness, our compassion. I'm sad you don't have it yourself, but those beliefs can't be destroyed."

Icarus shook his head. "Blind fools! I'm going to crush you all like ants—"

"We have no time for this," Iris interrupted, pushing Grant and Detective Crawford toward the gate. "We need to find my people and bring Alyx here."

"My granddaughter?" Detective Crawford asked, confused. "Why? She's just a baby. I don't want her involved in this."

"She's not exactly a baby anymore," Iris argued, watching as Icarus prepared another spell. "Come on, we don't have much time. Alyx is the key to defeating Icarus. Hurry!"

In confusion, Grant and Detective Crawford followed Iris, sprinting out of the cemetery. Icarus just watched and laughed as he caused more zombies to rise from their graves. Panting and out of breath, Iris led them toward the school, then Grant unlocked the doors.

They were all still in the gymnasium where Iris left them, crowding around a teenage girl. She was blonde, about sixteen or seventeen, and had grown into a new set of clothes. A plain t-shirt and jeans. Iris blinked, noticing the similarities between her, Princess Esme, and Noah.

When King Tedros heard them enter, he spun around. "Iris, there you are! My granddaughter has just hit her teenage years. What's going on?"

As everyone stared at Iris, she approached the teenage girl. "I think you know. It's what you were born to do. Do you feel it?"

The girl nodded. "I do. And I'm sorry, Mom and Dad ... but I need to do this."

"Do what?" Princess Esme asked, glancing between them. "I don't understand."

Iris silently gestured over her shoulder. The teenage girl nodded and followed. As the others chased after them, they left the school, then returned to the cemetery. Icarus was still there, raising the dead.

And waiting for their final confrontation. Iris hoped the teenage girl could stop him—that she wasn't just leading Princess Esme and Noah's only child to her death. Iris would never forgive herself if that was the case.

"Please, turn back!" Princess Esme cried. "He's going to kill you!"

"I have to do this, Mom," the girl shot back, heading toward Icarus. "It's my destiny. And judging by the zombies, he must be over there. *Icarus.* I feel it in my soul."

Her name was Alyx, Iris realized. And just a few hours ago, she had been a baby. Now, she was attempting to save the world. Iris was both nervous and impressed.

"Ah, you're here," Icarus said, smiling as everyone watched on. "You must feel it too. You know your power, yes?"

"I do," Alyx replied boldly. "And I'm here to end you. For good."

Icarus shook his head, preparing a potion. "Oh, but it's the other way around, my dear. I can finally end you now. Say goodbye to your family for me, will you?"

"No!" Iris cried.

Just as Icarus prepared to throw the vial, Detective Crawford leaped forward, protecting Alyx. He took the contents of the potion instead, the red liquid burning his skin. He cried out and fell to the ground.

"Dad, no!" Noah cried, rushing to his side.

Alyx watched in horror, her eyes hardening. Iris knew it— she was ready to strike the deadly blow. She only needed a weapon.

"Alyx, catch!" Iris cried, then tossed her sword to her.

Alyx caught the weapon, twirling it around. As Icarus

looked disappointed the potion hadn't landed, searching for another one to use, Alyx hesitated. Iris saw her brow furrow.

"What's wrong?" Iris asked. "You have him—Icarus is right there. Kill him, Alyx. End this, once and for all!"

"I ... I can't," Alyx whispered. "I'm ... scared. Scared of failing, scared of losing my parents. Scared of *him*."

Fear. Iris knew it well. She once feared losing Fairhaven, a fear that came true. Now she feared losing Grant and everything she had built here. Behind her, she heard Icarus searching for a new potion on his belt, muttering to himself. She had to convince Alyx to take the shot—before it was too late.

"It's okay to be afraid," Iris said, walking toward Alyx. "That's natural. Both for human *and* Fae. But you know what I've learned about fear?"

Alyx shook her head. Around her, Iris was aware of the sea of eyes watching. Icarus' chuckles meant his next potion would hit any second now. Time was ticking, beating on Iris like a drum.

"Fear is a liar," Iris continued. "It tells us we're weak, unworthy, alone. But you, Alyx? You are so loved and capable. You are strong—and you can do this. We all believe in you. And if you'd like, I'll put my hand on yours and help you land the killing blow." Her eyes hardened. "Now, prepare your sword and tell that necromancer that he can fuck off."

Iris watched as something changed on Alyx's face. Her brow softened; her eyes narrowed. She placed a hand over Alyx and nodded. They would do this together—defeat a great evil even while afraid.

They both screamed, then began running at Icarus with their sword drawn.

Before he could react, his next potion in hand, they both stabbed Iris's sword through his throat, making the immortal gurgle and groan. Then he fell to the ground, dead in a pool of his own blood before he faded to ashes. All the remaining zombies in the distance let out a groan and fell to the ground.

They faded to ash, then everything turned quiet.

"It's over," Alyx whispered. "Icarus is dead, and he won't be returning. Thank you, Iris. You can have your sword back now. But without you ... I don't think I would've had the strength to kill him. Even though I knew it was my birthright, I was still terrified."

"Nonsense. You always had it in you, Alyx. I just gave you a little boost of confidence."

She handed the sword back to Iris with a smile. "That you do. You'd be a great motivational speaker, you know."

"If being the general doesn't work out, I'll consider a career change." Iris glanced at Grant over her shoulder as Alyx's parents rushed to embrace her. "That was intense. Are you all right?"

"I am. I can't believe we made it," Grant said, cupping her face. "But I'm so glad we did. I love you, Iris."

"And I love you too."

As they kissed, they heard Noah and Princess Esme crying over their shoulder. They spun around, noticing that Detective Crawford had died of injuries from whatever potion Icarus had thrown. Princess Esme begged Fairy Godmother Odelia to help, but she shook her head.

"I'm sorry, but there's nothing I can do," she said softly. "May your father's soul rest in peace, Noah."

Noah continued to cry as Alyx bowed her head. "He died a hero. He died for *me*—so I could save the world. He had his destiny and so did I. I'll never forget him, even if I didn't have the chance to meet him yet."

As they took a moment, honoring Detective Crawford's sacrifice in silence, people began to poke their heads out of their homes. As the sky cleared, they worked up the courage to walk toward the cemetery and see what had happened.

When Iris spotted Michael Bond and his Exterminators approaching, carrying their guns, she lifted her sword and tried to shield her people with her body. "*You.* Why can't you just leave us alone?"

"Because you're dangerous. That immortal freak proved it," Michael spat, his pistol in hand. Sheila, Lisa, and the rest of his Exterminators stood proudly behind him. "The way I see it, we get rid of you, and we'll finally be free from all this stupid magic bullshit."

"You're already free," Alyx said, crossing her arms. "I killed Icarus—that was my destiny. The war is over and there's no more danger."

Michael sneered. "I don't recognize you. What, did you start adding new freaks to your group when I wasn't looking?"

"I'm the first hybrid. Princess Esme and Noah Crawford's child, the one my mother was pregnant with not that long ago. I know it seems strange, but Icarus made a potion that forced me to age quickly," Alyx said, making Michael's eyes widen. "And I won't let you destroy this era of peace. Things will be better now. I know they will. So, walk away—or this won't end well for you."

"The first ... hybrid? The child of a Fairhavener and human? That's an abomination," Michael spat, checking his watch. "And the twenty-four hours is almost up. I bet the city would thank me if I rid you all from our world—"

When several military trucks pulled up to the cemetery, Michael turned, seeing who it was. Prime Minister Lin stepped out of one of the trucks, followed by police officers, soldiers, and bodyguards. One officer immediately placed handcuffs around Michael's wrists and confiscated his weapon. He struggled against the officer, unable to move.

"Hey, what the hell are you doing?" Lisa demanded.

"Yeah, let my husband go!" Sheila cried out. "He's done nothing wrong."

"I beg to differ," Prime Minister Lin said. "Inciting violence, causing riots, walking the streets armed with the intention to kill. Canada doesn't have an open-carry law. And best of all? The lab *did* eventually find trace evidence of your DNA, Mr. Bond, on Bobby Blevins. It turns out Iris was right all along."

Michael sneered, still restrained. "I killed Bobby Blevins for the same reason I was going to kill these freaks—for the good of the world. Someone had to. It'd be a lot safer if they all vanished."

"I beg to differ," Prime Minister Lin said, gesturing for the officers to place handcuffs on the rest of Michael's gang. "You're all being arrested for your involvement, and you'll be read your rights. Officers, take them away."

As Michael and his Exterminators were led to the trucks, screaming and arguing, Iris felt bad for Justin. The boy would have no parents now—and who knew what would become of him. He deserved better role models.

But where was the German scientist, Dr. Koch? The same one Michael had kidnapped?

When Iris saw a red light appear on Prime Minister Lin's face, her eyes widened. "Watch out—everyone down!"

She jumped on the prime minister, pushing the woman to the ground with a thud. The others took cover as a single gunshot rang out. Iris looked up, noticing Dr. Koch on a nearby rooftop, aiming his sniper rifle again.

He was going to kill the prime minister.

Without hesitation, her bodyguards opened fire, shooting at Dr. Koch on the roof. Two bullets struck him in the chest before he fell off the roof to his death. They ran over, making sure he was dead in a pool of his own blood.

"My goodness," Prime Minister Lin muttered, rising to her feet. "You saved my life. Who was that?"

"The same scientist who kidnapped me," Iris said, her eyes on the truck where Michael had been brought. "And I have some questions. Excuse me."

Leaving the prime minister and everyone reeling over her shoulder, Iris walked toward the black SUV, finding Michael in handcuffs in the backseat. He was sneering at her as she opened the door.

"You took him, didn't you?" she asked. "Dr. Koch? Why didn't you kill him like Bobby Blevins?"

Michael shrugged. "I thought he could be useful. And he was—I ordered him to kill Prime Minister Lin so I could take her position. He agreed only so I would spare his life. That was the plan all along—to kill you and Prime Minister Lin. Then, maybe, humanity could have a fresh start."

Iris shook her head, noticing the bodyguards carrying Dr. Koch's corpse away. "Well, now, he's dead—for no good reason. I hope you're proud of yourself."

"Oh, I am," Michael said with a smile as he leaned forward. "You think you've won, don't you? That you defeated that immortal freak and stopped us? Well, you're wrong. Other people still oppose you. Someone is bound to stop you one of these days."

"You know, you make me sad. You've learned nothing from all your hate and violence. Let them come for us—I know kindness and justice will win in the end. I learned to be optimistic from a few friends of mine." Iris slammed his door shut. "Rot in prison, Michael. I pity your son."

As he yelled at her from the inside of the truck, enraged about Iris mentioning his son, she walked back over to her people. Grant immediately embraced her. Prime Minister Lin watched at Michael and his thugs were driven away by the police, then turned to Iris and her people.

"I'm sad to see Detective Crawford was killed," she said softly. "He was a good man and a fine detective. What happened here?"

"He sacrificed himself for me. His granddaughter," Alyx explained, making the prime minister's eyes widen. "Hi—I'm Alyx, the new Princess of Fairhaven. Now that it's gone, though, I'm not sure the title still applies."

"It's a long story," Princess Esme said, wiping her tears for the detective away. "But yes, this is our daughter. The first hybrid."

Prime Minister Lin studied Alyx for a while, turning to Iris. "I'm going to need a full report soon. Now, with this immortal gone, Bobby Blevins dead, and the Exterminators off the street ... is this city finally safe? Please say yes, for the love of all things holy."

"We think so, Prime Minister," Iris replied, holding onto Grant's hand. "Though they destroyed our church. So, we're homeless at the moment."

"I can make arrangements to find you new housing. And soon, I'll be giving a press conference on how you saved the world. That should make some humans come around to the idea of you. In the meantime, come with me—I want to know everything that happened here." Prime Minister Lin glanced at the crowd that had gathered, all murmuring and staring. "Maybe now ... there can be peace. Or the start of it, at least."

"We hope so," Iris said, squeezing Grant's hand. "No more magic, no more evil spells. Just the magic of love."

Grant smiled, kissing her again in front of the crowd. Gemma and Princess Esme's old friends pushed through the mass of people, hugging them all and expressing their condolences for the loss of Detective Crawford. They were all excited to meet Princess Esme's new daughter—who seemed to stop growing after Icarus was killed. Iris wondered if she and Maya would be friends. Maybe the next generation would start to embrace Fairhaveners.

When Ronan came running through the crowd, jumping into Iris's arms for a hug, she hugged him back tightly, relieved to see him all right. Even the Bhatias walked over, expressing their gratitude. For once, no one yelled or fought—not even Ronan's mother. She just smiled, though she kept her distance.

"... and you mean it?" Blanche was asking Fairy Godmother Odelia. "You'll let me out of my godmother pact?"

"That's right," Fairy Godmother Odelia said a smile, "now that Icarus is gone, you're free. With both mine and Gemma's blessing."

"Wow. I can do so much now. So much living." Blanche adjusted her hair, then checked to make sure she had fresh breath. "And you know what I want? I've had a crush on Gemma's father forever. I think it's time to shoot my shot."

Fairy Godmother Odelia smiled, watching as Blanche headed over to speak with him. "Good luck, dear!"

As Iris held onto Ronan, looking back at Grant over her shoulder, she hoped this was a fresh start for all of them. She couldn't save Fairhaven from Senator Remus, but she *had* helped Alyx save their new home—the entire world.

Now, all she had to do was explain the situation to Prime Minister Lin and hope the humans would embrace them in time. Maybe she could even stop for a coffee break along the way to relax for a change.

With Grant by her side, the way it should be.

Also by Dana Gricken

The Maidens of Fairhaven

Modern Fairytale

Enchantingly Yours

Spellbound Heart

The Soulless War Trilogy

The Dark Queen

The Dark Evolution

The Dark Cage

The Dragonwitch Chronicles Trilogy

The Girl Who Walked Through Fire

The Girl with the Invincible Blood

The Girl and The Silver Mark

The Hearts Companion

Ten Years: A Poetry Collection

Reverie: A Poetry Collection

Short Stories and Novellas

Whispers in the Woods: A Short Story Collection

Little Things: A horror novella

Drifting Darkly: A sci-fi novella

About the Author

Dana Gricken is an author from Ottawa, Ontario, Canada. The Dragonwitch Chronicles was her first series. Since then, she's published THE DARK QUEEN, THE DARK EVOLUTION, and THE DARK CAGE—the full trilogy in the Soulless War series. You can find those books at online retailers in both e-book and paperback forms.

In January 2020, she signed with Jessica Reino of the Metamorphosis Literary Agency. Please stay tuned for announcements on new books! In the meantime, if you've read and enjoyed her work, please don't hesitate to reach out to Dana on Twitter and Instagram—both @DanaGricken.

In her spare time, she enjoys watching Star Trek with her cats, reading, and playing video games. She hopes her books bring joy to people and wants to write over a hundred novels in her lifetime.